THE MYSTERY OF
ORCIVAL

On the bank of the river, among the stumps and flags, was stretched
the body of a woman.—Page 2.

THE MYSTERY
OF ORCIVAL

Translated from the French of

EMILE GABORIAU

Illustrated by

JULES GUERIN

WILDSIDE PRESS

LIST OF ILLUSTRATIONS

THE MYSTERY OF ORCIVAL

I

On Thursday, the 9th of July, 186-, Jean Bertaud
and his son, well known at Orcival as living by poaching and marauding, rose at three o'clock in the morning, just at daybreak, to go fishing.

Taking their tackle, they descended the charming
pathway, shaded by acacias, which you see from the
station at Evry, and which leads from the burg of Orcival to the Seine.

They made their way to their boat, moored as usual
some fifty yards above the wire bridge, across a field
adjoining Valfeuillu, the imposing estate of the Count
de Trémorel.

Having reached the river-bank, they laid down their
tackle, and Jean jumped into the boat to bail out the
water in the bottom.

While he was skilfully using the scoop, he perceived
that one of the oar-pins of the old craft, worn by the
oar, was on the point of breaking.

" Philippe," cried he, to his son, who was occupied
in unravelling a net, " bring me a bit of wood to make
a new oar-pin."

" All right," answered Philippe.

There was no tree in the field. The young man bent
his steps toward the park of Valfeuillu, a few rods dis-

tant; and, neglectful of Article 391 of the Penal Code, jumped across the wide ditch which surrounds M. de Trémorel's domain. He thought he would cut off a branch of one of the old willows, which at this place touch the water with their drooping branches.

He had scarcely drawn his knife from his pocket, while looking about him with the poacher's unquiet glance, when he uttered a low cry, "Father! Here! Father!"

"What's the matter?" responded the old marauder, without pausing from his work.

"Father, come here!" continued Philippe. "In Heaven's name, come here, quick!"

Jean knew by the tone of his son's voice that something unusual had happened. He threw down his scoop, and, anxiety quickening him, in three leaps was in the park. He also stood still, horror-struck, before the spectacle which had terrified Philippe.

On the bank of the river, among the stumps and flags, was stretched a woman's body. Her long, dishevelled locks lay among the water-shrubs; her dress —of gray silk—was soiled with mire and blood. All the upper part of the body lay in shallow water, and her face had sunk in the mud.

"A murder!" muttered Philippe, whose voice trembled.

"That's certain," responded Jean, in an indifferent tone. "But who can this woman be? Really one would say, the countess."

"We'll see," said the young man. He stepped toward the body; his father caught him by the arm.

"What would you do, fool?" said he. "You ought never to touch the body of a murdered person without legal authority."

" You think so? "

" Certainly. There are penalties for it."

" Then, come along and let's inform the Mayor."

" Why? as if people hereabouts were not against us enough already! Who knows that they would not accuse *us*——"

" But, father——"

" If we go and inform Monsieur Courtois, he will ask us how and why we came to be in Monsieur de Trémorel's park to find this out. What is it to you, that the countess has been killed? They'll find her body without you. Come, let's go away."

But Philippe did not budge. Hanging his head, his chin resting upon his palm, he reflected.

" We must make this known," said he, firmly. " We are not savages; we will tell Monsieur Courtois that in passing along by the park in our boat, we perceived the body."

Old Jean resisted at first; then, seeing that his son would, if need be, go without him, yielded.

They re-crossed the ditch, and leaving their fishing-tackle in the field, directed their steps hastily toward the mayor's house.

Orcival, situated a mile or more from Corbeil, on the right bank of the Seine, is one of the most charming villages in the environs of Paris, despite the infernal etymology of its name. The gay and thoughtless Parisian, who, on Sunday, wanders about the fields, more destructive than the rook, has not yet discovered this smiling country. The distressing odor of the frying from coffee-gardens does not there stifle the perfume of the honeysuckles. The refrains of bargemen, the brazen voices of boat-horns, have never awakened echoes there. Lazily situated on the gentle slopes of a bank washed by the Seine, the houses of Orcival are white, and there are delicious shades, and a bell-tower which is the pride of the place. On all sides vast pleasure domains, kept up at great cost, surround it. From the upper part, the weathercocks of twenty châteaux may be seen. On the right is the forest of Mauprévoir, and the pretty country-house of the Countess de la Brèche; opposite, on the other side of the river, is Mousseaux and Petit-Bourg, the ancient domain of Aguado, now the property of a famous coach-maker; on the left, those beautiful copses belong to the Count de Trémorel, that large park is d'Etiolles, and in the distance beyond is Corbiel; that vast building, whose roofs are higher than the oaks, is the Darblay mill.

The mayor of Orcival occupies a handsome, pleasant mansion, at the upper end of the village. Formerly a manufacturer of dry goods, M. Courtois entered business without a penny, and after thirty years of absorbing toil, he retired with four round millions of francs.

Then he proposed to live tranquilly with his wife and children, passing the winter at Paris and the summer at his country-house.

But all of a sudden he was observed to be disturbed and agitated. Ambition stirred his heart. He took vigorous measures to be forced to accept the mayoralty of Orcival. And he accepted it, quite in self-defence, as he will himself tell you. This office was at once his happiness and his despair; apparent despair, interior and real happiness.

It quite befits him, with clouded brow, to rail at the cares of power; he appears yet better when, his waist encircled with the gold-laced scarf, he goes in triumph at the head of the municipal body.

Everybody was sound asleep at the mayor's when the two Bertauds rapped the heavy knocker of the door. After a moment, a servant, half asleep, appeared at one of the ground-floor windows.

"What's the matter, you rascals?" asked he, growling.

Jean did not think it best to revenge an insult which his reputation in the village too well justified.

"We want to speak to Monsieur the Mayor," he answered. "There is terrible need of it. Go call him, Monsieur Baptiste; he won't blame you."

"I'd like to see anybody blame me," snapped out Baptiste.

It took ten minutes of talking and explaining to persuade the servant. Finally, the Bertauds were admitted to a little man, fat and red, very much annoyed at being dragged from his bed so early. It was M. Courtois.

They had decided that Philippe should speak.

"Monsieur Mayor," he said, "we have come to announce to you a great misfortune. A crime has been committed at Monsieur de Trémorel's."

M. Courtois was a friend of the count's; he became whiter than his shirt at this sudden news.

"My God!" stammered he, unable to control his emotion, "what do you say—a crime!"

"Yes; we have just discovered a body; and as sure as you are here, I believe it to be that of the countess."

The worthy man raised his arms heavenward, with a wandering air.

"But where, when?"

"Just now, at the foot of the park, as we were going to take up our nets."

"It is horrible!" exclaimed the good M. Courtois;

"what a calamity! So worthy a lady! But it is not possible—you must be mistaken; I should have been informed——"

"We saw it distinctly, Monsieur Mayor."

"Such a crime in my village! Well, you have done wisely to come here. I will dress at once, and will hasten off—no, wait." He reflected a moment, then called:

"Baptiste!"

The valet was not far off. With ear and eye alternately pressed against the key-hole, he heard and looked with all his might. At the sound of his master's voice he had only to stretch out his hand and open the door.

"Monsieur called me?"

"Run to the justice of the peace," said the mayor. "There is not a moment to lose. A crime has been committed—perhaps a murder—you must go quickly. And you," addressing the poachers, "await me here while I slip on my coat."

The justice of the peace at Orcival, M. Plantat—"Papa Plantat," as he was called—was formerly an attorney at Melun. At fifty, Mr. Plantat, whose career had been one of unbroken prosperity, lost in the same month, his wife, whom he adored, and his two sons, charming youths, one eighteen, the other twenty-two years old. These successive losses crushed a man whom thirty years of happiness left without defence against misfortune. For a long time his reason was despaired of. Even the sight of a client, coming to trouble his grief, to recount stupid tales of self-interest, exasperated him. It was not surprising that he sold out his professional effects and good-will at half price. He wished to establish himself at his ease in his grief, with the certainty of not being disturbed in its indulgence.

But the intensity of his mourning diminished, and the ills of idleness came. The justiceship of the peace at Orcival was vacant, and M. Plantat applied for and obtained it. Once installed in this office, he suffered less from ennui. This man, who saw his life drawing to an end, undertook to interest himself in the thousand diverse cases which came before him. He applied to these all the forces of a superior intelligence, the resources of a mind admirably fitted to separate the false from the true among the lies he was forced to hear. He persisted, besides, in living alone, despite the urging of M. Courtois; pretending that society fatigued him, and that an unhappy man is a bore in company.

Misfortune, which modifies characters, for good or bad, had made him, apparently, a great egotist. He declared that he was only interested in the affairs of life as a critic tired of its active scenes. He loved to make a parade of his profound indifference for everything, swearing that a rain of fire descending upon Paris, would not even make him turn his head. To move him seemed impossible. "What's that to me?" was his invariable exclamation.

Such was the man who, a quarter of an hour after Baptiste's departure, entered the mayor's house.

M. Plantat was tall, thin, and nervous. His physiognomy was not striking. His hair was short, his restless eyes seemed always to be seeking something, his very long nose was narrow and sharp. After his affliction, his mouth, formerly well shaped, became deformed; his lower lip had sunk, and gave him a deceptive look of simplicity.

"They tell me," said he, at the threshold, "that Madame de Trémorel has been murdered."

"These men here, at least, pretend so," answered the mayor, who had just reappeared.

M. Courtois was no longer the same man. He had had time to make his toilet a little. His face attempted to express a haughty coldness. He had been reproaching himself for having been wanting in dignity, in showing his grief before the Bertauds. "Nothing ought to agitate a man in my position," said he to himself. And, being terribly agitated, he forced himself to be calm, cold, and impassible.

M. Plantat was so naturally.

"This is a very sad event," said he, in a tone which he forced himself to make perfectly disinterested; "but after all, how does it concern us? We must, however, hurry and ascertain whether it is true. I have sent for the brigadier, and he will join us."

"Let us go," said M. Courtois; "I have my scarf in my pocket."

They hastened off. Philippe and his father went first, the young man eager and impatient, the old one sombre and thoughtful. The mayor, at each step, made some exclamation.

"I can't understand it," muttered he; "a murder in my commune! a commune where, in the memory of men, no crime has been committed!"

And he directed a suspicious glance toward the two Bertauds. The road which led toward the château of M. de Trémorel was an unpleasant one, shut in by walls a dozen feet high. On one side is the park of the Marchioness de Lanascol; on the other the spacious garden of Saint Jouan. The going and coming had taken time; it was nearly eight o'clock when the mayor, the justice, and their guides stopped before the gate of M. de Trémorel.

The mayor rang. The bell was very large; only a small gravelled court of five or six yards separated the gate from the house; nevertheless no one appeared.

The mayor rang more vigorously, then with all his strength; but in vain.

Before the gate of Mme. de Lanascol's château, nearly opposite, a groom was standing, occupied in cleaning and polishing a bridle-bit.

" It's of no use to ring, gentlemen," said this man; " there's nobody in the château."

" How! nobody?" asked the mayor, surprised.

" I mean," said the groom, " that there is no one there but the master and mistress. The servants all went away last evening by the 8.40 train to Paris, to the wedding of the old cook, Madame Denis. They ought to return this morning by the first train. I was invited myself——"

" Great God!" interrupted M. Courtois, " then the count and countess remained alone last night?"

" Entirely alone, Monsieur Mayor."

" It is horrible!"

M. Plantat seemed to grow impatient during this dialogue. " Come," said he, " we cannot stay forever at the gate. The gendarmes do not come; let us send for the locksmith." Philippe was about to hasten off, when, at the end of the road, singing and laughing were heard. Five persons, three women and two men, soon appeared.

" Ah, there are the people of the château," cried the groom, whom this morning visit seemed to annoy, " they ought to have a key."

The domestics, seeing the group about the gate, became silent and hastened their steps.   One of them began to run ahead of the others; it was the count's valet de chambre.

"These gentlemen perhaps wish to speak to Monsieur the Count?" asked he, having bowed to M. Plantat.

"We have rung five times, as hard as we could," said the mayor.

"It is surprising," said the valet de chambre, "the count sleeps very lightly.   Perhaps he has gone out."

"Horror!" cried Philippe.   "Both of them have been murdered!"   These words shocked the servants, whose gayety announced a reasonable number of healths drunk to the happiness of the newly wedded pair.   M. Courtois seemed to be studying the attitude of old Bertaud.

"A murder!" muttered the valet de chambre.   "It was for money then; it must have been known——"

"What?" asked the mayor.

"Monsieur the Count received a very large sum yesterday morning."

"Large! yes," added a chambermaid.   "He had a large package of bank-bills.   Madame even said to Monsieur that she should not shut her eyes the whole night, with this immense sum in the house."

There was a silence; each one looked at the others with a frightened air.   M. Courtois reflected.

"At what hour did you leave the château last evening?" asked he of the servants.

"At eight o'clock; we had dinner early."

"You went away all together?"

"Yes, sir."

"You did not leave each other?"

"Not a minute."

" And you returned all together? "

The servants exchanged a significant look.

" All," responded a chambermaid—" that is to say, no. One left us on reaching the Lyons station at Paris; it was Guespin."

" Ah!"

" Yes, sir; he went away, saying that he would rejoin us at Wepler's, in the Batignolles, where the wedding took place." The mayor nudged the justice with his elbow, as if to attract his attention, and continued to question the chambermaid.

" And this Guespin, as you call him—did you see him again? "

" No, sir. I asked several times during the evening in vain, what had become of him; his absence seemed to me suspicious." Evidently the chambermaid tried to show superior perspicacity. A little more, and she would have talked of presentiments.

" Has this Guespin been long in the house? "

" Since spring."

" What were his duties? "

" He was sent from Paris by the house of the ' Skilful Gardener,' to take care of the rare flowers in Madame's conservatory."

" And did he know of this money? "

The domestics again exchanged significant glances.

" Yes," they answered in chorus, " we had talked a great deal about it among ourselves."

The chambermaid added: " He even said to me, ' To think that Monsieur the Count has enough money in his cabinet to make all our fortunes.' "

" What kind of a man is this? "

This question absolutely extinguished the talkativeness of the servants. No one dared to speak, perceiving that the least word might serve as the basis of a terrible accusation.   But the groom of the house opposite, who burned to mix himself up in the affair, had none of these scruples.   " Guespin," answered he, " is a good fellow.   Lord, what jolly things he knows!   He knows everything you can imagine.   It appears he has been rich in times past, and if he wished—   But dame! he loves to have his work all finished, and go off on sprees.   He's a crack billiard-player, I can tell you."

Papa Plantat, while listening in an apparently absent-minded way to these depositions, or rather these scandals, carefully examined the wall and the gate. He now turned, and interrupting the groom :

" Enough of this," said he, to the great scandal of M. Courtois.   " Before pursuing this interrogatory, let us ascertain the crime, if crime there is ; for it is not proved.   Let whoever has the key, open the gate."

The valet de chambre had the key ; he opened the gate, and all entered the little court.   The gendarmes had just arrived.   The mayor told the brigadier to follow him, and placed two men at the gate, ordering them not to permit anyone to enter or go out, unless by his orders.   Then the valet de chambre opened the door of the house.

II

If there had been no crime, at least something extraordinary had taken place at the château ; the impassible justice might have been convinced of it, as soon as he had stepped into the vestibule.   The glass door leading to the garden was wide open, and three of the panes were shattered into a thousand pieces.   The carpeting of waxed canvas between the doors had been torn up, and on the white marble slabs large drops of blood were visible. At the foot of the staircase was a stain larger than the rest, and upon the lowest step a splash hideous to behold.

Unfitted for such spectacles, or for the mission he had now to perform, M. Courtois became faint. Luckily, he borrowed from the idea of his official importance, an energy foreign to his character. The more difficult the preliminary examination of this affair seemed, the more determined he was to carry it on with dignity.

" Conduct us to the place where you saw the body," said he to Bertaud. But Papa Plantat intervened.

" It would be wiser, I think," he objected, " and more methodical, to begin by going through the house."

" Perhaps—yes—true, that's my own view," said the mayor, grasping at the other's counsel, as a drowning man clings to a plank. And he made all retire excepting the brigadier and the valet de chambre, the latter remaining to serve as guide. " Gendarmes," cried he to the men guarding the gate, " see to it that no one goes out; prevent anybody from entering the house, and above all, let no one go into the garden."

Then they ascended the staircase. Drops of blood were sprinkled all along the stairs. There was also blood on the baluster, and M. Courtois perceived, with horror, that his hands were stained.

When they had reached the first landing-stage, the mayor said to the valet de chambre:

" Tell me, my friend, did your master and mistress occupy the same chamber? "

" Yes, sir."

" And where is their chamber? "

" There, sir."

As he spoke, the valet de chambre staggered back terrified, and pointed to a door, the upper panel of which betrayed the imprint of a bloody hand. Drops of perspiration overspread the poor mayor's forehead; he too was terrified, and could hardly keep on his feet. Alas, authority brings with it terrible obligations! The brigadier, an old soldier of the Crimea, visibly moved, hesitated.

M. Plantat alone, as tranquil as if he were in his garden, retained his coolness, and looked around upon the others.

" We must decide," said he.

He entered the room; the rest followed.

There was nothing unusual in the apartment; it was a boudoir hung in blue satin, furnished with a couch and four arm-chairs, covered also with blue satin. One of the chairs was overturned.

They passed on to the bed-chamber.

A frightful disorder appeared in this room. There was not an article of furniture, not an ornament, which did not betray that a terrible, enraged and merciless struggle had taken place between the assassins and their victims. In the middle of the chamber a small table was overturned, and all about it were scattered lumps of sugar, vermilion cups, and pieces of porcelain.

" Ah! " said the valet de chambre, " Monsieur and Madame were taking tea when the wretches came in! "

The mantel ornaments had been thrown upon the floor; the clock, in falling, had stopped at twenty minutes past three. Near the clock were the lamps; the globes were in pieces, the oil had been spilled.

The canopy of the bed had been torn down, and

covered the bed. Someone must have clutched desperately at the draperies. All the furniture was overturned. The coverings of the chairs had been hacked
by strokes of a knife, and in places the stuffing pro-
truded. The secretary had been broken open; the
writing-slide, dislocated, hung by its hinges; the
drawers were open and empty, and everywhere, blood
—blood upon the carpet, the furniture, the curtains—
above all, upon the bed-curtains.

"Poor wretches!" stammered the mayor. "They
were murdered here."

Everyone for a moment was appalled. But meanwhile, the justice of the peace devoted himself to a
minute scrutiny, taking notes upon his tablets, and
looking into every corner. When he had finished:

"Come," said he, "let us go into the other rooms."

Everywhere there was the same disorder. A band
of furious maniacs, or criminals seized with a frenzy,
had certainly passed the night in the house.

The count's library, especially, had been turned
topsy-turvy.· The assassins had not taken the trouble
to force the locks; they had gone to work with a
hatchet. Surely they were confident of not being overheard; for they must have struck tremendous blows to
make the massive oaken bureau fly in pieces.

Neither parlor nor smoking-room had been respected. Couches, chairs, canopies, were cut and torn as if
they had been lunged at with swords. Two spare
chambers for guests were all in confusion.

They then ascended to the second story.

There, in the first room which they penetrated, they
found, beside a trunk which had been assaulted, but
which was not yet opened, a hatchet for splitting wood,

which the valet de chambre recognized as belonging to the house.

" Do you understand now ? " said the mayor to M. Plantat. " The assassins were in force, that's clear. The murder accomplished, they scattered through the château, seeking everywhere the money they knew they would find here. One of them was engaged in breaking open this trunk, when the others, below, found the money ; they called him ; he hastened down, and thinking all further search useless, he left the hatchet here."

" I see it," said the brigadier, " just as if I had been here."

The ground-floor, which they next visited, had been respected. Only, after the crime had been committed, and the money secured, the murderers had felt the necessity of refreshing themselves. They found the remains of their supper in the dining-room. They had eaten up all the cold meats left in the cupboard. On the table, beside eight empty bottles of wine and liqueurs, were ranged five glasses.

" There were five of them," said the mayor.

By force of will, M. Courtois had recovered his self-possession.

" Before going to view the bodies," said he, " I will send word to the procureur oi Corbeil. In an hour, we will have a judge of instruction, who will finish our painful task."

A gendarme was instructed to harness the count's buggy, and to hasten to the procureur. Then the mayor and the justice, followed by the brigadier, the valet de chambre, and the two Bertauds, took their way toward the river.

The park of Valfeuillu was very wide from right to

left. From the house to the Seine it was almost two hundred steps. Before the house was a grassy lawn, interspersed with flower-beds. Two paths led across the lawn to the river-bank.

But the murderers had not followed the paths. Making a short cut, they had gone straight across the lawn. Their traces were perfectly visible. The grass was trampled and stamped down as if a heavy load had been dragged over it. In the midst of the lawn they perceived something red; M. Plantat went and picked it up. It was a slipper, which the valet de chambre recognized as the count's. Farther on, they found a white silk handkerchief, which the valet declared he had often seen around the count's neck. This handkerchief was stained with blood.

At last they arrived at the river-bank, under the willows from which Philippe had intended to cut off a branch; there they saw the body. The sand at this place was much indented by feet seeking a firm support. Everything indicated that here had been the supreme struggle.

M. Courtois understood all the importance of these traces.

" Let no one advance," said he, and, followed by the justice of the peace, he approached the corpse. Although the face could not be distinguished, both recognized the countess. Both had seen her in this gray robe, adorned with blue trimmings.

Now, how came she there?

The mayor thought that having succeeded in escaping from the hands of the murderers, she had fled wildly. They had pursued her, had caught up with her there, and she had fallen to rise no more. This version explained the traces of the struggle. It must

2

have been the count's body that they had dragged across the lawn.

M. Courtois talked excitedly, trying to impose his ideas on the justice. But M. Plantat hardly listened; you might have thought him a hundred leagues from Valfeuillu; he only responded by monosyllables— yes, no, perhaps. And the worthy mayor gave himself great pains; he went and came, measured steps, minutely scrutinized the ground.

There was not at this place more than a foot of water. A mud-bank, upon which grew some clumps of flags and some water-lilies, descended by a gentle decline from the bank to the middle of the river. The water was very clear, and there was no current; the slippery and slimy mire could be distinctly seen.

M. Courtois had gone thus far in his investigations, when he was struck by a sudden idea.

" Bertaud," said he, " come here."

The old poacher obeyed.

" You say that you saw the body from your boat?"

" Yes, Monsieur Mayor."

" Where is your boat?"

" There, hauled up to that field."

" Well, lead us to it."

It was clear to all that this order had a great effect upon the man. He trembled and turned pale under his rough skin, tanned as it was by sun and storm. He was even seen to cast a menacing look toward his son.

" Let us go," said he at last.

They were returning to the house when the valet proposed to pass over the ditch. " That will be the quickest way," said he, " I will go for a ladder which we will put across."

He went off, and quickly reappeared with his improvised foot-bridge. But at the moment he was adjusting it, the mayor cried out to him:

" Stop! "

The imprints left by the Bertauds on both sides of the ditch had just caught his eye.

" What is this? " said he; " evidently someone has crossed here, and not long ago; for the traces of the steps are quite fresh."

After an examination of some minutes he ordered that the ladder should be placed farther off. When they had reached the boat, he said to Jean, " Is this the boat with which you went to take up your nets this morning? "

" Yes."

" Then," resumed M. Courtois, " what implements did you use? your cast net is perfectly dry; this boat-hook and these oars have not been wet for twenty-four hours."

The distress of the father and son became more and more evident.

" Do you persist in what you say, Bertaud? " said the mayor.

" Certainly."

" And you, Philippe? "

" Monsieur," stammered the young man, " we have told the truth."

" Really! " said M. Courtois, in an ironical tone. " Then you will explain to the proper authorities how it was that you could see anything from a boat which you had not entered. It will be proved to you, also, that the body is in a position where it is impossible to see it from the middle of the river. Then you will still have to tell what these foot-prints on the grass are, which go from your boat to the place where the ditch has been crossed several times and by several persons."

The two Bertauds hung their heads.

" Brigadier," ordered the mayor, " arrest these two men in the name of the law, and prevent all communication between them."

Philippe seemed to be ill. As for old Jean, he contented himself with shrugging his shoulders and saying to his son:

" Well, you would have it so, wouldn't you? "

While the brigadier led the two poachers away, and shut them up separately, and under the guard of his men, the justice and the mayor returned to the park. " With all this," muttered M. Courtois, " no traces of the count."

They proceeded to take up the body of the countess.

The mayor sent for two planks, which, with a thousand precautions, they placed on the ground, being able thus to move the countess without effacing the imprints necessary for the legal examination. Alas! it was indeed she who had been the beautiful, the charming Countess de Trémorel! Here were her smiling face, her lovely, speaking eyes, her fine, sensitive mouth.

There remained nothing of her former self. The face was unrecognizable, so soiled and wounded was it. Her clothes were in tatters. Surely a furious frenzy had moved the monsters who had slain the poor lady! She had received more than twenty knife-wounds, and must have been struck with a stick, or rather with a hammer; she had been dragged by her feet and by her hair!

In her left hand she grasped a strip of common cloth, torn, doubtless, from the clothes of one of the assassins.

The mayor, in viewing the spectacle, felt his legs fail him, and supported himself on the arm of the impassible Plantat.

" Let us carry her to the house," said the justice, " and then we will search for the count."

The valet and brigadier (who had now returned) called on the domestics for assistance. The women rushed into the garden. There was then a terrible concert of cries, lamentations, and imprecations.

" The wretches! So noble a mistress! So good a lady! "

M. and Mme. de Trémorel, one could see, were adored by their people.

The countess had just been laid upon the billiard-table, on the ground-floor, when the judge of instruction and a physician were announced.

" At last! " sighed the worthy mayor; and in a lower tone he added, " the finest medals have their reverse."

For the first time in his life, he seriously cursed his ambition, and regretted being the most important personage in Orcival.

III

The judge of instruction of the tribunal at Corbeil, was M. Antoine Domini, a remarkable man, since called to higher functions. He was forty years of age, of a prepossessing person, and endowed with a very expressive, but too grave physiognomy. In him seemed typified the somewhat stiff solemnity of the magistracy. Penetrated with the dignity of his office, he sacrificed his life to it, rejecting the most simple distractions, and the most innocent pleasures.

He lived alone, seldom showing himself abroad;

rarely received his friends, not wishing, as he said, that the weaknesses of the man should derogate from the sacred character of the judge. This latter reason had deterred him from marrying, though he felt the need of a domestic sphere.

Always and everywhere he was the magistrate—that is, the representative, even to fanaticism, of what he thought the most august institution on the earth. Naturally gay, he would double-lock himself in when he wished to laugh. He was witty; but if a bright sally escaped him, you may be sure he repented of it. Body and soul he gave to his vocation; and no one could bring more conscientiousness to the discharge of what he thought to be his duty. He was also inflexible. It was monstrous, in his eyes, to discuss an article of the code. The law spoke; it was enough; he shut his eyes, covered his ears, and obeyed.

From the day when a legal investigation commenced, he did not sleep, and he employed every means to discover the truth. Yet he was not regarded as a good judge of instruction; to contend by tricks with a prisoner was repugnant to him; to lay a snare for a rogue he thought debasing; in short, he was obstinate —obstinate to foolishness, sometimes to absurdity, even to denying the existence of the sun at mid-day.

The mayor and Papa Plantat hastened to meet M. Domini. He bowed to them gravely, as if he had not known them, and presenting to them a man of some sixty years who accompanied him:

" Messieurs," said he, " this is Doctor Gendron."

Papa Plantat shook hands with the doctor; the mayor smiled graciously at him, for Dr. Gendron was well-known in those parts; he was even celebrated, despite the nearness of Paris. Loving his art and ex-

ercising it with a passionate energy, he yet owed his
renown less to his science than his manners. People
said: "He is an original;" they admired his affectation of independence, of scepticism, and rudeness.
He made his visits from five to nine in the morning—
all the worse for those for whom these hours were in-
convenient. After nine o'clock the doctor was not to
be had. The doctor was working for himself, the doctor was in his laboratory, the doctor was inspecting his
cellar. It was rumored that he sought for secrets of
practical chemistry, to augment still more his twenty
thousand livres of income. And he did not deny it;
for in truth he was engaged on poisons, and was per-
fecting an invention by which could be discovered
traces of all the alkaloids which up to that time had
escaped analysis. If his friends reproached him, even
jokingly, on sending away sick people in the afternoon,
he grew red with rage.

"Parbleu!" he answered, "I find you superb! I am
a doctor four hours in the day. I am paid by hardly a
quarter of my patients—that's three hours I give daily
to humanity, which I despise. Let each of you do as
much, and we shall see."

The mayor conducted the new-comers into the
drawing-room, where he installed himself to write
down the results of his examination.

"What a misfortune for my town, this crime!" said
he to M. Domini. "What shame! Orcival has lost its
reputation."

"I know nothing of the affair," returned the judge.
"The gendarme who went for me knew little about it."

M. Courtois recounted at length what his investigation had discovered, not forgetting the minutest detail,
dwelling especially on the excellent precautions which

he had had the sagacity to take. He told how the conduct of the Bertauds had at first awakened his suspicions ; how he had detected them, at least in a point-blank lie; how, finally, he had determined to arrest them. He spoke standing, his head thrown back, with wordy emphasis. The pleasure of speaking partially rewarded him for his recent distress.

" And now," he concluded, " I have just ordered the most exact search, so that doubtless we shall find the count's body. Five men, detailed by me, and all the people of the house, are searching the park. If their efforts are not crowned with success, I have here some fishermen who will drag the river."

M. Domini held his tongue, only nodding his head from time to time, as a sign of approbation. He was studying, weighing the details told him, building up in his mind a plan of proceeding.

" You have acted wisely," said he, at last. " The misfortune is a great one, but I agree with you that we are on the track of the criminals. These poachers, or the gardener who has disappeared, have something, perhaps, to do with this abominable crime."

Already, for some minutes, M. Plantat had rather awkwardly concealed some signs of impatience.

" The misfortune is," said he, " that if Guespin is guilty, he will not be such a fool as to show himself here."

" Oh, we'll find him," returned M. Domini. " Before leaving Corbeil, I sent a despatch to the prefecture of police at Paris, to ask for a police agent, who will doubtless be here shortly."

" While waiting," proposed the mayor, " perhaps you would like to see the scene of the crime ? "

M. Domini made a motion as if to rise; then sat down again.

"In fact, no," said he; "we will see nothing till the agent arrives. But I must have some information concerning the Count and Countess de Trémorel."

The worthy mayor again triumphed.

"Oh, I can give it to you," answered he quickly, "better than anybody. Ever since their advent here, I may say, I have been one of their best friends. Ah, sir, what charming people! excellent, and affable, and devoted——"

And at the remembrance of all his friends' good qualities, M. Courtois choked in his utterance.

"The Count de Trémorel," he resumed, "was a man of thirty-four years, handsome, witty to the tips of his nails. He had sometimes, however, periods of melancholy, during which he did not wish to see anybody; but he was ordinarily so affable, so polite, so obliging; he knew so well how to be noble without haughtiness, that everybody here esteemed and loved him."

"And the countess?" asked the judge of instruction.

"An angel, Monsieur, an angel on earth! Poor lady! You will soon see her remains, and surely you would not guess that she has been the queen of the country, by reason of her beauty."

"Were they rich?"

"Yes; they must have had, together, more than a hundred thousand francs income—oh, yes, much more; for within five or six months the count, who had not the bucolic tastes of poor Sauvresy, sold some lands to buy consols."

"Have they been married long?"

M. Courtois scratched his head; it was his appeal to memory.

" Faith," he answered, " it was in September of last year; just six months ago. I married them myself. Poor Sauvresy had been dead a year."

The judge of instruction looked up from his notes with a surprised air.

" Who is this Sauvresy," he inquired, " of whom you speak?"

Papa Plantat, who was furiously biting his nails in a corner, apparently a stranger to what was passing, rose abruptly.

" Monsieur Sauvresy," said he, " was the first husband of Madame de Trémorel. My friend Courtois has omitted this fact."

" Oh!" said the mayor, in a wounded tone, " it seems to me that under present circumstances——"

" Pardon me," interrupted the judge. " It is a detail such as may well become valuable, though apparently foreign to the case, and at the first view, insignificant."

" Hum!" grunted Papa Plantat. " Insignificant— foreign to it!"

His tone was so singular, his air so strange, that M. Domini was struck by it.

" Do you share," he asked, " the opinion of the mayor regarding the Trémorels?"

Plantat shrugged his shoulders.

" I haven't any opinions," he answered: " I live alone—see nobody; don't disturb myself about anything. But——"

" It seems to me," said M. Courtois, " that nobody should be better acquainted with people who were my friends than I myself."

" Then, you are telling the story clumsily," said M. Plantat, dryly.

The judge of instruction pressed him to explain him-

self. So M. Plantat, without more ado, to the great
scandal of the mayor, who was thus put into the background, proceeded to dilate upon the main features of
the count's and countess's biography.

"The Countess de Trémorel, *née* Bertha Lechaillu,
was the daughter of a poor village school-master. At
eighteen, her beauty was famous for three leagues
around, but as she only had for dowry her great blue
eyes and blond ringlets, but few serious lovers presented themselves. Already Bertha, by advice of her family, had resigned herself to take a place as a governess
—a sad position for so beautiful a maid—when the heir
of one of the richest domains in the neighborhood happened to see her, and fell in love with her.

"Clement Sauvresy was just thirty; he had no longer
any family, and possessed nearly a hundred thousand
livres income from lands absolutely free of incum-
brance. Clearly, he had the best right in the world to
choose a wife to his taste. He did not hesitate. He
asked for Bertha's hand, won it, and, a month after,
wedded her at mid-day, to the great scandal of the
neighboring aristocracy, who went about saying:
'What folly! what good is there in being rich, if it is
not to double one's fortune by a good marriage!'

"Nearly a month before the marriage, Sauvresy set
the laborers to work at Valfeuillu, and in no long time
had spent, in repairs and furniture, a trifle of thirty
thousand crowns. The newly married pair chose this
beautiful spot in which to spend their honeymoon.
They were so well-contented there that they established themselves permanently at Valfeuillu, to the
great satisfaction of the neighborhood.

"Bertha was one of those persons, it seemed, who are
born especially to marry millionnaires. Without awk-

wardness or embarrassment, she passed easily from the humble school-room, where she had assisted her father, to the splendid drawing-room of Valfeuillu. And when she did the honors of her château to all the neighboring aristocracy, it seemed as though she had never done anything else. She knew how to remain simple, approachable, modest, all the while that she took the tone of the highest society. She was beloved."

" But it appears to me," interrupted the mayor, "that I said the same thing, and it was really not worth while——"

A gesture from M. Domini closed his mouth, and M. Plantat continued:

" Sauvresy was also liked, for he was one of those golden hearts which know not how to suspect evil. He was one of those men with a robust faith, with obstinate illusions, whom doubts never disturb. He was one of those who thoroughly confide in the sincerity of their friends, in the love of their mistresses. This new domestic household ought to be happy; it was so. Bertha adored her husband—that frank man, who, before speaking to her a word of love, offered her his hand. Sauvresy professed for his wife a worship which few thought foolish. They lived in great style at Valfeuillu. They received a great deal. When autumn came all the numerous spare chambers were filled. The turn-outs were magnificent.

" Sauvresy had been married two years, when one evening he brought from Paris one of his old and intimate friends, a college comrade of whom he had often spoken, Count Hector de Trémorel. The count intended to remain but a short time at Valfeuillu; but weeks passed and then months, and he still remained. It was not surprising. Hector had passed a very stormy youth, full of debauchery, of clubs, of gambling, and of amours. He had thrown to the winds of his caprices an immense fortune; the relatively calm life of Valfeuillu was a relief. At first people said to him, 'You will soon have enough of the country.' He smiled, but said nothing. It was then thought, and rightly, perhaps, that having become poor, he cared little to display his ruin before those who had obscured his splendor. He absented himself rarely, and then only to go to Corbeil, almost always on foot. There he frequented the Belle Image hotel, the best in the town, and met, as if by chance, a young lady from Paris. They spent the afternoon together, and separated when the last train left."

"Peste!" growled the mayor, "for a man who lives alone, who sees nobody, who would not for the world have anything to do with other people's business, it seems to me our dear Monsieur Plantat is pretty well informed."

Evidently M. Courtois was jealous. How was it that he, the first personage in the place, had been absolutely ignorant of these meetings? His ill-humor was increasing, when Dr. Gendron answered:

"Pah! all Corbeil prated about that at the time."

M. Plantat made a movement with his lips as if to say, "I know other things besides." He went on, however, with his story.

"The visit of Count Hector made no change in the habits at the château. Monsieur and Madame Sauvresy had a brother; that was all. Sauvresy at this time made several journeys to Paris, where, as everybody knew, he was engaged in arranging his friend's affairs.

"This charming existence lasted a year. Happiness

seemed to be fixed forever beneath the delightful shades of Valfeuillu. But alas! one evening on returning from the hunt, Sauvresy became so ill that he was forced to take to his bed. A doctor was called; inflammation of the chest had set in. Sauvresy was young, vigorous as an oak; his state did not at first cause anxiety. A fort-night afterward, in fact, he was up and about. But he was imprudent and had a relapse. He again nearly recovered; a week afterward there was another relapse, and this time so serious, that a fatal end of his illness was foreseen. During this long sickness, the love of Bertha and the affection of Trémorel for Sauvresy were tenderly shown. Never was an invalid tended with such solicitude—surrounded with so many proofs of the purest devotion. His wife and his friend were al-ways at his couch, night and day. He had hours of suffering, but never a second of weariness. He re-peated to all who went to see him, that he had come to bless his illness. He said to himself, 'If I had not fallen ill, I should never have known how much I was be-loved.' "

"He said the same thing to me," interrupted the mayor, "more than a hundred times. He also said so to Madame Courtois, to Laurence, my eldest daugh-ter——"

"Naturally," continued M. Plantat. "But Sau-vresy's distemper was one against which the science of the most skilful physicians and the most constant care contend in vain.

"He said that he did not suffer much, but he faded perceptibly, and was no more than the shadow of his former self. At last, one night, toward two or three o'clock, he died in the arms of his wife and his friend. Up to the last moment, he had preserved the full force of his faculties. Less than an hour before expiring, he wished everyone to be awakened, and that all the servants of the castle should be summoned. When they were all gathered about the bedside, he took his wife's hand, placed it in that of the Count de Trémorel, and made them swear to marry each other when he was no more. Bertha and Hector began to protest, but he insisted in such a manner as to compel assent, praying and adjuring them, and declaring that their refusal would embitter his last moments. This idea of the marriage between his widow and his friend seems, besides, to have singularly possessed his thoughts toward the close of his life. In the preamble of his will, dictated the night before his death, to M. Bury, notary of Orcival, he says formally that their union is his dearest wish, certain as he is of their happiness, and knowing well that his memory will be piously kept."

" Had Monsieur and Madame Sauvresy no children? " asked the judge of instruction.

" No," answered the mayor.

M. Plantat continued:

" The grief of the count and the young widow was intense. M. de Trémorel, especially, seemed absolutely desperate, and acted like a madman. The countess shut herself up, forbidding even those whom she loved best from entering her chamber—even Madame Courtois. When the count and Madame Bertha reappeared, they were scarcely to be recognized, so much had both changed. Monsieur Hector seemed to have grown twenty years older. Would they keep the oath made at the death-bed of Sauvresy, of which everyone was apprised? This was asked with all the more curiosity, because their profound sorrow for a man who well merited it, was admired."

The judge of instruction stopped M. Plantat with a motion of his hand.

"Do you know," asked he, "whether the rendezvous at the Hôtel Belle Image had ceased?"

"I suppose so, sir; I think so."

"I am almost sure of it," said Dr. Gendron. "I have often heard it said—they know everything at Corbeil—that there was a heated explanation between M. de Trémorel and the pretty Parisian lady. After this quarrel, they were no longer seen at the Belle Image."

The old justice of the peace smiled.

"Melun is not at the end of the world," said he, "and there are hotels at Melun. With a good horse, one is soon at Fontainebleau, at Versailles, even at Paris. Madame de Trémorel might have been jealous; her husband had some first-rate trotters in his stables."

Did M. Plantat give an absolutely disinterested opinion, or did he make an insinuation? The judge of instruction looked at him attentively, to reassure himself, but his visage expressed nothing but a profound serenity. He told the story as he would any other, no matter what.

"Please go on, Monsieur," resumed M. Domini.

"Alas!" said M. Plantat, "nothing here below is eternal, not even grief. I know it better than anybody. Soon, to the tears of the first days, to violent despair, there succeeded, in the count and Madame Bertha, a reasonable sadness, then a soft melancholy. And in one year after Sauvresy's death Monsieur de Trémorel espoused his widow."

During this long narrative the mayor had several

times exhibited marks of impatience.   At the end, being able to hold in no longer, he exclaimed:

"There, those are surely exact details; but I question whether they have advanced us a step in this grave matter which occupies us all—to find the murderers of the count and countess."

M. Plantat, at these words, bent on the judge of instruction his clear and deep look, as if to search his conscience to the bottom.

"These details were indispensable," returned M. Domini, "and they are very clear.   Those rendezvous at the hotel struck me; one knows not to what extremities jealousy might lead a woman——"

He stopped abruptly, seeking, no doubt, some connection between the pretty Parisian and the murderers; then resumed:

"Now that I know the Trémorels as if I had lived with them intimately, let us proceed to the actual facts."

The brilliant eye of M. Plantat immediately grew dim; he opened his lips as if to speak; but kept his peace.   The doctor alone, who had not ceased to study the old justice of the peace, remarked the sudden change of his features.

"It only remains," said M. Domini, "to know how the new couple lived."

M. Courtois thought it due to his dignity to anticipate M. Plantat.

"You ask how the new couple lived," said he hastily; "they lived in perfect concord; nobody knows better about it than I, who was most intimate with them. The memory of poor Sauvresy was a bond of happiness between them; if they liked me so well, it was because I often talked of him.   Never a cloud, never a

3

cross word. Hector—I called him so, familiarly, this
poor, dear count—gave his wife the tender attentions
of a lover; those delicate cares, which I fear most married people soon dispense with."

"And the countess?" asked M. Plantat, in a tone
too marked not to be ironical.

"Bertha?" replied the worthy mayor—" she permitted me to call her thus, paternally—I have cited
her many and many a time as an example and model,
to Madame Courtois. She was worthy of Hector and
of Sauvresy, the two most worthy men I have ever
met!"

Then, perceiving that his enthusiasm somewhat surprised his hearers, he added, more softly:

"I have my reasons for expressing myself thus; and
I do not hesitate to do so before men whose profession
and character will justify my discretion. Sauvresy,
when living, did me a great service—when I was forced
to take the mayoralty. As for Hector, I knew well
that he had departed from the dissipations of his youth,
and thought I discerned that he was not indifferent to
my eldest daughter, Laurence; and I dreamed of a
marriage all the more proper, as, if the Count Hector
had a great name, I would give to my daughter a dowry
large enough to gild any escutcheon. Only events
modified my projects."

The mayor would have gone on singing the praises
of the Trémorels, and his own family, if the judge of
instruction had not interposed.

"Here I am fixed," he commenced, " now, it seems
to me——"

He was interrupted by a loud noise in the vestibule.
It seemed like a struggle, and cries and shouts reached
the drawing-room. Everybody rose.

" I know what it is," said the mayor, " only too well. They have just found the body of the Count de Tré-morel."

IV

The mayor was mistaken. The drawing-room door opened suddenly, and a man of slender form, who was struggling furiously, and with an energy which would not have been suspected, appeared, held on one side by a gendarme, and on the other by a domestic.

The struggle had already lasted long, and his clothes were in great disorder. His new coat was torn, his cravat floated in strips, the button of his collar had been wrenched off, and his open shirt left his breast bare. In the vestibule and court were heard the frantic cries of the servants and the curious crowd—of whom there were more than a hundred, whom the news of the crime had collected about the gate, and who burned to hear, and above all to see.

This enraged crowd cried:

" It is he! Death to the assassin! It is Guespin! See him!"

And the wretch, inspired by an immense fright, continued to struggle.

" Help!" shouted he hoarsely. " Leave me alone. I am innocent!"

He had posted himself against the drawing-room door, and they could not force him forward.

" Push him," ordered the mayor, " push him."

It was easier to command than to execute. Terror lent to Guespin enormous force. But it occurred to the doctor to open the second wing of the door; the support failed the wretch, and he fell, or rather rolled at the foot of the table at which the judge of instruction was seated.   He was straightway on his feet again, and his eyes sought a chance to escape.   Seeing none —for the windows and doors were crowded with the lookers-on—he fell into a chair.   The fellow appeared the image of terror, wrought up to paroxysm.   On his livid face, black and blue, were visible the marks of the blows he had received in the struggle; his white lips trembled, and he moved his jaws as if he sought a little saliva for his burning tongue; his staring eyes were bloodshot, and expressed the wildest distress; his body was bent with convulsive spasms.   So terrible was this spectacle, that the mayor thought it might be an example of great moral force.   He turned toward the crowd, and pointing to Guespin, said in a tragic tone:

"See what crime is!"

The others exchanged surprised looks.

"If he is guilty," muttered M. Plantat, "why on earth has he returned?"

It was with difficulty that the crowd was kept back; the brigadier was forced to call in the aid of his men. Then he returned and placed himself beside Guespin, thinking it not prudent to leave him alone with unarmed men.

But the man was little to be feared.   The reaction came; his over-excited energy became exhausted, his strained muscles flaccid, and his prostration resembled the agony of brain fever.   Meanwhile the brigadier recounted what had happened.

"Some of the servants of the château and the neighboring houses were chatting near the gate, about the crime, and the disappearance of Guespin last night, when all of a sudden, someone perceived him at a distance, staggering, and singing boisterously, as if he were drunk."

" Was he really drunk ? " asked M. Domini.

" Very," returned the brigadier.

" Then we owe it to the wine that we have caught him, and thus all will be explained."

" On perceiving this wretch," pursued the gendarme, who seemed not to have the shadow of a doubt of Guespin's guilt, " François, the count's valet de chambre, and Baptiste, the mayor's servant, who were there, hastened to meet him, and seized him. He was so tipsy that he thought they were fooling with him. When he saw my men, he was undeceived. Just then one of the women cried out, ' Brigand, it was you who have this night assassinated the count and the countess!' He immediately became paler than death, and remained motionless and dumb. Then he began to struggle so violently that he nearly escaped. Ah! he's strong, the rogue, although he does not look like it."

" And he said nothing ? " said Plantat.

" Not a word; his teeth were so tightly shut with rage that I'm sure he couldn't say ' bread.' But we've got him. I've searched him, and this is what I have found in his pockets: a handkerchief, a pruning-knife, two small keys, a scrap of paper covered with figures, and an address of the establishment of ' Vulcan's Forges.' But that's not all——"

The brigadier took a step, and eyed his auditors mysteriously; he was preparing his effect.

" That's not all. While they were bringing him along in the court-yard, he tried to get rid of his wallet. Happily I had my eyes open, and saw the dodge. I picked up the wallet, which he had thrown among the flowers near the door; here it is. In it are a one-hundred-franc note, three napoleons, and seven francs in change. Yesterday the rascal hadn't a sou——"

" How do you know that?" asked M. Domini.

" Dame! Monsieur Judge, he borrowed of the valet François (who told me of it) twenty-five francs, pretending that it was to pay his share of the wedding expenses."

" Tell François to come here," said the judge of instruction. " Now, sir," he continued, when the valet presented himself, " do you know whether Guespin had any money yesterday?"

" He had so little, Monsieur," answered François promptly, " that he asked me to lend him twenty-five francs during the day, saying that otherwise he could not go to the wedding, not having enough even to pay his railway fare."

" But he might have some savings—a hundred-franc note, for instance, which he didn't like to change."

François shook his head with an incredulous smile.

" Guespin isn't the man to have savings," said he. " Women and cards exhaust all his wages. No longer ago than last week, the keeper of the Café du Commerce came here and made a row on account of what he owed him, and threatened to go to the count about it."

Perceiving the effect of what he said, the valet, as if to correct himself, hastened to add:

" I have no ill-will toward Guespin; before to-day I've always considered him a clever fellow, though he was too much of a practical joker; he was, perhaps, a little proud, considering his bringing up——"

" You may go," said the judge, cutting the disquisition of M. François short; the valet retired.

During this colloquy, Guespin had little by little

come to himself. The judge of instruction, Plantat, and the mayor narrowly watched the play of his countenance, which he had not the coolness to compose, while the doctor held his pulse and counted its beating.

" Remorse, and fear of punishment," muttered the mayor.

" Innocence, and the impossibility of proving it," responded Plantat in a low tone.

M. Domini heard both these exclamations, but did not appear to take notice of them. His opinion was not formed, and he did not wish that anyone should be able to foretell, by any word of his, what it would be.

" Are you better, my friend?" asked Dr. Gendron, of Guespin.

The poor fellow made an affirmative sign. Then, having looked around with the anxious glance of a man who calculates a precipice over which he has fallen, he passed his hand across his eyes and stammered:

" Something to drink!"

A glass of water was brought, and he drank it at a draught, with an expression of intense satisfaction. Then he got upon his feet.

" Are you now in a fit state to answer me?" asked the judge.

Guespin staggered a little, then drew himself up. He continued erect before the judge, supporting himself against a table. The nervous trembling of his hands diminished, the blood returned to his cheeks, and as he listened, he arranged the disorder of his clothes.

" You know the events of this night, don't you?" commenced the judge; " the Count and Countess de

Trémorel have been murdered. You went away yesterday with all the servants of the château; you left
them at the Lyons station about nine o'clock; you have
just returned, alone. Where have you passed the
night? "

Guespin hung his head and remained silent.

" That is not all," continued M. Domini; " yesterday you had no money, the fact is well known; one of
your fellow-servants has just proved it. To-day, one
hundred and sixty-seven francs are found in your wallet. Where did you get this money? "

The unhappy creature's lip moved as if he wished
to answer; a sudden thought seemed to check him, for
he did not speak.

" More yet. What is this card of a hardware establishment that has been found in your pocket? "

Guespin made a sign of desperation, and stammered:
" I am innocent."

" I have not as yet accused you," said the judge of
instruction, quickly. " You knew, perhaps, that the
count received a considerable sum yesterday? "

A bitter smile parted Guespin's lips as he answered:
" I know well enough that everything is against me."

There was a profound silence. The doctor, the
mayor, and Plantat, seized with a keen curiosity, dared
not move. Perhaps nothing in the world is more
thrilling than one of these merciless duels between
justice and a man suspected of a crime. The questions
may seem insignificant, the answers irrelevant; both
questions and answers envelop terrible, hidden meanings. The smallest gesture, the most rapid movement
of physiognomy may acquire deep significance, a
fugitive light in the eye betray an advantage gained;

an imperceptible change in the voice may be confession.

The coolness of M. Domini was disheartening.

" Let us see," said he after a pause.: " where did you pass the night? How did you get this money? And what does this address mean? "

" Eh! " cried Guespin, with the rage of powerlessness, " I should tell you what you would not believe."

The judge was about to ask another question, but Guespin cut him short.

" No; you wouldn't believe me," he repeated, his eyes glistening with anger. " Do men like you believe men like me? I have a past, you know, of antecedents, as you would say. The past! They throw that in my face, as if the future depended on the past. Well, yes; it's true, I'm a debauchee, a gambler, a drunkard, an idler, but what of it? It's true I have been before the police court, and condemned for night poaching—what does that prove? I have wasted my life, but whom have I wronged if not myself? My past! Have I not sufficiently expiated it? "

Guespin was self-possessed, and finding in himself sensations which awoke a sort of eloquence, he expressed himself with a savage energy well calculated to strike his hearers.

" I have not always served others," he continued; " my father was in easy circumstances—almost rich. He had large gardens, near Saumur, and he passed for one of the best gardeners of that region. I was educated, and when sixteen years old, began to study law. Four years later they thought me a talented youth. Unhappily for me, my father died. He left me a landed property worth a hundred thousand francs: I sold it out for sixty thousand and went to Paris. I was a fool then. I had the fever of pleasure-seeking, a thirst for all sorts of pastimes, perfect health, plenty of money. I found Paris a narrow limit for my vices; it seemed to me that the objects of my desires were wanting. I thought my sixty thousand francs would last forever."

Guespin paused; a thousand memories of those times rushed into his thoughts and he muttered: "Those were good times."

"My sixty thousand francs," he resumed, "held out eight years. Then I hadn't a sou, yet I longed to continue my way of living. You understand, don't you? About this time, the police, one night, arrested me. I was 'detained' six months. You will find the records of the affair at the prefecture. Do you know what it will tell you? It will tell you that on leaving prison I fell into that shameful and abominable misery which exists in Paris. It will tell you that I have lived among the worst and lowest outcasts of Paris—and it is the truth."

The worthy mayor was filled with consternation.

"Good Heaven!" thought he, "what an audacious and cynical rascal! and to think that one is liable at any time to admit such servants into his house!"

The judge held his tongue. He knew that Guespin was in such a state that, under the irresistible impulse of passion, he might betray his innermost thoughts.

"But there is one thing," continued the suspected man, "that the record will not tell you; that, disgusted with this abject life, I was tempted to suicide. It will not tell you anything of my desperate attempts, my repentance, my relapses. At last, I was able in part to reform. I got work; and after being in four situations, engaged myself here. I found myself well off. I always spent my month's wages in advance, it's true—

but what would you have? And ask if anyone has ever had to complain of me."

It is well known that among the most intelligent criminals, those who have had a certain degree of education, and enjoyed some good fortune, are the most redoubtable. According to this, Guespin was decidedly dangerous. So thought those who heard him. Meanwhile, exhausted by his excitement, he paused and wiped his face, covered with perspiration.

M. Domini had not lost sight of his plan of attack.

" All that is very well," said he, " we will return to your confession at the proper time and place. But just now the question is, how you spent your night, and where you got this money."

This persistency seemed to exasperate Guespin.

" Eh! " cried he, " how do you want me to answer? The truth? You wouldn't credit it. As well keep silent. It is a fatality."

" I warn you for your own sake," resumed the judge, " that if you persist in refusing to answer, the charges which weigh upon you are such that I will have you arrested as suspected of this murder."

This menace seemed to have a remarkable effect on Guespin. Great tears filled his eyes, up to that time dry and flashing, and silently rolled down his cheeks. His energy was exhausted; he fell on his knees, crying:

" Mercy! I beg you, Monsieur, not to arrest me; I swear I am innocent, I swear it! "

" Speak, then."

" You wish it," said Guespin, rising. Then he suddenly changed his tone. " No, I will not speak, I cannot! One man alone could save me; it is the count; and he is dead. I am innocent; yet if the guilty are not found, I am lost. Everything is against me. I know it too well. Now, do with me as you please; I will not say another word."

Guespin's determination, confirmed by his look, did not surprise the judge.

"You will reflect," said he, quietly, "only, when you have reflected, I shall not have the same confidence in what you say as I should have now. Possibly," and the judge spoke slowly and with emphasis, "you have only had an indirect part in this crime; if so——"

"Neither indirect nor direct," interrupted Guespin; and he added, violently, "what misery! To be innocent, and not able to defend myself."

"Since it is so," resumed M. Domini, "you should not object to be placed before Mme. de Trémorel's body?"

The accused did not seem affected by this menace. He was conducted into the hall whither they had fetched the countess. There, he examined the body with a cold and calm eye. He said, simply:

"She is happier than I; she is dead, she suffers no longer; and I, who am not guilty, am accused of her death."

M. Domini made one more effort.

"Come, Guespin; if in any way you know of this crime, I conjure you, tell me. If you know the murderers, name them. Try to merit some indulgence for your frankness and repentance."

Guespin made a gesture as if resigned to persecution. "By all that is most sacred," he answered, "I am innocent. Yet I see clearly that if the murderer is not found, I am lost."

Little by little M. Domini's conviction was formed and confirmed. An inquest of this sort is not so diffi-

cult as may be imagined.   The difficulty is to seize at
the beginning, in the entangled skein, the main thread,
which must lead to the truth through all the mazes, the
ruses, silence, falsehoods of the guilty.   M. Domini
was certain that he held this precious thread.   Having
one of the assassins, he knew well that he would secure
the others.   Our prisons, where good soup is eaten, and
good beds are provided, have tongues, as well as the
dungeons of the mediæval ages.

The judge ordered the brigadier to arrest Guespin,
and told him not to lose sight of him.   He then sent for
old Bertaud.   This worthy personage was not one of
the people who worry themselves.   He had had so
many affairs with the men of law, that one inquisition
the more disturbed him little.

"This man has a bad reputation in my commune,"
whispered the mayor to M. Domini.

Bertaud heard it, however, and smiled.

Questioned by the judge of instruction, he recounted very clearly and exactly what had happened in the
morning, his resistance, and his son's determination.
He explained the reason for the falsehood they told;
and here again the chapter of antecedents came up.

"Look here; I'm better than my reputation, after
all," said he.   "There are many folks who can't say
as much.   You see many things when you go about at
night—enough."

He was urged to explain his allusions, but in vain.

When he was asked where and how he had passed
the night, he answered, that having left the cabaret at
ten o'clock, he went to put down some traps in Mauprévoir wood; and had gone home and to bed about
one o'clock.

"By the bye," added he, "there ought to be some game in those traps by this time."

"Can you bring a witness to prove that you went home at one?" asked the mayor, who bethought him of the count's clock, stopped at twenty minutes past three.

"Don't know, I'm sure," carelessly responded the poacher, "it's quite likely that my son didn't wake up when I went to bed."

He added, seeing the judge reflect:

"I suspect that you are going to imprison me until the murderers are discovered. If it was winter, I wouldn't complain much; a fellow is well off in prison then, for it's warm there. But just at the time for hunting, it's provoking. It will be a good lesson for that Philippe; it'll teach him what it costs to render a service to gentlefolks."

"Enough!" interrupted M. Domini, sternly. "Do you know Guespin?"

This name suddenly subdued the careless insolence of the marauder; his little gray eyes experienced a singular restlessness.

"Certainly," he answered in an embarrassed tone, "we have often made a party at cards, you understand, while sipping our ' gloria.' " *

The man's inquietude struck the four who heard him. Plantat, especially, betrayed profound surprise. The old vagabond was too shrewd not to perceive the effect which he produced.

"Faith, so much the worse!" cried he: " I'll tell you everything. Every man for himself, isn't it? If Guespin has done the deed, it will not blacken him any more, nor make him any the worse off. I know him,

* Coffee and brandy.

simply because he used to sell me the grapes and straw-
berries from the count's conservatories; I *suppose* he
stole them; we divided the money, and I left."

Plantat could not refrain from an exclamation of satisfaction, as if to say, "Good luck! I knew it well
enough!"

When he said he would be sent to prison, Bertaud
was not wrong. The judge ordered his arrest.

It was now Philippe's turn.

The poor fellow was in a pitiable state; he was crying bitterly.

"To accuse me of such a crime, *me!*" he kept re-
peating.

On being questioned he told the pure and simple
truth, excusing himself, however, for having dared to
penetrate into the park. When he was asked at what
hour his father reached home, he said he knew nothing
about it; he had gone to bed about nine, and had not
awoke until morning. He knew Guespin, from having seen him at his father's several times. He knew
that the old man had some transactions with the gardener, but he was ignorant as to what they were. He
had never spoken four times to Guespin. The judge
ordered Philippe to be set at liberty, not that he was
wholly convinced of his innocence, but because if the
crime had been committed by several persons, it was
well to have one of them free; he could be watched,
and he would betray the whereabouts of the rest.

Meanwhile the count's body was nowhere to be
found. The park had been rigidly searched, but in
vain. The mayor suggested that he had been thrown
into the river, which was also M. Domini's opinion;
and some fishermen were sent to drag the Seine, com-

mencing their search a little above the place where the
countess was found.

It was then nearly three o'clock. M. Plantat remarked that probably no one had eaten anything during the day. Would it not be wise to take something,
he suggested, if the investigations were to be pursued
till night? This appeal to the trivial necessities of our
frail humanity highly displeased the worthy mayor;
but the rest readily assented to the suggestion, and M.
Courtois, though not in the least hungry, followed the
general example. Around the table which was yet
wet with the wine spilt by the assassins, the judge, M.
Plantat, the mayor, and the doctor sat down, and par-
took of an improvised collation.

V

The staircase had been put under guard, but the
vestibule had remained free. People were heard coming and going, tramping and coughing; then rising
above this continuous noise, the oaths of the gendarmes trying to keep back the crowd. From time to
time, a scared face passed by the dining-room door,
which was ajar. These were curious folks who, more
daring than the rest, wished to see the " men of justice " eating, and tried to hear a word or two, to report them, and so become important in the eyes of the
others. But the " men of justice "—as they said at
Orcival—took care to say nothing of moment while
the doors were open, and while a servant was passing
to and fro. Greatly moved by this frightful crime,
disturbed by the mystery which surrounded it, they
hid their impressions. Each, on his part, studied the

probability of his suspicions, and kept his opinion to himself.

M. Domini, as he ate, put his notes in order, numbering the leaves, marking certain peculiarly significant answers of the suspected persons with a cross. He was, perhaps, the least tormented of the four companions at this funereal repast. The crime did not seem to him one of those which keep judges of instruction sleepless through the night; he saw clearly the motive of it; and he had Bertaud and Guespin, two of the assassins, or at least accomplices, secure.

M. Plantat and Dr. Gendron, seated next each other, were talking of the illness which carried off Sauvresy. M. Courtois listened to the hubbub without.

The news of the double murder was soon noised about the neighborhood, and the crowd increased every minute. It filled the court, and became bolder and bolder; the gendarmes were overwhelmed. Then or never was the time for the mayor to show his authority. "I am going to make these people listen to reason," said he, "and make them retire." And at once, wiping his mouth, he threw his tumbled napkin on the table, and went out.

It was time. The brigadier's injunctions were no longer heeded. Some curious people, more eager than the rest, had flanked the position and were forcing an entrance through the gate leading to the garden. The mayor's presence did not perhaps intimidate the crowd much, but it redoubled the energy of the gendames; the vestibule was cleared, amid murmurings against the arm of the law.

What a chance for a speech! M. Courtois was not wanting to the occasion. He believed that his eloquence, endowed with the virtues of a cold shower-bath, would calm this unwonted effervescence of his constituency. He stepped forward upon the steps, his left hand resting in the opening of his vest, gesturing with his right in the proud and impassible attitude which the sculptor lends to great orators. It was thus that he posed before his council when, finding unexpected opposition, he undertook to impose his will upon them, and recall the recalcitrant members to their duty.

His speech, in fragments, penetrated to the dining-room. According as he turned to the right or to the left, his voice was clear and distinct, or was lost in space. He said:

"Fellow-citizens, an atrocious crime, unheard of before in our commune, has shocked our peaceable and honest neighborhood. I understand and excuse your feverish emotion, your natural indignation. As well as you, my friends, more than you—I cherished and esteemed the noble Count de Trémorel, and his virtuous wife. We mourn them together——"

"I assure you," said Dr. Gendron to M. Plantat, "that the symptoms you describe are not uncommon after pleurisy. From the acute state, the inflammation passes to the chronic state, and becomes complicated with pneumonia."

"But nothing," pursued the mayor, "can justify a curiosity, which by its importunate attempts to be satisfied, embarrasses the investigation, and is, at all events, a punishable interference with the cause of justice. Why this unwonted gathering? Why these rumors and noises? These premature conjectures?"

"There were several consultations," said M. Plantat, "which did not have favorable results. Sauvresy suffered altogether strange and unaccountable tortures. He complained of troubles so unwonted, so absurd, if you'll excuse the word, that he discouraged all the conjectures of the most experienced physicians."

" Was it not R——, of Paris, who attended him ? "

" Exactly. He came daily, and often remained overnight. Many times I have seen him ascending the principal street of the village, with troubled countenance, as he went to give his prescription to the apothecary."

" Be wise enough," cried M. Courtois, " to moderate your just anger; be calm; be dignified."

" Surely," continued Dr. Dendron, " your apothecary is an intelligent man; but you have at Orcival a fellow who quite outdoes him, a fellow who knows how to make money; one Robelot——"

" Robelot, the bone-setter? "

" That's the man. I suspect him of giving consultations, and prescribing *sub rosa.* He is very clever. In fact I educated him. Five or six years ago, he was my laboratory boy, and even now I employ him when I have a delicate operation on hand——"

The doctor stopped, struck by the alteration in the impassible Plantat's features.

" What is the matter, my friend? " he asked. " Are you ill? "

The judge left his notes, to look at him.

" Why," said he, " Monsieur Plantat is very pale——"

But M. Plantat speedily resumed his habitual expression.

" 'Tis nothing," he answered, " really nothing. With my abominable stomach, as soon as I change my hour of eating——"

Having reached his peroration, M. Courtois raised his voice.

"Return," said he, "to your peaceable homes, your quiet avocations. Rest assured the law protects you. Already justice has begun its work; two of the criminals are in its power, and we are on the track of their accomplices."

"Of all the servants of the château," remarked M. Plantat, "there remains not one who knew Sauvresy. The domestics have one by one been replaced."

"No doubt," answered the doctor, "the sight of the old servants would be disagreeable to Monsieur de Trémorel."

He was interrupted by the mayor, who re-entered, his eyes glowing, his face animated, wiping his forehead.

"I have let the people know," said he, "the indecency of their curiosity. They have all gone away. They were anxious to get at Philippe Bertaud, the brigadier says; public opinion has a sharp scent."

Hearing the door open, he turned, and found himself face to face with a man whose features were scarcely visible, so profoundly did he bow, his hat pressed against his breast.

"What do you wish?" sternly asked M. Courtois. "By what right have you come in here? Who are you?"

The man drew himself up.

"I am Monsieur Lecoq," he replied, with a gracious smile. "Monsieur Lecoq of the detective force, sent by the prefect of police in reply to a telegram, for this affair."

This declaration clearly surprised all present, even the judge of instruction.

In France, each profession has its special externals, as it were, insignia, which betray it at first view. Each profession has its conventional type, and when public opinion has adopted a type, it does not admit it possible that the type should be departed from. What is a doctor? A grave man, all in black, with a white cravat. A gentleman with a capacious stomach, adorned with heavy gold seals, can only be a banker. Everybody knows that the artist is a merry liver, with a peaked hat, a velvet vest, and enormous ruffles. By virtue of this rule, the detective of the prefecture ought to have an eye full of mystery, something suspicious about him, a negligence of dress, and imitation jewelry. The most obtuse shopkeeper is sure that he can scent a detective at twenty paces; a big man with mustaches, and a shining felt hat, his throat imprisoned by a collar of hair, dressed in a black, threadbare surtout, carefully buttoned up on account of the entire absence of linen. Such is the type. But, according to this, M. Lecoq, as he entered the dining-room at Valfeuillu, had by no means the air of a detective. True, M. Lecoq can assume whatever air he pleases. His friends declare that he has a physiognomy peculiar to himself, which he resumes when he enters his own house, and which he retains by his own fireside, with his slippers on; but the fact is not well proved. What is certain, is that his mobile face lends itself to strange metamorphoses; that he moulds his features according to his will, as the sculptor moulds clay for modelling. He changes everything, even his look.

" So," said the judge of instruction, " the prefect has sent you to me, in case certain investigations become necessary."

" Yes, Monsieur, quite at your service."

M. Lecoq had on this day assumed a handsome wig of lank hair, of that vague color called Paris blonde, parted on the side by a line pretentiously fanciful; whiskers of the same color puffed out with bad pomade, encircled a pallid face. His big eyes seemed congealed within their red border, an open smile rested on his thick lips, which, in parting, discovered a range of long yellow teeth. His face, otherwise, expressed nothing in particular. It was a nearly equal mixture of timidity, self-sufficiency, and contentment. It was quite impossible to concede the least intelligence to the possessor of such a phiz. One involuntarily looked for a goitre. The retail haberdashers, who, having cheated for thirty years in their threads and needles, retire with large incomes, should have such heads as this. His apparel was as dull as his person. His coat resembled all coats, his trousers all trousers. A hair chain, the same color as his whiskers, was attached to a large silver watch, which bulged out his left waistcoat pocket. While speaking, he fumbled with a confection-box made of transparent horn, full of little square lozenges, and adorned by a portrait of a very homely, well-dressed woman—" the defunct," no doubt. As the conversation proceeded, according as he was satisfied or disturbed, M. Lecoq munched a lozenge, or directed glances toward the portrait which were quite a poem in themselves.

Having examined the man a long time, the judge of instruction shrugged his shoulders. " Well," said M. Domini, finally, " now that you are here, we will explain to you what has occurred."

" Oh, that's quite useless," responded Lecoq, with a satisfied air, " perfectly useless, sir."

"Nevertheless, it is necessary that you should know——"

"What? that which monsieur the judge knows?" interrupted the detective, "for that I already know. Let us agree there has been a murder, with theft as its motive; and start from that point. The countess's body has been found—not so that of the count. What else? Bertaud, an acknowledged rogue, is arrested; he merits a little punishment, doubtless. Guespin came back drunk; ah, there are sad charges against this Guespin! His past is deplorable; it is not known where he passed the night, he refuses to answer, he brings no alibi—this is indeed grave!"

M. Plantat gazed at the detective with visible pleasure.

"Who has told you about these things?" asked M. Domini.

"Well—everybody has told me a little."

"But where?"

"Here: I've already been here two hours, and even heard the mayor's speech."

And, satisfied with the effect he had produced, M. Lecoq munched a lozenge.

"You were not aware, then," resumed the judge, "that I was waiting for you?"

"Pardon me," said the detective; "I hope you will be kind enough to hear me. You see, it is indispensable to study the ground; one must look about, establish his batteries. I am anxious to catch the general rumor—public opinion, as they say, so as to distrust it."

"All this," answered M. Domini, severely, "does not justify your delay."

M. Lecoq glanced tenderly at the portrait.

" Monsieur the judge," said he, " has only to inquire
at the prefecture, and he will learn that I know my profession. The great thing requisite, in order to make
an effective search, is to remain unknown. The police
are not popular. Now, if they knew who I was, and
why I was here, I might go out, but nobody would tell
me anything ; I might ask questions—they'd serve me
a hundred lies ; they would distrust me, and hold their
tongues."

" Quite true—quite true," murmured Plantat, coming to the support of the detective.

M. Lecoq went on :

" So that when I was told that I was going into the
country, I put on my country face and clothes. I arrive here and everybody, on seeing me, says to himself, ' Here's a curious bumpkin, but not a bad fellow.'
Then I slip about, listen, talk, make the rest talk ! I
ask this question and that, and am answered frankly ;
I inform myself, gather hints, no one troubles himself
about me. These Orcival folks are positively charming ; why, I've already made several friends, and am
invited to dine this very evening."

M. Domini did not like the police, and scarcely concealed it. He rather submitted to their co-operation
than accepted it, solely because he could not do without them. While listening to M. Lecoq, he could not
but approve of what he said ; yet he looked at him with
an eye by no means friendly.

" Since you know so much about the matter," observed he, dryly, " we will proceed to examine the
scene of the crime."

" I am quite at Monsieur the judge's orders," returned the detective, laconically. As everyone was

getting up, he took the opportunity to offer M. Plantat his lozenge-box.

"Monsieur perhaps uses them?"

Plantat, unwilling to decline, appropriated a lozenge, and the detective's face became again serene. Public sympathy was necessary to him, as it is to all great comedians.

VI

M. Lecoq was the first to reach the staircase, and the spots of blood at once caught his eye.

"Oh," cried he, at each spot he saw, "oh, oh, the wretches!"

M. Courtois was much moved to find so much sensibility in a detective. The latter, as he continued to ascend, went on:

"The wretches! They don't often leave traces like this everywhere—or at least they wipe them out."

On gaining the first landing, and the door of the boudoir which led into the chamber, he stopped, eagerly scanning, before he entered, the position of the rooms.

Then he entered the boudoir, saying:

"Come; I don't see my way clear yet."

"But it seems to me," remarked the judge, "that we have already important materials to aid your task. It is clear that Guespin, if he is not an accomplice, at least knew something about the crime."

M. Lecoq had recourse to the portrait in the lozenge-box. It was more than a glance, it was a confidence. He evidently said something to the dear defunct, which he dared not say aloud.

"I see that Guespin is seriously compromised," re-

sumed he. " Why didn't he want to tell where he
passed the night? But, then, public opinion is against
him, and I naturally distrust *that*."

The detective stood alone in the middle of the room,
the rest, at his request, remained at the threshold,
and looking keenly about him, searched for some explanation of the frightful disorder of the apartment.

" Fools!" cried he, in an irritated tone, " double
brutes! Because they murder people so as to rob
them, is no reason why they should break everything
in the house. Sharp folks don't smash up furniture;
they carry pretty picklocks, which work well and make
no noise. Idiots! one would say——"

He stopped with his mouth wide open.

" Eh! Not so bungling, after all, perhaps."

The witnesses of this scene remained motionless at
the door, following, with an interest mingled with surprise, the detective's movements.

Kneeling down, he passed his flat palm over the
thick carpet, among the broken porcelain.

" It's damp; very damp. The tea was not all drunk,
it seems, when the cups were broken."

" Some tea might have remained in the teapot," suggested Plantat.

" I know it," answered M. Lecoq, " just what I was
going to say. So that this dampness cannot tell us
the exact moment when the crime was committed."

" But the clock does, and very exactly," interrupted
the mayor.

" The mayor," said M. Domini, " in his notes, well
explains that the movements of the clock stopped when
it fell."

" But see here," said M. Plantat, " it was the odd
hour marked by that clock that struck me. The hands

point to twenty minutes past three; yet we know that
the countess was fully dressed, when she was struck.
Was she up taking tea at three in the morning?   It's
hardly probable."

" I, too, was struck with that circumstance," returned M. Lecoq, " and that's why I said, ' not so stupid!'   Well, let's see."

He lifted the clock with great care, and replaced it
on the mantel, being cautious to set it exactly upright.
The hands continued to point to twenty minutes past
three.

" Twenty past three! " muttered he, while slipping a
little wedge under the stand.   " People don't take tea
at *that* hour.   Still less common is it that people are
murdered at daylight."

He opened the clock-case with some difficulty, and
pushed the longer hand to the figure of half-past three.

The clock struck eleven!

" Good," cried M. Lecoq, triumphantly.   " That is
the truth! " and drawing the lozenge-box from his
pocket, he excitedly crushed a lozenge between his
teeth.

The simplicity of this discovery surprised the specta-
tors; the idea of trying the clock in this way had occurred to no one.   M. Courtois, especially, was be-
wildered.

" There's a fellow," whispered he to the doctor,
" who knows what he's about."

" *Ergo*," resumed M. Lecoq (who knew Latin), " we
have here, not brutes, as I thought at first, but rascals
who looked beyond the end of their knife.   They intended to put us off the scent, by deceiving us as to the
hour."

"I don't see their object very clearly," said M. Courtois, timidly.

"Yet it is easy to see it," answered M. Domini. "Was it not for their interest to make it appear that the crime was committed after the last train for Paris had left? Guespin, leaving his companions at the Lyons station at nine, might have reached here at ten, murdered the count and countess, seized the money which he knew to be in the count's possession, and returned to Paris by the last train."

"These conjectures are very shrewd," interposed M. Plantat; "but how is it that Guespin did not rejoin his comrades in the Batignolles? For in that way, to a certain degree, he might have provided a kind of alibi."

Dr. Gendron had been sitting on the only unbroken chair in the chamber, reflecting on Plantat's sudden embarrassment, when he had spoken of Robelot the bone-setter. The remarks of the judge drew him from his revery; he got up, and said:

"There is another point; putting forward the time was perhaps useful to Guespin, but it would greatly damage Bertaud, his accomplice."

"But," answered M. Domini, "it might be that Bertaud was not consulted. As to Guespin, he had no doubt good reasons for not returning to the wedding. His restlessness, after such a deed, would possibly have betrayed him."

M. Lecoq had not thought fit to speak as yet. Like a doctor at a sick bedside, he wanted to be sure of his diagnosis. He had returned to the mantel, and again pushed forward the hands of the clock. It sounded, successively, half-past eleven, then twelve, then half-past twelve, then one.

As he moved the hands, he kept muttering:

"Apprentices—chance brigands! You are malicious, parbleu, but you don't think of everything. You give a push to the hands, but don't remember to put the striking in harmony with them. Then comes along a detective, an old rat who knows things, and the dodge is discovered."

M. Domini and Plantat held their tongues. M. Lecoq walked up to them.

"Monsieur the Judge," said he, "is perhaps now convinced that the deed was done at half-past ten."

"Unless," interrupted M. Plantat, "the machinery of the clock has been out of order."

"That often happens," added M. Courtois. "The clock in my drawing-room is in such a state that I never know the time of day."

M. Lecoq reflected.

"It is possible," said he, "that Monsieur Plantat is right. The probability is in favor of my theory; but probability, in such an affair, is not sufficient; we must have certainty. There happily remains a mode of testing the matter—the bed; I'll wager it is rumpled up." Then addressing the mayor, "I shall need a servant to lend me a hand."

"I'll help you," said Plantat, "that will be a quicker way."

They lifted the top of the bed and set it on the floor, at the same time raising the curtains.

"Hum!" cried M. Lecoq, "was I right?"

"True," said M. Domini, surprised, "the bed is rumpled."

"Yes; and yet no one has lain in it."

"But—" objected M. Courtois.

"I am sure of what I say," interrupted the detective. "The sheets, it is true, have been thrown back, per-

haps someone has rolled about in the bed; the pillows
have been tumbled, the quilts and curtains ruffled, but
this bed has not the appearance of having been slept in.
It is, perhaps, more difficult to rumple up a bed than to
put it in order again.   To make it up, the coverings
must be taken off, and the mattresses turned.   To dis-
arrange it, one must actually lie down in it, and warm
it with the body.   A bed is one of those terrible witnesses which never misguide, and against which no
counter testimony can be given.   Nobody has gone to
bed in this——"

"The countess," remarked Plantat, "was dressed;
but the count might have gone to bed first."

"No," answered M. Lecoq, "I'll prove to the contrary.   The proof is easy, indeed, and a child of ten,
having heard it, wouldn't think of being deceived by
this intentional disorder of the bedclothes."

M. Lecoq's auditors drew up to him.   He put the
coverings back upon the middle of the bed, and went
on:

"Both of the pillows are much rumpled, are they
not?   But look under the bolster—it is all smooth, and
you find none of those wrinkles which are made by the
weight of the head and the moving about of the arms.
That's not all; look at the bed from the middle to the
foot.   The sheets being laid carefully, the upper and
under lie close together everywhere.   Slip your hand
underneath—there—you see there is a resistance to
your hand which would not occur if the legs had been
stretched in that place.   Now Monsieur de Trémorel
was tall enough to extend the full length of the bed."

This demonstration was so clear, its proof so palpable, that it could not be gainsaid.

"This is nothing," continued M. Lecoq.   "Let us

examine the second mattress. When a person pur- posely disarranges a bed, he does not think of the sec- ond mattress."

He lifted up the upper mattress, and observed that the covering of the under one was perfectly even.

" H'm, the second mattress," muttered M. Lecoq, as if some memory crossed his mind.

" It appears to be proved," observed the judge, " that Monsieur de Trémorel had not gone to bed."

" Besides," added the doctor, " if he had been mur- dered in his bed, his clothes would be lying here some- where."

" Without considering," suggested M. Lecoq, " that some blood must have been found on the sheets. De- cidedly, these criminals were not shrewd."

" What seems to me surprising," M. Plantat ob- served to the judge, " is that anybody would succeed in killing, except in his sleep, a young man so vigorous as Count Hector."

" And in a house full of weapons," added Dr. Gendron; " for the count's cabinet is full of guns, swords and hunting knives; it's a perfect arsenal."

" Alas!" sighed M. Courtois, " we know of worse catastrophies. There is not a week that the papers don't——"

He stopped, chagrined, for nobody was listening to him. Plantat claimed the general attention, and con- tinued:

" The confusion in the house seems to you surpris- ing; well now, I'm surprised that it is not worse than it is. I am, so to speak, an old man; I haven't the en- ergy of a young man of thirty-five; yet it seems to me that if assassins should get into my house, when I was there, and up, it would go hard with them. I don't know what I would do; probably I should be killed; but surely I would give the alarm. I would defend myself, and cry out, and open the windows, and set the house afire."

" Let us add," insisted the doctor, " that it is not easy to surprise a man who is awake. There is always an unexpected noise which puts one on his guard. Perhaps it is a creaking door, or a cracking stair. However cautious the murderer, he does not surprise his victim."

" They may have used fire-arms," struck in the worthy mayor, " that has been done. You are quietly sitting in your chamber; it is summer, and your windows are open; you are chatting with your wife, and sipping a cup of tea; outside, the assassins are supplied with a short ladder; one ascends to a level with the window, sights you at his ease, presses the trigger, the bullet speeds——"

" And," continued the doctor, " the whole neighborhood, aroused by it, hastens to the spot."

" Permit me, pardon, permit me," said M. Courtois, testily, " that would be so in a populous town. Here, in the midst of a vast park, no. Think, doctor, of the isolation of this house. The nearest neighbor is a long way off, and between there are many large trees, intercepting the sound. Let us test it by experience. I will fire a pistol in this room, and I'll wager that you will not hear the echo in the road."

" In the daytime, perhaps, but not in the night."

" Well," said M. Domini, who had been reflecting while M. Courtois was talking, " if against all hope, Guespin does not decide to speak to-night, or to-morrow, the count's body will afford us a key to the mystery."

During this discussion, M. Lecoq had continued his investigations, lifting the furniture, studying the fractures, examining the smallest pieces, as if they might betray the truth. Now and then, he took out an instrument-case, from which he produced a shank, which he introduced and turned in the locks. He found several keys on the carpet, and on a rack, a towel, which he carefully put one side, as if he deemed it important. He came and went from the bedroom to the count's cabinet, without losing a word that was said; noting in his memory, not so much the phrases uttered, as the diverse accents and intonations with which they were spoken. In an inquest such as that of the crime of Orcival, when several officials find themselves face to face, they hold a certain reserve toward each other. They know each other to have nearly equal experience, to be shrewd, clear-headed, equally interested in discovering the truth, not disposed to confide in appearances, difficult to surprise. Each one, likely enough, gives a different interpretation to the facts revealed; each may have a different theory of the deed; but a superficial observer would not note these differences. Each, while dissimulating his real thoughts, tries to penetrate those of his neighbor, and if they are opposed to his own, to convert him to his opinion. The great importance of a single word justifies this caution. Men who hold the liberty and lives of others in their hands, a scratch of whose pen condemns to death, are apt to feel heavily the burden of their responsibility. It is an ineffable solace, to feel that this burden is shared by others. This is why no one dares take the initiative, or express himself openly; but each awaits other opinions, to adopt or oppose them. They exchange fewer affirmations than sug-

5

gestions. They proceed by insinuation; then they utter commonplaces, ridiculous suppositions, asides, provocative, as it were, of other explanations.

In this instance, the judge of instruction and Plantat were far from being of the same opinion; they knew it before speaking a word. But M. Domini, whose opinion rested on material and palpable facts, which appeared to him indisputable, was not disposed to provoke contradiction. Plantat, on the contrary, whose system seemed to rest on *impressions*, on a series of logical deductions, would not clearly express himself, without a positive and pressing invitation. His last speech, impressively uttered, had not been replied to; he judged that he had advanced far enough to sound the detective.

" Well, Monsieur Lecoq," asked he, " have you found any new traces ? "

M. Lecoq was at that moment curiously examining a large portrait of the Count Hector, which hung opposite the bed. Hearing M. Plantat's question, he turned.

" I have found nothing decisive," answered he, " and I have found nothing to refute my conjectures. But——"

He did not finish; perhaps he too, recoiled before his share of the responsibility.

" What ? " insisted M. Domini, sternly.

" I was going to say," resumed M. Lecoq, " that I am not yet satisfied. I have my lantern and a candle in it; I only need a match——"

" Please preserve your decorum," interrupted the judge severely.

" Very well, then," continued M. Lecoq, in a tone too humble to be serious, " I still hesitate. If the doctor, now, would kindly proceed to examine the countess's body, he would do me a great service."

" I was just going to ask the same favor, Doctor," said M. Domini.

The doctor answering, " Willingly," directed his steps toward the door.

M. Lecoq caught him by the arm.

" If you please," said he, in a tone totally unlike that he had used up to this time, " I would like to call your attention to the wounds on the head, made by a blunt instrument, which I suppose to be a hammer. I have studied these wounds, and though I am no doctor, they seem to me suspicious."

" And to me," M. Plantat quickly added. " It seemed to me, that in the places struck, there was no emission of blood in the cutaneous vessels."

" The nature of these wounds," continued M. Lecoq, " will be a valuable indication, which will fix my opinion." And, as he felt keenly the brusque manner of the judge, he added:

" It is you, Doctor, who hold the match."

M. Gendron was about to leave the room, when Baptiste, the mayor's servant—the man who wouldn't be scolded—appeared. He bowed and said:

" I have come for Monsieur the Mayor."

" For me? why? " asked M. Courtois. " What's the matter? They don't give me a minute's rest! Answer that I am busy."

" It's on account of madame," resumed the placid Baptiste; " she isn't at all well." The excellent mayor grew slightly pale.

" My wife! " cried he, alarmed. " What do you mean? Explain yourself."

" The postman arrived just now," returned Baptiste

with a most tranquil air, " and I carried the letters to
madame, who was in the drawing-room.   Hardly had
I turned on my heels when I heard a shriek, and the
noise of someone falling to the floor."   Baptiste spoke
slowly, taking artful pains to prolong his master's anguish.

" Speak! go on!" cried the mayor, exasperated.
" Speak, won't you?"

" I naturally opened the drawing-room door again.
What did I see? madame, at full length on the floor.
I called for help; the chambermaid, cook, and others
came hastening up, and we carried madame to her bed.
Justine said that it was a letter from Mademoiselle
Laurence which overcame my mistress——"

At each word Baptiste hesitated, reflected; his eyes,
giving the lie to his solemn face, betrayed the great
satisfaction he felt in relating his master's misfortunes.

His master was full of consternation.   As it is with
all of us, when we know not exactly what ill is about
to befall us, he dared not ask any questions.   He stood
still, crushed; lamenting, instead of hastening home.
M. Plantat profited by the pause to question the servant, with a look which Baptiste dared not disobey.

" What, a letter from Mademoiselle Laurence?
Isn't she here, then?"

" No, sir: she went away a week ago, to pass a
month with one of her aunts."

" And how is madame?"

" Better, sir; only she cries piteously."

The unfortunate mayor had now somewhat recovered his presence of mind.   He seized Baptiste by the
arm.

" Come along," cried he, " come along!"

They hastened off.

" Poor man ! " said the judge of instruction. " Perhaps his daughter is dead."

M. Plantat shook his head.

" If it were only that ! " muttered he. He added, turning to M. Domini:

" Do you recall the allusions of Bertaud, Monsieur ? "

VII

The judge of instruction, the doctor, and M. Plantat exchanged a significant look. What misfortune had befallen M. Courtois, this worthy, and despite his faults, excellent person ? Decidedly, this was an ill-omened day !

" If we are to speak of Bertaud's allusions," said M. Lecoq, " I have heard two very curious stories, though I have been here but a few hours. It seems that this Mademoiselle Laurence——"

M. Plantat abruptly interrupted the detective.

" Calumnies ! odious calumnies ! The lower classes, to annoy the rich, do not hesitate to say all sorts of things against them. Don't you know it ? Is it not always so ? The gentry, above all, those of a provincial town, live in glass houses. The lynx eyes of envy watch them steadily night and day, spy on them, surprise what they regard as their most secret actions to arm themselves against them. The bourgeois goes on, proud and content ; his business prospers ; he possesses the esteem and friendship of his own class ; all this while, he is vilified by the lower classes, his name dragged in the dust, soiled by suppositions the most mischievous. Envy, Monsieur, respects nothing, no one."

"If Laurence has been slandered," observed Dr. Gendron, smiling, "she has a good advocate to defend her."

The old justice of the peace (the man of bronze, as M. Courtois called him) blushed slightly, a little embarrassed.

"There are causes," said he, quietly, "which defend themselves. Mademoiselle Courtois is one of those young girls who has a right to all respect. But there are evils which no laws can cure, and which revolt me. Think of it, monsieurs, our reputations, the honor of our wives and daughters, are at the mercy of the first petty rascal who has imagination enough to invent a slander. It is not believed, perhaps; but it is repeated, and spreads. What can be done? How can we know what is secretly said against us; will we ever know it?"

"Eh!" replied the doctor, "what matters it? There is only one voice, to my mind, worth listening to—that of conscience. As to what is called 'public opinion,' as it is the aggregate opinion of thousands of fools and rogues, I only despise it."

This discussion might have been prolonged, if the judge of instruction had not pulled out his watch, and made an impatient gesture.

"While we are talking, time is flying," said he. "We must hasten to the work that still remains."

It was then agreed that while the doctor proceeded to his autopsy, the judge should draw up his report of the case. M. Plantat was charged with watching Lecoq's investigations.

As soon as the detective found himself alone with M. Plantat:

"Well," he said, drawing a long breath, as if relieved of a heavy burden, "now we can get on."

Plantat smiled; the detective munched a lozenge, and added:

"It was very annoying to find the investigation already going on when I reached here. Those who were here before me have had time to get up a theory, and if I don't adopt it at once, there is the deuce to pay!"

M. Domini's voice was heard in the entry, calling out to his clerk.

"Now there's the judge of instruction," continued Lecoq, "who thinks this a very simple affair; while I, Lecoq, the equal at least of Gévrol, the favorite pupil of Papa Tabaret—I do not see it at all clearly yet."

He stopped, and after apparently going over in his mind the result of his discoveries, went on: "No; I'm off the track, and have almost lost my way. I see something underneath all this—but what? what?"

M. Plantat's face remained placid, but his eyes shone.

"Perhaps you are right," said he, carelessly; "perhaps there is something underneath." The detective looked at him; he didn't stir. His face seemed the most undisturbed in the world. There was a long silence, by which M. Lecoq profited to confide to the portrait of the defunct the reflections which burdened his brain.

"See here, my dear darling," said he, "this worthy person seems a shrewd old customer, and I must watch his actions and gestures carefully. He does not argue with the judge; he's got an idea that he doesn't dare to tell, and we must find it out. At the very first he guessed me out, despite these pretty blond locks. As long as he thought he could, by misleading me, make me follow M. Domini's tack, he followed and aided me, showing me the way. Now that he sees me on the scent, he crosses his arms and retires. He wants to leave me the honor of the discovery. Why? He lives here—perhaps he is afraid of making enemies. No. He isn't a man to fear much of anything. What then? He shrinks from his own thoughts. He has found something so amazing, that he dares not explain himself."

A sudden reflection changed the course of M. Lecoq's confidences.

"A thousand imps!" thought he. "Suppose I'm wrong! Suppose this old fellow is not shrewd at all! Suppose he hasn't discovered anything, and only obeys the inspirations of chance! I've seen stranger things. I've known so many of these folks whose eyes seem so very mysterious, and announce such wonders; after all, I found nothing, and was cheated. But I intend to sound this old fellow well."

And, assuming his most idiotic manner, he said aloud:

"On reflection, Monsieur, little remains to be done. Two of the principals are in custody, and when they make up their minds to talk—they'll do it, sooner or later, if the judge is determined they shall—we shall know all."

A bucket of ice-water falling on M. Plantat's head could not have surprised him more, or more disagreeably, than this speech.

"What!" stammered he, with an air of frank amazement, "do you, a man of experience, who——"

Delighted with the success of his ruse, Lecoq could not keep his countenance, and Plantat, who perceived that he had been caught in the snare, laughed heartily.

Not a word, however, was exchanged between these two men, both subtle in the science of life, and equally cunning in its mysteries. They quite understood each other.

"My worthy old buck," said the detective to himself, "you've got something in your sack; only it's so big, so monstrous, that you won't exhibit it, not for a cannon-ball. You wish your hand forced, do you? Ve-ry well!"

"He's sly," thought M. Plantat. "He knows that I've got an idea; he's trying to get at it—and I believe he will."

M. Lecoq had restored his lozenge-box to his pocket, as he always did when he went seriously to work. His amour-propre was enlisted; he played a part—and he was a rare comedian.

"Now," cried he, "let's to horse. According to the mayor's account, the instrument with which all these things were broken has been found."

"In the room in the second story," answered M. Plantat, "overlooking the garden, we found a hatchet on the floor, near a piece of furniture which had been assailed, but not broken open; I forbade anyone to touch it."

"And you did well. Is it a heavy hatchet?"

"It weighs about two pounds."

"Good. Let's see it."

They ascended to the room in question, and M. Lecoq, forgetting his part of a haberdasher, and regardless of his clothes, went down flat on his stomach, alternately scrutinizing the hatchet—which was a heavy, terrible weapon—and the slippery and well-waxed oaken floor.

"I suppose," observed M. Plantat, "that the assassins brought this hatchet up here and assailed this cupboard, for the sole purpose of putting us off our scent, and to complicate the mystery. This weapon, you see, was by no means necessary for breaking open the cupboard, which I could smash with my fist. They gave one blow—only one—and quietly put the hatchet down."

The detective got up and brushed himself.

" I think you are mistaken," said he. " This hatchet wasn't put on the floor gently; it was thrown with a violence betraying either great terror or great anger. Look here; do you see these three marks, near each other, on the floor? When the assassin threw the hatchet, it first fell on the edge—hence this sharp cut; then it fell over on one side; and the flat, or hammer end left this mark here, under my finger. Therefore, it was thrown with such violence that it turned over itself and that its edge a second time cut in the floor, where you see it now."

" True," answered M. Plantat. The detective's conjectures doubtless refuted his own theory, for he added, with a perplexed air:

" I don't understand anything about it."

M. Lecoq went on:

" Were the windows open this morning as they are now ? "

" Yes."

" Ah ! The wretches heard some noise or other in the garden, and they went and looked out. What did they see? I can't tell. But I do know that what they saw terrified them, that they threw down the hatchet furiously, and made off. Look at the position of these cuts—they are slanting of course—and you will see that the hatchet was thrown by a man who was standing, not by the cupboard, but close by the open window."

Plantat in his turn knelt down, and looked long and carefully. The detective was right. He got up confused, and after meditating a moment, said:

"This perplexes me a little; however——"

He stopped, motionless, in a revery, with one of his hands on his forehead.

"All might yet be explained," he muttered, mentally searching for a solution of the mystery, "and in that case the time indicated by the clock would be true."

M. Lecoq did not think of questioning his companion. He knew that he would not answer, for pride's sake.

"This matter of the hatchet puzzles me, too," said he. "I thought that these assassins had worked leisurely; but that can't be so. I see they were surprised and interrupted."

Plantat was all ears.

"True," pursued M. Lecoq, slowly, "we ought to divide these indications into two classes. There are the traces left on purpose to mislead us—the jumbled-up bed, for instance; then there are the real traces, undesigned, as are these hatchet cuts. But here I hesitate. Is the trace of the hatchet true or false, good or bad? I thought myself sure of the character of these assassins: but now——"

He paused; the wrinkles on his face, the contraction of his mouth, betrayed his mental effort.

"But now?" asked M. Plantat.

M. Lecoq, at this question, seemed like a man just roused from sleep.

"I beg your pardon," said he. "I forgot myself.

I've a bad habit of reflecting aloud. That's why I almost always insist on working alone. My uncertainty, hesitation, the vacillation of my suspicions, lose me
the credit of being an astute detective—of being an
agent for whom there's no such thing as a mystery."

Worthy M. Plantat gave the detective an indulgent
smile.

" I don't usually open my mouth," pursued M. Lecoq, " until my mind is satisfied; then I speak in a
peremptory tone, and say—this is thus, or this is so.
But to-day I am acting without too much restraint, in
the company of a man who knows that a problem such
as this seems to me to be, is not solved at the first attempt. So I permit my gropings to be seen without
shame. You cannot always reach the truth at a
bound, but by a series of diverse calculations, by deductions and inductions. Well, just now my logic is
at fault."

" How so? "

" Oh, it's very simple. I thought I understood the
rascals, and knew them by heart; and yet I have only
recognized imaginary adversaries. Are they fools, or
are they mighty sly? That's what I ask myself. The
tricks played with the bed and clock had, I supposed,
given me the measure and extent of their intelligence
and invention. Making deductions from the known
to the unknown, I arrived, by a series of very simple
consequences, at the point of foreseeing all that they
could have imagined, to throw us off the scent. My
point of departure admitted, I had only, in order to
reach the truth, to take the contrary of that which appearances indicated. I said to myself:

" A hatchet has been found in the second story;

therefore the assassins carried it there, and designedly forgot it.

"They left five glasses on the dining-room table; therefore they were more or less than five, but they were not five.

"There were the remains of a supper on the table; therefore they neither drank nor ate.

"The countess's body was on the river-bank; therefore it was placed there deliberately. A piece of cloth was found in the victim's hand; therefore it was put there by the murderers themselves.

"Madame de Trémorel's body is disfigured by many dagger-strokes, and horribly mutilated; therefore she was killed by a single blow——"

"Bravo, yes, bravo," cried M. Plantat, visibly charmed.

"Eh! no, not bravo yet," returned M. Lecoq. "For here my thread is broken; I have reached a gap. If my deductions were sound, this hatchet would have been very carefully placed on the floor."

"Once more, bravo," added the other, "for this does not at all affect our general theory. It is clear, nay certain, that the assassins intended to act as you say. An unlooked-for event interrupted them."

"Perhaps; perhaps that's true. But I see something else——"

"What?"

"Nothing—at least, for the moment. Before all, I must see the dining-room and the garden."

They descended at once, and Plantat pointed out the glasses and bottles, which he had put one side. The detective took the glasses, one after another, held them level with his eye, toward the light, and scrutinized the moist places left on them.

"No one has drank from these glasses," said he, firmly.

"What, from neither one of them?"

The detective fixed a penetrating look upon his companion, and in a measured tone, said:

"From neither one."

M. Plantat only answered by a movement of the lips, as if to say, "You are going too far."

The other smiled, opened the door, and called:

"François!"

The valet hastened to obey the call. His face was suffused with tears; he actually bewailed the loss of his master.

"Hear what I've got to say, my lad," said M. Lecoq, with true detective-like familiarity. "And be sure and answer me exactly, frankly, and briefly."

"I will, sir."

"Was it customary here at the château, to bring up the wine before it was wanted?"

"No, sir; before each meal, I myself went down to the cellar for it."

"Then no full bottles were ever kept in the dining-room?"

"Never."

"But some of the wine might sometimes remain in draught?"

"No; the count permitted me to carry the dessert wine to the servants' table."

"And where were the empty bottles put?"

"I put them in this corner cupboard, and when they amounted to a certain number, I carried them down cellar."

"When did you last do so?"

" Oh "—François reflected—" at least five or six days ago."

" Good. Now, what liqueurs did the count drink? "

" The count scarcely ever drank liqueurs. If, by chance, he took a notion to have a small glass of eau-de-vie, he got it from the liqueur closet, there, over the stove."

" There were no decanters of rum or cognac in any of the cupboards? "

" No."

" Thanks ; you may retire."

As François was going out, M. Lecoq called him back.

" While we are about it, look in the bottom of the closet, and see if you find the right number of empty bottles."

The valet obeyed, and looked into the closet.

" There isn't one there."

" Just so," returned M. Lecoq. " This time, show us your heels for good."

As soon as François had shut the door, M. Lecoq turned to Plantat and asked:

" What do you think now? "

" You were perfectly right."

The detective then smelt successively each glass and bottle.

" Good again! Another proof in aid of my guess."

" What more? "

" It was not wine that was at the bottom of these glasses. Among all the empty bottles put away in the bottom of that closet, there was one—here it is—which had contained *vinegar;* and it was from this bottle that they turned what they thought to be wine into the glasses."

Seizing a glass, he put it to M. Plantat's nose, adding:

"See for yourself."

There was no disputing it; the vinegar was good, its odor of the strongest; the villains, in their haste, had left behind them an incontestable proof of their intention to mislead the officers of justice. While they were capable of shrewd inventions, they did not have the art to perform them well. All their oversights could, however, be accounted for by their sudden haste, caused by the occurrence of an unlooked-for incident. "The floors of a house where a crime has just been committed," said a famous detective, "burn the feet." M. Lecoq seemed exasperated, like a true artist, before the gross, pretentious, and ridiculous work of some green and bungling scholar.

"These are a parcel of vulgar ruffians, truly! able ones, certainly; but they don't know their trade yet, the wretches."

M. Lecoq, indignant, ate three or four lozenges at a mouthful.

"Come, now," said Plantat, in a paternally severe tone. "Don't let's get angry. The people have failed in address, no doubt; but reflect that they could not, in their calculations, take account of the craft of a man like you."

M. Lecoq, who had the vanity which all actors possess, was flattered by the compliment, and but poorly dissimulated an expression of pleasure.

"We must be indulgent; come now," pursued Plantat. "Besides," he paused a moment to give more weight to what he was going to say, "besides, you haven't seen everything yet."

No one could tell when M. Lecoq was playing a

comedy. He did not always know, himself. This great artist, devoted to his art, practised the feigning of all the emotions of the human soul, just as he accustomed himself to wearing all sorts of costumes. He was very indignant against the assassins, and gesticulated about in great excitement; but he never ceased to watch Plantat slyly, and the last words of the latter made him prick up his ears.

"Let's see the rest, then," said he.

As he followed his worthy comrade to the garden, he renewed his confidences to the dear defunct.

"Confound this old bundle of mystery! We can't take this obstinate fellow by surprise, that's clear. He'll give us the word of the riddle when we have guessed it; not before. He is as strong as we, my darling; he only needs a little practice. But look you —if he has found something which has escaped us, he must have previous information, that we don't know of."

Nothing had been disturbed in the garden.

"See here, Monsieur Lecoq," said the old justice of the peace, as he followed a winding pathway which led to the river. "It was here that one of the count's slippers was found; below there, a little to the right of these geraniums, his silk handkerchief was picked up."

They reached the river-bank, and lifted, with great care, the planks which had been placed there to preserve the foot-prints.

"We suppose," said M. Plantat, "that the countess, in her flight, succeeded in getting to this spot; and that here they caught up with her and gave her a finishing blow."

Was this really Plantat's opinion, or did he only report the morning's theory? M. Lecoq could not tell.

6

"According to my calculations," he said, "the countess could not have fled, but was brought here already dead, or logic is not logic. However, let us examine this spot carefully."

He knelt down and studied the sand on the path, the stagnant water, and the reeds and water-plants. Then going along a little distance, he threw a stone, approaching again to see the effect produced on the mud. He next returned to the house, and came back again under the willows, crossing the lawn, where were still clearly visible traces of a heavy burden having been dragged over it. Without the least respect for his pantaloons, he crossed the lawn on all-fours, scrutinizing the smallest blades of grass, pulling away the thick tufts to see the earth better, and minutely observing the direction of the broken stems. This done, he said:

"My conclusions are confirmed. The countess was carried across here."

"Are you sure of it?" asked Plantat.

There was no mistaking the old man's hesitation this time; he was clearly undecided, and leaned on the other's judgment for guidance.

"There can be no error, possibly."

The detective smiled, as he added:

"Only, as two heads are better than one, I will ask you to listen to me, and then, you will tell me what you think."

M. Lecoq had, in searching about, picked up a little flexible stick, and while he talked, he used it to point out this and that object, like the lecturer at the panorama.

"No," said he, "Madame de Trémorel did not fly from her murderers. Had she been struck down here, she would have fallen violently; her weight, therefore,

would have made the water spirt to some distance, as
well as the mud; and we should certainly have found
some splashes."

"But don't you think that, since morning, the
sun——"

"The sun would have absorbed the water; but the
stain of dry mud would have remained. I have found
nothing of the sort anywhere. You might object, that
the water and mud would have spirted right and left;
but just look at the tufts of these flags, lilies, and stems
of cane—you find a light dust on every one. Do you
find the least trace of a drop of water? No. There
was then no splash, therefore no violent fall; therefore
the countess was not killed here; therefore her body
was brought here, and carefully deposited where you
found it."

M. Plantat did not seem to be quite convinced yet.

"But there are the traces of a struggle in the sand,"
said he.

His companion made a gesture of protest.

"Monsieur deigns to have his joke; those marks
would not deceive a school-boy."

"It appears to me, however——"

"There can be no mistake, Monsieur Plantat. Certain it is that the sand has been disturbed and thrown
about. But all these trails that lay bare the earth which
was covered by the sand, were made by the same foot.
Perhaps you don't believe it. They were made, too,
with the end of the foot; that you may see for yourself."

"Yes, I perceive it."

"Very well, then; when there has been a struggle
on ground like this, there are always two distinct kinds
of traces—those of the assailant and those of the vic-

tim. The assailant, throwing himself forward, necessarily supports himself on his toes, and imprints the
fore part of his feet on the earth. The victim, on the
contrary, falling back, and trying to avoid the assault,
props himself on his heels, and therefore buries the
heels in the soil. If the adversaries are equally strong,
the number of imprints of the toes and the heels will
be nearly equal, according to the chances of the struggle. But what do we find here?"

M. Plantat interrupted:

" Enough; the most incredulous would now be convinced." After thinking a moment, he added:

" No, there is no longer any possible doubt of it."

M. Lecoq thought that his argument deserved a reward, and treated himself to two lozenges at a mouthful.

" I haven't done yet," he resumed. " Granted, that
the countess could not have been murdered here; let's
add that she was not carried hither, but dragged along.
There are only two ways of dragging a body; by the
shoulders, and in this case the feet, scraping along the
earth, leave two parallel trails; or by the legs—in
which case the head, lying on the earth, leaves a single
furrow, and that a wide one."

Plantat nodded assent.

" When I examined the lawn," pursued M. Lecoq,
" I found the parallel trails of the feet, but yet the grass
was crushed over a rather wide space. How was that?
Because it was the body, not of a man, but of a woman,
which was dragged across the lawn—of a woman full-
dressed, with heavy petticoats; that, in short, of the
countess, and not of the count."

M. Lecoq paused, in expectation of a question, or a
remark.

But the old justice of the peace did not seem to be listening, and appeared to be plunged in the deepest meditation. Night was falling; a light fog hung like smoke over the Seine.

" We must go in," said M. Plantat, abruptly, " and see how the doctor has got on with his autopsy."

They slowly approached the house. The judge of instruction awaited them on the steps. He appeared to have a satisfied air.

" I am going to leave you in charge," said he to M. Plantat, " for if I am to see the procureur, I must go at once. When you sent for him this morning, he was absent."

M. Plantat bowed.

" I shall be much obliged if you will watch this affair to the end. The doctor will have finished in a few minutes, he says, and will report to-morrow morning. I count on your co-operation to put seals wherever they are necessary, and to select the guard over the château. I shall send an architect to draw up an exact plan of the house and garden. Well, sir," asked M. Domini, turning to the detective, " have you made any fresh discoveries? "

" I have found some important facts; but I cannot speak decisively till I have seen everything by daylight. If you will permit me, I will postpone making my report till to-morrow afternoon. I think I may say, however, that complicated as this affair is——"

M. Domini did not let him finish.

" I see nothing complicated in the affair at all; everything strikes me as very simple."

" But," objected M. Lecoq, " I thought——"

" I sincerely regret," continued the judge, " that you were so hastily called, when there was really no serious reason for it. The evidences against the arrested men are very conclusive."

Plantat and Lecoq exchanged a long look, betraying their great surprise.

" What! " exclaimed the former, " have you discovered any new indications? "

" More than indications, I believe," responded M. Domini. " Old Bertaud, whom I have again questioned, begins to be uneasy. He has quite lost his arrogant manner. I succeeded in making him contradict himself several times, and he finished by confessing that he saw the assassins."

" The assassins! " exclaimed M. Plantat. " Did he say assassins? "

" He saw at least one of them. He persists in declaring that he did not recognize him. That's where we are. But prison walls have salutary terrors. To-morrow after a sleepless night, the fellow will be more explicit, if I mistake not."

" But Guespin," anxiously asked the old man, " have you questioned him? "

" Oh, as for him, everything is clear."

" Has he confessed? " asked M. Lecoq, stupefied.

The judge half turned toward the detective, as if he were displeased that M. Lecoq should dare to question him.

" Guespin has *not* confessed," he answered, " but his case is none the better for that. Our searchers have returned. They haven't yet found the count's body, and I think it has been carried down by the current. But they found at the end of the park, the count's other slipper, among the roses; and under the bridge, in the middle of the river, they discovered a thick vest which still bears the marks of blood."

" And that vest is Guespin's? "

" Exactly so. It was recognized by all the domestics, and Guespin himself did not hesitate to admit that it belonged to him. But that is not all——"

M. Domini stopped as if to take breath, but really to keep Plantat in suspense. As they differed in their theories, he thought Plantat betrayed a stupid opposition to him; and he was not sorry to have a chance for a little triumph.

" That is not all," he went on; " this vest had, in the right pocket, a large rent, and a piece of it had been torn off. Do you know what became of that piece of Guespin's vest? "

" Ah," muttered M. Plantat, " it was that which we found in the countess's hand."

" You are right, Monsieur. And what think you of this proof, pray, of the prisoner's guilt? "

M. Plantat seemed amazed; his arms fell at his side. As for M. Lecoq, who, in presence of the judge, had resumed his haberdasher manner, he was so much surprised that he nearly strangled himself with a lozenge.

" A thousand devils!" exclaimed he. " That's tough, that is! " He smiled sillily, and added in a low tone, meant only for Plantat's ear:

" Mighty tough! Though quite foreseen in our calculations. The countess held a piece of cloth tightly in her hand; therefore it was put there, *intentionally*, by the murderers."

M. Domini did not hear this remark. He shook hands with M. Plantat and made an appointment to meet him on the morrow, at the court-house. Then he went away with his clerk.

Guespin and old Bertaud, handcuffed, had a few

minutes before been led off to the prison of Corbeil, under the guard of the Orcival gendarmes.

VIII

Dr. Gendron had just finished his sad task in the billiard-room. He had taken off his long coat, and pulled up his shirt-sleeves above his elbows. His instruments lay on a table near him; he had covered the body with a long white sheet. Night had come, and a large lamp, with a crystal globe, lighted up the gloomy scene. The doctor, leaning over a water-basin, was washing his hands, when the old justice of the peace and the detective entered.

" Ah, it's you, Plantat," said the doctor in a suppressed tone; " where is Monsieur Domini? "

" Gone."

The doctor did not take the trouble to repress a vexed motion.

" I must speak with him, though," said he, " it's absolutely necessary—and the sooner the better; for perhaps I am wrong—I may be mistaken——"

M. Lecoq and M. Plantat approached him, having carefully closed the door. The doctor was paler than the corpse which lay under the sheet. His usually calm features betrayed great distress. This change could not have been caused by the task in which he had been engaged. Of course it was a painful one; but M. Gendron was one of those experienced practitioners who have felt the pulse of every human misery, and whose disgust had become torpid by the most hideous spectacles. He must have discovered something extraordinary.

"I am going to ask you what you asked me a while ago," said M. Plantat. "Are you ill or suffering?"

M. Gendron shook his head sorrowfully, and answered, slowly and emphatically:

"I will answer you, as you did me; 'tis nothing, I am already better."

Then these two, equally profound, turned away their heads, as if fearing to exchange their ideas; they doubted lest their looks should betray them.

M. Lecoq advanced and spoke.

"I believe I know the cause of the doctor's emotion. He has just discovered that Madame de Trémorel was killed by a single blow, and that the assassins afterward set themselves to disfiguring the body, when it was nearly cold."

The doctor's eyes fastened on the detective, with a stupefied expression.

"How could you divine that?" he asked.

"Oh, I didn't guess it alone; I ought to share the honor of the theory which has enabled us to foresee this fact, with Monsieur Plantat."

"Oh," cried the doctor, striking his forehead, "now, I recollect your advice; in my worry, I must say, I had quite forgotten it. Well," he added, "your foresight is confirmed. Perhaps not so much time as you suppose elapsed between the first blow and the rest; but I am convinced that the countess had ceased to live nearly three hours, when the last blows were struck."

M. Gendron went to the billiard-table, and slowly raised the sheet, discovering the head and part of the bust.

"Let us inform ourselves, Plantat," he said.

The old justice of the peace took the lamp, and passed to the other side of the table. His hand trembled so that the globe tingled. The vacillating light cast gloomy shadows upon the walls. The countess's face had been carefully bathed, the blood and mud effaced. The marks of the blows were thus more visible, but they still found upon that livid countenance, the traces of its beauty. M. Lecoq stood at the head of the table, leaning over to see more clearly.

"The countess," said Dr. Gendron, "received eighteen blows from a dagger. Of these, but one is mortal; it is this one, the direction of which is nearly vertical—a little below the shoulder, you see." He pointed out the wound, sustaining the body in his left arm. The eyes had preserved a frightful expression. It seemed as if the half-open mouth were about to cry "Help! Help!"

Plantat, the man with a heart of stone, turned away his head, and the doctor, having mastered his first emotion, continued in a professionally apathetic tone:

"The blade must have been an inch wide, and eight inches long. All the other wounds—those on the arms, breast, and shoulders, are comparatively slight. They must have been inflicted at least two hours after that which caused death."

"Good," said M. Lecoq.

"Observe that I am not positive," returned the doctor quickly. "I merely state a probability. The phenomena on which I base my own conviction are too fugitive, too capricious in their nature, to enable me to be absolutely certain."

This seemed to disturb M. Lecoq.

"But, from the moment when——"

"What I can affirm," interrupted Dr. Gendron, "what I would affirm under oath, is, that all the wounds on the head, excepting one, were inflicted after

death.   No doubt of that whatever—none whatever.
Here, above the eye, is the blow given while the countess was alive."

" It seems to me, Doctor," observed M. Lecoq, "that
we may conclude from the proved fact that the countess, after death, was struck by a flat implement, that
she had also ceased to live when she was mutilated by
the knife."

M. Gendron reflected a moment.

" It is possible that you are right; as for me, I am
persuaded of it.   Still the conclusions in my report will
not be yours.   The physician consulted by the law,
should only pronounce upon patent, demonstrated
facts.   If he has a doubt, even the slightest, he should
hold his tongue.   I will say more; if there is any uncertainty, my opinion is that the accused, and not the
prosecution, should have the benefit of it."

This was certainly not the detective's opinion, but
he was cautious not to say so.   He had followed Dr.
Gendron with anxious attention, and the contraction
of his face showed the travail of his mind.

" It seems to me now possible," said he, " to deter-
mine how and where the countess was struck."

The doctor had covered the body, and Plantat had
replaced the lamp on the little table.   Both asked M.
Lecoq to explain himself.

" Very well," resumed the detective.   " The direction of the wound proves to me that the countess was
in her chamber taking tea, seated, her body inclined a
little forward, when she was murdered.   The assassin
came up behind her with his arm raised; he chose his
position coolly, and struck her with terrific force.   The
violence of the blow was such that the victim fell forward, and in the fall, her forehead struck the end of the

table; she thus gave herself the only fatal blow which we have discovered on the head."

M. Gendron looked from one to the other of his companions, who exchanged significant glances. Perhaps he suspected the game they were playing.

"The crime must evidently have been committed as you say," said he.

There was another embarrassing silence. M. Lecoq's obstinate muteness annoyed Plantat, who finally asked him:

"Have you seen all you want to see?"

"All for to-day; I shall need daylight for what remains. I am confident, indeed, that with the exception of one detail that worries me, I have the key to the mystery."

"We must be here, then, early to-morrow morning."

"I will be here at any hour you will name."

"Your search finished, we will go together to Monsieur Domini, at Corbeil."

"I am quite at your orders."

There was another pause.

M. Plantat perceived that M. Lecoq guessed his thoughts, and did not understand the detective's capriciousness; a little while before, he had been very loquacious, but now held his tongue. M. Lecoq, on the other hand, was delighted to puzzle the old man a little, and formed the intention to astonish him the next morning, by giving him a report which should faithfully reflect all his ideas. Meanwhile he had taken out his lozenge-box, and was intrusting a hundred secrets to the portrait.

"Well," said the doctor, "there remains nothing more to be done, except to retire."

"I was just going to ask permission to do so," said
M. Lecoq. "I have been fasting ever since morning."

M. Plantat now took a bold step.

"Shall you return to Paris to-night, Monsieur Lecoq?" asked he, abruptly.

"No; I came prepared to remain over-night; I've
brought my night-gown, which I left, before coming
up here, at the little roadside inn below. I shall sup
and sleep there."

"You will be poorly off at the Faithful Grenadier,"
said the old justice of the peace. "You will do better
to come and dine with me."

"You are really too good, Monsieur——"

"Besides, we have a good deal to say, and so you
must remain the night with me; we will get your
night-clothes as we pass along."

M. Lecoq bowed, flattered and grateful for the invitation.

"And I shall carry you off, too, Doctor," continued
M. Plantat, "whether you will or not. Now, don't
say no. If you insist on going to Corbeil to-night, we
will carry you over after supper."

The operation of fixing the seals was speedily concluded; narrow strips of parchment, held by large
waxen seals, were affixed to all the doors, as well as to
the bureau in which the articles gathered for the pur-
poses of the investigation had been deposited.

IX

Despite the haste they made, it was nearly ten
o'clock when M. Plantat and his guests quitted the
château of Valfeuillu. Instead of taking the high
road, they cut across a pathway which ran along be-

side Mme. de Lanascol's park, and led diagonally to
the wire bridge; this was the shortest way to the inn
where M. Lecoq had left his slight baggage. As they
went along, M. Plantat grew anxious about his good
friend, M. Courtois.

"What misfortune can have happened to him?" said
he to Dr. Gendron.

"Thanks to the stupidity of that rascal of a servant,
we learned nothing at all. This letter from Mademoiselle Laurence has caused the trouble, somehow."

They had now reached the Faithful Grenadier.

A big red-faced fellow was smoking a long pipe at
the door, his back against the house. He was talking
with a railway employee. It was the landlord.

"Well, Monsieur Plantat," he cried, "what a horrible affair this is! Come in, come in; there are several folks in the hall who saw the assassins. What a
villain old Bertaud is! And that Guespin; ah, I would
willingly trudge to Corbeil to see them put up the
scaffold!"

"A little charity, Master Lenfant; you forget that
both these men were among your best customers."

Master Lenfant was confused by this reply; but his
native impudence soon regained the mastery.

"Fine customers, parbleu!" he answered, "this
thief of a Guespin has got thirty francs of mine which
I'll never see again."

"Who knows?" said Plantat, ironically. "Besides, you are going to make more than that to-night,
there's so much company at the Orcival festival."

During this brief conversation, M. Lecoq entered the
inn for his night-gown. His office being no longer a
secret, he was not now welcomed as when he was taken
for a simple retired haberdasher. Mme. Lenfant, a lady

who had no need of her husband's aid to show penniless sots the door, scarcely deigned to answer him.
When he asked how much he owed, she responded,
with a contemptuous gesture, " Nothing." When he
returned to the door, his night-gown in hand, M. Plantat said :

" Let's hurry, for I want to get news of our poor
mayor."

The three hastened their steps, and the old justice of
the peace, oppressed with sad presentiments, and trying to combat them, continued :

" If anything had happened at the mayor's, I should
certainly have been informed of it by this time. Perhaps Laurence has written that she is ill, or a little indisposed. Madame Courtois, who is the best woman
in the world, gets excited about nothing; she probably
wanted to send her husband for Laurence at once.
You'll see that it's some false alarm."

No; some catastrophe had happened. A number of
the village women were standing before the mayor's
gate. Baptiste, in the midst of the group, was ranting
and gesticulating. But at M. Plantat's approach, the
women fled like a troop of frightened gulls. The old
man's unexpected appearance annoyed the placid Baptiste not a little, for he was interrupted, by the sudden
departure of his audience, in the midst of a superb ora-
torical flight. As he had a great fear of M. Plantat,
however, he dissimulated his chagrin with his habitual
smile.

" Ah, sir," cried he, when M. Plantat was three steps
off, " ah, what an affair! I was going for you——"

" Does your master wish me? "

" More than you can think. He ran so fast from
Valfeuillu here, that I could scarcely keep up with him.

He's not usually fast, you know; but you ought to have seen him this time, fat as he is!"

M. Plantat stamped impatiently.

"Well, we got here at last," resumed the man, "and monsieur rushed into the drawing-room, where he found madame sobbing like a Magdalene. He was so out of breath he could scarcely speak. His eyes stuck out of his head, and he stuttered like this—'What's—the—matter? What's the—matter?' Madame, who couldn't speak either, held out mademoiselle's letter, which she had in her hand."

The three auditors were on coals of fire; the rogue perceived it, and spoke more and more slowly.

"Then monsieur took the letter, went to the window, and at a glance read it through. He cried out hoarsely, thus: 'Oh!' then he went to beating the air with his hands, like a swimming dog; then he walked up and down and fell, pouf! like a bag, his face on the floor. That was all."

"Is he dead?" cried all three in the same breath.

"Oh, no; you shall see," responded Baptiste, with a placid smile.

M. Lecoq was a patient man, but not so patient as you might think. Irritated by the manner of Baptiste's recital, he put down his bundle, seized the man's arm with his right hand, while with the left he whisked a light flexible cane, and said:

"Look here, fellow, I want you to hurry up, you know."

That was all he said; the servant was terribly afraid of this little blond man, with a strange voice, and a fist harder than a vice. He went on very rapidly this time, his eye fixed on M. Lecoq's rattan.

"Monsieur had an attack of vertigo. All the house

was in confusion; everybody except I, lost their heads;
it occurred to me to go for a doctor, and I started off
for one—for Doctor Gendron, whom I knew to be at
the château, or the doctor near by, or the apothecary—
it mattered not who. By good luck, at the street corner, I came upon Robelot, the bone-setter—' Come,
follow me,' said I. He did so; sent away those who
were tending monsieur, and bled him in both arms.
Shortly after, he breathed, then he opened his eyes, and
then he spoke. Now he is quite restored, and is lying
on one of the drawing-room lounges, crying with all
his might. He told me he wanted to see Monsieur
Plantat, and I——"

   " And—Mademoiselle Laurence? " asked M. Plantat, with a trembling voice. Baptiste assumed a tragic
pose.

   " Ah, gentlemen," said he, " don't ask me about her
—'tis heartrending! "

   The doctor and M. Plantat heard no more, but hur-
ried in; M. Lecoq followed, having confided his night-
gown to Baptiste, with, " Carry that to M. Plantat's—
quick! "

   Misfortune, when it enters a house, seems to leave
its fatal imprint on the very threshold. Perhaps it is
not really so, but it is the feeling which those who are
summoned to it experience. As the physician and the
justice of the peace traversed the court-yard, this house,
usually so gay and hospitable, presented a mournful
aspect. Lights were seen coming and going in the
upper story. Mlle. Lucile, the mayor's youngest
daughter, had had a nervous attack, and was being
tended. A young girl, who served as Laurence's
maid, was seated in the vestibule, on the lower stair,
weeping bitterly. Several domestics were there also,

7

frightened, motionless, not knowing what to do in all this fright. The drawing-room door was wide open; the room was dimly lighted by two candles; Mme. Courtois lay rather than sat in a large arm-chair near the fireplace. Her husband was reclining on a lounge near the windows at the rear of the apartment. They had taken off his coat and had torn away his shirt-sleeves and flannel vest, when he was to be bled. There were strips of cotton wrapped about his naked arms. A small man, habited like a well-to-do Parisian artisan, stood near the door, with an embarrassed expression of countenance. It was Robelot, who had remained, lest any new exigency for his services should arise.

The entrance of his friend startled M. Courtois from the sad stupor into which he had been plunged. He got up and staggered into the arms of the worthy Plantat, saying, in a broken voice:

" Ah, my friend, I am most miserable—most wretched ! "

The poor mayor was so changed as scarcely to be recognizable. He was no longer the happy man of the world, with smiling face, firm look, the pride of which betrayed plainly his self-importance and prosperity. In a few hours he had grown twenty years older. He was broken, overwhelmed; his thoughts wandered in a sea of bitterness. He could only repeat, vacantly, again and again:

" Wretched ! most wretched ! "

M. Plantat was the right sort of a friend for such a time. He led M. Courtois back to the sofa and sat down beside him, and taking his hand in his own, forced him to calm his grief. He recalled to him that his wife, the companion of his life, remained to him, to mourn the dear departed with him. Had he not another daughter to cherish? But the poor man was in no state to listen to all this.

"Ah, my friend," said he shuddering, "you do not know all! If she had died here, in the midst of us, comforted by our tender care, my despair would be great; but nothing compared with that which now tortures me. If you only knew——"

M. Plantat rose, as if terrified by what he was about to hear.

"But who can tell," pursued the wretched man, "where or how she died? Oh, my Laurence, was there no one to hear your last agony and save you? What has become of you, so young and happy?"

He rose, shaking with anguish and cried:

"Let us go, Plantat, and look for her at. the Morgue." Then he fell back again, muttering the lugubrious word, "the Morgue."

The witnesses of this scene remained mute, motionless, rigid, holding their breath. The stifled sobs and groans of Mme. Courtois and the little maid alone broke the silence.

"You know that I am your friend—your best friend," said M. Plantat, softly; "confide in me—tell me all."

"Well," commenced M. Courtois, "know"—but his tears choked his utterance, and he could not go on. Holding out a crumpled letter, wet with tears, he stammered:

"Here, read—it is her last letter."

M. Plantat approached the table, and, not without difficulty, read:

" Dearly Beloved Parents—

" Forgive, forgive, I beseech you, your unhappy
daughter, the distress she is about to cause you. Alas!
I have been very guilty, but the punishment is terrible!
In a day of wandering, I forgot all—the example and
advice of my dear, sainted mother, my most sacred
duty, and your tenderness.   I could not, no, I *could* not
resist him who wept before me in swearing for me an
eternal love—and who has abandoned me.   Now, all
is over; I am lost, lost.   I cannot long conceal my
dreadful sin.   Oh, dear parents, do not curse me.   I
am your daughter—I cannot bear to face contempt, I
will not survive my dishonor.

" When this letter reaches you, I shall have ceased to
live; I shall have quitted my aunt's, and shall have
gone far away, where no one will find me.   There I
shall end my misery and despair. Adieu, then, oh, beloved parents, adieu!   I would that I could, for the
last time, beg your forgiveness on my knees.   My dear
mother, my good father, have pity on a poor wanderer;
pardon me, forgive me.   Never let my sister Lucile
know.   Once more, adieu—I have courage—honor
commands!   For you is the last prayer and supreme
thought of your poor   Laurence."

Great tears rolled silently down the old man's cheeks
as he deciphered this sad letter.   A cold, mute, terrible anger shrivelled the muscles of his face.   When he
had finished, he said, in a hoarse voice:

" Wretch! "

M. Courtois heard this exclamation.

" Ah, yes, wretch indeed," he cried, " this vile villain
who has crept in in the dark, and stolen my dearest
treasure, my darling child!   Alas, she knew nothing of

life. He whispered into her ear those fond words
which make the hearts of all young girls throb; she
had faith in him; and now he abandons her. Oh, if
I knew who he was—if I knew——"

He suddenly interrupted himself. A ray of intelligence had just illumined the abyss of despair into
which he had fallen.

"No," said he, "a young girl is not thus abandoned,
when she has a dowry of a million, unless for some
good reason. Love passes away; avarice remains.
The infamous wretch was not free—he was married.
He could only be the Count de Trémorel. It is he who
has killed my child."

The profound silence which succeeded proved to him
that his conjecture was shared by those around him.

"I was blind, blind!" cried he. "For I received
him at my house, and called him my friend. Oh, have
I not a right to a terrible vengeance?"

But the crime at Valfeuillu occurred to him; and it
was with a tone of deep disappointment that he resumed:

"And not to be able to revenge myself! I could
not, then, kill him with my own hands, see him suffer
for hours, hear him beg for mercy! He is dead. He
has fallen under the blows of assassins, less vile than
himself."

The doctor and M. Plantat strove to comfort the unhappy man; but he went on, excited more and more
by the sound of his own voice.

"Oh, Laurence, my beloved, why did you not confide in me? You feared my anger, as if a father would
ever cease to love his child. Lost, degraded, fallen to
the ranks of the vilest, I would still love thee. Were
you not my own? Alas! you knew not a father's

heart. A father does not pardon; he forgets. You might still have been happy, my lost love."

He wept; a thousand memories of the time when Laurence was a child and played about his knees recurred to his mind; it seemed as though it were but yesterday.

"Oh, my daughter, was it that you feared the world —the wicked, hypocritical world? But we should have gone away. I should have left Orcival, resigned my office. We should have settled down far away, in the remotest corner of France, in Germany, in Italy. With money all is possible. All? No! I have millions, and yet my daughter has killed herself."

He concealed his face in his hands; his sobs choked him.

"And not to know what has become of her!" he continued. "Is it not frightful? What death did she choose? You remember, Doctor, and you, Plantat, her beautiful curls about her pure forehead, her great, trembling eyes, her long curved lashes? Her smile —do you know, it was the sun's ray of my life. I *so* loved her voice, and her mouth so fresh, which gave me such warm, loving kisses. Dead! Lost! And not to know what has become of her sweet form—perhaps abandoned in the mire of some river. Do you recall the countess's body this morning? It will kill me! Oh, my child—that I might see her one hour— one minute—that I might give her cold lips one last kiss!"

M. Lecoq strove in vain to prevent a warm tear which ran from his eyes, from falling. M. Lecoq was a stoic on principle, and by profession. But the desolate words of the poor father overcame him. Forgetting that his emotion would be seen, he came out from the shadow where he had stood, and spoke to M. Courtois:

"I, Monsieur Lecoq, of the detectives, give you my honor that I will find Mademoiselle Laurence's body."

The poor mayor grasped desperately at this promise, as a drowning man to a straw.

"Oh, yes, we will find her, won't we? You will help me. They say that to the police nothing is impossible—that they see and know everything. We will see what has become of my child."

He went toward M. Lecoq, and taking him by the hand:

"Thank you," added he, "you are a good man. I received you ill a while ago, and judged you with foolish pride: forgive me. We will succeed—you will see, we will aid each other, we will put all the police on the scent, we will search through France, money will do it—I have it—I have millions—take them——"

His energies were exhausted: he staggered and fell heavily on the lounge.

"He must not remain here long," muttered the doctor in Plantat's ear, "he must get to bed. A brain fever, after such excitement, would not surprise me."

The old justice of the peace at once approached Mme. Courtois, who still reclined in the arm-chair, apparently having seen or heard nothing of what had passed, and oblivious in her grief.

"Madame!" said he, "Madame!"

She shuddered and rose, with a wandering air.

"It is my fault," said she, "my miserable fault! A mother should read her daughter's heart as in a book. I did not suspect Laurence's secret; I am a most unhappy mother."

The doctor also came to her.

"Madame," said he, in an imperious tone, "your husband must be persuaded to go to bed at once. His condition is very serious, and a little sleep is absolutely necessary. I will have a potion prepared——"

"Oh, my God!" cried the poor lady, wringing her hands, in the fear of a new misfortune, as bitter as the first; which, however, restored her to her presence of mind. She called the servants, who assisted the mayor to regain his chamber. Mme. Courtois also retired, followed by the doctor. Three persons only remained in the drawing-room—Plantat, Lecoq, and Robelot, who still stood near the door.

"Poor Laurence!" murmured Plantat. "Poor girl!"

"It seems to me that her father is most to be pitied," remarked M. Lecoq. "Such a blow, at his age, may be more than he can bear. Even should he recover, his life is broken."

"I had a sort of presentiment," said the other, "that this misfortune would come. I had guessed Laurence's secret, but I guessed it too late."

"And you did not try——"

"What? In a delicate case like this, when the honor of a family depends on a word, one must be circumspect. What could I do? Put Courtois on his guard? Clearly not. He would have refused to believe me. He is one of those men who will listen to nothing, and whom the brutal fact alone can undeceive."

"You might have dealt with the Count de Trémorel."

"The count would have denied all. He would have asked what right I had to interfere in his affairs."

"But the girl?"

M. Plantat sighed heavily.

"Though I detest mixing up with what does not concern me, I did try one day to talk with her. With infinite precaution and delicacy, and without letting her see that I knew all, I tried to show her the abyss near which she was drawing."

"And what did she reply?"

"Nothing. She laughed and joked, as women who have a secret which they wish to conceal, do. Besides, I could not get a quarter of an hour alone with her, and it was necessary to act, I knew—for I was her best friend—before committing this imprudence of speaking to her. Not a day passed that she did not come to my garden and cull my rarest flowers—and I would not, look you, give one of my flowers to the Pope himself. She had instituted me her florist in ordinary. For her sake I collected my briars of the Cape——"

He was talking on so wide of his subject that M. Lecoq could not repress a roguish smile. The old man was about to proceed when he heard a noise in the hall, and looking up he observed Robelot for the first time. His face at once betrayed his great annoyance.

"*You* were there, were you?" he said.

The bone-setter smiled obsequiously.

"Yes, Monsieur, quite at your service."

"You have been listening, eh?"

"Oh, as to that, I was waiting to see if Madame Courtois had any commands for me."

A sudden reflection occurred to M. Plantat; the expression of his eye changed. He winked at M. Lecoq to call his attention, and addressing the bone-setter in a milder tone, said: "Come here, Master Robelot."

M. Lecoq had read the man at a glance. Robelot

was a small, insignificant-looking man, but really of herculean strength. His hair, cut short behind, fell over his large, intelligent forehead. His eyes shone with the fire of covetousness, and expressed, when he forgot to guard them, a cynical boldness. A sly smile was always playing about his thin lips, beneath which there was no beard. A little way off, with his slight figure and his beardless face, he looked like a Paris gamin—one of those little wretches who are the essence of all corruption, whose imagination is more soiled than the gutters where they search for lost pennies.

Robelot advanced several steps, smiling and bowing.

" Perhaps," said he, " Monsieur has, by chance, need of me? "

" None whatever, Master Robelot, I only wish to congratulate you on happening in so apropos, to bleed Monsieur Courtois. Your lancet has, doubtless, saved his life."

" It's quite possible."

" Monsieur Courtois is generous—he will amply recompense this great service."

" Oh, I shall ask him nothing. Thank God, I want nobody's help. If I am paid my due, I am content."

" I know that well enough; you are prosperous— you ought to be satisfied."

M. Plantat's tone was friendly, almost paternal. He was deeply interested, evidently, in Robelot's prosperity.

" Satisfied ! " resumed the bone-setter. " Not so much as you might think. Life is very dear for poor people."

" But, haven't you just purchased an estate near d'Evry? "

" Yes."

" And a nice place, too, though a trifle damp. Happily you have stone to fill it in with, on the land that you bought of the widow Frapesle."

Robelot had never seen the old justice of the peace so talkative, so familiar; he seemed a little surprised.

" Three wretched pieces of land! " said he.

" Not so bad as you talk about. Then you've also bought something in the way of mines, at auction, haven't you? "

" Just a bunch of nothing at all."

" True, but it pays well. It isn't so bad, you see, to be a doctor without a diploma."

Robelot had been several times prosecuted for illegal practicing; so he thought he ought to protest against this.

" If I cure people," said he, " I'm not paid for it."

" Then your trade in herbs isn't what has enriched you."

The conversation was becoming a cross-examination. The bone-setter was beginning to be restless.

" Oh, I make something out of the herbs," he answered.

" And as you are thrifty, you buy land."

" I've also got some cattle and horses, which bring in something. I raise horses, cows, and sheep."

" Also without diploma? "

Robelot waxed disdainful.

" A piece of parchment does not make science. I don't fear the men of the schools. I study animals in the fields and the stable, without bragging. I haven't my equal for raising them, nor for knowing their diseases."

M. Plantat's tone became more and more winning.

"I know that you are a bright fellow, full of experience. Doctor Gendron, with whom you served, was praising your cleverness a moment ago."

The bone-setter shuddered, not so imperceptibly as to escape Plantat, who continued: "Yes, the good doctor said he never had so intelligent an assistant. 'Robelot,' said he, 'has such an aptitude for chemistry, and so much taste for it besides, that he understands as well as I many of the most delicate operations.'"

"Parbleu! I did my best, for I was well paid, and I was always fond of learning."

"And you were an apt scholar at Doctor Gendron's, Master Robelot; he makes some very curious studies. His work and experience on poisons are above all remarkable."

Robelot's uneasiness became apparent; his look wavered.

"Yes," returned he, "I have seen some strange experiments."

"Well, you see, you may think yourself lucky—for the doctor is going to have a splendid chance to study this sort of thing, and he will undoubtedly want you to assist him."

But Robelot was too shrewd not to have already guessed that this cross-examination had a purpose. What was M. Plantat after? he asked himself, not without a vague terror. And, going over in his mind the questions which had been asked, and the answers he had given, and to what these questions led, he trembled. He thought to escape further questioning by saying:

"I am always at my old master's orders when he needs me."

"He'll need you, be assured," said M. Plantat, who

added, in a careless tone, which his rapid glance at
Robelot belied, " The interest attaching to this case
will be intense, and the task difficult. Monsieur Sauvresy's body is to be disinterred."

Robelot was certainly prepared for something
strange, and he was armed with all his audacity. But
the name of Sauvresy fell upon his head like the stroke
of a club, and he stammered, in a choked voice :

" Sauvresy ! "

M. Plantat had already turned his head, and continued in an indifferent tone :

" Yes, Sauvresy is to be exhumed. It is suspected
that his death was not wholly a natural one. You see,
justice always has its suspicions."

Robelot leaned against the wall so as not to fall.
M. Plantat proceeded :

" So Doctor Gendron has been applied to. He has,
as you know, found reactive drugs which betray the
presence of an alkaloid, whatever it may be, in the
substances submitted to him for analysis. He has
spoken to me of a certain sensitive paper——"

Appealing to all his energy, Robelot forced himself
to stand up and resume a calm countenance.

" I know Doctor Gendron's process," said he, " but
I don't see who could be capable of the suspicions of
which you speak."

" I think there are more than suspicions," resumed
M. Plantat. " Madame de Trémorel, you know, has
been murdered : her papers have, of course, been examined ; letters have been found, with very damaging
revelations, receipts, and so on."

Robelot, apparently, was once more self-possessed ;
he forced himself to answer :

" Bast ! let us hope that justice is in the wrong."

Then, such was this man's self-control, despite a nervous trembling which shook his whole body as the wind does the leaves, that he added, constraining his thin lips to form a smile:

" Madame Courtois does not come down; I am waited for at home, and will drop in again to-morrow. Good-evening, gentlemen."

He walked away, and soon the sand in the court was heard creaking with his steps. As he went, he staggered like a drunken man.

M. Lecoq went up to M. Plantat, and taking off his hat:

" I surrender," said he, " and bow to you; you are great, like my master, the great Tabaret."

The detective's amour-propre was clearly aroused; his professional zeal was inspired; he found himself before a great crime—one of those crimes which triple the sale of the *Gazette of the Courts.* Doubtless many of its details escaped him: he was ignorant of the starting-point; but he saw the way clearing before him. He had surprised Plantat's theory, and had followed the train of his thought step by step; thus he discovered the complications of the crime which seemed so simple to M. Domini. His subtle mind had connected together all the circumstances which had been disclosed to him during the day, and now he sincerely admired the old justice of the peace. As he gazed at his beloved portrait, he thought, " Between the two of us—this old fox and I—we will unravel the whole web." He would not, however, show himself to be inferior to his companion.

" Monsieur," said he, " while you were questioning this rogue, who will be very useful to us, I did not lose any time. I've been looking about, under the furniture and so on, and have found this slip of paper."

" Let's see."

" It is the envelope of the young lady's letter. Do you know where her aunt, whom she was visiting, lives ? "

" At Fontainebleau, I believe."

" Ah ; well, this envelope is stamped ' Paris,' Saint-Lazare branch post-office. I know this stamp proves nothing——"

" It is, of course, an indication."

" That is not all ; I have read the letter itself—it was here on the table."

M. Plantat frowned involuntarily.

" It was, perhaps, a liberty," resumed M. Lecoq, " but the end justifies the means. Well, you have read this letter ; but have you studied it, examined the handwriting, weighed the words, remarked the context of the sentences ? "

" Ah," cried Plantat, " I was not mistaken then— you had the same idea strike you that occurred to me ! "

And, in the energy of his excitement he seized the detective's hands and pressed them as if he were an old friend. They were about to resume talking when a step was heard on the staircase ; and presently Dr. Gendron appeared.

" Courtois is better," said he, " he is in a doze, and will recover."

" We have nothing more, then, to keep us here," returned M. Plantat. " Let's be off. Monsieur Lecoq must be half dead with hunger."

As they went away, M. Lecoq slipped Laurence's letter, with the envelope, into his pocket.

X

M. Plantat's house was small and narrow; a philosopher's house. Three large rooms on the ground-floor, four chambers in the first story, an attic under the roof for the servants, composed all its apartments. Everywhere the carelessness of a man who has withdrawn from the world into himself, for years, ceasing to have the least interest in the objects which surround him, was apparent. The furniture was shabby, though it had been elegant; the mouldings had come off, the clocks had ceased to keep time, the chairs showed the stuffing of their cushions, the curtains, in places, were faded by the sun. The library alone betrayed a daily care and attention.

Long rows of books in calf and gilt were ranged on the carved oaken shelves, a movable table near the fireplace contained M. Plantat's favorite books, the discreet friends of his solitude. A spacious conservatory, fitted with every accessory and convenience, was his only luxury. In it flourished one hundred and thirty-seven varieties of briars.

Two servants, the widow Petit, cook and housekeeper, and Louis, gardener, inhabited the house. If they did not make it a noisy one, it was because Plantat, who talked little, detested also to hear others talk. Silence was there a despotic law. It was very hard for Mme. Petit, especially at first. She was very talkative, so talkative that when she found no one to chat with, she went to confession; to confess was to chat. She came near leaving the place twenty times; but the thought of an assured pension restrained her. Gradually she became accustomed to govern her tongue, and to this cloistral silence.   But she revenged herself outside for the privations of the household, and regained among the neighbors the time lost at home.

She was very much wrought up on the day of the murder.   At eleven o'clock, after going out for news, she had prepared monsieur's dinner; but he did not appear.   She waited one, two hours, five hours, keeping her water boiling for the eggs; no monsieur.   She wanted to send Louis to look for him, but Louis being a poor talker and not curious, asked her to go herself. The house was besieged by the female neighbors, who, thinking that Mme. Petit ought to be well posted, came for news; no news to give.

Toward five o'clock, giving up all thought of breakfast, she began to prepare for dinner.   But when the village bell struck eight o'clock, monsieur had not made his appearance.   At nine, the good woman was beside herself, and began to scold Louis, who had just come in from watering the garden, and, seated at the kitchen table, was soberly eating a plate of soup.

The bell rung.

" Ah, there's monsieur, at last."

No, it was not monsieur, but a little boy, whom M. Plantat had sent from Valfeuillu to apprise Mme. Petit that he would soon return, bringing with him two guests who would dine and sleep at the house.   The worthy woman nearly fainted.   It was the first time that M. Plantat had invited anyone to dinner for five years.   There was some mystery at the bottom of it —so thought Mme. Petit, and her anger doubled with her curiosity.

" To order a dinner at this hour," she grumbled. " Has he got common-sense, then?"   But reflecting that time pressed, she continued:

8

" Go along, Louis; this is not the moment for two feet to stay in one shoe.   Hurry up, and wring three chickens' heads ; see if there ain't some ripe grapes in the conservatory; bring on some preserves; fetch up some wine from the cellar ! "   The dinner was well advanced when the bell rung again.   This time Baptiste appeared, in exceeding bad humor, bearing M. Lecoq's night-gown.

" See here," said he to the cook, " what the person, who is with your master, gave me to bring here."

" What person ? "

" How do I know?   He's a spy sent down from Paris about this Valfeuillu affair; not much good, probably—ill-bred—a brute—and a wretch."

" But he's not alone with monsieur ? "

" No ; Doctor Gendron is with them."

Mme. Petit burned to get some news out of Baptiste ; but Baptiste also burned to get back and know what was taking place at his master's—so off he went, without having left any news behind.

An hour or more passed, and Mme. Petit had just angrily declared to Louis that she was going to throw the dinner out the window, when her master at last appeared, followed by his guests.   They had not exchanged a word after they left the mayor's.   Aside from the fatigues of the evening, they wished to reflect, and to resume their self-command.   Mme. Petit found it useless to question their faces—they told her nothing.   But she did not agree with Baptiste about M. Lecoq: she thought him good-humored, and rather silly.   Though the party was less silent at the dinner-table, all avoided, as if by tacit consent, any allusion to the events of the day.   No one would ever have thought that they had just been witnesses of, almost actors in, the Valfeuillu drama, they were so calm, and talked so glibly of indifferent things.   From time to time, indeed, a question remained unanswered, or a reply came tardily; but nothing of the sensations and thoughts, which were concealed beneath the uttered commonplaces, appeared on the surface.

Louis passed to and fro behind the diners, his white cloth on his arm, carving and passing the wine. Mme. Petit brought in the dishes, and came in thrice as often as was necessary, her ears wide open, leaving the door ajar as often as she dared.   Poor woman! she had prepared an excellent dinner, and nobody paid any attention to it.

M. Lecoq was fond of tit-bits; yet, when Louis placed on the table a dish of superb grapes—quite out of season—his mouth did not so much as expand into a smile.   Dr. Gendron would have been puzzled to say what he had eaten.   The dinner was nearly over, when M. Plantat began to be annoyed by the constraint which the presence of the servants put upon the party.   He called to the cook:

" You will give us our coffee in the library, and may then retire, as well as Louis."

" But these gentlemen do not know their rooms," insisted Mme. Petit, whose eavesdropping projects were checked by this order.   " They will, perhaps, need something."

" I will show them their rooms," said M. Plantat, dryly.   " And if they need anything, I shall be here."

They went into the library.   M. Plantat brought out a box of cigars and passed them round:

" It will be healthful to smoke a little before retiring."

M. Lecoq lit an aromatic weed, and remarked:

"You two may go to bed if you like; I am condemned, I see, to a sleepless night.   But before I go
to writing, I wish to ask you a few things, Monsieur
Plantat."

M. Plantat bowed in token of assent.

"We must resume our conversation," continued the
detective, "and compare our inferences. All our
lights are not too much to throw a little daylight upon
this affair, which is one of the darkest I have ever met
with.   The situation is dangerous, and time presses.
On our acuteness depends the fate of several innocent
persons, upon whom rest very serious charges.   We
have a theory: but Monsieur Domini also has one, and
his, let us confess, is based upon material facts, while
ours rests upon very disputable sensations and logic."

"We have more than sensations," responded M.
Plantat.

"I agree with you," said the doctor, "but we must
prove it."   ,

"And I *will* prove it, parbleu," cried M. Lecoq,
eagerly.   "The affair is complicated and difficult—so
much the better.   Eh! If it were simple, I would go
back to Paris instanter, and to-morrow I would send
you one of my men.   I leave easy riddles to infants.
What I want is the inexplicable enigmas, so as to unravel it; a struggle, to show my strength; obstacles, to
conquer them."

M. Plantat and the doctor looked steadily at the
speaker.   He was as if transfigured.   It was the same
yellow-haired and whiskered man, in a long overcoat:
yet the voice, the physiognomy, the very features, had
changed.   His eyes shone with the fire of his enthusiasm, his voice was metallic and vibrating, his imperi-

ous gesture affirmed the audacity and energy of his resolution.

"If you think, my friends," pursued he, "that they don't manufacture detectives like me at so much a year, you are right. When I was twenty years old, I took service with an astronomer, as his calculator, after a long course of study. He gave me my breakfasts and seventy francs a month; by means of which I dressed well, and covered I know not how many square feet with figures daily."

M. Lecoq puffed vigorously at his cigar a moment, casting a curious glance at M. Plantat. Then he resumed:

"Well, you may imagine that I wasn't the happiest of men. I forgot to mention that I had two little vices: I loved the women, and I loved play. All are not perfect. My salary seemed too small, and while I added up my columns of figures, I was looking about for a way to make a rapid fortune. There is, indeed, but one means; to appropriate somebody else's money, shrewdly enough not to be found out. I thought about it day and night. My mind was fertile in expedients, and I formed a hundred projects, each more practicable than the others. I should frighten you if I were to tell you half of what I imagined in those days. If many thieves of my calibre existed, you'd have to blot the word 'property' out of the dictionary. Precautions, as well as safes, would be useless. Happily for men of property, criminals are idiots."

"What is he coming to?" thought the doctor.

"One day, I became afraid of my own thoughts. I had just been inventing a little arrangement by which a man could rob any banker whatever of 200,000 francs without any more danger or difficulty than I raise this cup. So I said to myself, ' Well, my boy, if this goes on a little longer, a moment will come when, from the idea, you will naturally proceed to the practice.' Having, however, been born an honest lad—a mere chance —and being determined to use the talents which nature had given me, eight days afterward I bid my astronomer good-morning, and went to the prefecture. My fear of being a burglar drove me into the police.'

" And you are satisfied with the exchange? " asked Dr. Gendron.

" I' faith, Doctor, my first regret is yet to come. I am happy, because I am free to exercise my peculiar faculties with usefulness to my race. Existence has an enormous attraction for me, because I have still a passion which overrides all others—curiosity."

The detective smiled, and continued:

" There are people who have a mania for the theatre. It is like my own mania. Only, I can't understand how people can take pleasure in the wretched display of fictions, which are to real life what a tallow dip is to the sun. It seems to me monstrous that people can be interested in sentiments which, though well represented, are fictitious. What! can you laugh at the witticisms of a comedian, whom you know to be the struggling father of a family? Can you pity the sad fate of the poor actress who poisons herself, when you know that on going out you will meet her on the boulevards? It's pitiable! "

" Let's shut up the theatres," suggested Dr. Gendron.

" I am more difficult to please than the public," returned M. Lecoq. " I must have veritable comedies, or real dramas. My theatre is—society. My actors laugh honestly, or weep with genuine tears. A crime is committed—that is the prologue; I reach the scene, the first act begins. I seize at a glance the minutest shades of the scenery. Then I try to penetrate the motives, I group the characters, I link the episodes to the central fact, I bind in a bundle all the circumstances. The action soon reaches the crisis, the thread of my inductions conducts me to the guilty person; I divine him, arrest him, deliver him up. Then comes the great scene; the accused struggles, tries tricks, splits straws; but the judge, armed with the arms I have forged for him, overwhelms the wretch; he does not confess, but he is confounded. And how many secondary personages, accomplices, friends, enemies, witnesses are grouped about the principal criminal! Some are terrible, frightful, gloomy—others grotesque. And you know not what the ludicrous in the horrible is. My last scene is the court of assize. The prosecutor speaks, but it is I who furnished his ideas; his phrases are embroideries set around the canvass of my report. The president submits his questions to the jury; what emotion! The fate of my drama is being decided. The jury, perhaps, answers, ' Not guilty;' very well, my piece was bad, I am hissed. If ' Guilty,' on the contrary, the piece was good, I am applauded, and victorious. The next day I can go and see my hero, and slapping him on the shoulder, say to him, ' You have lost, old fellow, I am too much for you!' "

Was M. Lecoq in earnest now, or was he playing a part? What was the object of this autobiography? Without appearing to notice the surprise of his companions, he lit a fresh cigar; then, whether designedly or not, instead of replacing the lamp with which he lit it on the table, he put it on one corner of the mantel.

Thus M. Plantat's face was in full view, while that of M. Lecoq remained in shadow.

"I ought to confess," he continued, "without false modesty, that I have rarely been hissed. Like every man I have my Achilles heel. I have conquered the demon of play, but I have not triumphed over my passion for woman."

He sighed heavily, with the resigned gesture of a man who has chosen his path. "It's this way. There is a woman, before whom I am but an idiot. Yes, I the detective, the terror of thieves and murderers, who have divulged the combinations of all the sharpers of all the nations, who for ten years have swum amid vice and crime; who wash the dirty linen of all the corruptions, who have measured the depths of human infamy; I who know all, who have seen and heard all; I, Lecoq, am before her, more simple and credulous than an infant. She deceives me—I see it—and she proves that I have seen wrongly. She lies—I know it, I prove it to her—and I believe her. It is because this is one of those passions," he added, in a low, mournful tone, "that age, far from extinguishing, only fans, and to which the consciousness of shame and powerlessness adds fire. One loves, and the certainty that he cannot be loved in return is one of those griefs which you must have felt to know its depth. In a moment of reason, one sees and judges himself; he says, no, it's impossible, she is almost a child, I almost an old man. He says this—but always, in the heart, more potent than reason, than will, than experience, a ray of hope remains, and he says to himself, 'who knows —perhaps!' He awaits, what—a miracle? There are none, nowadays. No matter, he hopes on."

M. Lecoq stopped, as if his emotion prevented his

going on. M. Plantat had continued to smoke mechanically, puffing the smoke out at regular intervals;
but his face seemed troubled, his glance was unsteady,
his hands trembled. He got up, took the lamp from
the mantel and replaced it on the table, and sat down
again. The significance of this scene at last struck
Dr. Gendron.

In short, M. Lecoq, without departing widely from
the truth, had just attempted one of the most daring
experiments of his repertoire, and he judged it useless
to go further. He knew now what he wished to know.
After a moment's silence, he shuddered as though
awaking from a dream, and pulling out his watch,
said:

" Par le Dieu!   How I chat on, while time flies ! "

" And Guespin is in prison," remarked the doctor.

" We will have him out," answered the detective,
" if, indeed, he is innocent; for this time I have mastered the mystery, my romance, if you wish, and without any gap. There is, however, one fact of the utmost importance, that I by myself cannot explain."

" What ? " asked M. Plantat.

" Is it possible that Monsieur de Trémorel had a very
great interest in finding something—a deed, a letter, a
paper of some sort—something of a small size, secreted
in his own house ? "

" Yes—that is possible," returned the justice of the
peace.

" But I must know for certain."

M. Plantat reflected a moment.

" Well then," he went on, " I am sure, perfectly sure,
that if Madame de Trémorel had died suddenly, the
count would have ransacked the house to find a certain

paper, which he knew to be in his wife's possession, and which I myself have had in my hands."

"Then," said M. Lecoq, "there's the drama complete. On reaching Valfeuillu, I, like you, was struck with the frightful disorder of the rooms. Like you, I thought at first that this disorder was the result of design. I was wrong; a more careful scrutiny has convinced me of it. The assassin, it is true, threw everything into disorder, broke the furniture, hacked the chairs in order to make us think that some furious villains had been there. But amid these acts of premeditated violence I have followed up the involuntary traces of an exact, minute, and I may say patient search. Everything seemed turned topsy-turvy by chance; articles were broken open with the hatchet, which might have been opened with the hands; drawers had been forced which were not shut, and the keys of which were in the locks. Was this folly? No. For really no corner or crevice where a letter might be hid has been neglected. The table and bureau-drawers had been thrown here and there, but the narrow spaces between the drawers had been examined—I saw proofs of it, for I found the imprints of fingers on the dust which lay in these spaces. The books had been thrown pell-mell upon the floor, but every one of them had been handled, and some of them with such violence that the bindings were torn off. We found the mantel-shelves in their places, but every one had been lifted up. The chairs were not hacked with a sword, for the mere purpose of ripping the cloth—the seats were thus examined. My conviction of the certainty that there had been a most desperate search, at first roused my suspicions. I said to myself, 'The villains have

been looking for the money which was concealed;
therefore they did not belong to the household.' "

"But," observed the doctor, "they might belong to
the house, and yet not know the money was hidden;
for Guespin——"

"Permit me," interrupted M. Lecoq, "I will explain
myself. On the other hand, I found indications that
the assassin must have been closely connected with
Madame de Trémorel—her lover, or her husband.
These were the ideas that then struck me."

"And now?"

"Now," responded the detective, "with the certainty
that something besides booty might have been the
object of the search, I am not far from thinking that
the guilty man is he whose body is being searched for
—the Count Hector de Trémorel."

M. Plantat and Dr. Gendron had divined the name;
but neither had as yet dared to utter his suspicions.
They awaited this name of Trémorel; and yet, pronounced as it was in the middle of the night, in this
great sombre room, by this at least strange personage,
it made them shudder with an indescribable fright.

"Observe," resumed M. Lecoq, "what I say; I believe it to be so. In my eyes, the count's guilt is only
as yet extremely probable. Let us see if we three can
reach the certainty of it. You see, gentlemen, the inquest of a crime is nothing more nor less than the solution of a problem. Given the crime, proved, patent,
you commence by seeking out all the circumstances,
whether serious or superficial; the details and the particulars. When these have been carefully gathered,
you classify them, and put them in their order and
date. You thus know the victim, the crime, and the
circumstances; it remains to find the third term of the
problem, that is, x, the unknown quantity—the guilty

party. The task is a difficult one, but not so difficult as is imagined. The object is to find a man whose guilt explains all the circumstances, all the details found—all, understand me. Find such a man, and it is probable—and in nine cases out of ten, the probability becomes a reality—that you hold the perpetrator of the crime."

So clear had been M. Lecoq's exposition, so logical his argument, that his hearers could not repress an admiring exclamation:

"Very good! Very good!"

"Let us then examine together if the assumed guilt of the Count de Trémorel explains all the circumstances of the crime at Valfeuillu."

He was about to continue when Dr. Gendron, who sat near the window, rose abruptly.

"There is someone in the garden," said he.

All approached the window. The weather was glorious, the night very clear, and a large open space lay before the library window; they looked out, but saw no one.

"You are mistaken, Doctor," said Plantat, resuming his arm-chair.

M. Lecoq continued:

"Now let us suppose that, under the influence of certain events that we will examine presently, Monsieur de Trémorel had made up his mind to get rid of his wife. The crime once resolved upon, it was clear that the count must have reflected, and sought out the means of committing it with impunity; he must have weighed the circumstances, and estimated the perils of his act. Let us admit, also, that the events which led him to this extremity were such that he feared to be disturbed, and that he also feared that a search would be made for certain things, even should his wife die a natural death."

"That is true," said M. Plantat, nodding his head.

"Monsieur de Trémorel, then, determined to kill his wife, brutally, with a knife, with the idea of so arranging everything, as to make it believed that he too had been assassinated; and he also decided to endeavor to thrust suspicion on an innocent person, or at least, an accomplice infinitely less guilty than he.

"He made up his mind in advance, in adopting this course, to disappear, fly, conceal himself, change his personality; to suppress, in short, Count Hector de Trémorel, and make for himself, under another name, a new position and identity. These hypotheses, easily admitted, suffice to explain the whole series of otherwise inconsistent circumstances. They explain to us in the first place, how it was that on the very night of the murder, there was a large fortune in ready money at Valfeuillu; and this seems to me decisive. Why, when a man receives sums like this, which he proposes to keep by him, he conceals the fact as carefully as possible. Monsieur de Trémorel had not this common prudence. He shows his bundles of bank-notes freely, handles them, parades them; the servants see them, almost touch them. He wants everybody to know and repeat that there is a large sum in the house, easy to take, carry off, and conceal. And what time of all times, does he choose for this display? Exactly the moment when he knows, and everyone in the neighborhood knows, that he is going to pass the night at the château, alone with Madame de Trémorel.

"For he is aware that all his servants are invited, on the evening of July 8th to the wedding of the former cook. So well aware of it is he, that he defrays the wedding expenses, and himself names the day. You will perhaps say that it was by chance that this money was sent to Valfeuillu on the very night of the crime. At the worst that might be admitted. But believe me, there was no chance about it, and I will prove it. We will go to-morrow to the count's banker, and will inquire whether the count did not ask him, by letter or verbally, to send him these funds precisely on July 8th. Well, if he says yes, if he shows us such a letter, or if he declares that the money was called for in person, you will confess, no doubt, that I have more than a probability in favor of my theory."

Both his hearers bowed in token of assent.

" So far, then, there is no objection."

" Not the least," said M. Plantat.

" My conjectures have also the advantage of shedding light on Guespin's position. Honestly, his appearance is against him, and justifies his arrest. Was he an accomplice or entirely innocent? We certainly cannot yet decide. But it is a fact that he has fallen into an admirably well-laid trap. The count, in selecting him for his victim, took all care that every doubt possible should weigh upon him. I would wager that Monsieur de Trémorel, who knew this fellow's history, thought that his antecedents would add probability to the suspicions against him, and would weigh with a terrible weight in the scales of justice. Perhaps, too, he said to himself that Guespin would be sure to prove his innocence in the end, and he only wished to gain time to elude the first search. It is impossible that we can be deceived. We know that the countess died of the first blow, as if thunderstruck. She did not struggle; therefore she could not have torn a piece of cloth off the assassin's vest. If you admit Guespin's guilt, you admit that he was idiot enough to put a piece of his vest in his victim's hand; you admit that he was such a fool as to go and throw this torn and bloody vest into the Seine, from a bridge, in a place where he might know search would be made—and all this, without taking the common precaution of attaching it to a stone to carry it to the bottom.   That would be absurd.

"To me, then, this piece of cloth, this smeared vest, indicate at once Guespin's innocence and the count's guilt."

"But," objected Dr. Gendron, "if Guespin is innocent, why don't he talk?   Why don't he prove an alibi?   How was it he had his purse full of money?"

"Observe," resumed the detective, "that I don't say he is innocent; we are still among the probabilities. Can't you suppose that the count, perfidious enough to set a trap for his servant, was shrewd enough to deprive him of every means of proving an alibi?"

"But you yourself deny the count's shrewdness."

"I beg your pardon; please hear me.   The count's plan was excellent, and shows a superior kind of perversity; the execution alone was defective.   This is because the plan was conceived and perfected in safety, while when the crime had been committed, the murderer, distressed, frightened at his danger, lost his coolness and only half executed his project.   But there are other suppositions.   It might be asked whether, while Madame de Trémorel was being murdered, Guespin might not have been committing some other crime elsewhere."

This conjecture seemed so improbable to the doctor that he could not avoid objecting to it.   "Oh!" muttered he.

" Don't forget," replied Lecoq, " that the field of conjectures has no bounds. Imagine whatever complication of events you may, I am ready to maintain that such a complication has occurred or will present itself. Lieuben, a German lunatic, bet that he would succeed in turning up a pack of cards in the order stated in the written agreement. He turned and turned ten hours per day for twenty years. He had repeated the operation 4,246,028 times, when he succeeded."

M. Lecoq was about to proceed with another illustration, when M. Plantat interrupted him by a gesture.

" I admit your hypotheses; I think they are more than probable—they are true."

M. Lecoq, as he spoke, paced up and down between the window and the book-shelves, stopping at emphatic words, like a general who dictates to his aids the plan of the morrow's battle. To his auditors, he seemed a new man, with serious features, an eye bright with intelligence, his sentences clear and concise—the Lecoq, in short, which the magistrates who have employed his talents, would recognize.

" Now," he resumed, " hear me. It is ten o'clock at night. No noise without, the road deserted, the village lights extinguished, the château servants away at Paris. The count and countess are alone at Valfeuillu.

" They have gone to their bedroom.

" The countess has seated herself at the table where tea has been served. The count, as he talks with her, paces up and down the chamber.

" Madame de Trémorel has no ill presentiment; her husband, the past few days, has been more amiable, more attentive than ever. She mistrusts nothing, and so the count can approach her from behind, without her thinking of turning her head.

"When she hears him coming up softly, she imagines that he is going to surprise her with a kiss. He, meanwhile, armed with a long dagger, stands beside his wife. He knows where to strike that the wound may be mortal. He chooses the place at a glance; takes aim; strikes a terrible blow—so terrible that the handle of the dagger imprints itself on both sides of the wound. The countess falls without a sound, bruising her forehead on the edge of the table, which is overturned. Is not the position of the terrible wound below the left shoulder thus explained—a wound almost vertical, its direction being from right to left?"

The doctor made a motion of assent.

"And who, besides a woman's lover or her husband is admitted to her chamber, or can approach her when she is seated without her turning round?"

"That's clear," muttered M. Plantat.

"The countess is now dead," pursued M. Lecoq. "The assassin's first emotion is one of triumph. He is at last rid of her who was his wife, whom he hated enough to murder her, and to change his happy, splendid, envied existence for a frightful life, henceforth without country, friend, or refuge, proscribed by all nations, tracked by all the police, punishable by the laws of all the world! His second thought is of this letter or paper, this object of small size which he knows to be in his wife's keeping, which he has demanded a hundred times, which she would not give up to him, and which he must have."

"Add," interrupted M. Plantat, "that this paper was one of the motives of the crime."

"The count thinks he knows where it is. He im-

9

agines that he can put his hand on it at once. He is mistaken. He looks into all the drawers and bureaus used by his wife—and finds nothing. He searches every corner, he lifts up the shelves, overturns everything in the chamber—nothing. An idea strikes him. Is this letter under the mantel-shelf? By a turn of the arm he lifts it—down the clock tumbles and stops. It is not yet half-past ten."

"Yes," murmured the doctor, "the clock betrays that."

"The count finds nothing under the mantel-shelf except the dust, which has retained traces of his fingers. Then he begins to be anxious. Where can this paper be, for which he has risked his life? He grows angry. How search the locked drawers? The keys are on the carpet—I found them among the débris of the tea service—but he does not see them. He must have some implement with which to break open everything. He goes downstairs for a hatchet. The drunkenness of blood and vengeance is dissipated on the staircase; his terrors begin. All the dark corners are peopled, now, with those spectres which form the cortege of assassins; he is frightened, and hurries on. He soon goes up again, armed with a large hatchet—that found on the second story—and makes the pieces of wood fly about him. He goes about like a maniac, rips up the furniture at hazard; but he pursues a desperate search, the traces of which I have followed, among the débris. Nothing, always nothing! Everything in the room is topsy-turvy; he goes into his cabinet and continues the destruction; the hatchet rises and falls without rest. He breaks his own bureau, since he may find something concealed there of which he is ignorant. This bureau belonged to the first husband

—to Sauvresy. He takes out all the books in the library, one by one, shakes them furiously, and throws them about the floor. The infernal paper is undiscoverable. His distress is now too great for him to pursue the search with the least method. His wandering reason no longer guides him. He staggers, without calculation, from one thing to another, fumbling a dozen times in the same drawer, while he completely forgets others just by him. Then he thinks that this paper may have been hid in the stuffing of a chair. He seizes a sword, and to be certain, he slashes up the drawing-room chairs and sofas and those in the other rooms."

M. Lecoq's voice, accent, gestures, gave a vivid character to his recital. The hearer might imagine that he saw the crime committed, and was present at the terrible scenes which he described. His companions held their breath, unwilling by a movement to distract his attention.

" At this moment," pursued he, " the count's rage and terror were at their height. He had said to himself, when he planned the murder, that he would kill his wife, get possession of the letter, execute his plan quickly, and fly. And now all his projects were baffled! How much time was being lost, when each minute diminished the chances of escape! Then the probability of a thousand dangers which had not occurred to him, entered his mind. What if some friend should suddenly arrive, expecting his hospitality, as had occurred twenty times? What if a passer-by on the road should notice a light flying from room to room? Might not one of the servants return? When he is in the drawing-room, he thinks he hears someone ring at the gate; such is his terror, that he lets his candle fall—for I have found the marks of it on the

carpet.   He hears strange noises, such as never before
assailed his ears; he thinks he hears walking in the
next room; the floor creaks.   Is his wife really dead;
will she not suddenly rise up, run to the window, and
scream for help?   Beset by these terrors, he returns
to the bedroom, seizes his dagger, and again strikes
the poor countess.   But his hand is so unsteady that
the wounds are light.   You have observed, doctor,
that all these wounds take the same direction.   They
form right angles with the body, proving that the victim was lying down when they were inflicted.   Then,
in the excess of his frenzy, he strikes the body with his
feet, and his heels form the contusions discovered by
the autopsy."

M. Lecoq paused to take breath.   He not only narrated the drama, he acted it, adding gesture to word;
and each of his phrases made a scene, explained a fact,
and dissipated a doubt.   Like all true artists who wrap
themselves up in the character they represent, the detective really felt something of the sensations which
he interpreted, and his expressive face was terrible in
its contortions.

" That," he resumed, " is the first act of the drama.
An irresistible prostration succeeds the count's furious
passion.   The various circumstances which I am describing to you are to be noticed in nearly all great
crimes.   The assassin is always seized, after the murder, with a horrible and singular hatred against his
victim, and he often mutilates the body.   Then comes
the period of a prostration so great, of torpor so irresistible, that murderers have been known literally to go
to sleep in the blood, that they have been surprised
sleeping, and that it was with great difficulty that they
were awakened.   The count, when he has frightfully

disfigured the poor lady, falls into an arm-chair; indeed, the cloth of one of the chairs has retained some wrinkles, which shows that someone had sat in it. What are then the count's thoughts? He reflects on the long hours which have elapsed, upon the few hours which remain to him. He reflects that he has found nothing; that he will hardly have time, before day, to execute his plans for turning suspicion from him, and assure his safety, by creating an impression that he, too, has been murdered. And he must fly at once—fly, without that accursed paper. He summons up his energies, rises, and do you know what he does? He seizes a pair of scissors and cuts off his long, carefully cultivated beard."

"Ah!" interrupted M. Plantat, "that's why you examined the portrait so closely."

M. Lecoq was too intent on following the thread of his deductions to note the interruption.

"This is one of those vulgar details," pursued he, "whose very insignificance makes them terrible, when they are attended by certain circumstances. Now imagine the Count de Trémorel, pale, covered with his wife's blood, shaving himself before his glass, rubbing the soap over his face, in that room all topsy-turvy, while three steps off lies the still warm and palpitating body! It was an act of terrible courage, believe me, to look at himself in the glass after a murder—one of which few criminals are capable. The count's hands, however, trembled so violently that he could scarcely hold his razor, and his face must have been cut several times."

"What!" said Dr. Gendron, "do you imagine that the count spared the time to shave?"

"I am positively sure of it, pos-i-tive-ly. A towel

on which I have found one of those marks which a
razor leaves when it is wiped—and one only—has put
me on the track of this fact. I looked about, and found
a box of razors, one of which had recently been used,
for it was still moist; and I have carefully preserved
both the towel and the box. And if these proofs are
not enough, I will send to Paris for two of my men,
who will find, somewhere in the house or the garden,
both the count's beard and the cloth with which he
wiped his razor. As to the fact which surprises you,
Doctor, it seems to me very natural; more, it is the
necessary result of the plan he adopted. Monsieur de
Trémorel has always worn his full beard: he cuts it
off, and his appearance is so entirely altered, that if he
met anyone in his flight, he would not be recognized."

The doctor was apparently convinced, for he cried:

" It's clear—it's evident."

" Once thus disguised, the count hastens to carry
out the rest of his plan, to arrange everything to throw
the law off the scent, and to make it appear that he,
as well as his wife, has been murdered. He hunts up
Guespin's vest, tears it out at the pocket, and puts a
piece of it in the countess's hand. Then taking the
body in his arms, crosswise, he goes downstairs. The
wounds bleed frightfully—hence the numerous stains
discovered all along his path. Reaching the foot of
the staircase he is obliged to put the countess down, in
order to open the garden-door. This explains the
large stain in the vestibule. The count, having opened
the door, returns for the body and carries it in his arms
as far as the edge of the lawn; there he stops carrying
it, and drags it by the shoulders, walking backward,
trying thus to create the impression that his own body
has been dragged across there and thrown into the

Seine.   But the wretch forgot two things which betray
him to us.   He did not reflect that the countess's skirts,
in being dragged along the grass, pressing it down and
breaking it for a considerable space, spoiled his trick.
Nor did he think that her elegant and well-curved feet,
encased in small high-heeled boots, would mould themselves in the damp earth of the lawn, and thus leave
against him a proof clearer than the day."

M. Plantat rose abruptly.

" Ah," said he, " you said nothing of this before."

" Nor of several other things, either.   But I was before ignorant of some facts which I now know ; and as
I had reason to suppose that you were better informed
than I, I was not sorry to avenge myself for a caution
which seemed to me mysterious."

" Well, you are avenged," remarked the doctor,
smiling.

" On the other side of the lawn," continued M. Lecoq, " the count again took up the countess's body.
But forgetting the effect of water when it spirts, or—
who knows?—disliking to soil himself, instead of
throwing her violently in the river, he put her down
softly, with great precaution.   That's not all.   He
wished it to appear that there had been a terrible struggle.   What does he do?   Stirs up the sand with the
end of his foot.   And he thinks that will deceive the
police ! "

" Yes, yes," muttered Plantat, " exactly so—I saw
it."

" Having got rid of the body, the count returns to
the house.   Time presses, but he is still anxious to find
the paper.   He hastens to take the last measures to
assure his safety.   He smears his slippers and handkerchief with blood.   He throws his handkerchief and

one of his slippers on the sward, and the other slipper into the river. His haste explains the incomplete execution of his manœuvres. He hurries—and commits blunder after blunder. He does not reflect that his valet will explain about the empty bottles which he puts on the table. He thinks he is turning wine into the five glasses—it is vinegar, which will prove that no one has drunk out of them. He ascends, puts forward the hands of the clock, but forgets to put the hands and the striking bell in harmony. He rumples up the bed, but he does it awkwardly—and it is impossible to reconcile these three facts, the bed crumpled, the clock showing twenty minutes past three, and the countess dressed as if it were mid-day. He adds as much as he can to the disorder of the room. He smears a sheet with blood; also the bed-curtains and furniture. Then he marks the door with the imprint of a bloody hand, too distinct and precise not to be done designedly. Is there so far a circumstance or detail of the crime, which does not explain the count's guilt?"

"There's the hatchet," answered M. Plantat, "found on the second story, the position of which seemed so strange to you."

"I am coming to that. There is one point in this mysterious affair, which, thanks to you, is now clear. We know that Madame de Trémorel, known to her husband, possessed and concealed a paper or a letter, which he wanted, and which she obstinately refused to give up in spite of all his entreaties. You have told us that the anxiety—perhaps the necessity—to have this paper, was a powerful motive of the crime. We will not be rash then in supposing that the importance of this paper was immense—entirely beyond an ordi-

nary affair. It must have been, somehow, very damaging to one or the other. To whom? To both, or
only the count? Here I am reduced to conjectures.
It is certain that it was a menace—capable of being executed at any moment—suspended over the head of
him or them concerned by it. Madame de Trémorel
surely regarded this paper either as a security, or as
a terrible arm which put her husband at her mercy.
It was surely to deliver himself from this perpetual menace that the count killed his wife."

The logic was so clear, the last words brought the
evidence out so lucidly and forcibly, that his hearers
were struck with admiration. They both cried:

"Very good!"

"Now," resumed M. Lecoq, "from the various ele-
ments which have served to form our conviction, we
must conclude that the contents of this letter, if it can
be found, will clear away our last doubts, will explain
the crime, and will render the assassin's precautions
wholly useless. The count, therefore, must do everything in the world, must attempt the impossible, not to
leave this danger behind him. His preparations for
flight ended, Hector, in spite of his deadly peril, of the
speeding time, of the coming day, instead of flying
recommences with more desperation than ever his useless search. Again he goes through all the furniture,
the books, the papers—in vain. Then he determines
to search the second story, and armed with his hatchet,
goes up to it. He has already attacked a bureau, when
he hears a cry in the garden. He runs to the window
—what does he see? Philippe and old Bertaud are
standing on the river-bank under the willows, near the
corpse. Can you imagine his immense terror? Now,
there's not a second to lose—he has already delayed

too long. The danger is near, terrible. Daylight has come, the crime is discovered, they are coming, he sees himself lost beyond hope. He must fly, fly at once, at the peril of being seen, met, arrested. He throws the hatchet down violently—it cuts the floor. He rushes down, slips the bank-notes in his pocket, seizes Guespin's torn and smeared vest, which he will throw into the river from the bridge, and saves himself by the garden. Forgetting all caution, confused, beside himself, covered with blood, he runs, clears the ditch, and it is he whom old Bertaud sees making for the forest of Mauprévior, where he intends to arrange the disorder of his clothes. For the moment he is safe. But he leaves behind him this letter, which is, believe me, a formidable witness, which will enlighten justice and will betray his guilt and the perfidy of his projects. For he has not found it, but we will find it; it is necessary for us to have it to defeat Monsieur Domini, and to change our doubts into certainty."

XI

A long silence followed the detective's discourse. Perhaps his hearers were casting about for objections. At last Dr. Gendron spoke:

" I don't see Guespin's part in all this."

" Nor I, very clearly," answered M. Lecoq. " And here I ought to confess to you not only the strength, but the weakness also, of the theory I have adopted. By this method, which consists of reconstructing the crime before discovering the criminal, I can be neither right nor wrong by halves. Either all my inferences are correct, or not one of them is. It's all, or nothing. If I am right, Guespin has not been mixed up with this crime, at least directly; for there isn't a single circumstance which suggests outside aid. If, on the other hand, I am wrong——"

M. Lecoq paused. He seemed to have heard some unexpected noise in the garden.

" But I am not wrong. I have still another charge against the count, of which I haven't spoken, but which seems to be conclusive."

" Oh," cried the doctor, " what now? "

" Two certainties are better than one, and I always doubt. When I was left alone a moment with François, the valet, I asked him if he knew exactly the number of the count's shoes; he said yes, and took me to a closet where the shoes are kept. A pair of boots, with green Russia leather tops, which François was sure the count had put on the previous morning, was missing. I looked for them carefully everywhere, but could not find them. Again, the blue cravat with white stripes which the count wore on the 8th, had also disappeared."

" There," cried M. Plantat, " that is indisputable proof that your supposition about the slippers and handkerchief was right."

" I think that the facts are sufficiently established to enable us to go forward. Let's now consider the events which must have decided——"

M. Lecoq again stopped, and seemed to be listening. All of a sudden, without a word he jumped on the window-sill and from thence into the garden, with the bound of a cat which pounces on a mouse. The noise of a fall, a stifled cry, an oath, were heard, and then a stamping as if a struggle were going on. The doctor and M. Plantat hastened to the window. Day was breaking, the trees shivered in the fresh wind of the early morning, objects were vaguely visible without distinct forms across the white mist which hangs, on summer nights, over the valley of the Seine. In the middle of the lawn, at rapid intervals, they heard the blunt noise of a clinched fist striking a living body, and saw two men, or rather two phantoms, furiously swinging their arms. Presently the two shapes formed but one, then they separated, again to unite; one of the two fell, rose at once, and fell again.

"Don't disturb yourselves," cried M. Lecoq's voice. "I've got the rogue."

The shadow of the detective, which was upright, bent over, and the conflict was recommenced. The shadow stretched on the ground defended itself with the dangerous strength of despair; his body formed a large brown spot in the middle of the lawn, and his legs, kicking furiously, convulsively stretched and contracted. Then there was a moment when the lookers-on could not make out which was the detective. They rose again and struggled; suddenly a cry of pain escaped, with a ferocious oath.

"Ah, wretch!"

And almost immediately a loud shout rent the air, and the detective's mocking tones were heard:

"There he is! I've persuaded him to pay his respects to us—light me up a little."

The doctor and his host hastened to the lamp; their zeal caused a delay, and at the moment that the doctor raised the lamp, the door was rudely pushed open.

"I beg to present to you," said M. Lecoq, "Master Robelot, bone-setter of Orcival, herborist by prudence, and poisoner by vocation."

The stupefaction of the others was such that neither could speak.

It was really the bone-setter, working his jaws nervously. His adversary had thrown him down by the famous knee-stroke which is the last resort of the worst prowlers about the Parisian barriers. But it was not so much Robelot's presence which surprised M. Plantat and his friend. Their stupor was caused by the detective's appearance; who, with his wrist of steel—as rigid as handcuffs—held the doctor's ex-assistant, and pushed him forward. The voice was certainly Lecoq's; there was his costume, his big-knotted cravat, his yellow-haired watch-chain—still it was no longer Lecoq. He was blond, with highly cultivated whiskers, when he jumped out the window; he returned, brown, with a smooth face. The man who had jumped out was a middle-aged person, with an expressive face which was in turn idiotic and intelligent; the man who returned by the door was a fine young fellow of thirty-five, with a beaming eye and a sensitive lip; a splendid head of curly black hair, brought out vividly the pallor of his complexion, and the firm outline of his head and face. A wound appeared on his neck, just below the chin.

"Monsieur Lecoq!" cried M. Plantat, recovering his voice.

"Himself," answered the detective, "and this time the true Lecoq." Turning to Robelot, he slapped him on the shoulder and added:

"Go on, you."

Robelot fell upon a sofa, but the detective continued to hold him fast.

"Yes," he continued, "this rascal has robbed me of my blond locks. Thanks to him and in spite of myself, you see me as I am, with the head the Creator gave me, and which is really my own." He gave a

careless gesture, half angry, half good-humored. " I
am the true Lecoq; and to tell the truth, only three
persons besides yourselves really know him—two trusted friends, and one who is infinitely less so—she of
whom I spoke a while ago."

The eyes of the other two met as if to question each
other, and M. Lecoq continued:

" What can a fellow do? All is not rose color in my
trade. We run such dangers, in protecting society, as
should entitle us to the esteem, if not the affection of
our fellow-men. Why, I am condemned to death, at
this moment, by seven of the most dangerous criminals
in France. I have caught them, you see, and they
have sworn—they are men of their word, too—that I
should only die by their hands. Where are these
wretches? Four at Cayenne, one at Brest; I've had
news of them. But the other two? I've lost their
track. Who knows whether one of them hasn't followed me here, and whether to-morrow, at the turning
of some obscure road, I shall not get six inches of cold
steel in my stomach? "

He smiled sadly.

" And no reward," pursued he, " for the perils which
we brave. If I should fall to-morrow, they would take
up my body, carry it to my house, and that would be
the end." The detective's tone had become bitter, the
irritation of his voice betrayed his rancor. " My precautions happily are taken. While I am performing
my duties, I suspect everything, and when I am on my
guard I fear no one. But there are days when one is
tired of being on his guard, and would like to be able
to turn a street corner without looking for a dagger.
On such days I again become myself; I take off my
false beard, throw down my mask, and my real self

emerges from the hundred disguises which I assume in turn.   I have been a detective fifteen years, and no one at the prefecture knows either my true face or the color of my hair."

Master Robelot, ill at ease on his lounge, attempted to move.

"Ah, look out!" cried M. Lecoq, suddenly changing his tone.   "Now get up here, and tell us what you were about in the garden?"

"But you are wounded!" exclaimed Plantat, observing stains of blood on M. Lecoq's shirt.

"Oh, that's nothing—only a scratch that this fellow gave me with a big cutlass he had."

M. Plantat insisted on examining the wound, and was not satisfied until the doctor declared it to be a very slight one.

"Come, Master Robelot," said the old man, "what were you doing here?"

The bone-setter did not reply.

"Take care," insisted M. Plantat, "your silence will confirm us in the idea that you came with the worst designs."

But it was in vain that M. Plantat wasted his persuasive eloquence.   Robelot shut himself up in a ferocious and dogged silence.   M. Gendron, hoping, not without reason, that he might have some influence over his former assistant, spoke:

"Answer us; what did you come for?"

Robelot made an effort; it was painful, with his broken jaw, to speak.

"I came to rob; I confess it."

"To rob—what?"

"I don't know."

" But you didn't scale a wall and risk the jail without a definite object ? "

" Well, then, I wanted——"

He stopped.

" What ?   Go on."

" To get some rare flowers in the conservatory."

" With your cutlass, hey ? " said M. Lecoq.

Robelot gave him a terrible look; the detective continued :

" You needn't look at me that way—you don't scare me.   And don't talk like a fool, either.   If you think we are duller than you, you are mistaken—I warn you of it."

" I wanted the flower-pots," stammered the man.

" Oh, come now," cried M. Lecoq, shrugging his shoulders, " don't repeat such nonsense.   You, a man that buys large estates for cash, steal flower-pots !   Tell that to somebody else.   You've been turned over to-night, my boy, like an old glove.   You've let out in spite of yourself a secret that tormented you furiously, and you came here to get it back again.   You thought that perhaps Monsieur Plantat had not told it to anybody, and you wanted to prevent him from speaking again forever."

Robelot made a sign of protesting.

" Shut up now," said M. Lecoq.   " And your cutlass ? "

While this conversation was going on, M. Plantat reflected.

" Perhaps," he murmured, " I've spoken too soon."

" Why so ? " asked M. Lecoq.   " I wanted a palpable proof for Monsieur Domini ; we'll give him this rascal, and if he isn't satisfied, he's difficult to please."

" But what shall we do with him ? "

" Shut him up somewhere in the house ; if necessary, I'll tie him up."

" Here's a dark closet."

" Is it secure ? "

" There are thick walls on three sides of it, and the fourth is closed with a double door; no openings, no windows, nothing."

" Just the place."

M. Plantat opened the closet, a black-looking hole, damp, narrow, and full of old books and papers.

" There," said M. Lecoq to his prisoner, " in here you'll be like a little king," and he pushed him into the closet. Robelot did not resist, but he asked for some water and a light. They gave him a bottle of water and a glass.

" As for a light," said M. Lecoq, " you may dispense with it. You'll be playing us some dirty trick."

M. Plantat, having shut the closet-door, took the detective's hand.

" Monsieur," said he, earnestly, " you have probably just saved my life at the peril of your own ; I will not thank you. The day will come, I trust, when I may——"

The detective interrupted him with a gesture.

" You know how I constantly expose myself," said he, " once more or less does not matter much. Besides, it does not always serve a man to save his life." He was pensive a moment, then added: " You will thank me after awhile, when I have gained other titles to your gratitude."

M. Gendron also cordially shook the detective's hand, saying:

" Permit me to express my admiration of you. I had no idea what the resources of such a man as you

10

were. You got here this morning without information, without details, and by the mere scrutiny of the
scene of the crime, by the sole force of reasoning, have
found the criminal: more, you have proved to us that
the criminal could be no other than he whom you have
named."

M. Lecoq bowed modestly. These praises evidently
pleased him greatly.

" Still," he answered, " I am not yet quite satisfied.
The guilt of the Count de Trémorel is of course abun-
dantly clear to me. But what motives urged him?
How was he led to this terrible impulse to kill his wife,
and make it appear that he, too, had been murdered?"

" Might we not conclude," remarked the doctor,
" that, disgusted with Madame de Trémorel, he has got
rid of her to rejoin another woman, adored by him to
madness?"

M. Lecoq shook his head.

" People don't kill their wives for the sole reason that
they are tired of them and love others. They quit their
wives, live with the new loves—that's all. That happens every day, and neither the law nor public opinion
condemns such people with great severity."

" But it was the wife who had the fortune."

" That wasn't the case here. I have been posting
myself up. M. de Trémorel had a hundred thousand
crowns, the remains of a colossal fortune saved by his
friend Sauvresy; and his wife by the marriage contract
made over a half million to him. A man can live in
ease anywhere on eight hundred thousand francs. Besides, the count was master of all the funds of the estate. He could sell, buy, realize, borrow, deposit, and
draw funds at will."

The doctor had nothing to reply. M. Lecoq went

on, speaking with a certain hesitation, while his eyes interrogated M. Plantat.

"We must find the reasons of this murder, and the motives of the assassin's terrible resolution—in the past. Some crime so indissolubly linked the count and countess, that only the death of one of them could free the other. I suspected this crime the first thing this morning, and have seen it all the way through; and the man that we have just shut up in there—Robelot—who wanted to murder Monsieur Plantat, was either the agent or the accomplice of this crime."

The doctor had not been present at the various episodes which, during the day at Valfeuillu and in the evening at the mayor's, had established a tacit understanding between Plantat and Lecoq. He needed all the shrewdness he possessed to fill up the gaps and understand the hidden meanings of the conversation to which he had been listening for two hours. M. Lecoq's last words shed a ray of light upon it all, and the doctor cried, "Sauvresy!"

"Yes—Sauvresy," answered M. Lecoq. "And the paper which the murderer hunted for so eagerly, for which he neglected his safety and risked his life, must contain the certain proof of the crime."

M. Plantat, despite the most significant looks and the direct provocation to make an explanation, was silent. He seemed a hundred leagues off in his thoughts, and his eyes, wandering in space, seemed to follow forgotten episodes in the mists of the past. M. Lecoq, after a brief pause, decided to strike a bold blow.

"What a past that must have been," exclaimed he, "which could drive a young, rich, happy man like Hector de Trémorel to plan in cool blood such a crime, to resign himself to disappear after it, to cease to exist, as it were to lose all at once his personality, his position, his honor and his name! What a past must be that which drives a young girl of twenty to suicide!"

M. Plantat started up, pale, more moved than he had yet appeared.

"Ah," cried he, in an altered voice, "you don't believe what you say! Laurence never knew about it, never!"

The doctor, who was narrowly watching the detective, thought he saw a faint smile light up his mobile features. The old justice of the peace went on, now calmly and with dignity, in a somewhat haughty tone:

"You didn't need tricks or subterfuge, Monsieur Lecoq, to induce me to tell what I know. I have evinced enough esteem and confidence in you to deprive you of the right to arm yourself against me with the sad secret which you have surprised."

M. Lecoq, despite his cool-headedness, was disconcerted.

"Yes," pursued M. Plantat, "your astonishing genius for penetrating dramas like this has led you to the truth. But you do not know all, and even now I would hold my tongue, had not the reasons which compelled me to be silent ceased to exist."

He opened a secret drawer in an old oaken desk near the fireplace and took out a large paper package, which he laid on the table.

"For four years," he resumed, "I have followed, day by day—I might say, hour by hour—the various phases of the dreadful drama which ended in blood last night at Valfeuillu. At first, the curiosity of an old retired attorney prompted me. Later, I hoped to save the life and honor of one very dear to me. Why did I say nothing of my discoveries? That, my friends,

is the secret of my conscience—it does not reproach
me.   Besides, I shut my eyes to the evidence even up
to yesterday; I needed the brutal testimony of this
deed!"

Day had come.   The frightened blackbirds flew
whistling by.   The pavement resounded with the
wooden shoes of the workmen going fieldward.   No
noise troubled the sad stillness of the library, unless
it were the rustling of the leaves which M. Plantat was
turning over, or now and then a groan from Robelot.

"Before commencing," said the old man, "I ought
to consider your weariness; we have been up twenty-
four hours——"

But the others protested that they did not need repose.   The fever of curiosity had chased away their
exhaustion.   They were at last to know the key of the
mystery.

"Very well," said their host, "listen to me."

XII

The Count Hector de Trémorel, at twenty-six, was
the model and ideal of the polished man of the world,
proper to our age; a man useless alike to himself and
to others, harmful even, seeming to have been placed
on earth expressly to play at the expense of all.   Young,
noble, elegant, rich by millions, endowed with vigorous health, this last descendant of a great family squan-
dered most foolishly and ignobly both his youth and
his patrimony.   He acquired by excesses of all kinds
a wide and unenviable celebrity.   People talked of his
stables, his carriages, his servants, his furniture, his
dogs, his favorite loves.   His cast-off horses still took
prizes, and a jade distinguished by his notice was eager-

ly sought by the young bloods of the town. Do not
think, however, that he was naturally vicious; he had
a warm heart, and even generous emotions at twenty.
Six years of unhealthy pleasures had spoiled him to
the marrow. Foolishly vain, he was ready to do anything to maintain his notoriety. He had the bold and
determined egotism of one who has never had to think
of anyone but himself, and has never suffered. Intoxicated by the flatteries of the so-called friends who drew
his money from him, he admired himself, mistaking
his brutal cynicism for wit, and his lofty disdain of all
morality and his idiotic scepticism, for character. He
was also feeble; he had caprices, but never a will;
feeble as a child, a woman, a girl. His biography was
to be found in the petty journals of the day, which re-
tailed his sayings—or what he might have said; his
least actions and gestures were reported.

One night when he was supping at the Café de Paris,
he threw all the plates out the window. It cost him
twenty thousand francs. Bravo! One morning gos-
siping Paris learned with stupefaction that he had
eloped to Italy with the wife of X——, the banker, a
lady nineteen years married. He fought a duel, and
killed his man. The week after, he was wounded in
another. He was a hero! On one occasion he went
to Baden, where he broke the bank. Another time,
after playing sixty hours, he managed to lose one hundred and twenty thousand francs—won by a Russian
prince.

He was one of those men whom success intoxicates,
who long for applause, but who care not for what they
are applauded. Count Hector was more than ravished
by the noise he made in the world. It seemed to him
the acme of honor and glory to have his name or ini-

tials constantly in the columns of the *Parisian World*.
He did not betray this, however, but said, with charming modesty, after each new adventure:

" When will they stop talking about me? "

On great occasions, he borrowed from Louis XIV.
the epigram:

" After me the deluge."

The deluge came in his lifetime.

One April morning, his valet, a villainous fellow,
drilled and dressed up by the count—woke him at nine
o'clock with this speech:

" Monsieur, a bailiff is downstairs in the ante-chamber, and has come to seize your furniture."

Hector turned on his pillow, yawned, stretched, and
replied:

" Well, tell him to begin operations with the stables
and carriage-house; and then come up and dress me."

He did not seem disturbed, and the servant retired
amazed at his master's coolness. The count had at
least sense enough to know the state of his finances;
and he had foreseen, nay, expected the bailiff's visit.
Three years before, when he had been laid up for six
weeks in consequence of a fall from his horse, he had
measured the depth of the gulf toward which he was
hastening. Then, he might yet have saved himself.
But he must have changed his whole course of life, re-
formed his household, learned that twenty-one franc
pieces made a napoleon. Fie, never! After mature
reflection he had said to himself that he would go on to
the end. When the last hour came, he would fly to
the other end of France, erase his name from his linen,
and blow his brains out in some forest.

This hour had now come.

By contracting debts, signing bills, renewing obligations, paying interests and compound interests, giving commissions by always borrowing, and never paying, Hector had consumed the princely heritage—nearly four millions in lands—which he had received at his father's death. The winter just past had cost him fifty thousand crowns. He had tried eight days before to borrow a hundred thousand francs, and had failed. He had been refused, not because his property was not as much as he owed, but because it was known that property sold by a bankrupt does not bring its value.

Thus it was that when the valet came in and said, "The bailiff is here," he seemed like a spectre commanding suicide.

Hector took the announcement coolly and said, as he got up:

"Well, here's an end of it."

He was very calm, though a little confused. A little confusion is excusable when a man passes from wealth to beggary. He thought he would make his last toilet with especial care. Parbleu! The French nobility goes into battle in court costume! He was ready in less than an hour. He put on his bejewelled watch-chain; then he put a pair of little pistols, of the finest quality, in his overcoat pocket; then he sent the valet away, and opening his desk, he counted up what funds he had left. Ten thousand and some hundreds of francs remained. He might with this sum take a journey, prolong his life two or three months; but he repelled with disdain the thought of a miserable subterfuge, of a reprieve in disguise. He imagined that with this money he might make a great show of generosity, which would be talked of in the world; it would be chivalrous to breakfast with his inamorata and make her a present of this money at dessert. During the

meal he would be full of nervous gayety, of cynical humor, and then he would announce his intention to kill
himself.   The girl would not fail to narrate the scene
everywhere; she would repeat his last conversation, his
last will and gift; all the cafés would buzz with it at
night; the papers would be full of it.

This idea strangely excited him, and comforted him
at once.   He was going out, when his eyes fell upon
the mass of papers in his desk.   Perhaps there was
something there which might dim the positiveness of
his resolution.   He emptied all the drawers without
looking or choosing, and put all the papers in the fire.
He looked with pride upon this conflagration; there
were bills, love letters, business letters, bonds, patents
of nobility, deeds of property.   Was it not his brilliant
past which flickered and consumed in the fireplace?

The bailiff occurred to him, and he hastily descended.   He was the most polite of bailiffs, a man of taste
and wit, a friend of artists, himself a poet at times.
He had already seized eight horses in the stables with
all their harness and trappings, and five carriages with
their equipage, in the carriage-house.

"I'm going on slowly, Count," said he, bowing.
"Perhaps you wish to arrest the execution.   The sum
is large, to be sure, but a man in your position——"

"Believe that you are here because it suits me," interrupted Hector, proudly, "this house doesn't suit me;
I shall never enter it again.   So, as you are master, go
on."

And wheeling round on his heel he went off.

The astonished bailiff proceeded with his work.   He
went from room to room, admiring and seizing.   He
seized cups gained at the races, collections of pipes and

arms, and the library, containing many sporting-books, superbly bound.

Meanwhile the Count de Trémorel, who was resolved more than ever on suicide, ascending the boulevards came to his inamorata's house, which was near the Madeleine. He had introduced her some six months before into the *demi-monde* as Jenny Fancy. Her real name was Pélagie Taponnet, and although the count did not know it, she was his valet's sister. She was pretty and lively, with delicate hands and a tiny foot, superb chestnut hair, white teeth, and great impertinent black eyes, which were languishing, caressing, or provoking, at will. She had passed suddenly from the most abject poverty to a state of extravagant luxury. This brilliant change did not astonish her as much as you might think. Forty-eight hours after her removal to her new apartments, she had established order among the servants; she made them obey a glance or a gesture; and she made her dressmakers and milliners submit with good grace to her orders. Jenny soon began to languish, in her fine rooms, for new excitement; her gorgeous toilets no longer amused her. A woman's happiness is not complete unless seasoned by the jealousy of rivals. Jenny's rivals lived in the Faubourg du Temple, near the barrier; they could not envy her splendor, for they did not know her, and she was strictly forbidden to associate with and so dazzle them. As for Trémorel, Jenny submitted to him from necessity. He seemed to her the most tiresome of men. She thought his friends the dreariest of beings. Perhaps she perceived beneath their ironically polite manner, a contempt for her, and understood of how little consequence she was to these rich people, these high livers, gamblers, men of the world. Her pleasures comprised an evening with someone of her own class, card-playing, at which she won, and a midnight supper. The rest of the time she suffered ennui. She was wearied to death. A hundred times she was on the point of discarding Trémorel, abandoning all this luxury, money, servants, and resuming her old life. Many a time she packed up; her vanity always checked her at the last moment.

Hector de Trémorel rang at her door at eleven on the morning in question. She did not expect him so early, and she was evidently surprised when he told her he had come to breakfast, and asked her to hasten the cook, as he was in a great hurry.

She had never, she thought, seen him so amiable, so gay. All through breakfast he sparkled, as he promised himself he would, with spirit and fun. At last, while they were sipping their coffee, Hector spoke:

"All this, my dear, is only a preface, intended to prepare you for a piece of news which will surprise you. I am a ruined man."

She looked at him with amazement, not seeming to comprehend him.

"I said—ruined," said he, laughing bitterly, "as ruined as man can be."

"Oh, you are making fun of me, joking——"

"I never spoke so seriously in my life. It seems strange to you, doesn't it? Yet it's sober truth."

Jenny's large eyes continued to interrogate him.

"Why," he continued, with lofty carelessness, "life, you know, is like a bunch of grapes, which one either eats gradually, piece by piece, or squeezes into a glass to be tossed off at a gulp. I've chosen the latter way. My grape was four million francs; they are drunk up to the dregs. I don't regret them, I've had a jolly life

for my money.   But now I can flatter myself that I am
as much of a beggar as any beggar in France.   Everything at my house is in the bailiff's hands—I am without a domicile, without a penny."

He spoke with increasing animation as the multitude
of diverse thoughts passed each other tumultuously in
his brain.   And he was not playing a part.   He was
speaking in all good faith.

"But—then—" stammered Jenny.

"What?   Are you free?   Just so——"

She hardly knew whether to rejoice or mourn.

"Yes," he continued, "I give you back your liberty."

Jenny made a gesture which Hector misunderstood.

"Oh! be quiet," he added quickly, "I sha'n't leave
you thus; I would not desert you in a state of need.
This furniture is yours, and I have provided for you besides.   Here in my pocket are five hundred napoleons;
it is my all; I have brought it to give to you."

He passed the money over to her on a plate, laughingly, imitating the restaurant waiters.   She pushed it
back with a shudder.

"Oh, well," said he, "that's a good sign, my dear;
very good, very good.   I've always thought and said
that you were a good girl—in fact, too good; you
needed correcting."

She did, indeed, have a good heart; for instead of
taking Hector's bank-notes and turning him out of
doors, she tried to comfort and console him.   Since he
had confessed to her that he was penniless, she ceased
to hate him, and even commenced to love him.   Hector, homeless, was no longer the dreaded man who paid
to be master, the millionnaire who, by a caprice, had
raised her from the gutter.   He was no longer the ex-

ecrated tyrant. Ruined, he descended from his pedes-
tal, he became a man like others, to be preferred to
others, as a handsome and gallant youth. Then Jenny
mistook the last artifice of a discarded vanity for a generous impulse of the heart, and was deeply touched by
this splendid last gift.

" You are not as poor as you say," she said, " for you
still have so large a sum."

" But, dear child, I have several times given as much
for diamonds which you envied."

She reflected a moment, then as if an idea had struck
her, exclaimed:

" That's true enough ; but I can spend, oh, a great
deal less, and yet be just as happy. Once, before I
knew you, when I was young (she was now nineteen),
ten thousand francs seemed to me to be one of those
fabulous sums which were talked about, but which few
men ever saw in one pile, and fewer still held in their
hands."

She tried to slip the money into the count's pocket ;
but he prevented it.

" Come, take it back, keep it——"

" What shall I do with it? "

" I don't know, but wouldn't this money bring in
more? Couldn't you speculate on the Bourse, bet at
the races, play at Baden, or something? I've heard of
people that are now rich as kings, who commenced
with nothing, and hadn't your talents either. Why
don't you do as they did? "

She spoke excitedly, as a woman does who is anxious to persuade. He looked at her, astonished to find
her so sensitive, so disinterested.

" You will, won't you? " she insisted, " now, won't
you? "

"You are a good girl," said he, charmed with her, "but you must take this money. I give it to you, don't be worried about anything."

"But you—have you still any money? What have you?"

"I have yet——"

He stopped, searched his pockets, and counted the money in his purse.

"Faith, here's three hundred and forty francs—more than I need. I must give some napoleons to your servants before I go."

"And what for Heaven's sake will become of you?"

He sat back in his chair, negligently stroked his handsome beard, and said:

"I am going to blow my brains out."

"Oh!"

Hector thought that she doubted what he said. He took his pistols out of his pockets, showed them to her, and went on:

"You see these toys? Well, when I leave you, I shall go somewhere—no matter where—put the muzzle to my temple, thus, press the trigger—and all will be over!"

She gazed at him, her eyes dilated with terror, pale, breathing hard and fast. But at the same time, she admired him. She marvelled at so much courage, at this calm, this careless railing tone. What superb disdain of life! To exhaust his fortune and then kill himself, without a cry, a tear, or a regret, seemed to her an act of heroism unheard of, unexampled. It seemed to her that a new, unknown, beautiful, radiant man stood before her. She loved him as she had never loved before!

"No!" she cried, "no! It shall not be!"

And rising suddenly, she rushed to him and seized him by the arm.

" You will not kill yourself, will you? Promise me, swear it to me. It isn't possible, you would not! I love you—I couldn't bear you before. Oh, I did not know you, but now—come, we will be happy. You, who have lived with millions don't know how much ten thousand francs are—but I know. We can live a long time on that, and very well, too. Then, if we are obliged to sell the useless things—the horses, carriages, my diamonds, my green cashmere, we can have three or four times that sum. Thirty thousand francs —it's a fortune! Think how many happy days——"

The Count de Trémorel shook his head, smilingly. He was ravished; his vanity was flattered by the heat of the passion which beamed from the poor girl's eyes. How he was beloved! How he would be regretted! What a hero the world was about to lose!

" For we will not stay here," Jenny went on, " we will go and conceal ourselves far from Paris, in a little cottage. Why, on the other side of Belleville you can get a place surrounded by gardens for a thousand francs a year. How well off we should be there! You would never leave me, for I should be jealous—oh, so jealous! We wouldn't have any servants, and you should see that I know how to keep house."

Hector said nothing.

" While the money lasts," continued Jenny, " we'll laugh away the days. When it's all gone, if you are still decided, you will kill yourself—that is, we will kill ourselves together. But not with a pistol—No! We'll light a pan of charcoal, sleep in one another's arms, and that will be the end. They say one doesn't suffer that way at all."

This idea drew Hector from his torpor, and awoke in him a recollection which ruffled all his vanity.

Three or four days before, he had read in a paper the account of the suicide of a cook, who, in a fit of love and despair, had bravely suffocated himself in his garret. Before dying he had written a most touching letter to his faithless love. The idea of killing himself like a cook made him shudder. He saw the possibility of the horrible comparison. How ridiculous! And the Count de Trémorel had a wholesome fear of ridicule. To suffocate himself, at Belleville, with a grisette, how dreadful! He almost rudely pushed Jenny's arms away, and repulsed her.

"Enough of that sort of thing," said he, in his careless tone. "What you say, child, is all very pretty, but utterly absurd. A man of my name dies, and doesn't choke." And taking the bank-notes from his pocket, where Jenny had slipped them, he threw them on the table.

"Now, good-by."

He would have gone, but Jenny, red and with glistening eyes, barred the door with her body.

"You shall not go!" she cried, "I won't have you; you are mine—for I love you; if you take one step, I will scream."

The count shrugged his shoulders.

"But we must end all this!"

"You sha'n't go!"

"Well, then, I'll blow my brains out here." And taking out one of his pistols, he held it to his forehead, adding, "If you call out and don't let me pass, I shall fire." He meant the threat for earnest.

But Jenny did not call out; she could not; she uttered a deep groan and fainted.

"At last!" muttered Hector, replacing the pistol in his pocket.

He went out, not taking time to lift her from the floor where she had fallen, and shut the door. Then he called the servants into the vestibule, gave them ten napoleons to divide among them, and hastened away.

XIII

The Count de Trémorel, having reached the street, ascended the boulevard. All of a sudden he bethought him of his friends. The story of the execution must have already spread.

"No; not that way," he muttered.

This was because, on the boulevard, he would certainly meet some of his very dear cronies, and he desired to escape their condolence and offers of service. He pictured to himself their sorry visages, concealing a hidden and delicious satisfaction. He had wounded so many vanities that he must look for terrible revenges. The friends of an insolently prosperous man are rejoiced in his downfall.

Hector crossed the street, went along the Rue Duphot, and reached the quays. Where was he going? He did not know, and did not even ask himself. He walked at random, enjoying the physical content which follows a good meal, happy to find himself still in the land of the living, in the soft April sunlight.

The weather was superb, and all Paris was out of doors. There was a holiday air about the town. The flower-women at the corners of the bridges had their baskets full of odorous violets. The count bought a bouquet near the Pont Neuf and stuck it in his buttonhole, and without waiting for his change, passed on.

11

He reached the large square at the end of the Bourdon boulevard, which is always full of jugglers and curiosity shows; here the noise, the music, drew him from his torpor, and brought his thoughts back to his present situation.

" I must leave Paris," thought he.

He crossed toward the Orleans station at a quicker pace. He entered the waiting-room, and asked what time the train left for Etampes. Why did he choose Etampes? A train had just gone, and there would not be another one for two hours. He was much annoyed at this, and as he could not wait there two hours, he wended his way, to kill time, toward the Jardin des Plantes. He had not been there for ten or twelve years—not since, when at school, his teachers had brought him there to look at the animals. Nothing had changed. There were the groves and parterres, the lawns and lanes, the beasts and birds, as before. The principal avenue was nearly deserted. He took a seat opposite the mineralogical museum. He reflected on his position. He glanced back through the departed years, and did not find one day among those many days which had left him one of those gracious memories which delight and console. Millions had slipped through his prodigal hands, and he could not recall a single useful expenditure, a really generous one, amounting to twenty francs. He, who had had so many friends, searched his memory in vain for the name of a single friend whom he regretted to part from. The past seemed to him like a faithful mirror; he was surprised, startled at the folly of the pleasures, the inane delights, which had been the end and aim of his existence. For what had he lived? For others.

"Ah, what a fool I was!" he muttered, "what a fool!"

After living for others, he was going to kill himself for others. His heart became softened. Who would think of him, eight days hence? Not one living being. Yes—Jenny, perhaps. Yet, no. She would be consoled with a new lover in less than a week.

The bell for closing the garden rang. Night had come, and a thick and damp mist had covered the city. The count, chilled to the bones, left his seat.

"To the station again," muttered he.

It was a horrible idea to him now—this of shooting himself in the silence and obscurity of the forest. He pictured to himself his disfigured body, bleeding, lying on the edge of some ditch. Beggars or robbers would despoil him. And then? The police would come and take up this unknown body, and doubtless would carry it, to be identified, to the Morgue.

"Never!" cried he, at this thought, "no, never!"

How die, then? He reflected, and it struck him that he would kill himself in some second-class hotel on the left bank of the Seine.

"Yes, that's it," said he to himself.

Leaving the garden with the last of the visitors, he wended his way toward the Latin Quarter. The carelessness which he had assumed in the morning gave way to a sad resignation. He was suffering; his head was heavy, and he was cold.

"If I shouldn't die to-night," he thought, "I shall have a terrible cold in the morning."

This mental sally did not make him smile, but it gave him the consciousness of being firm and determined. He went into the Rue Dauphine and looked about for a hotel. Then it occurred to him that it was not yet

seven o'clock, and it might arouse suspicions if he
asked for a room at that early hour.   He reflected that
he still had over one hundred francs, and resolved to
dine.   It should be his last meal.   He went into a restaurant and ordered it.   But he in vain tried to throw
off the anxious sadness which filled him.   He drank,
and consumed three bottles of wine without changing
the current of his thoughts.

The waiters were surprised to see him scarcely touch
the dishes set before him, and growing more gloomy
after each potation.   His dinner cost ninety francs;
he threw his last hundred-franc note on the table, and
went out.   As it was not yet late, he went into another
restaurant where some students were drinking, and sat
down at a table in the farther corner of the room.   He
ordered coffee and rapidly drank three or four cups.
He wished to excite himself, to screw up his courage to
do what he had resolved upon ; but he could not ; the
drink seemed only to make him more and more irreso-
lute.

A waiter, seeing him alone at the table, offered him a
newspaper.   He took it mechanically, opened it, and
read :

" Just as we are going to press, we learn that a well-
known person has disappeared, after announcing his
intention to commit suicide.   The statements made to
us are so strange, that we defer details till to-morrow,
not having time to send for fuller information now."

These lines startled Hector.   They were his death
sentence, not to be recalled, signed by the tyrant whose
obsequious courtier he had always been—public opinion.

" They will never cease talking about me," he muttered angrily. Then he added, firmly, " Come, I must make an end of this."

He soon reached the Hôtel Luxembourg. He rapped at the door, and was speedily conducted to the best room in the house. He ordered a fire to be lighted. He also asked for sugar and water, and writing materials. At this moment he was as firm as in the morning.

" I must not hesitate," he muttered, " nor recoil from my fate."

He sat down at the table near the fireplace, and wrote in a firm hand a declaration which he destined for the police.

" No one must be accused of my death," he commenced ; and he went on by asking that the hotel-keeper should be indemnified.

The hour by the clock was five minutes before eleven ; he placed his pistols on the mantel.

" I will shoot myself at midnight," thought he. " I have yet an hour to live."

The count threw himself in an arm-chair and buried his face in his hands. Why did he not kill himself at once? Why impose on himself this hour of waiting, of anguish and torture? He could not have told. He began again to think over the events of his life, reflecting on the headlong rapidity of the occurrences which had brought him to that wretched room. How time had passed ! It seemed but yesterday that he first began to borrow. It does little good, however, to a man who has fallen to the bottom of the abyss, to know the causes why he fell.

The large hand of the clock had passed the half hour after eleven.

He thought of the newspaper item which he had just

read.   Who furnished the information?   Doubtless it
was Jenny.   She had come to her senses, tearfully
hastened after him.   When she failed to find him on
the boulevard, she had probably gone to his house,
then to his club, then to some of his friends.   So that
to-night, at this very moment, the world was discussing him.

" Have you heard the news? "

" Ah, yes, poor Trémorel!   What a romance!   A
good fellow, only——"

He thought he heard this " only " greeted with
laughter and innuendoes.   Time passed on.   The ringing vibration of the clock was at hand; the hour had
come.

The count got up, seized his pistols, and placed himself near the bed, so as not to fall on the floor.

The first stroke of twelve; he did not fire.

Hector was a man of courage; his reputation for
bravery was high.   He had fought at least ten duels,
and his cool bearing on the ground had always been
admiringly remarked.   One day he had killed a man,
and that night he slept very soundly.

But he did not fire.

There are two kinds of courage.   One, false courage, is that meant for the public eye, which needs the
excitement of the struggle, the stimulus of rage, and the
applause of lookers-on.   The other, true courage, despises public opinion, obeys conscience, not passion;
success does not sway it, it does its work noiselessly.

Two minutes after twelve—Hector still held the pistol against his forehead.

" Am I going to be afraid? " he asked himself.

He was afraid, but would not confess it to himself.

The Count threw himself into an arm-chair and buried his face in his
hands.

He put his pistols back on the table and returned to his seat near the fire.   All his limbs were trembling.

"It's nervousness," he muttered.   "It'll pass off."

He gave himself till one o'clock.   He tried to convince himself of the necessity of committing suicide. If he did not, what would become of him?   How would he live?   Must he make up his mind to work?   Besides, could he appear in the world, when all Paris knew of his intention?   This thought goaded him to fury; he had a sudden courage, and grasped his pistols.   But the sensation which the touch of the cold steel gave him, caused him to drop his arm and draw away shuddering.

"I cannot," repeated he, in his anguish.   "I cannot!"

The idea of the physical pain of shooting himself filled him with horror.   Why had he not a gentler death?   Poison, or perhaps charcoal—like the little cook?   He did not fear the ludicrousness of this now; all that he feared was, that the courage to kill himself would fail him.

He went on extending his time of grace from half-hour to half-hour.   It was a horrible night, full of the agony of the last night of the criminal condemned to the scaffold.   He wept with grief and rage and wrung his hands and prayed.   Toward daylight he fell exhausted into an uneasy slumber, in his arm-chair.   He was awakened by three or four heavy raps on the door, which he hastily opened.   It was the waiter, who had come to take his order for breakfast, and who started back with amazement on seeing Hector, so disordered was his clothing and so livid the pallor of his features.

"I want nothing," said the count.   "I'm going down."

He had just enough money left to pay his bill, and six sous for the waiter. He quitted the hotel where he had suffered so much, without end or aim in view. He was more resolved than ever to die, only he yearned for several days of respite to nerve himself for the deed. But how could he live during these days? He had not so much as a centime left. An idea struck him—the pawnbrokers!

He knew that at the Monte-de-Pieté * a certain amount would be advanced to him on his jewelry. But where find a branch office? He dared not ask, but hunted for one at hazard. He now held his head up, walked with a firmer step; he was seeking something, and had a purpose to accomplish. He at last saw the sign of the Monte-de-Pieté on a house in the Rue Condé, and entered. The hall was small, damp, filthy, and full of people. But if the place was gloomy, the borrowers seemed to take their misfortunes good-humoredly. They were mostly students and women, talking gayly as they waited for their turns. The Count de Trémorel advanced with his watch, chain, and a brilliant diamond that he had taken from his finger. He was seized with the timidity of misery, and did not know how to open his business. A young woman pitied his embarrassment.

" See," said she, " put your articles on this counter, before that window with green curtains."

A moment after he heard a voice which seemed to proceed from the next room:

" Twelve hundred francs for the watch and ring."

This large amount produced such a sensation as to arrest all the conversation. All eyes were turned tow-

* The public pawnbroker establishment of Paris, which has branch bureaus through the city.

ard the millionnaire who was going to pocket such a fortune. The millionnaire made no response.

The same woman who had spoken before nudged his arm.

"That's for you," said she. "Answer whether you will take it or not."

"I'll take it," cried Hector.

He was filled with a joy which made him forget the night's torture. Twelve hundred francs! How many days it would last! Had he not heard there were clerks who hardly got that in a year?

Hector waited a long time, when one of the clerks, who was writing at a desk, called out:

"Whose are the twelve hundred francs?"

The count stepped forward.

"Mine," said he.

"Your name?"

Hector hesitated. He would never give his name aloud in such a place as this. He gave the first name that occurred to him.

"Durand."

"Where are your papers?"

"What papers?"

"A passport, a receipt for lodgings, a license to hunt——"

"I haven't any."

"Go for them, or bring two well-known witnesses."

"But——"

"There is no but. The next——"

Hector was provoked by the clerk's abrupt manner.

"Well, then," said he, "give me back the jewelry."

The clerk looked at him jeeringly.

"Can't be done. No goods that are registered, can be returned without proof of rightful possession." So saying, he went on with his work. "One French shawl, thirty-five francs, whose is it?"

Hector meanwhile went out of the establishment. He had never suffered so much, had never imagined that one could suffer so much. After this ray of hope, so abruptly put out, the clouds lowered over him thicker and more hopelessly. He was worse off than the shipwrecked sailor; the pawnbroker had taken his last resources. All the romance with which he had invested the idea of his suicide now vanished, leaving bare the stern and ignoble reality. He must kill himself, not like the gay gamester who voluntarily leaves upon the roulette table the remains of his fortune, but like the Greek, who surprised and hunted, knows that every door will be shut upon him. His death would not be voluntary; he could neither hesitate nor choose the fatal hour; he must kill himself because he had not the means of living one day longer.

And life never before seemed to him so sweet a thing as now. He never felt so keenly the exuberance of his youth and strength. He suddenly discovered all about him a crowd of pleasures each more enviable than the others, which he had never tasted. He who flattered himself that he had squeezed life to press out its pleasures, had not really lived. He had had all that is to be bought or sold, nothing of what is given or achieved. He already not only regretted giving the ten thousand francs to Jenny, but the two hundred francs to the servants—nay the six sous given to the waiter at the restaurant, even the money he had spent on the bunch of violets. The bouquet still hung in his buttonhole, faded and shrivelled. What good did it do him? While the sous which he had paid for it—!

He did not think of his wasted millions, but could not drive away the thought of that wasted franc!

True, he might, if he chose, find plenty of money still, and easily. He had only to return quietly to his house, to discharge the bailiffs, and to resume the possession of his remaining effects. But he would thus confront the world, and confess his terrors to have overcome him at the last moment; he would have to suffer glances more cruel than the pistol-ball. The world must not be deceived; when a man announces that he is going to kill himself—he must kill himself.

So Hector was going to die because he had said he would, because the newspapers had announced the fact. He confessed this to himself as he went along, and bitterly reproached himself.

He remembered a pretty spot in Viroflay forest, where he had once fought a duel; he would commit the deed there. He hastened toward it. The weather was fine, and he met many groups of young people going into the country for a good time. Workmen were drinking and clinking their glasses under the trees along the river-bank. All seemed happy and contented, and their gayety seemed to insult Hector's wretchedness. He left the main road at the Sèvres bridge, and descending the embankment reached the borders of the Seine. Kneeling down, he took up some water in the palm of his hand, and drank—an invincible lassitude crept over him. He sat, or rather fell, upon the sward. The fever of despair came, and death now seemed to him a refuge, which he could almost welcome with joy. Some feet above him the windows of a Sèvres restaurant opened toward the river. He could be seen from them, as well as from the bridge; but he did not mind this, nor anything else.

"As well here as elsewhere," he said to himself.

He had just drawn his pistol out, when he heard someone call:

"Hector! Hector!"

He jumped up at a bound, concealed the pistol, and looked about. A man was running down the embankment toward him with outstretched arms. This was a man of his own age, rather stout, but well shaped, with a fine open face and large black eyes in which one read frankness and good-nature; one of those men who are sympathetic at first sight, whom one loves on a week's acquaintance.

Hector recognized him. It was his oldest friend, a college mate; they had once been very intimate, but the count not finding the other fast enough for him, had little by little dropped his intimacy, and had now lost sight of him for two years.

"Sauvresy!" he exclaimed, stupefied.

"Yes," said the young man, hot, and out of breath, "I've been watching you the last two minutes; what were you doing here?"

"Why—nothing."

"How! What they told me at your house this morning was true, then! I went there."

"What did they say?"

"That nobody knew what had become of you, and that you declared to Jenny when you left her the night before that you were going to blow your brains out. The papers have already announced your death, with details."

This news seemed to have a great effect on the count.

" You see, then," he answered tragically, " that I must kill myself! "

" Why? In order to save the papers from the inconvenience of correcting their error? "

" People will say that I shrunk——"

" Oh, 'pon my word now! According to you, a man must make a fool of himself because it has been reported that he would do it. Absurd, old fellow. What do you want to kill yourself for? "

Hector reflected; he almost saw the possibility of living.

" I am ruined," answered he, sadly.

" And it's for this that—stop, my friend, let me tell you, you are an ass! Ruined! It's a misfortune, but when a man is of your age he rebuilds his fortune. Besides, you aren't as ruined as you say, because I've got an income of a hundred thousand francs."

" A hundred thousand francs——"

" Well, my fortune is in land, which brings in about four per cent."

Trémorel knew that his friend was rich, but not that he was as rich as this. He answered with a tinge of envy in his tone:

" Well, I had more than that; but I had no breakfast this morning."

" And you did not tell me! But true, you are in a pitiable state; come along, quick! "

And he led him toward the restaurant.

Trémorel reluctantly followed this friend, who had just saved his life. He was conscious of having been surprised in a distressingly ridiculous situation. If a man who is resolved to blow his brains out is accosted, he presses the trigger, he doesn't conceal his pistol. There was one alone, among all his friends, who loved

him enough not to see the ludicrousness of his position; one alone generous enough not to torture him
with raillery; it was Sauvresy.

But once seated before a well-filled table, Hector
could not preserve his rigidity. He felt the joyous ex-
pansion of spirit which follows assured safety after
terrible peril. He was himself, young again, once
more strong. He told Sauvresy everything; his vain
boasting, his terror at the last moment, his agony at
the hotel, his fury, remorse, and anguish at the pawnbroker's.

"Ah!" said he. "You have saved me! You are
my friend, my only friend, my brother."

They talked for more than two hours.

"Come," said Sauvresy at last, "let us arrange our
plans. You want to disappear awhile; I see that.
But to-night you must write four lines to the papers.
To-morrow I propose to take your affairs in hand,
that's a thing I know how to do. I don't know exactly
how you stand; but I will agree to save something
from the wreck. We've got money, you see; your
creditors will be easy with us."

"But where shall I go?" asked Hector, whom the
mere idea of isolation terrified.

"What? You'll come home with me, parbleu, to
Valfeuillu. Don't you know that I am married? Ah,
my friend, a happier man than I does not exist! I've
married—for love—the loveliest and best of women.
You will be a brother to us. But come, my carriage
is right here near the door."

XIV

M. Plantat stopped. His companions had not suffered a gesture or a word to interrupt him. M. Lecoq,
as he listened, reflected. He asked himself where M.
Plantat could have got all these minute details. Who
had written Trémorel's terrible biography? As he
glanced at the papers from which Plantat read, he saw
that they were not all in the same handwriting.

The old justice of the peace pursued the story:

Bertha Lechaillu, though by an unhoped-for piece
of good fortune she had become Madame Sauvresy,
did not love her husband. She was the daughter of a
poor country school-master, whose highest ambition
had been to be an assistant teacher in a Versailles
school; yet she was not now satisfied. Absolute queen
of one of the finest domains in the land, surrounded
by every luxury, spending as she pleased, beloved,
adored, she was not content. Her life, so well regulated, so constantly smooth, without annoyances and
disturbance, seemed to her insipid. There were always
the same monotonous pleasures, always recurring each
in its season. There were parties and receptions, horse
rides, hunts, drives—and it was always thus! Alas, this
was not the life she had dreamed of; she was born for
more exciting pleasures. She yearned for unknown
emotions and sensations, the unforeseen, abrupt transitions, passions, adventures. She had not liked Sauvresy from the first day she saw him, and her secret
aversion to him increased in proportion as her influence over him grew more certain. She thought him
common, vulgar, ridiculous. She thought the simplicity of his manners, silliness. She looked at him, and

saw nothing in him to admire. She did not listen to him when he spoke, having already decided in her wisdom that he could say nothing that was not tedious or commonplace. She was angry that he had not been a wild young man, the terror of his family.

He had, however, done as other young men do. He had gone to Paris and tried the sort of life which his friend Trémorel led. He had enough of it in six months, and hastily returned to Valfeuillu, to rest after such laborious pleasures. The experience cost him a hundred thousand francs, but he said he did not regret purchasing it at this price.

Bertha was wearied with the constancy and adoration of her husband. She had only to express a desire to be at once obeyed, and this blind submission to all her wishes appeared to her servile in a man. A man is born, she thought, to command, and not to obey; to be master, and not slave. She would have preferred a husband who would come in in the middle of the night, still warm from his orgy, having lost at play, and who would strike her if she upbraided him. A tyrant, but a man. Some months after her marriage she suddenly took it into her head to have absurd freaks and extravagant caprices. She wished to prove him, and see how far his constant complacence would go. She thought she would tire him out. It was intolerable to feel absolutely sure of her husband, to know that she so filled his heart that he had room for no other, to have nothing to fear, not even the caprice of an hour. Perhaps there was yet more than this in Bertha's aversion. She knew herself, and confessed to herself that had Sauvresy wished, she would have been his without being his wife. She was so lonely at her father's, so wretched in her poverty, that she would have fled from her home, even for this. And she despised her husband because he had not despised her enough!

People were always telling her that she was the happiest of women. Happy! And there were days when she wept when she thought that she was married. Happy! There were times when she longed to fly, to seek adventure and pleasure, all that she yearned for, what she had not had and never would have. The fear of poverty—which she knew well—restrained her. This fear was caused in part by a wise precaution which her father, recently dead, had taken. Sauvresy wished to insert in the marriage-contract a settlement of five hundred thousand francs on his affianced. The worthy Lechaillu had opposed this generous act.

"My daughter," he said, "brings you nothing. Settle forty thousand francs on her if you will, not a sou more; otherwise there shall be no marriage."

As Sauvresy insisted, the old man added:

"I hope that she will be a good and worthy wife; if so, your fortune will be hers. But if she is not, forty thousand francs will be none too little for her. Of course, if you are afraid that you will die first, you can make a will."

Sauvresy was forced to yield. Perhaps the worthy school-master knew his daughter; if so he was the only one. Never did so consummate a hypocrisy minister to so profound a perversity, and a depravity so inconceivable in a young and seemingly innocent girl. If, at the bottom of her heart, she thought herself the most wretched of women, there was nothing of it apparent—it was a well-kept secret. She knew how to show to her husband, in place of the love she did not feel, the appearance of a passion at once burning and

modest, betraying furtive glances and a flush as of
pleasure, when he entered the room.

All the world said:

" Bertha is foolishly fond of her husband."

Sauvresy was sure of it, and he was the first to say,
not caring to conceal his joy:

" My wife adores me."

Such were man and wife at Valfeuillu when Sauvresy found Trémorel on the banks of the Seine with
a pistol in his hand. Sauvresy missed his dinner that
evening for the first time since his marriage, though
he had promised to be prompt, and the meal was kept
waiting for him. Bertha might have been anxious
about this delay; she was only indignant at what she
called inconsiderateness. She was asking herself how
she should punish her husband, when, at ten o'clock
at night, the drawing-room door was abruptly thrown
open, and Sauvresy stood smiling upon the threshold.

" Bertha," said he, " I've brought you an apparition."

She scarcely deigned to raise her head. Sauvresy
continued:

" An apparition whom you know, of whom I have
often spoken to you, whom you will like because I
love him, and because he is my oldest comrade, my
best friend."

And standing aside, he gently pushed Hector into
the room.

" Madame Sauvresy, permit me to present to you
Monsieur the Count de Trémorel."

Bertha rose suddenly, blushing, confused, agitated
by an indefinable emotion, as if she saw in reality an
apparition. For the first time in her life she was

abashed, and did not dare to raise her large, clear blue eyes.

"Monsieur," she stammered, "you are welcome."

She knew Trémorel's name well. Sauvresy had often mentioned it, and she had seen it often in the papers, and had heard it in the drawing-rooms of all her friends. He who bore it seemed to her, after what she had heard, a great personage. He was, according to his reputation, a hero of another age, a social Don Quixote, a terribly fast man of the world. He was one of those men whose lives astonish common people, whom the well-to-do citizen thinks faithless and lawless, whose extravagant passions overleap the narrow bounds of social prejudice ; a man who tyrannizes over others, whom all fear, who fights on the slightest provocation, who scatters gold with a prodigal hand, whose iron health resists the most terrible excesses. She had often in her miserable reveries tried to imagine what kind of man this Count de Trémorel was. She awarded him with such qualities as she desired for her fancied hero, with whom she could fly from her husband in search of new adventures. And now, of a sudden, he appeared before her.

"Give Hector your hand, dear," said Sauvresy.

She held out her hand, which Trémorel lightly pressed, and his touch seemed to give her an electric shock.

Sauvresy threw himself into an arm-chair.

"You see, Bertha," said he, "our friend Hector is exhausted with the life he has been leading. He has been advised to rest, and has come to seek it here, with us."

"But, dear," responded Bertha, "aren't you afraid that the count will be bored a little here?"

" Why ? "

" Valfeuillu is very quiet, and we are but dull country folks."

Bertha talked for the sake of talking, to break a silence which embarrassed her, to make Trémorel speak,
and hear his voice. As she talked she observed him,
and studied the impression she made on him. Her
radiant beauty usually struck those who saw her for the
first time with open admiration. He remained impassible. She recognized the worn-out rake of title, the
fast man who has tried, experienced, exhausted all
things, in his coldness and superb indifference. And
because he did not admire her she admired him the
more.

" What a difference," thought she, " between him
and that vulgar Sauvresy, who is surprised at everything, whose face shows all that he thinks, whose eye
betrays what he is going to say before he opens his
mouth."

Bertha was mistaken. Hector was not as cold and
indifferent as she imagined. He was simply wearied,
utterly exhausted. He could scarcely sit up after the
terrible excitements of the last twenty-four hours. He
soon asked permission to retire. Sauvresy, when left
alone with his wife, told her all that happened, and the
events which resulted in Trémorel's coming to Valfeuillu ; but like a true friend omitted everything that
would cast ridicule upon his old comrade.

" He's a big child," said he, " a foolish fellow, whose
brain is weak ; but we'll take care of him and cure
him."

Bertha never listened to her husband so attentively
before. She seemed to agree with him, but she really
admired Trémorel. Like Jenny, she was struck with

the heroism which could squander a fortune and then commit suicide.

"Ah!" sighed she, "Sauvresy would not have done it!"

No, Sauvresy was quite a different man from the Count de Trémorel. The next day he declared his intention to adjust his friend's affairs. Hector had slept well, having spent the night on an excellent bed, undisturbed by pressing anxieties; and he appeared in the morning sleek and well-dressed, the disorder and desperation of the previous evening having quite disappeared. He had a nature not deeply impressible by events; twenty-four hours consoled him for the worst catastrophes, and he soon forgot the severest lessons of life. If Sauvresy had bid him begone, he would not have known where to go; yet he had already resumed the haughty carelessness of the millionnaire, accustomed to bend men and circumstances to his will. He was once more calm and cold, coolly joking, as if years had passed since that night at the hotel, and as if all the disasters to his fortune had been repaired. Bertha was amazed at this tranquillity after such great reverses, and thought this childish recklessness force of character.

"Now," said Sauvresy, "as I've become your man of business, give me my instructions, and some valuable hints. What is, or was, the amount of your fortune?"

"I haven't the least idea."

Sauvresy provided himself with a pencil and a large sheet of paper, ready to set down the figures. He seemed a little surprised.

"All right," said he, "we'll put x down as the unknown quantity of the assets; now for the liabilities.

Hector made a superbly disdainful gesture.

" Don't know, I'm sure, what they are."

" What, can't you give a rough guess? "

" Oh, perhaps. For instance, I owe between five and six hundred thousand francs to Clair & Co., five hundred thousand to Dervoy; about as much to Dubois, of Orleans——"

" Well? "

" I can't remember any more."

" But you must have a memorandum of your loans somewhere? "

" No."

" You have at least kept your bonds, bills, and the sums of your various debts? "

" None of them. I burnt up all my papers yesterday."

Sauvresy jumped up from his chair in astonishment; such a method of doing business seemed to him monstrous; he could not suppose that Hector was lying. Yet he was lying, and this affectation of ignorance was a conceit of the aristocratic man of the world. It was very noble, very distingué, to ruin one's self without knowing how!

" But, my dear fellow," cried Sauvresy, " how can we clear up your affairs? "

" Oh, don't clear them up at all; do as I do—let the creditors act as they please, they will know how to settle it all, rest assured; let them sell out my property."

" Never! Then you would be ruined, indeed! "

" Well, it's only a little more or a little less."

" What splendid disinterestedness! " thought Bertha; " what coolness, what admirable contempt of money, what noble disdain of the petty details which annoy common people! Was Sauvresy capable of all this?"

She could not at least accuse him of avarice, since for her he was as prodigal as a thief; he had never refused her anything; he anticipated her most extravagant fancies. Still he had a strong appetite for gain, and despite his large fortune, he retained the hereditary respect for money. When he had business with one of his farmers, he would rise very early, mount his horse, though it were mid-winter, and go several leagues in the snow to get a hundred crowns. He would have ruined himself for her if she had willed it, this she was convinced of; but he would have ruined himself economically, in an orderly way.

Sauvresy reflected.

"You are right," said he to Hector, "your creditors ought to know your exact position. Who knows that they are not acting in concert? Their simultaneous refusal to lend you a hundred thousand makes me suspect it. I will go and see them."

"Clair & Co., from whom I received my first loans, ought to be the best informed."

"Well, I will see Clair & Co. But look here, do you know what you would do if you were reasonable?"

"What?"

"You would go to Paris with me, and both of us——"

Hector turned very pale, and his eyes shone.

"Never!" he interrupted, violently, "never!"

His "dear friends" still terrified him. What! Reappear on the theatre of his glory, now that he was fallen, ruined, ridiculous by his unsuccessful suicide? Sauvresy had held out his arms to him. Sauvresy was a noble fellow, and loved Hector sufficiently not to perceive the falseness of his position, and not to judge him a coward because he shrank from suicide. But the others!——

"Don't talk to me about Paris," said he in a calmer tone. "I shall never set my foot in it again."

"All right—so much the better; stay with us; I sha'n't complain of it, nor my wife either. Some fine day we'll find you a pretty heiress in the neighborhood. But," added Sauvresy, consulting his watch, "I must go if I don't want to lose the train."

"I'll go to the station with you," said Trémorel.

This was not solely from a friendly impulse. He wanted to ask Sauvresy to look after the articles left at the pawnbroker's in the Rue de Condé, and to call on Jenny. Bertha, from her window, followed with her eyes the two friends, who, with arms interlocked, ascended the road toward Orcival. "What a difference," thought she, "between these two men! My husband said he wished to be his friend's steward; truly he has the air of a steward. What a noble gait the count has, what youthful ease, what real distinction! And yet I'm sure that my husband despises him, because he has ruined himself by dissipation. He affected—I saw it—an air of protection. Poor youth! But everything about the count betrays an innate or acquired superiority; even his name, Hector—how it sounds!" And she repeated "Hector" several times, as if it pleased her, adding, contemptuously, "My husband's name is Clement!"

M. de Trémorel returned alone from the station, as gayly as a convalescent taking his first airing. As soon as Bertha saw him she left the window. She wished to remain alone, to reflect upon this event which had happened so suddenly, to analyze her sensations, listen to her presentiments, study her impressions and decide, if possible, upon her line of conduct. She only reappeared when the tea was set for her husband, who returned at eleven in the evening. Sauvresy was faint from hunger, thirst, and fatigue, but his face glowed with satisfaction.

"Victory!" exclaimed he, as he ate his soup. "We'll snatch you from the hands of the Philistines yet. Parbleu! The finest feathers of your plumage will remain, after all, and you will be able to save enough for a good cosey nest."

Bertha glanced at her husband.

"How is that?" said she.

"It's very simple. At the very first, I guessed the game of our friend's creditors. They reckoned on getting a sale of his effects; would have bought them in a lump dirt cheap, as it always happens, and then sold them in detail, dividing the profits of the operation."

"And can you prevent that?" asked Trémorel, incredulously.

"Certainly. Ah, I've completely checkmated these gentlemen. I've succeeded by chance—I had the good luck to get them all together this evening. I said to them, you'll let us sell this property as we please, voluntarily, or I'll outbid you all, and spoil your cards. They looked at me in amazement. My notary, who was with me, remarked that I was Monsieur Sauvresy, worth two millions. Our gentlemen opened their eyes very wide, and consented to grant my request."

Hector, notwithstanding what he had said, knew enough about his affairs to see that this action would save him a fortune—a small one, as compared with what he had possessed, yet a fortune.

The certainty of this delighted him, and moved by

a momentary and sincere gratitude, he grasped both of Sauvresy's hands in his.

"Ah, my friend," cried he, "you give me my honor, after saving my life! How can I ever repay you?"

"By committing no imprudences or foolishnesses, except reasonable ones. Such as this," added Sauvresy, leaning toward Bertha and embracing her.

"And there is nothing more to fear?"

"Nothing! Why I could have borrowed the two millions in an hour, and they knew it. But that's not all. The search for you is suspended. I went to your house, took the responsibility of sending away all your servants except your valet and a groom. If you agree, we'll send the horses to be sold to-morrow, and they'll fetch a good price; your own saddle-horse shall be brought here."

These details annoyed Bertha. She thought her husband exaggerated his services, carrying them even to servility.

"Really," thought she, "he was born to be a steward."

"Do you know what else I did?" pursued Sauvresy. "Thinking that perhaps you were in want of a wardrobe, I had three or four trunks filled with your clothes, sent them out by rail, and one of the servants has just gone after them."

Hector, too, began to find Sauvresy's services excessive, and thought he treated him too much like a child who could foresee nothing. The idea of having it said before a woman that he was in want of clothes irritated him. He forgot that he had found it a very simple thing in the morning to ask his friend for some linen.

Just then a noise was heard in the vestibule. Doubt-

less the trunks had come.   Bertha went out to give the
necessary orders.

"Quick!" cried Sauvresy.   "Now that we are
alone, here are your trinkets.   I had some trouble in
getting them.   They are suspicious at the pawnbroker's.   I think they began to suspect that I was one of a
band of thieves."

"You didn't mention my name, did you?"

"That would have been useless.   My notary was
with me, fortunately.   One never knows how useful
one's notary may be.   Don't you think society is un-
just toward notaries?"

Trémorel thought his friend talked very lightly about
a serious matter, and this flippancy vexed him.

"To finish up, I paid a visit to Miss Jenny.   She
has been abed since last evening, and her chambermaid
told me she had not ceased sobbing bitterly ever since
your departure."

"Had she seen no one?"

"Nobody at all.   She really thought you dead, and
when I told her you were here with me, alive and well,
I thought she would go mad for joy.   Do you know,
Hector, she's really pretty."

"Yes—not bad."

"And a very good little body, I imagine.   She told
me some very touching things.   I would wager, my
friend, that she don't care so much for your money as
she does for yourself."

Hector smiled superciliously.

"In short, she was anxious to follow me, to see and
speak to you.   I had to swear with terrible oaths that
she should see you to-morrow, before she would let
me go; not at Paris, as you said you would never go
there, but at Corbeil."

" Ah, as for that——"

" She will be at the station to-morrow at twelve. We will go down together, and I will take the train for Paris. You can get into the Corbeil train, and breakfast with Miss Jenny at the hotel of the Belle Image."

Hector began to offer an objection. Sauvresy stopped him with a gesture.

" Not a word," said he. " Here is my wife."

XV

On going to bed, that night, the count was less enchanted than ever with the devotion of his friend Sauvresy. There is not a diamond on which a spot cannot be found with a microscope.

" Here he is," thought he, " abusing his privileges as the saver of my life. Can't a man do you a service, without continually making you feel it? It seems as though because he prevented me from blowing my brains out, I had somehow become something that belongs to him! He came very near upbraiding me for Jenny's extravagance. Where will he stop? "

The next day at breakfast he feigned indisposition so as not to eat, and suggested to Sauvresy that he would lose the train.

Bertha, as on the evening before, crouched at the window to see them go away. Her troubles during the past eight-and-forty hours had been so great that she hardly recognized herself. She scarcely dared to reflect or to descend to the depths of her heart. What mysterious power did this man possess, to so violently affect her life? She wished that he would go, never to return, while at the same time she avowed to herself that in going he would carry with him all her thoughts.

She struggled under the charm, not knowing whether she ought to rejoice or grieve at the inexpressible emotions which agitated her, being irritated to submit to an influence stronger than her own will.

She decided that to-day she would go down to the drawing-room. He would not fail—were it only for politeness—to go in there; and then, she thought, by seeing him nearer, talking with him, knowing him better, his influence over her would vanish. Doubtless he would return, and so she watched for him, ready to go down as soon as she saw him approaching. She waited with feverish shudderings, anxiously believing that this first *tête-à-tête* in her husband's absence would be decisive. Time passed; it was more than two hours since he had gone out with Sauvresy, and he had not reappeared. Where could he be?

At this moment, Hector was awaiting Jenny at the Corbeil station. The train arrived, and Jenny soon appeared. Her grief, joy, emotion had not made her forget her toilet, and never had she been so rollickingly elegant and pretty. She wore a green dress with a train, a velvet mantle, and the jauntiest little hat in the world. As soon as she saw Hector standing near the door, she uttered a cry, pushed the people aside, and rushed into his arms, laughing and crying at the same time. She spoke quite loud, with wild gestures, so that everyone could hear what she said.

" You didn't kill yourself, after all," said she. " Oh, how I have suffered; but what happiness I feel to-day! "

Trémorel struggled with her as he could, trying to calm her enthusiastic exclamations, softly repelling her, charmed and irritated at once, and exasperated at all these eyes rudely fixed on him. For none of the passengers had gone out. They were all there, staring and gazing. Hector and Jenny were surrounded by a circle of curious folks.

" Come along," said Hector, his patience exhausted.

He drew her out of the door, hoping to escape this prying curiosity; but he did not succeed. They were persistently followed. Some of the Corbeil people who were on the top of the omnibus begged the conductor to walk his horses, that this singular couple might not be lost to view, and the horses did not get into a trot until they had disappeared in the hotel.

Sauvresy's foresight in recommending the place of meeting had thus been disconcerted by Jenny's sensational arrival. Questions were asked; the hostess was adroitly interrogated, and it was soon known that this person, who waited for eccentric young ladies at the Corbeil station, was an intimate friend of the owner of Valfeuillu. Neither Hector nor Jenny doubted that they formed the general topic of conversation. They breakfasted gayly in the best room at the Belle Image, during which Trémorel recounted a very pretty story about his restoration to life, in which he played a part, the heroism of which was well calculated to redouble the little lady's admiration. Then Jenny in her turn unfolded her plans for the future, which were, to do her justice, most reasonable. She had resolved more than ever to remain faithful to Hector now that he was ruined, to give up her elegant rooms, sell her furniture, and undertake some honest trade. She had found one of her old friends, who was now an accomplished dressmaker, and who was anxious to obtain a partner who had some money, while she herself furnished the experience. They would purchase an establishment in the Breda quarter, and between them could scarcely fail

THE MYSTERY OF ORCIVAL

to prosper. Jenny talked with a pretty, knowing, busi-
ness-like air, which made Hector laugh. These projects seemed very comic to him; yet he was touched
by this unselfishness on the part of a young and pretty
woman, who was willing to work in order to please
him.

But, unhappily, they were forced to part. Jenny had
gone to Corbeil intending to stay a week; but the
count told her this was absolutely impossible. She
cried bitterly at first, then got angry, and finally consoled herself with a plan to return on the following
Tuesday.

" Good-by," said she, embracing Hector, " think of
me." She smilingly added, " I ought to be jealous;
for they say your friend's wife is perhaps the hand-
somest woman in France. Is it true? "

" Upon my word, I don't know. I've forgotten to
look at her."

Hector told the truth. Although he did not betray
it, he was still under the surprise of his chagrin at the
failure of his attempt at suicide. He felt the dizziness
which follows great moral crises as well as a heavy
blow on the head, and which distracts the attention
from exterior things. But Jenny's words, " the hand-
somest woman in France," attracted his notice, and
he could, that very evening, repair his forgetfulness.
When he returned to Valfeuillu, his friend had not returned; Mme. Sauvresy was alone reading, in the
brilliantly lighted drawing-room. Hector seated himself opposite her, a little aside, and was thus able to
observe her at his ease, while engaging her in conversation. His first impression was an unfavorable one.
He found her beauty too sculptural and polished. He
sought for imperfections, and finding none, was almost

terrified by this lovely, motionless face, these clear, cold eyes. Little by little, however, he accustomed himself to pass the greater part of the afternoon with Bertha, while Sauvresy was away arranging his affairs —selling, negotiating, using his time in cutting down interests and discussing with agents and attorneys. He soon perceived that she listened to him with pleasure, and he judged from this that she was a decidedly superior woman, much better than her husband. He had no wit, but possessed an inexhaustible fund of anecdotes and adventures. He had seen so many things and known so many people that he was as interesting as a chronicle. He had a sort of frothy fervor, not wanting in brilliancy, and a polite cynicism which, at first, surprised one. Had Bertha been unimpassioned, she might have judged him at his value; but she had lost her power of insight. She heard him, plunged in a foolish ecstasy, as one hears a traveller who has returned from far and dangerous countries, who has visited peoples of whose language the hearer is ignorant, and lived in the midst of manners and customs incomprehensible to ourselves.

Days, weeks, months passed on, and the Count de Trémorel did not find life at Valfeuillu as dull as he had thought. He insensibly slipped along the gentle slope of material well-being, which leads directly to brutishness. A physical and moral torpor had succeeded the fever of the first days, free from disagreeable sensations, though wanting in excitement. He ate and drank much, and slept twelve round hours. The rest of the time, when he did not talk with Bertha, he wandered in the park, lounged in a rocking-chair, or took a jaunt in the saddle. He even went fishing under the willows at the foot of the garden; and grew fat. His best days were those which he spent at Corbeil with Jenny. He found in her something of his past, and she always quarrelled with him, which woke him up. Besides, she brought him the gossip of Paris and the small talk of the boulevards. She came regularly every week, and her love for Hector, far from diminishing, seemed to grow with each interview. The poor girl's affairs were in a troubled condition. She had bought her establishment at too high a price, and her partner at the end of the first month decamped, carrying off three thousand francs. She knew nothing about the trade which she had undertaken, and she was robbed without mercy on all sides. She said nothing of these troubles to Hector, but she intended to ask him to come to her assistance. It was the least that he could do.

At first, the visitors to Valfeuillu were somewhat astonished at the constant presence there of a young man of leisure; but they got accustomed to him. Hector assumed a melancholy expression of countenance, such as a man ought to have who had undergone unheard-of misfortunes, and whose life had failed of its promise. He appeared inoffensive; people said:

" The count has a charming simplicity."

But sometimes, when alone, he had sudden and terrible relapses. " This life cannot last," thought he; and he was overcome with childish rage when he contrasted the past with the present. How could he shake off this dull existence, and rid himself of these stiffly good people who surrounded him, these friends of Sauvresy? Where should he take refuge? He was not tempted to return to Paris; what could he do there? His house had been sold to an old leather merchant; and he had no money except that which he borrowed

13.

of Sauvresy. Yet Sauvresy, to Hector's mind, was a most uncomfortable, wearisome, implacable friend; he did not understand half-way measures in desperate situations.

"Your boat is foundering," he said to Hector; "let us begin by throwing all that is superfluous into the sea. Let us keep nothing of the past; that is dead; we will bury it, and nothing shall recall it. When your situation is relieved, we will see."

The settlement of Hector's affairs was very laborious. Creditors sprung up at every step, on every side, and the list of them seemed never to be finished. Some had even come from foreign lands. Several of them had been already paid, but their receipts could not be found, and they were clamorous. Others, whose demands had been refused as exorbitant, threatened to go to law, hoping to frighten Sauvresy into paying. Sauvresy wearied his friend by his incessant activity. Every two or three days he went to Paris, and he attended the sales of the property in Burgundy and Orleans. The count at last detested and hated him; Sauvresy's happy, cheerful air annoyed him; jealousy stung him. One thought—that a wretched one—consoled him a little. "Sauvresy's happiness," said he to himself, "is owing to his imbecility. He thinks his wife dead in love with him, whereas she can't bear him."

Bertha had, indeed, permitted Hector to perceive her aversion to her husband. She no longer studied the emotions of her heart; she loved Trémorel, and confessed it to herself. In her eyes he realized the ideal of her dreams. At the same time she was exasperated to see in him no signs of love for her. Her beauty was

not, then, irresistible, as she had often been told. He
was gallant and courteous to her—nothing more.

"If he loved me," thought she, "he would tell me
so, for he is bold with women and fears no one."

Then she began to hate the girl, her rival, whom
Hector went to meet at Corbeil every week. She
wished to see her, to know her. Who could she be?
Was she handsome? Hector had been very reticent
about Jenny. He evaded all questions about her, not
sorry to let Bertha's imagination work on his mysterious visits.

The day at last came when she could no longer resist the intensity of her curiosity. She put on the sim-
plest of her toilets, in black, threw a thick veil over her
head, and hastened to the Corbeil station at the hour
that she thought the unknown girl would present herself there. She took a seat on a bench in the rear of
the waiting-room. She had not long to wait. She
soon perceived the count and a young girl coming
along the avenue, which she could see from where she
sat. They were arm in arm, and seemed to be in a
very happy mood. They passed within a few steps of
her, and as they walked very slowly, she was able to
scrutinize Jenny at her ease. She saw that she was
pretty, but that was all. Having seen that which she
wished, and become satisfied that Jenny was not to be
feared (which showed her inexperience) Bertha directed her steps homeward. But she chose her
time of departure awkwardly; for as she was passing along behind the cabs, which concealed her,
Hector came out of the station. They crossed each
other's paths at the gate, and their eyes met. Did he
recognize her? His face expressed great surprise, yet
he did not bow to her. "Yes, he recognized me,"

thought Bertha, as she returned home by the river-road; and surprised, almost terrified by her boldness, she asked herself whether she ought to rejoice or mourn over this meeting. What would be its result? Hector cautiously followed her at a little distance. He was greatly astonished. His vanity, always on the watch, had already apprised him of what was passing in Bertha's heart, but, though modesty was no fault of his, he was far from guessing that she was so much enamoured of him as to take such a step.

" She loves me! " he repeated to himself, as he went along. " She loves me! "

He did not yet know what to do. Should he fly? Should he still appear the same in his conduct toward her, pretending not to have seen her? He ought to fly that very evening, without hesitation, without turning his head; to fly as if the house were about to tumble about his head. This was his first thought. It was quickly stifled under the explosion of the base passions which fermented in him. Ah, Sauvresy had saved him when he was dying! Sauvresy, after saving him, had welcomed him, opened to him his heart, purse, house; at this very moment he was making untiring efforts to restore his fortunes. Men like Trémorel can only receive such services as outrages. Had not his sojourn at Valfeuillu been a continual suffering? Was not his self-conceit tortured from morning till night? He might count the days by their humiliations. What! Must he always submit to—if he was not grateful for —the superiority of a man whom he had always been wont to treat as his inferior?

" Besides," thought he, judging his friend by himself, " he only acts thus from pride and ostentation. What am I at his house, but a living witness of his

generosity and devotion? He seems to live for me—
it's Trémorel here and Trémorel there! He triumphs
over my misfortunes, and makes his conduct a glory
and title to the public admiration."

He could not forgive his friend for being so rich, so
happy, so highly respected, for having known how to
regulate his life, while he had exhausted his own fortune at thirty. And should he not seize so good an
opportunity to avenge himself for the favors which
overwhelmed him?

" Have I run after his wife? " said he to himself, trying to impose silence on his conscience. " She comes
to me of her own will, herself, without the least temptation from me. I should be a fool if I repelled her."

Conceit has irresistible arguments. Hector, when
he entered the house, had made up his mind. He did
not fly. Yet he had the excuse neither of passion nor
of temptation; he did not love her, and his infamy
was deliberate, coldly premeditated. Between her and
him a chain more solid than mutual attraction was
riveted; their common hatred of Sauvresy. They
owed too much to him. His hand had held both from
degradation.

The first hours of their mutual understanding were
spent in angry words, rather than the cooings of love.
They perceived too clearly the disgrace of their conduct not to try to reassure each other against their remorse. They tried to prove to each other that Sauvresy was ridiculous and odious; as if they were ab-
solved by his deficiencies, if deficiencies he had. If indeed trustfulness is foolishness, Sauvresy was indeed
a fool, because he could be deceived under his own
eyes, in his own house, because he had perfect faith in
his wife and his friend. He suspected nothing, and

every day he rejoiced that he had been able to keep
Trémorel by him. He often repeated to his wife:

"I am too happy."

Bertha employed all her art to encourage these joyous illusions. She who had before been so capricious,
so nervous, wilful, became little by little submissive to
the degree of an angelic softness. The future of her
love depended on her husband, and she spared no pains
to prevent the slightest suspicion from ruffling his calm
confidence. Such was their prudence that no one in
the house suspected their state. And yet Bertha was
not happy. Her love did not yield her the joys she had
expected. She hoped to be transported to the clouds,
and she remained on the earth, hampered by all the
miserable ties of a life of lies and deceit.

Perhaps she perceived that she was Hector's revenge
on her husband, and that he only loved in her the dishonored wife of an envied friend. And to crown all,
she was jealous. For several months she tried to persuade Trémorel to break with Jenny. He always had
the same reply, which, though it might be prudent,
was irritating.

"Jenny is our security—you must think of that."

The fact was, however, that he was trying to devise
some means of getting rid of Jenny. It was a difficult
matter. The poor girl, having fallen into comparative
poverty, became more and more tenacious of Hector's
affection. She often gave him trouble by telling him
that he was no longer the same, that he was changed;
she was sad, and wept, and had red eyes.

One evening, in a fit of anger, she menaced him with
a singular threat.

"You love another," she said. "I know it, for I
have proofs of it. Take care! If you ever leave me,

my anger will fall on her head, and I will not have any mercy on her."

The count foolishly attached no importance to these words; they only hastened the separation.

" She is getting very troublesome," thought he. " If some day I shouldn't go when she was expecting me, she might come up to Valfeuillu, and make a wretched scandal."

He armed himself with all his courage, which was assisted by Bertha's tears and entreaties, and started for Corbeil resolved to break off with Jenny. He took every precaution in declaring his intentions, giving the best reasons for his decision that he could think of.

" We must be careful, you know, Jenny," said he, " and cease to meet for a while. I am ruined, you know, and the only thing that can save me is marriage."

Hector had prepared himself for an explosion of fury, piercing cries, hysterics, fainting-fits. To his great surprise, Jenny did not answer a word. She became as white as her collar, her ruddy lips blanched, her eyes stared.

" So," said she, with her teeth tightly shut to contain herself, " so you are going to get married? "

" Alas, I must," he answered with a hypocritical sigh. " You know that lately I have only been able to get money for you by borrowing from my friend; his purse will not be at my service forever."

Jenny took Hector by the hand, and led him to the window. There, looking intently at him, as if her gaze could frighten the truth out of him, she said, slowly:

" It is really true, is it, that you are going to leave me to get married? "

Hector disengaged one of his hands, and placed it on his heart.

"I swear it on my honor," said he.

"I ought to believe you, then."

Jenny returned to the middle of the room. Standing erect before the mirror, she put on her hat, quietly disposing its ribbons as if nothing had occurred. When she was ready to go, she went up to Trémorel.

"For the last time," said she, in a tone which she forced to be firm, and which belied her tearful, glistening eyes. "For the last time, Hector, are we really to part?"

"We must."

Jenny made a gesture which Trémorel did not see; her face had a malicious expression; her lips parted to utter some sarcastic response; but she recovered herself almost immediately.

"I am going, Hector," said she, after a moment's reflection. "If you are really leaving me to get married, you shall never hear of me again."

"Why, Jenny, I hope I shall still remain your friend."

"Well, only if you abandon me for another reason, remember what I tell you; you will be a dead man, and she, a lost woman."

She opened the door; he tried to take her hand; she repulsed him.

"Adieu!"

Hector ran to the window to assure himself of her departure. She was ascending the avenue leading to the station.

"Well, that's over," thought he, with a sigh of relief. "Jenny was a good girl."

XVI

The count told half a truth when he spoke to Jenny of his marriage. Sauvresy and he had discussed the subject, and if the matter was not as ripe as he had represented, there was at least some prospect of such an event. Sauvresy had proposed it in his anxiety to complete his work of restoring Hector to fortune and society.

One evening, about a month before the events just narrated, he had led Hector into the library, saying:

" Give me your ear for a quarter of an hour, and don't answer me hastily. What I am going to propose to you deserves serious reflection."

" Well, I can be serious when it is necessary."

" Let's begin with your debts. Their payment is not yet completed, but enough has been done to enable us to foresee the end.   It is certain that you will have, after all debts are paid, from three to four hundred thousand francs."

Hector had never, in his wildest hopes, expected such success.

" Why, I'm going to be rich," exclaimed he joyously.

" No, not rich, but quite above want. There is, too, a mode in which you can regain your lost position."

" A mode? what? "

Sauvresy paused a moment, and looked steadily at his friend.

" You must marry," said he at last.

This seemed to surprise Hector, but not disagreeably.

" I, marry? It's easier to give that advice than to follow it."

" Pardon me—you ought to know that I do not speak rashly. What would you say to a young girl of good family, pretty, well brought up, so charming that, excepting my own wife, I know of no one more attractive, and who would bring with her a dowry of a million ? "

" Ah, my friend, I should say that I adore her! And do you know such an angel ? "

" Yes, and you too, for the angel is Mademoiselle Laurence Courtois."

Hector's radiant face overclouded at this name, and he made a discouraged gesture.

" Never," said he. " That stiff and obstinate old merchant, Monsieur Courtois, would never consent to give his daughter to a man who has been fool enough to waste his fortune."

Sauvresy shrugged his shoulders.

" Now, there's what it is to have eyes, and not see. Know that this Courtois, whom you think so obstinate, is really the most romantic of men, and an ambitious old fellow to boot. It would seem to him a grand good speculation to give his daughter to the Count Hector de Trémorel, cousin of the Duke of Samblemeuse, the relative of the Commarins, even though you hadn't a sou. What wouldn't he give to have the delicious pleasure of saying, Monsieur the Count, my son-in-law ; or my daughter, Madame the Countess Hector ! And you aren't ruined, you know, you are going to have an income of twenty thousand francs, and perhaps enough more to raise your capital to a million."

Hector was silent. He had thought his life ended, and now, all of a sudden, a splendid perspective unrolled itself before him. He might then rid himself of the patronizing protection of his friend; he would be free, rich, would have a better wife, as he thought, than Bertha; his house would outshine Sauvresy's. The thought of Bertha crossed his mind, and it occurred to him that he might thus escape a lover who although beautiful and loving, was proud and bold, and whose domineering temper began to be burdensome to him.

"I may say," said he, seriously to his friend, "that I have always thought Monsieur Courtois an excellent and honorable man, and Mademoiselle Laurence seems to me so accomplished a young lady, that a man might be happy in marrying her even without a dowry."

"So much the better, my dear Hector, so much the better. But you know, the first thing is to engage Laurence's affections; her father adores her, and would not, I am sure, give her to a man whom she herself had not chosen."

"Don't disturb yourself," answered Hector, with a gesture of triumph, "she will love me."

The next day he took occasion to encounter M. Courtois, who invited him to dinner. The count employed all his practised seductions on Laurence, which were so brilliant and able that they were well fitted to surprise and dazzle a young girl. It was not long before the count was the hero of the mayor's household. Nothing formal had been said, nor any direct allusion or overture made; yet M. Courtois was sure that Hector would some day ask his daughter's hand, and that he should freely answer, "yes;" while he thought it certain that Laurence would not say "no."

Bertha suspected nothing; she was now very much worried about Jenny, and saw nothing else. Sauvresy, after spending an evening with the count at the mayor's, during which Hector had not once quitted the whist-table, decided to speak to his wife of the proposed marriage, which he thought would give her an agreeable surprise. At his first words, she grew pale. Her emotion was so great that, seeing she would betray herself, she hastily retired to her boudoir. Sauvresy, quietly seated in one of the bedroom arm-chairs, continued to expatiate on the advantages of such a marriage—raising his voice, so that Bertha might hear him in the neighboring room.

" Do you know," said he, " that our friend has an income of sixty thousand crowns? We'll find an estate for him near by, and then we shall see him and his wife every day. They will be very pleasant society for us in the autumn months. Hector is a fine fellow, and you've often told me how charming Laurence is."

Bertha did not reply. This unexpected blow was so terrible that she could not think clearly, and her brain whirled.

" You don't say anything," pursued Sauvresy. " Don't you approve of my project? I thought you'd be enchanted with it."

She saw that if she were silent any longer, her husband would go in and find her sunk upon a chair, and would guess all. She made an effort and said, in a strangled voice, without attaching any sense to her words:

" Yes, yes; it is a capital idea."

" How you say that! Do you see any objections? "

She was trying to find some objection, but could not.

" I have a little fear of Laurence's future," said she at last.

"Bah! Why?"

"I only say what I've heard you say. You told me that Monsieur Trémorel has been a libertine, a gambler, a prodigal——"

"All the more reason for trusting him. His past follies guarantee his future prudence. He has received a lesson which he will not forget. Besides, he will love his wife."

"How do you know?"

"Barbleu, he loves her already."

"Who told you so?"

"Himself."

And Sauvresy began to laugh about Hector's passion, which he said was becoming quite pastoral.

"Would you believe," said he, laughing, "that he thinks our worthy Courtois a man of wit? Ah, what spectacles these lovers look through! He spends two or three hours every day with the mayor. What do you suppose he does there?"

Bertha, by great effort, succeeded in dissembling her grief; she reappeared with a smiling face. She went and came, apparently calm, though suffering the bitterest anguish a woman can endure. And she could not run to Hector, and ask him if it were true!

For Sauvresy must be deceiving her. Why? She knew nòt. No matter. She felt her hatred of him increasing to disgust; for she excused and pardoned her lover, and she blamed her husband alone. Whose idea was this marriage? His. Who had awakened Hector's hopes, and encouraged them? He, always he. While he had been harmless, she had been able to pardon him for having married her; she had compelled herself to bear him, to feign a love quite foreign to her heart. But now he became hateful; should she submit to his interference in a matter which was life or death to her?

She did not close her eyes all night; she had one of those horrible nights in which crimes are conceived. She did not find herself alone with Hector until after breakfast the next day, in the billiard-hall.

" Is it true? " she asked.

The expression of her face was so menacing that he quailed before it. He stammered:

" True—what? "

" Your marriage."

He was silent at first, asking himself whether he should tell the truth or equivocate. At last, irritated by Bertha's imperious tone, he replied:

" Yes."

She was thunderstruck at this response. Till then, she had a glimmer of hope. She thought that he would at least try to reassure her, to deceive her. There are times when a falsehood is the highest homage. But no—he avowed it. She was speechless; words failed her.

Trémorel began to tell her the motives which prompted his conduct. He could not live forever at Valfeuillu. What could he, with his habits and tastes, do with a few thousand crowns a year? He was thirty; he must, now or never, think of the future. M. Courtois would give his daughter a million, and at his death there would be a great deal more. Should he let this chance slip? He cared little for Laurence, it was the dowry he wanted. He took no pains to conceal his meanness; he rather gloried in it, speaking of the marriage as simply a bargain, in which he gave his name and title in exchange for riches. Bertha stopped him with a look full of contempt.

"Spare yourself," said she. "You love Laurence."

He would have protested; he really disliked her.

"Enough," resumed Bertha. "Another woman would have reproached you; I simply tell you that this marriage shall not be; I do not wish it. Believe me, give it up frankly, don't force me to act."

She retired, shutting the door violently; Hector was furious.

"How she treats me!" said he to himself. "Just as a queen would speak to a serf. Ah, she don't want me to marry Laurence!" His coolness returned, and with it serious reflections. If he insisted on marrying, would not Bertha carry out her threats? Evidently; for he knew well that she was one of those women who shrink from nothing, whom no consideration could arrest. He guessed what she would do, from what she had said in a quarrel with him about Jenny. She had told him, "I will confess everything to Sauvresy, and we will be the more bound together by shame than by all the ceremonies of the church."

This was surely the mode she would adopt to break a marriage which was so hateful to her; and Trémorel trembled at the idea of Sauvresy knowing all.

"What would he do," thought he, "if Bertha told him? He would kill me off-hand—that's what I would do in his place. Suppose he didn't; I should have to fight a duel with him, and if I killed him, quit the country. Whatever would happen, my marriage is irrevocably broken, and Bertha seems to be on my hands for all time."

He saw no possible way out of the horrible situation in which he had put himself.

"I must wait," thought he.

And he waited, going secretly to the mayor's, for he really loved Laurence. He waited, devoured by anxiety, struggling between Sauvresy's urgency and Bertha's threats. How he detested this woman who held him, whose will weighed so heavily on him! Nothing could curb her ferocious obstinacy. She had one fixed idea. He had thought to conciliate her by dismissing Jenny. It was a mistake. When he said to her:

"Bertha, I shall never see Jenny again."

She answered, ironically:

"Mademoiselle Courtois will be very grateful to you!"

That evening, while Sauvresy was crossing the courtyard, he saw a beggar at the gate, making signs to him.

"What do you want, my good man?"

The beggar looked around to see that no one was listening.

"I have brought you a note," said he, rapidly, and in a low tone. "I was told to give it only to you, and to ask you to read it when you are alone."

He mysteriously slipped a note, carefully sealed, into Sauvresy's hand.

"It comes from a pretty girl," added he, winking.

Sauvresy, turning his back to the house, opened it and read:

"SIR—You will do a great favor to a poor and unhappy girl, if you will come to-morrow to the Belle Image, at Corbeil, where you will be awaited all day.
      "Your humble servant,
                  "JENNY F——."

There was also a postscript.

"Please, sir, don't say a word of this to the Count de Trémorel."

"Ah ha," thought Sauvresy, "there's some trouble about Hector, that's bad for the marriage."

"I was told, sir," said the beggar, "there would be an answer."

"Say that I will come," answered Sauvresy, throwing him a franc piece.

XVII

The next day was cold and damp. A fog, so thick that one could not discern objects ten steps off, hung over the earth. Sauvresy, after breakfast, took his gun and whistled to his dogs.

"I'm going to take a turn in Mauprévoir wood," said he.

"A queer idea," remarked Hector, "for you wont see the end of your gun-barrel in the woods."

"No matter, if I see some pheasants."

This was only a pretext, for Sauvresy, on leaving Valfeuillu, took the direct road to Corbeil, and half an hour later, faithful to his promise, he entered the Belle Image tavern.

Jenny was waiting for him in the large room which had always been reserved for her since she became a regular customer of the house. Her eyes were red with recent tears; she was very pale, and her marble color showed that she had not slept. Her breakfast lay untouched on the table near the fireplace, where a bright fire was burning. When Sauvresy came in, she rose to meet him, and took him by the hand with a friendly motion.

"Thank you for coming," said she. "Ah, you are very good."

Jenny was only a girl, and Sauvresy detested girls;

14

but her grief was so sincere and seemed so deep, that
he was touched.

"You are suffering, Madame?" asked he.

"Oh, yes, very much."

Her tears choked her, and she concealed her face
in her handkerchief.

"I guessed right," thought Sauvresy. "Hector has
deserted her. Now I must smooth the wound, and yet
make future meetings between them impossible."

He took the weeping Jenny's hand, and softly pulled
away the handkerchief.

"Have courage," said he.

She lifted her tearful eyes to him, and said:

"You know, then?"

"I know nothing, for, as you asked me, I have said
nothing to Trémorel; but I can imagine what the
trouble is."

"He will not see me any more," murmured Jenny.
"He has deserted me."

Sauvresy summoned up all his eloquence. The moment to be persuasive and paternal had come. He
drew a chair up to Jenny's, and sat down.

"Come, my child," pursued he, "be resigned. People are not always young, you know. A time comes
when the voice of reason must be heard. Hector does
not desert you, but he sees the necessity of assuring
his future, and placing his life on a domestic foundation; he feels the need of a home."

Jenny stopped crying. Nature took the upper hand,
and her tears were dried by the fire of anger which
took possession of her. She rose, overturning her
chair, and walked restlessly up and down the room.

"Do you believe that?" said she. "Do you believe
that Hector troubles himself about his future? I see

you don't know his character. He dream of a home, or a family? He never has and never will think of anything but himself. If he had any heart, would he have gone to live with you as he has? He had two arms to gain his bread and mine. I was ashamed to ask money of him, knowing that what he gave me came from you."

"But he is my friend, my dear child."

"Would you do as he has done?"

Sauvresy did not know what to say; he was embarrassed by the logic of this daughter of the people, judging her lover rudely, but justly.

"Ah, I know him, I do," continued Jenny, growing more excited as her mind reverted to the past. "He has only deceived me once—the morning he came and told me he was going to kill himself. I was stupid enough to think him dead, and to cry about it. He, kill himself? Why, he's too much of a coward to hurt himself! Yes, I love him, but I don't esteem him. That's our fate, you see, only to love the men we despise."

Jenny talked loud, gesticulating, and every now and then thumping the table with her fist so that the bottles and glasses jingled. Sauvresy was somewhat fearful lest the hotel people should hear her; they knew him, and had seen him come in. He began to be sorry that he had come, and tried to calm the girl.

"But Hector is not deserting you," repeated he. "He will assure you a good position."

"Humph! I should laugh at such a thing! Have I any need of *him?* As long as I have ten fingers and good eyes, I shall not be at the mercy of any man. He made me change my name, and wanted to accustom me to luxury! And now there is neither a Miss Jenny, nor riches, but there is a Pélagie, who proposes to get her fifty sous a day, without much trouble."

" No," said Sauvresy, " you will not need——"

" What? To work? But I like work; I am not a do-nothing. I will go back to my old life. I used to breakfast on a sou's worth of biscuit and a sou's worth of potatoes, and was well and happy. On Sundays, I dined at the Turk for thirty sous. I laughed more then in one afternoon, than in all the years I have known Trémorel."

She no longer cried, nor was she angry; she was laughing. She was thinking of her old breakfasts, and her feasts at the Turk.

Sauvresy was stupefied. He had no idea of this Parisian nature, detestable and excellent, emotional to excess, nervous, full of transitions, which laughs and cries, caresses and strikes in the same minute, which a passing idea whirls a hundred leagues from the present moment.

" So," said Jenny, more calmly, " I snap my fingers at Hector "—she had just said exactly the contrary, and had forgotten it—" I don't care for him, but I will not let him leave me in this way. It sha'n't be said that he left me for another. I won't have it."

Jenny was one of those women who do not reason, but who feel; with whom it is folly to argue, for their fixed idea is impregnable to the most victorious arguments. Sauvresy asked himself why she had asked him to come, and said to himself that the part he had intended to play would be a difficult one. But he was patient.

" I see, my child," he commenced, " that you haven't understood or even heard me. I told you that Hector was intending to marry."

"He!" answered Jenny, with an ironical gesture. "He get married."

She reflected a moment, and added:

"If it were true, though——"

"I tell you it is so."

"No," cried Jenny, "no, that can't be possible. He loves another, I am sure of it, for I have proofs."

Sauvresy smiled; this irritated her.

"What does this letter mean," cried she warmly, "which I found in his pocket, six months ago? It isn't signed to be sure, but it must have come from a woman."

"A letter?"

"Yes, one that destroys all doubts. Perhaps you ask, why I did not speak to him about it? Ah, you see, I did not dare. I loved him. I was afraid if I said anything, and it was true he loved another, I should lose him. And so I resigned myself to humiliation, I concealed myself to weep, for I said to myself, he will come back to me. Poor fool!"

"Well, but what will you do?"

"Me? I don't know—anything. I didn't say anything about the letter, but I kept it; it is my weapon— I will make use of it. When I want to, I shall find out who she is, and then——"

"You will compel Trémorel, who is kindly disposed toward you, to use violence."

"He? What can he do to me? Why, I will follow him like his shadow—I will cry out everywhere the name of this other. Will he have me put in St. Lazare prison? I will invent the most dreadful calumnies against him. They will not believe me at first; later, part of it will be believed. I have nothing to fear—I have no parents, no friends, nobody on earth who cares for me. That's what it is to raise girls from the gutter. I have fallen so low that I defy him to push me lower. So, if you are his friend, sir, advise him to come back to me."

Sauvresy was really alarmed; he saw clearly how real and earnest Jenny's menaces were. There are persecutions against which the law is powerless. But he dissimulated his alarm under the blandest air he could assume.

"Hear me, my child," said he. "If I give you my word of honor to tell you the truth, you'll believe me, won't you?"

She hesitated a moment, and said:

"Yes, you are honorable; I will believe you."

"Then, I swear to you that Trémorel hopes to marry a young girl who is immensely rich, whose dowry will secure his future."

"He tells you so; he wants you to believe it."

"Why should he? Since he came to Valfeuillu, he could have had no other affair than this with you. He lives in my house, as if he were my brother, between my wife and myself, and I could tell you how he spends his time every hour of every day as well as what I do myself."

Jenny opened her mouth to reply, but a sudden reflection froze the words on her lips. She remained silent and blushed violently, looking at Sauvresy with an indefinable expression. He did not observe this, being inspired by a restless though aimless curiosity. This proof, which Jenny talked about, worried him.

"Suppose," said he, "you should show me this letter."

She seemed to feel at these words an electric shock.

"To you?" she said, shuddering. "Never!"

If, when one is sleeping, the thunder rolls and the storm bursts, it often happens that the sleep is not troubled; then suddenly, at a certain moment, the imperceptible flutter of a passing insect's wing awakens one.

Jenny's shudder was like such a fluttering to Sauvresy. The sinister light of doubt struck on his soul. Now his confidence, his happiness, his repose, were gone forever. He rose with a flashing eye and trembling lips.

"Give me the letter," said he, in an imperious tone.

Jenny recoiled with terror. She tried to conceal her agitation, to smile, to turn the matter into a joke.

"Not to-day," said she. "Another time; you are too curious."

But Sauvresy's anger was terrible; he became as purple as if he had had a stroke of apoplexy, and he repeated, in a choking voice:

"The letter, I demand the letter."

"Impossible," said Jenny. "Because," she added, struck with an idea, "I haven't got it here."

"Where is it?"

"At my room, in Paris."

"Come, then, let us go there."

She saw that she was caught; and she could find no more excuses, quick-witted as she was. She might, however, easily have followed Sauvresy, put his suspicions to sleep with her gayety, and when once in the Paris streets, might have eluded him and fled. But she did not think of that. It occurred to her that she might have time to reach the door, open it, and rush downstairs. She started to do so. Sauvresy caught her at a bound, shut the door, and said, in a low, hoarse voice:

"Wretched girl! Do you wish me to strike you?"

He pushed her into a chair, returned to the door, double locked it, and put the keys in his pocket.

"Now," said he, returning to the girl, "the letter."

Jenny had never been so terrified in her life. This man's rage made her tremble; she saw that he was beside himself, that she was completely at his mercy; yet she still resisted him.

"You have hurt me very much," said she, crying, "but I have done you no harm."

He grasped her hands in his, and bending over her, repeated:

"For the last time, the letter; give it to me, or I will take it by force."

It would have been folly to resist longer.

"Leave me alone," said she. "You shall have it."

He released her, remaining, however, close by her side, while she searched in all her pockets. Her hair had been loosened in the struggle, her collar was torn, she was tired, her teeth chattered, but her eyes shone with a bold resolution.

"Wait—here it is—no. It's odd—I am sure I've got it though—I had it a minute ago——"

And, suddenly, with a rapid gesture, she put the letter, rolled into a ball, into her mouth, and tried to swallow it. But Sauvresy as quickly grasped her by the throat, and she was forced to disgorge it.

He had the letter at last. His hands trembled so that he could scarcely open it.

It was, indeed, Bertha's writing.

Sauvresy tottered with a horrible sensation of dizziness; he could not see clearly; there was a red cloud before his eyes; his legs gave way under him, he staggered, and his hands stretched out for a support.

Jenny, somewhat recovered, hastened to give him
help; but her touch made him shudder, and he repulsed her. What had happened he could not tell. Ah,
he wished to read this letter and could not. He went
to the table, turned out and drank two large glasses of
water one after another. The cold draught restored
him, his blood resumed its natural course, and he could
see. The note was short, and this was what he read:

" Don't go to-morrow to Petit-Bourg; or rather, return before breakfast. He has just told me that he
must go to Melun, and that he should return late. A
whole day! "

" He "—that was himself. This other lover of Hector's was Bertha, his wife. For a moment he saw nothing but that; all thought was crushed within him. His
temples beat furiously, he heard a dreadful buzzing in
his ears, it seemed to him as if the earth were about to
swallow him up. He fell into a chair; from purple he
became ashy white. Great tears trickled down his
cheeks.

Jenny understood the miserable meanness of her
conduct when she saw this great grief, this silent despair, this man with a broken heart. Was she not the
cause of all? She had guessed who the writer of the
note was. She thought when she asked Sauvresy to
come to her, that she could tell him all, and thus avenge
herself at once upon Hector and her rival. Then, on
seeing this man refusing to comprehend her hints, she
had been full of pity for him. She had said to herself
that he would be the one who would be most cruelly
punished; and then she had recoiled—but too late—
and he had snatched the secret from her.

She approached Sauvresy and tried to take his
hands; he still repulsed her.

" Let me alone," said he.

" Pardon me, sir—I am a wretch, I am horrified at myself."

He rose suddenly ; he was gradually coming to himself.

" What do you want ? "

" That letter—I guessed——"

He burst into a loud, bitter, discordant laugh, and replied :

" God forgive me ! Why, my dear, did you dare to suspect my wife ? "

While Jenny was muttering confused excuses, he drew out his pocket-book and took from it all the money it contained—some seven or eight hundred francs—which he put on the table.

" Take this, from Hector," said he, " he will not permit you to suffer for anything ; but, believe me, you had best let him get married."

Then he mechanically took up his gun, opened the door, and went out. His dogs leaped upon him to caress him ; he kicked them off. Where was he going ? What was he going to do ?

XVIII

A small, fine, chilly rain had succeeded the morning fog ; but Sauvresy did not perceive it. He went across the fields with his head bare, wandering at hazard, without aim or discretion. He talked aloud as he went, stopping ever and anon, then resuming his course. The peasants who met him—they all knew him— turned to look at him after having saluted him, asking themselves whether the master of Valfeuillu had not gone mad. Unhappily he was not mad. Overwhelmed by an unheard-of, unlooked-for catastrophe, his brain had been for a moment paralyzed. But one by one he collected his scattered ideas and acquired the faculty of thinking and of suffering. Each one of his reflections increased his mortal anguish. Yes, Bertha and Hector had deceived, had dishonored him. She, beloved to idolatry; he, his best and oldest friend, a wretch that he had snatched from misery, who owed him everything. And it was in his house, under his own roof, that this infamy had taken place. They had taken advantage of his noble trust, had made a dupe of him. The frightful discovery not only embittered the future, but also the past. He longed to blot out of his life these years passed with Bertha, with whom, but the night before, he had recalled these " happiest years of his life." The memory of his former happiness filled his soul with disgust. But how had this been done? When? How was it he had seen nothing of it? And now things came into his mind which should have warned him had he not been blind. He recalled certain looks of Bertha, certain tones of voice, which were an avowal. At times, he tried to doubt. There are misfortunes so great that to be believed there must be more than evidence.

" It is not possible! " muttered he.

Seating himself upon a prostrate tree in the midst of Mauprévoir forest, he studied the fatal letter for the tenth time within four hours.

" It proves all," said he, " and it proves nothing."

And he read once more.

" Do not go to-morrow to Petit-Bourg——"

Well, had he not again and again, in his idiotic confidence, said to Hector:

"I shall be away to-morrow, stay here and keep Bertha company."

This sentence, then, had no positive signification. But why add:

"Or rather, return before breakfast."

This was what betrayed fear, that is, the fault. To go away and return again anon, was to be cautious, to avoid suspicion. Then, why " he," instead of, " Clement?" This word was striking. " He "—that is, the dear one, or else, the master that one hates. There is no medium—'tis the husband, or the lover. " He," is never an indifferent person. A husband is lost when his wife, in speaking of him, says, " He."

But when had Bertha written these few lines? Doubtless some evening after they had retired to their room. He had said to her, " I'm going to-morrow to Melun," and then she had hastily scratched off this note and given it, in a book, to Hector.

Alas! the edifice of his happiness, which had seemed to him strong enough to defy every tempest of life, had crumbled, and he stood there lost in the midst of its débris. No more happiness, joys, hopes—nothing! All his plans for the future rested on Bertha; her name was mingled in his every dream, she was at once the future and the dream. He had so loved her that she had become something of himself, that he could not imagine himself without her. Bertha lost to him, he saw no direction in life to take, he had no further reason for living. He perceived this so vividly that the idea of suicide came to him. He had his gun, powder and balls; his death would be attributed to a hunting accident, and all would be over.

Oh, but the guilty ones!

They would doubtless go on in their infamous

comedy—would seem to mourn for him, while really their hearts would bound with joy. No more husband, no more hypocrisies or terrors. His will giving his fortune to Bertha, they would be rich. They would sell everything, and would depart rejoicing to some distant clime. As to his memory, poor man, it would amuse them to think of him as the cheated and despised husband.

"Never!" cried he, drunk with fury, "never! I must kill myself, but first, I must avenge my dishonor!"

But he tried in vain to imagine a punishment cruel or terrible enough. What chastisement could expiate the horrible tortures which he endured? He said to himself that, in order to assure his vengeance, he must wait—and he swore that he would wait. He would feign the same stolid confidence, and resigned himself to see and hear everything.

"My hypocrisy will equal theirs," thought he.

Indeed a cautious duplicity was necessary. Bertha was most cunning, and at the first suspicion would fly with her lover. Hector had already—thanks to him— several hundred thousand francs. The idea that they might escape his vengeance gave him energy and a clear head.

It was only then that he thought of the flight of time, the rain falling in torrents, and the state of his clothes.

"Bah!" thought he, "I will make up some story to account for myself."

He was only a league from Valfeuillu, but he was an hour and a half reaching home. He was broken, exhausted; he felt chilled to the marrow of his bones. But when he entered the gate, he had succeeded in assuming his usual expression, and the gayety which so well

hinted his perfect trustfulness. He had been waited
for, but in spite of his resolutions, he could not sit at
table between this man and woman, his two most cruel
enemies. He said that he had taken cold, and would
go to bed. Bertha insisted in vain that he should take
at least a bowl of broth, and a glass of claret.

" Really," said he, " I don't feel well."

When he had retired, Bertha said:

" Did you notice, Hector? "

" What? "

" Something unusual has happened to him."

" Very likely, after being all day in the rain."

" No. His eye had a look I never saw before."

" He seemed to be very cheerful, as he always is."

" Hector, my husband suspects! "

" He? Ah, my poor good friend has too much confidence in us to think of being jealous."

" You deceive yourself, Hector; he did not embrace
me when he came in, and it is the first time since our
marriage."

Thus, at the very first, he had made a blunder. He
knew it well; but it was beyond his power to embrace
Bertha at that moment; and he was suffering more
than he thought he should. When his wife and his
friend ascended to his room, after dinner, they found
him shivering under the sheets, red, his forehead burning, his throat dry, and his eyes shining with an unusual brilliancy. A fever soon came on, attended by
delirium. A doctor was called, who at first said he
would not answer for him. The next day he was worse.
From this time both Hector and Bertha conceived for
him the most tender devotion. Did they think they
should thus in some sort expiate their crime? It is
doubtful. More likely they tried to impose on the peo-

ple about them; everyone was anxious for Sauvresy.
They never deserted him for a moment, passing the
night by turns near his bed. And it was painful to
watch over him; a furious delirium never left him. Several times force had to be used to keep him on the
bed; he tried to throw himself out of the window. The
third day he had a strange fancy; he did not wish to
stay in his chamber. He kept crying out:

"Carry me away from here, carry me away from
here."

The doctor advised that he should be humored; so
a bed was made up for him in a little room on the
ground-floor, overlooking the garden. His wander-
ings did not betray anything of his suspicions; perhaps
the firm will was able even to control the delirium. The
fever finally yielded on the ninth day. His breathing
became calmer, and he slept. When he awoke, reason
had returned. That was a frightful moment. He had,
so to speak, to take up the burden of his misery. At
first he thought it the memory of a horrid night-mare;
but no. He had not dreamed. He recalled the Belle
Image, Jenny, the forest, the letter. What had become
of the letter? Then, having the vague impression of a
serious illness, he asked himself if he had said anything
to betray the source of his misery. This anxiety prevented his making the slightest movement, and he
opened his eyes softly and cautiously. It was eleven
at night, and all the servants had gone to bed. Hector and Bertha alone were keeping watch; he was reading a paper, she was crocheting. Sauvresy saw by their
placid countenances that he had betrayed nothing. He
moved slightly; Bertha at once arose and came to him.

"How are you, dear Clement?" asked she, kissing
him fondly on the forehead.

" I am no longer in pain."

" You see the result of being careless."

" How many days have I been sick? "

" Eight days."

" Why was I brought here? "

" Because you wished it."

Trémorel had approached the bedside.

" You refused to stay upstairs," said he, " you were ungovernable till we had you brought here."

" Ah! "

" But don't tire yourself," resumed Hector. " Go to sleep again, and you will be well by to-morrow. And good-night, for I am going to bed now, and shall return and wake your wife at four o'clock."

He went out, and Bertha, having given Sauvresy something to drink, returned to her seat.

" What a friend Trémorel is," murmured she.

Sauvresy did not answer this terribly ironical exclamation. He shut his eyes, pretended to sleep, and thought of the letter. What had he done with it? He remembered that he had carefully folded it and put it in the right-hand pocket of his vest. He must have this letter. It would balk his vengeance, should it fall into his wife's hands; and this might happen at any moment. It was a miracle that his valet had not put it on the mantel, as he was accustomed to do with the things which he found in his master's pockets. He was reflecting on some means of getting it, of the possibility of going up to his bedroom, where his vest ought to be, when Bertha got up softly. She came to the bed and whispered gently:

" Clement, Clement! "

He did not open his eyes, and she, persuaded that

he was sleeping, though very lightly, stole out of the room, holding her breath as she went

"Oh, the wretch!" muttered Sauvresy, "she is going to *him!*"

At the same time the necessity of recovering the letter occurred to him more vividly than ever.

"I can get to my room," thought he, "without being seen, by the garden and back-stairs. She thinks I'm asleep; I shall get back and abed before she returns."

Then, without asking himself whether he were not too feeble, or what danger there might be in exposing himself to the cold, he got up, threw a gown around him, put on his slippers and went toward the door.

"If anyone sees me, I will feign delirium," said he to himself.

The vestibule lamp was out and he found some difficulty in opening the door; finally, he descended into the garden. It was intensely cold, and snow had fallen. The wind shook the limbs of the trees crusted with ice. The front of the house was sombre. One window only was lighted—that of Trémorel's room; that was lighted brilliantly, by a lamp and a great blazing fire. The shadow of a man—of Hector—rested on the muslin curtains; the shape was distinct. He was near the window, and his forehead was pressed against the panes. Sauvresy instinctively stopped to look at his friend, who was so at home in his house, and who, in exchange for the most brotherly hospitality, had brought dishonor, despair and death.

Hector made a sudden movement, and turned around as if he was surprised by an unwonted noise. What was it? Sauvresy only knew too well. Another shadow appeared on the curtain—that of Bertha. And he had forced himself to doubt till now! Now proofs

15

had come without his seeking. What had brought her to that room, at that hour? She seemed to be talking excitedly. He thought he could hear that full, sonorous voice, now as clear as metal, now soft and caressing, which had made all the chords of passion vibrate in him. He once more saw those beautiful eyes which had reigned so despotically over his heart, and whose expressions he knew so well. But what was she doing? Doubtless she had gone to ask Hector something, which he refused her, and she was pleading with him; Sauvresy saw that she was supplicating, by her motions; he knew the gesture well. She lifted her clasped hands as high as her forehead, bent her head, half shut her eyes. What languor had been in her voice when she used to say:

"Say, dear Clement, you will, will you not?"

And now she was using the same blandishments on another. Sauvresy was obliged to support himself against a tree. Hector was evidently refusing what she wished; then she shook her finger menacingly, and tossed her head angrily, as if she were saying:

"You won't? You shall see, then."

And then she returned to her supplications.

"Ah," thought Sauvresy. "*he* can resist her prayers; *I* never had such courage. He can preserve his coolness, his will, when she looks at him; I never said no to her; rather, I never waited for her to ask anything of me; I have passed my life in watching her lightest fancies, to gratify them. Perhaps that is what has ruined me!"

Hector was obstinate, and Bertha was roused little by little; she must be angry. She recoiled, holding out her arms, her head thrown back; she was threatening him. At last he was conquered; he nodded, "Yes."

Then she flung herself upon him, and the two shadows were confounded in a long embrace.

Sauvresy could not repress an agonized cry, which was lost amid the noises of the night. He had asked for certainty; here it was. The truth, indisputable, evident, was clear to him. He had to seek for nothing more, now, except for the means to punish surely and terribly. Bertha and Hector were talking amicably. Sauvresy saw that she was about to go downstairs, and that he could not now go for the letter. He went in hurriedly, forgetting, in his fear of being discovered, to lock the garden door. He did not perceive that he had been standing with naked feet in the snow, till he had returned to his bedroom again; he saw some flakes on his slippers, and they were damp; quickly he threw them under the bed, and jumped in between the clothes, and pretended to be asleep.

It was time, for Bertha soon came in. She went to the bed, and thinking that he had not woke up, returned to her embroidery by the fire. Trémorel also soon reappeared; he had forgotten to take his paper, and had come back for it. He seemed uneasy.

" Have you been out to-night, Madame? " asked he, in a low voice.

" No."

" Have all the servants gone to bed? "

" I suppose so; but why do you ask? "

" Since I have been upstairs, somebody has gone out into the garden, and come back again."

Bertha looked at him with a troubled glance.

" Are you sure of what you say? "

" Certainly. Snow is falling, and whoever went out brought some back on his shoes. This has melted in the vestibule——"

Mme. Sauvresy seized the lamp, and interrupting Hector, said:

" Come."

Trémorel was right. Here and there on the vestibule pavement were little puddles.

" Perhaps this water has been here some time," suggested Bertha.

" No. It was not there an hour ago, I could swear. Besides, see, here is a little snow that has not melted yet."

" It must have been one of the servants."

Hector went to the door and examined it.

" I do not think so," said he. " A servant would have shut the bolts; here they are, drawn back. Yet I myself shut the door to-night, and distinctly recollect fastening the bolts."

" It's very strange! "

" And all the more so, look you, because the traces of the water do not go much beyond the drawing-room door."

They remained silent, and exchanged anxious looks. The same terrible thought occurred to them both.

" If it were he? "

But why should he have gone into the garden? It could not have been to spy on them.

They did not think of the window.

" It couldn't have been Clement," said Bertha, at last. " He was asleep when I went back, and he is in a calm and deep slumber now."

Sauvresy, stretched upon his bed, heard what his enemies were saying. He cursed his imprudence.

" Suppose," thought he, " they should think of looking at my gown and slippers! "

Happily this simple idea did not occur to them; after

reassuring each other as well as they were able, they separated; but each heart carried an anxious doubt. Sauvresy on that night had a terrible crisis in his illness. Delirium, succeeding this ray of reason, renewed its possession of his brain. The next morning Dr. R—— pronounced him in more danger than ever; and sent a despatch to Paris, saying that he would be detained at Valfeuillu three or four days. The distemper redoubled in violence; very contradictory symptoms appeared. Each day brought some new phase of it, which confounded the foresight of the doctors. Every time that Sauvresy had a moment of reason, the scene at the window recurred to him, and drove him to madness again.

On that terrible night when he had gone out into the snow, he had not been mistaken; Bertha was really begging something of Hector. This was it:

M. Courtois, the mayor, had invited Hector to accompany himself and his family on an excursion to Fontainebleau on the following day. Hector had cordially accepted the invitation. Bertha could not bear the idea of his spending the day in Laurence's company, and begged him not to go. She told him there were plenty of excuses to relieve him from his promise; for instance, he might urge that it would not be seemly for him to go when his friend lay dangerously ill. At first he positively refused to grant her prayer, but by her supplications and menaces she persuaded him, and she did not go downstairs until he had sworn that he would write to M. Courtois that very evening declining the invitation. He kept his word, but he was disgusted by her tyrannical behavior. He was tired of forever sacrificing his wishes and his liberty, so that he could plan nothing, say or promise nothing without consulting this jealous woman, who would scarcely let him wander out of her sight. The chain became heavier and heavier to bear, and he began to see that sooner or later it must be wrenched apart. He had never loved either Bertha or Jenny, or anyone, probably; but he now loved the mayor's daughter. Her dowry of a million had at first dazzled him, but little by little he had been subdued by Laurence's charms of mind and person. He, the dissipated rake, was seduced by such grave and naïve innocence, such frankness and beauty; he would have married Laurence had she been poor—as Sauvresy married Bertha. But he feared Bertha too much to brave her suddenly, and so he waited. The next day after the quarrel about Fontainebleau, he declared that he was indisposed, attributed it to the want of exercise, and took to the saddle for several hours every day afterward. But he did not go far; only to the mayor's. Bertha at first did not perceive anything suspicious in Trémorel's rides; it reassured her to see him go off on his horse. After some days, however, she thought she saw in him a certain feeling of satisfaction concealed under the semblance of fatigue. She began to have doubts, and these increased every time he went out; all sorts of conjectures worried her while he was away. Where did he go? Probably to see Laurence, whom she feared and detested. The suspicion soon became a certainty with her. One evening Hector appeared, carrying in his button-hole a flower which Laurence herself had put there, and which he had forgotten to take out. Bertha took it gently, examined it, smelt it, and, compelling herself to smile:

" Why," said she, " what a pretty flower ! "

"So I thought," answered Hector, carelessly, "though I don't know what it is called."

"Would it be bold to ask who gave it to you?"

"Not at all. It's a present from our good Plantat."

All Orcival knew that M. Plantat, a monomaniac on flowers, never gave them away to anyone except Mlle. Laurence. Hector's evasion was an unhappy one, and Bertha was not deceived.

"You promised me, Hector," said she, "not to see Laurence any more, and to give up this marriage."

He tried to reply.

"Let me speak," she continued, "and explain yourself afterward. You have broken your word—you are deceiving my confidence! But I tell you, you shall not marry her!" Then, without awaiting his reply, she overwhelmed him with reproaches. Why had he come here at all? She was happy in her home before she knew him. She did not love Sauvresy, it was true; but she esteemed him, and he was good to her. Ignorant of the happiness of true love, she did not desire it. But he had come, and she could not resist his fascination. And now, after having engaged her affection, he was going to desert her, to marry another! Trémorel listened to her, perfectly amazed at her audacity. What! She dared to pretend that it was *he* who had abused her innocence, when, on the contrary, he had sometimes been astonished at her persistency! Such was the depth of her corruption, as it seemed to him, that he wondered whether he were her first or her twentieth lover. And she had so led him on, and had so forcibly made him feel the intensity of her will, that he had been fain still to submit to this despotism. But he had now determined to resist on the first opportunity; and he resisted.

"Well, yes," said he, frankly, "I did deceive you;
I have no fortune—this marriage will give me one; I
shall get married." He went on to say that he loved
Laurence less than ever, but that he coveted her money
more and more every day. "To prove this," he pursued, "if you will find me to-morrow a girl who
has twelve hundred thousand francs instead of a million, I will marry her in preference to Mademoiselle
Courtois."

She had never suspected he had so much courage.
She had so long moulded him like soft wax, and this
unexpected conduct disconcerted her. She was indignant, but at the same time she felt that unhealthy satisfaction that some women feel, when they meet a master
who subdues them; and she admired Trémorel more
than ever before. This time, he had taken a tone which
conquered her; she despised him enough to think him
quite capable of marrying for money. When he had
done, she said:

"It's really so, then; you only care for the million
of dowry?"

"I've sworn it to you a hundred times."

"Truly now, don't you love Laurence?"

"I have never loved her, and never shall."

He thought that he would thus secure his peace until
the wedding-day; once married, he cared not what
would happen. What cared he for Sauvresy? Life is
only a succession of broken friendships. What is a
friend, after all? One who can and ought to serve you.
Ability consists in breaking with people, when they
cease to be useful to you.

Bertha reflected.

"Hear me, Hector," said she at last. "I cannot
calmly resign myself to the sacrifice which you demand.

Let me have but a few days, to accustom myself to this dreadful blow. You owe me as much—let Clement get well, first."

He did not expect to see her so gentle and subdued; who would have looked for such concessions, so easily obtained? The idea of a snare did not occur to him. In his delight he betrayed how he rejoiced in his liberty, which ought to have undeceived Bertha; but she did not perceive it. He grasped her hand, and cried:

" Ah, you are very good—you really love me."

XIX

The Count de Trémorel did not anticipate that the respite which Bertha begged would last long. Sauvresy had seemed better during the last week. He got up every day, and commenced to go about the house; he even received numerous visits from the neighbors; without apparent fatigue. But alas, the master of Valfeuillu was only the shadow of himself. His friends would never have recognized in that emaciated form and white face, and burning, haggard eye, the robust young man with red lips and beaming visage whom they remembered. He had suffered so! He did not wish to die before avenging himself on the wretches who had filched his happiness and his life. But what punishment should he inflict? This fixed idea burning in his brain, gave his look a fiery eagerness. Ordinarily, there are three modes in which a betrayed husband may avenge himself. He has the right, and it is almost a duty—to deliver the guilty ones up to the law, which is on his side. He may adroitly watch them, surprise them and kill them. There is a law which does

not absolute, but excuses him, in this. Lastly, he may
affect a stolid indifference, laugh the first and loudest
at his misfortune, drive his wife from his roof, and leave
her to starve. But what poor, wretched methods of
vengeance. Give up his wife to the law? Would not
that be to offer his name, honor, and life to public ridicule? To put himself at the mercy of a lawyer, who
would drag him through the mire. They do not defend
the erring wife, they attack her husband. And what
satisfaction would he get? Bertha and Trémorel would
be condemned to a year's imprisonment, perhaps eighteen months, possibly two years. It seemed to him
simpler to kill them. He might go in, fire a revolver
at them, and they would not have time to comprehend
it, for their agony would be but for a moment; and
then? Then, he must become a prisoner, submit to a
trial, invoke the judge's mercy, and risk conviction.
As to turning his wife out of doors, that was to hand
her over quietly to Hector. He imagined them leaving Valfeuillu, hand in hand, happy and smiling, and
laughing in his face. At this thought he had a fit of
cold rage; his self-esteem adding the sharpest pains
to the wounds in his heart. None of these vulgar methods could satisfy him. He longed for some revenge
unheard-of, strange, monstrous, as his tortures were.
Then he thought of all the horrible tales he had read,
seeking one to his purpose; he had a right to be particular, and he was determined to wait until he was
satisfied. There was only one thing that could balk
his progress—Jenny's letter. What had become of it?
Had he lost it in the woods? He had looked for it
everywhere, and could not find it.

He accustomed himself, however, to feign, finding
a sort of fierce pleasure in the constraint. He learned

to assume a countenance which completely hid his thoughts. He submitted to his wife's caresses without an apparent shudder; and shook Hector by the hand as heartily as ever. In the evening, when they were gathered about the drawing-room table, he was the gayest of the three. He built a hundred air-castles, pictured a hundred pleasure-parties, when he was able to go abroad again. Hector rejoiced at his returning health.

"Clement is getting on finely," said he to Bertha, one evening.

She understood only too well what he meant.

"Always thinking of Laurence?"

"Did you not permit me to hope?"

"I asked you to wait, Hector, and you have done well not to be in a hurry. I know a young girl who would bring you, not one, but three millions as dowry."

This was a painful surprise. He really had no thoughts for anyone but Laurence, and now a new obstacle presented itself.

"And who is that?"

She leaned over, and whispered tremblingly in his ear:

"I am Clement's sole heiress; perhaps he'll die; I might be a widow to-morrow."

Hector was petrified.

"But Sauvresy, thank God! is getting well fast."

Bertha fixed her large, clear eyes upon him, and with frightful calmness said:

"What do you know about it?"

Trémorel dared not ask what these strange words meant. He was one of those men who shun explanations, and who, rather than put themselves on their guard in time, permit themselves to be drawn on by circumstances; soft and feeble beings, who deliberately bandage their eyes so as not to see the danger which threatens them, and who prefer the sloth of doubt, and acts of uncertainty to a definite and open position, which they have not the courage to face.

Besides, Hector experienced a childish satisfaction in seeing Bertha's distress, though he feared and detested her. He conceived a great opinion of his own value and merit, when he saw the persistency and desperation with which she insisted on keeping her hold on him.

" Poor woman! " thought he. " In her grief at losing me, and seeing me another's, she has begun to wish for her husband's death! "

Such was the torpor of his moral sense that he did not see the vileness of Bertha's and his own thoughts.

Meanwhile Sauvresy's state was not reassuring for Hector's hopes and plans. On the very day when he had this conversation with Bertha, her husband was forced to take to his bed again. This relapse took place after he had drank a glass of quinine and water, which he had been accustomed to take just before supper; only, this time, the symptoms changed entirely, as if one malady had yielded to another of a very different kind. He complained of a pricking in his skin, of vertigo, of convulsive twitches which contracted and twisted his limbs, especially his arms. He cried out with excruciating neuralgic pains in the face. He was seized with a violent, persistent, tenacious craving for pepper, which nothing could assuage. He was sleepless, and morphine in large doses failed to bring him slumber; while he felt an intense chill within him, as if the body's temperature were gradually diminishing. Delirium had completely disappeared, and the sick man

retained perfectly the clearness of his mind. Sauvresy
bore up wonderfully under his pains, and seemed to
take a new interest in the business of his estates. He
was constantly in consultation with bailiffs and agents,
and shut himself up for days together with notaries and
attorneys. Then, saying that he must have distractions,
he received all his friends, and when no one called, he
sent for some acquaintance to come and chat with him
in order to forget his illness. He gave no hint of what
he was doing and thinking, and Bertha was devoured
by anxiety. She often watched for her husband's agent,
when, after a conference of several hours, he came out
of his room; and making herself as sweet and fascinat-
ing as possible, she used all her cunning to find out
something which would enlighten her as to what he was
about. But no one could, or at least would, satisfy her
curiosity; all gave evasive replies, as if Sauvresy had
cautioned them, or as if there were nothing to tell.

No complaints were heard from Sauvresy. He
talked constantly of Bertha and Hector; he wished all
the world to know their devotion to him; he called
them his " guardian angels," and blessed Heaven that
had given him such a wife and such a friend. Sauvresy's illness now became so serious that Trémorel
began to despair; he became alarmed; what position
would his friend's death leave him in? Bertha, having
become a widow, would be implacable. He resolved to
find out her inmost thoughts at the first opportunity;
she anticipated him, and saved him the trouble of
broaching the subject. One afternoon, when they
were alone, M. Plantat being in attendance at the sick
man's bedside, Bertha commenced.

" I want some advice, Hector, and you alone can
give it to me. How can I find out whether Clement,

within the past day or two, has not changed his will in regard to me?"

" His will?"

" Yes, I've already told you that by a will of which I myself have a copy, Sauvresy has left me his whole fortune. I fear that he may perhaps revoke it."

" What an idea!"

" Ah, I have reasons for my apprehensions. What are all these agents and attorneys doing at Valfeuillu? A stroke of this man's pen may ruin me. Don't you see that he can deprive me of his millions, and reduce me to my dowry of fifty thousand francs?"

" But he will not do it; he loves you——"

" Are you sure of it? I've told you, there are three millions; I must have this fortune—not for myself, but for you; I want it, I *must* have it! But how can I find out—how? how?"

Hector was very indignant. It was to this end, then, that his delays had conducted him! She thought that she had a right now to dispose of him in spite of himself, and, as it were, to purchase him. And he could not, dared not, say anything!

" We must be patient," said he, " and wait——"

" Wait—for what? Till he's dead?"

" Don't speak so."

" Why not?" Bertha went up to him, and in a low voice, muttered:

" He has only a week to live; and see here——"

She drew a little vial from her pocket, and held it up to him.

" That is what convinces me that I am not mistaken."

Hector became livid, and could not stifle a cry of horror. He comprehended all now—he saw how it was that Bertha had been so easily subdued, why she had

refrained from speaking of Laurence, her strange
words, her calm confidence.

"Poison!" stammered he, confounded.

"Yes, poison."

"You have not used it?"

She fixed a hard, stern look upon him—the look
which had subdued his will, against which he had struggled in vain—and in a calm voice, emphasizing each
word, answered:

"I have used it."

The count was, indeed, a dangerous man, unscrupulous, not recoiling from any wickedness when his passions were to be indulged, capable of everything; but
this horrible crime awoke in him all that remained of
honest energy.

"Well," he cried, in disgust, "you will not use it
again!"

He hastened toward the door, shuddering; she
stopped him.

"Reflect before you act," said she, coldly. "I will
betray the fact of your relations with me; who will
then believe that you are not my accomplice?"

He saw the force of this terrible menace, coming
from Bertha.

"Come," said she, ironically, "speak—betray me if
you choose. Whatever happens, for happiness or misery, we shall no longer be separated; our destinies will
be the same."

Hector fell heavily into a chair, more overwhelmed
than if he had been struck with a hammer. He held
his bursting forehead between his hands; he saw himself shut up in an infernal circle, without outlet.

"I am lost!" he stammered, without knowing what
he said, "I am lost!"

He was to be pitied; his face was terribly haggard, great drops of perspiration stood at the roots of his hair, his eyes wandered as if he were insane. Bertha shook him rudely by the arm, for his cowardice exasperated her.

"You are afraid," she said. "You are trembling! Lost? You would not say so, if you loved me as I do you. Will you be lost because I am to be your wife, because we shall be free to love in the face of all the world? Lost! Then you have no idea of what I have endured? You don't know, then, that I am tired of suffering, fearing, feigning."

"Such a crime!"

She burst out with a laugh that made him shudder.

"You ought to have said so," said she, with a look full of contempt, "the day you won me from Sauvresy —the day that you stole the wife of this friend who saved your life. Do you think that was a less horrid crime? You knew as well as I did how much my husband loved me, and that he would have preferred to die, rather than lose me thus."

"But he knows nothing, suspects nothing of it."

"You are mistaken; Sauvresy knows all."

"Impossible!"

"All, I tell you—and he has known all since that day when he came home so late from hunting. Don't you remember that I noticed his strange look, and said to you that my husband suspected something? You shrugged your shoulders. Do you forget the steps in the vestibule, the night I went to your room? He had been spying on us. Well, do you want a more certain proof? Look at this letter, which I found, crumpled up and wet, in one of his vest pockets."

She showed him the letter which Sauvresy had forcibly taken from Jenny, and he recognized it well.

"It is a fatality," said he, overwhelmed. "But we can separate and break off with each other. Bertha, I can go away."

"It's too late. Believe me, Hector, we are to-day defending our lives. Ah, you don't know Clement! You don't know what the fury of a man like him can be, when he sees that his confidence has been outrageously abused, and his trust vilely betrayed. If he has said nothing to me, and has not let us see any traces of his implacable anger, it is because he is meditating some frightful vengeance."

This was only too probable, and Hector saw it clearly.

"What shall we do?" he asked, in a hoarse voice; he was almost speechless.

"Find out what change he has made in his will."

"But how?"

"I don't know yet. I came to ask your advice, and I find you more cowardly than a woman. Let me act, then; don't do anything yourself; I will do all."

He essayed an objection.

"Enough," said she. "He must not ruin us after all—I will see—I will think."

Someone below called her. She went down, leaving Hector overcome with despair.

That evening, during which Bertha seemed happy and smiling, his face finally betrayed so distinctly the traces of his anguish, that Sauvresy tenderly asked him if he were not ill?

"You exhaust yourself tending on me, my good Hector," said he. "How can I ever repay your devotion?"

Trémorel had not the strength to reply.

16

"And that man knows all," thought he. "What courage! What fate can he be reserving for us?"

The scene which was passing before Hector's eyes made his flesh creep. Every time that Bertha gave her husband his medicine, she took a hair-pin from her tresses, and plunged it into the little vial which she had shown him, taking up thus some small, white grains, which she dissolved in the potions prescribed by the doctor.

It might be supposed that Trémorel, enslaved by his horrid position, and harassed by increasing terror, would renounce forever his proposed marriage with Laurence. Not so. He clung to that project more desperately than ever. Bertha's threats, the great obstacles now intervening, his anguish, crime, only augmented the violence of his love for her, and fed the flame of his ambition to secure her as his wife. A small and flickering ray of hope which lighted the darkness of his despair, consoled and revived him, and made the present more easy to bear. He said to himself that Bertha could not be thinking of marrying him the day after her husband's death. Months, a whole year must pass, and thus he would gain time; then some day he would declare his will. What would she have to say? Would she divulge the crime, and try to hold him as her accomplice? Who would believe her? How could she prove that he, who loved and had married another woman, had any interest in Sauvresy's death? People don't kill their friends for the mere pleasure of it. Would she provoke the law to exhume her husband? She was now in a position, thought he, wherein she could, or would not exercise her reason. Later on, she would reflect, and then she would be arrested by

the probability of those dangers, the certainty of which
did not now terrify her.

He did not wish that she should ever be his wife at
any price. He would have detested her had she possessed millions; he hated her now that she was poor,
ruined, reduced to her own narrow means. And that
she was so, there was no doubt, Sauvresy indeed knew
all. He was content to wait; he knew that Laurence
loved him enough to wait for him one, or three years,
if necessary. He already had such absolute power over
her, that she did not try to combat the thoughts of him,
which gently forced themselves on her, penetrated to
her soul, and filled her mind and heart. Hector said
to himself that in the interest of his designs, perhaps it
was well that Bertha was acting as she did. He forced
himself to stifle his conscience in trying to prove that
he was not guilty. Who thought of this crime? Bertha.
Who was executing it? She alone. He could only
be reproached with moral complicity in it, a complicity
involuntary, forced upon him, imposed somehow by
the care for his own life. Sometimes, however, a bitter
remorse seized him. He could have understood a sudden, violent, rapid murder; could have explained to
himself a knife-stroke; but this slow death, given drop
by drop, horribly sweetened by tenderness, veiled under
kisses, appeared to him unspeakably hideous. He was
mortally afraid of Bertha, as of a reptile, and when she
embraced him he shuddered from head to foot.

She was so calm, so engaging, so natural; her voice
had the same soft and caressing tones, that he could
not forget it. She plunged her hair-pin into the fatal
vial without ceasing her conversation, and he did not
surprise her in any shrinking or shuddering, nor even
a trembling of the eyelids. She must have been made

of brass. Yet he thought that she was not cautious enough, and that she put herself in danger of discovery; and he told her of these fears, and how she made him tremble every moment.

" Have confidence in me," she answered. " I want to succeed—I am prudent."

" But you may be suspected."

" By whom? "

" Eh! How do I know? Everyone—the servants, the doctor."

" No danger. And suppose they did suspect? "

" They would make examinations, Bertha; they would make a minute scrutiny."

She gave a smile of the most perfect security.

" They might examine and experiment as much as they pleased, they would find nothing. Do you think I am such a fool as to use arsenic? "

" For Heaven's sake, hush! "

" I have procured one of those poisons which are as yet unknown, and which defy all analysis; one of which many doctors—and learned ones, too—could not even tell the symptoms! "

" But where did you get this—this——"

He dared not say, " poison."

" Who gave you *that?* " resumed he.

" What matters it? I have taken care that he who gave it to me should run the same danger as myself, and he knows it. There's nothing to fear from that quarter. I've paid him enough to smother all his regrets."

An objection came to his lips; he wanted to say, " It's too slow; " but he had not the courage, though she read his thought in his eyes.

" It is slow, because that suits me," said she. " Before all, I must know about the will—and that I am trying to find out."

She occupied herself constantly about this will, and during the long hours that she passed at Sauvresy's bedside, she gradually, with the greatest craft and delicacy, led her husband's mind in the direction of his last testament, with such success that he himself mentioned the subject which so absorbed Bertha.

He said that he did not comprehend why people did not always have their worldly affairs in order, and their wishes fully written down, in case of accident. What difference did it make whether one were ill or well? At these words Bertha attempted to stop him. Such ideas, she said, pained her too much. She even shed real tears, which fell down her cheeks and made her more beautiful and irresistible than before; real tears which moistened her handkerchief.

" You dear silly creature," said Sauvresy, " do you think that makes one die ? "

" No ; but I do not wish it."

" But, dear, have we been any the less happy because, on the day after our marriage, I made a will bequeathing you all my fortune? And, stop; you have a copy of it, haven't you? If you were kind, you would go and fetch it for me."

She became very red, then very pale. Why did he ask for this copy? Did he want to tear it up? A sudden thought reassured her; people do not tear up a document which can be cancelled by a scratch of the pen on another sheet of paper. Still, she hesitated a moment.

" I don't know where it can be."

" But I do. It is in the left-hand drawer of the glass cupboard; come, please me by getting it."

While she was gone, Sauvresy said to Hector:

"Poor girl! Poor dear Bertha! If I died, she nevei would survive me!"

Trémorel thought of nothing to reply; his anxiety was intense and visible.

"And this man," thought he, "suspects something! No; it is not possible."

Bertha returned.

"I have found it," said she.

"Give it to me."

He took the copy of his will, and read it with evident satisfaction, nodding his head at certain passages in which he referred to his love for his wife. When he had finished reading, he said:

"Now give me a pen and some ink."

Hector and Bertha reminded him that it would fatigue him to write; but he insisted. The two guilty ones, seated at the foot of the bed and out of Sauvresy's sight, exchanged looks of alarm. What was he going to write? But he speedily finished it.

"Take this," said he to Trémorel, "and read aloud what I have just added."

Hector complied with his friend's request, with trembling voice:

"This day, being sound in mind, though much suffering, I declare that I do not wish to change a line of this will. Never have I loved my wife more—never have I so much desired to leave her the heiress of all I possess, should I die before her.

"CLEMENT SAUVRESY."

Mistress of herself as Bertha was, she succeeded in concealing the unspeakable satisfaction with which she was filled. All her wishes were accomplished, and yet she was able to veil her delight under an apparent sadness.

"Of what good is this?" said she, with a sigh.

She said this, but half an hour afterward, when she was alone with Hector, she gave herself up to the extravagance of her delight.

"Nothing more to fear," exclaimed she. "Nothing! Now we shall have liberty, fortune, love, pleasure, life! Why, Hector, we shall have at least three millions; you see, I've got this will myself, and I shall keep it. No more agents or notaries shall be admitted into this house henceforth. Now I must hasten!"

The count certainly felt a satisfaction in knowing her to be rich, for he could much more easily get rid of a millionnaire widow than of a poor penniless woman. Sauvresy's conduct thus calmed many sharp anxieties. Her restless gayety, however, her confident security, seemed monstrous to Hector. He would have wished for more solemnity in the execution of the crime; he thought that he ought at least to calm Bertha's delirium.

"You will think more than once of Sauvresy," said he, in a graver tone.

She answered with a "prrr," and added vivaciously:

"Of him? when and why? Oh, his memory will not weigh on me very heavily. I trust that we shall be able to live still at Valfeuillu, for the place pleases me; but we must also have a house at Paris—or we will buy yours back again. What happiness, Hector!"

The mere prospect of this anticipated felicity so shocked Hector, that his better self for the moment got the mastery; he essayed to move Bertha.

"For the last time," said he, "I implore you to renounce this terrible, dangerous project. You see

that you were mistaken—that Sauvresy suspects nothing, but loves you as well as ever."

The expression of Bertha's face suddenly changed;
she sat quite still, in a pensive revery.

"Don't let's talk any more of that," said she, at last.
"Perhaps I was mistaken. Perhaps he only had doubts
—perhaps, although he has discovered something, he
hopes to win me back by his goodness. But you
see——"

She stopped. Doubtless she did not wish to alarm
him.

He was already much alarmed. The next day he
went off to Melun without a word, being unable to bear
the sight of this agony, and fearing to betray himself.
But he left his address, and when she sent word that
Sauvresy was always crying out for him, he hastily returned. Her letter was most imprudent and absurd,
and made his hair stand on end. He had intended, on
his arrival, to reproach her; but it was she who upbraided him.

"Why this flight?"

"I could not stay here—I suffered, trembled, felt as
if I were dying."

"What a coward you are!"

He would have replied, but she put her finger on his
mouth, and pointed with her other hand to the door
of the next room.

"Sh! Three doctors have been in consultation there
for the past hour, and I haven't been able to hear a
word of what they said. Who knows what they are
about? I shall not be easy till they go away."

Bertha's fears were not without foundation. When
Sauvresy had his last relapse, and complained of a severe neuralgia in the face and an irresistible craving for

pepper, Dr. R—— had uttered a significant exclamation. It was nothing, perhaps—yet Bertha had heard it, and she thought she surprised a sudden suspicion on the doctor's part; and this now disturbed her, for she thought that it might be the subject of the consultation. The suspicion, however, if there had ever been any, quickly vanished. The symptoms entirely changed twelve hours later, and the next day the sick man felt pains quite the opposite of those which had previously distressed him. This very inconstancy of the distemper served to puzzle the doctor's conclusions. Sauvresy, in these latter days, had scarcely suffered at all, he said, and had slept well at night; but he had, at times, strange and often distressing sensations. He was evidently failing hourly; he was dying—everyone perceived it. And now Dr. R—— asked for a consultation, the result of which had not been reached when Trémorel returned.

The drawing-room door at last swung open, and the calm faces of the physicians reassured the poisoner. Their conclusions were that the case was hopeless; everything had been tried and exhausted; no human resources had been neglected; the only hope was in Sauvresy's strong constitution.

Bertha, colder than marble, motionless, her eyes full of tears, seemed so full of grief on hearing this cruel decision, that all the doctors were touched.

" Is there no hope then? Oh, my God ! " cried she, in agonizing tones.

Dr. R—— hardly dared to attempt to comfort her; he answered her questions evasively.

" We must never despair," said he, " when the invalid is of Sauvresy's age and constitution ; nature often works miracles when least expected."

The doctor, however, lost no time in taking Hector apart and begging him to prepare the poor, devoted, loving young lady for the terrible blow about to ensue.

"For you see," added he, "I don't think Monsieur Sauvresy can live more than two days!"

Bertha, with her ear at the keyhole, had heard the doctor's prediction; and when Hector returned from conducting the physician to the door, he found her radiant. She rushed into his arms.

"Now," cried she, "the future truly belongs to us. Only one black point obscured our horizon, and it has cleared away. It is for me to realize Doctor R——'s prediction." They dined together, as usual, in the dining-room, while one of the chambermaids remained beside the sick-bed. Bertha was full of spirits which she could scarcely control. The certainty of success and safety, the assurance of reaching the end, made her imprudently gay. She spoke aloud, even in the presence of the servants, of her approaching liberty. During the evening she was more reckless than ever. If any of the servants should have a suspicion, or a shadow of one, she might be discovered and lost. Hector constantly nudged her under the table and frowned at her, to keep her quiet; he felt his blood run cold at her conduct; all in vain. There are times when the armor of hypocrisy becomes so burdensome that one is forced, cost what it may, to throw it off if only for an instant.

While Hector was smoking his cigar, Bertha was more freely pursuing her dream. She was thinking that she could spend the period of her mourning at Valfeuillu, and Hector, for the sake of appearances, would hire a pretty little house somewhere in the suburbs. The worst of it all was that she would be forced to seem to mourn for Sauvresy, as she had pretended to

love him during his lifetime. But at last a day would
come when, without scandal, she might throw off her
mourning clothes, and then they would get married.
Where? At Paris or Orcival?

Hector's thoughts ran in the same channel. He, too,
wished to see his friend under the ground to end his
own terrors, and to submit to Bertha's terrible yoke.

XX

Time passed. Hector and Bertha repaired to Sauvresy's room; he was asleep. They noiselessly took
chairs beside the fire, as usual, and the maid retired.
In order that the sick man might not be disturbed by
the light of the lamp, curtains had been hung so that,
when lying down, he could not see the fireplace and
mantel. In order to see these, he must have raised
himself on his pillow and leaned forward on his right
arm. But now he was asleep, breathing painfully, feverish, and shuddering convulsively. Bertha and Hector did not speak; the solemn and sinister silence was
only broken by the ticking of the clock, or by the leaves
of the book which Hector was reading. Ten o'clock
struck; soon after Sauvresy moved, turned over, and
awoke. Bertha was at his side in an instant; she saw
that his eyes were open.

"Do you feel a little better, dear Clement?" she
asked.

"Neither better nor worse."

"Do you want anything?"

"I am thirsty."

Hector, who had raised his eyes when his friend
spoke, suddenly resumed his reading.

Bertha, standing by the mantel, began to prepare with great care Dr. R.——'s last prescription; when it was ready, she took out the fatal little vial as usual, and thrust one of her hair-pins into it.

She had not time to draw it out before she felt a light touch upon her shoulder. A shudder shook her from head to foot; she suddenly turned and uttered a loud scream, a cry of terror and horror.

"Oh!"

The hand which had touched her was her husband's.

While she was busied with the poison at the mantel, Sauvresy had softly raised himself; more softly still, he had pulled the curtain aside, and had stretched out his arm and touched her. His eyes glittered with hate and anger.

Bertha's cry was answered by another dull cry, or rather groan; Trémorel had seen and comprehended all; he was overwhelmed.

"All is discovered!" Their eyes spoke these three words to each other. They saw them everywhere, written in letters of fire. There was a moment of stupor, of silence so profound that Hector heard his temples beat. Sauvresy had got back under the bed-clothes again. He laughed loudly, wildly, just as a skeleton might have laughed whose jaws and teeth rattled together.

But Bertha was not one of those persons who are overcome by a single blow, terrible as it might be. She trembled like a leaf; her legs staggered; but her mind was already at work seeking a subterfuge. What had Sauvresy seen—anything? What did he know? For even had he seen the vial, this might be explained. It could only have been by simple chance that he had touched her at the moment when she was using the poison. All these thoughts flashed across her mind in a moment, as rapid as lightning shooting between the clouds. And then she dared to approach the bed, and, with a frightfully constrained smile, to say:

" How you frightened me then ! "

He looked at her a moment, which seemed to her an age—and simply replied:

" I understand it."

There was no longer any uncertainty. Bertha saw only too well in her husband's eyes that he knew something. But what—how much? She nerved herself to go on:

" Are you still suffering? "

" No."

" Then why did you get up? "

He raised himself upon his pillow, and with a sudden strength, he continued:

" I got up to tell you that I have had enough of these tortures, that I have reached the limits of human energy, that I cannot endure one day longer the agony of seeing myself put to death slowly, drop by drop, by the hands of my wife and my best friend ! "

He stopped. Hector and Bertha were thunderstruck.

" I wanted to tell you also, that I have had enough of your cruel caution, and that I suffer. Ah, don't you see that I suffer horribly? Hurry, cut short my agony! Kill me, and kill me at a blow—poisoners ! "

At the last word, the Count de Trémorel sprang up as if he had moved by a spring, his eyes haggard, his arms stretched out. Sauvresy, seeing this, quickly slipped his hand under the pillow, pulled out a revolver, and pointed the barrel at Hector, crying out:

" Don't advance a step ! "

He thought that Trémorel, seeing that they were

discovered, was going to rush upon him and strangle him; but he was mistaken. It seemed to Hector as though he were losing his mind. He fell down as heavily as if he were a log. Bertha was more self-possessed; she tried to resist the torpor of terror which she felt coming on.

"You are worse, my Clement," said she. "This is that dreadful fever which frightens me so. Delirium——"

"Have I really been delirious?" interrupted he, with a surprised air.

"Alas, yes, dear, that is what haunts you, and fills your poor sick head with horrid visions."

He looked at her curiously. He was really stupefied by this boldness, which constantly grew more bold.

"What! you think that we, who are so dear to you, your friends, I, your——"

Her husband's implacable look forced her to stop, and the words expired on her lips.

"Enough of these lies, Bertha," resumed Sauvresy, "they are useless. No, I have not been dreaming, nor have I been delirious. The poison is only too real, and I could tell you what it is without your taking it out of your pocket."

She recoiled as if she had seen her husband's hand stretched out to snatch the blue vial.

"I guessed it and recognized it at the very first; for you have chosen one of those poisons which, it is true, leave scarcely any trace of themselves, but the symptoms of which are not deceptive. Do you remember the day when I complained of a morbid taste for pepper? The next day I was certain of it, and I was not the only one. Doctor R——, too, had a suspicion."

Bertha tried to stammer something; her husband interrupted her.

"People ought to try their poisons," pursued he, in an ironical tone, "before they use them. Didn't you understand yours, or what its effects were? Why, your poison gives intolerable neuralgia, sleeplessness, and you saw me without surprise, sleeping soundly all night long! I complained of a devouring fire within me, while your poison freezes the blood and the entrails, and yet you are not astonished. You see all the symptoms change and disappear, and that does not enlighten you. You are fools, then. Now see what I had to do to divert Doctor R——'s suspicions. I hid the real pains which your poison caused, and complained of imaginary, ridiculous ones. I described sensations just the opposite of those which I felt. You were lost, then —and I saved you."

Bertha's malignant energy staggered beneath so many successive blows. She wondered whether she were not going mad; had she heard aright? Was it really true that her husband had perceived that he was being poisoned, and yet said nothing; nay, that he had even deceived the doctor? Why? What was his purpose?

Sauvresy paused several minutes, and then went on:

"I have held my tongue and so saved you, because the sacrifice of my life had already been made. Yes, I had been fatally wounded in the heart on the day that I learned that you were faithless to me."

He spoke of his death without apparent emotion; but at the words, "You were faithless to me," his voice faltered and trembled.

"I would not, could not believe it at first. I doubted the evidence of my senses, rather than doubt you. But

I was forced to believe at last. I was no longer anything in my house but a laughing-stock. But I was in
your way. You and your lover needed more room and
liberty. You were tired of constraint and hypocrisy.
Then it was that, believing that my death would make
you free and rich, you brought in poison to rid yourselves of me."

Bertha had at least the heroism of crime. All was
discovered; well, she threw down the mask. She tried
to defend her accomplice, who lay unconscious in a
chair.

" It is I that have done it all," cried she. " He is
innocent."

Sauvresy turned pale with rage.

" Ah, really," said he, " my friend Hector is innocent! It wasn't he, then, who, to pay me up—not for
his life, for he was too cowardly to kill himself; but
for his honor, which he owes to me—took my wife from
me? Wretch! I hold out my hand to him when he is
drowning, I welcome him like a brother, and in return,
he desolates my hearth! . . . And you knew what
you were doing, my friend Hector—for I told you a
hundred times that my wife was my all here below, my
present and my future, my dream and happiness and
hope and very life! You knew that for me to lose her
was to die. But if you had loved her—no, it was not
that you loved her; you hated me. Envy devoured
you, and you could not tell me to my face, " You are
too happy." Then, like a coward, you hishonored me
in the dark. Bertha was only the instrument of your
rancor; and she weighs upon you to-day—you despise
and fear her. My friend, Hector, you have been in this
house the vile lackey who thinks to avenge his base-

ness by spitting upon the meats which he puts on his master's table!"

The count only responded by a shudder. The dying man's terrible words fell more cruelly on his conscience than blows upon his cheek.

" See, Bertha," continued Sauvresy, " that's the man whom you have preferred to me, and for whom you have betrayed me. You never loved me—I see it now —your heart was never mine. And I—I loved you so! From the day I first saw you, you were my only thought; as if your heart had beaten in place of mine. Everything about you was dear and precious to me; I adored your whims, caprices, even your faults. There was nothing I would not do for a smile from you, so that you would say to me, Thank you, between two kisses. You don't know that for years after our marriage it was my delight to wake up first so as to gaze upon you as you lay asleep, to admire and touch your lovely hair, lying dishevelled across the pillow. Bertha!"

He softened at the remembrance of these past joys, which would not come again. He forgot their presence, the infamous treachery, the poison; that he was about to die, murdered by this beloved wife; and his eyes filled with tears, his voice choked.

Bertha, more motionless and pallid than marble, listened to him breathlessly.

" It is true, then," continued the sick man, " that these lovely eyes conceal a soul of filth! Ah, who would not have been deceived, as I was? Bertha, what did you dream of when you were sleeping in my arms? Trémorel came, and you thought you saw in him the ideal of your dreams. You admired the precocious wrinkles which betrayed an exhausted life, like the fatal

17

seal which marks the fallen archangel's forehead. Your love, without thought of mine, rushed toward him, though he did not think of you. You went to evil as if it were your nature. And yet I thought you more immaculate than the Alpine snows. You did not even have a struggle with yourself; you betrayed no confusion which would reveal your first fault to me. You brought me your forehead soiled with *his* kisses without blushing."

Weariness overcame his energies; his voice became little by little feebler and less distinct.

" You had your happiness in your hands, Bertha, and you carelessly destroyed it, as the child breaks the toy of whose value he is ignorant. What did you expect from this wretch for whom you had the frightful courage to kill me, with a kiss upon your lips, slowly, hour by hour? You thought you loved him, but disgust ought to have come at last. Look at him, and judge between us. See which is the man—I, extended on this bed where I shall soon die, or he shivering there in a corner. You have the energy of crime, but he has only the baseness of it. Ah, if my name was Hector de Trémorel, and a man had spoken as I have just done, that man should live no longer, even if he had ten revolvers like this I am holding to defend himself with!"

Hector, thus taunted, tried to get up and reply; but his legs would not support him, and his throat only gave hoarse, unintelligible sounds. Bertha, as she looked at the two men, recognized her error with rage and indignation. Her husband, at this moment, seemed to her sublime; his eyes gleamed, his face was radiant; while the other—the other! She felt sick with disgust when she but glanced toward him.

Thus all these deceptive chimeras after which she

had run, love, passion, poetry, were already hers; she had held them in her hands and she had not been able to perceive it. But what was Sauvresy's purpose?

He continued, painfully:

" This then, is our situation; you have killed me, you are going to be free, yet you hate and despise each other——"

He stopped, and seemed to be suffocating; he tried to raise himself on his pillow and to sit up in bed, but found himself too feeble.

" Bertha," said he, " help me get up."

She leaned over the bed, and taking her husband in her arms, succeeded in placing him as he wished. He appeared more at ease in his new position, and took two or three long breaths.

" Now," he said, " I should like something to drink. The doctor lets me take a little old wine, if I have a fancy for it; give me some."

She hastened to bring him a glass of wine, which he emptied and handed back to her.

" There wasn't any poison in it, was there? " he asked.

This ghastly question and the smile which accompanied it, melted Bertha's callousness; remorse had already taken possession of her, as her disgust of Trémorel increased.

" Poison? " she cried, eagerly, " never! "

" You must give me some, though, presently, so as to help me to die."

" You die, Clement? No; I want you to live, so that I may redeem the past. I am a wretch, and have committed a hideous crime—but you are good. You will live; I don't ask to be your wife, but only your servant. I will love you, humiliate myself, serve you on my knees, so that some day, after ten, twenty years of expiation, you will forgive me!"

Hector in his mortal terror and anguish, was scarcely able to distinguish what was taking place. But he saw a dim ray of hope in Bertha's gestures and accent, and especially in her last words; he thought that perhaps it was all going to end and be forgotten, and that Sauvresy would pardon them. Half-rising, he stammered:

"Yes, forgive us, forgive us!"

Sauvresy's eyes glittered, and his angry voice vibrated as if it came from a throat of metal.

"Forgive!" cried he, "pardon! Did you have pity on me during all this year that you have been playing with my happiness, during this fortnight that you have been mixing poison in all my potions? Pardon? What, are you fools? Why do you think I held my tongue, when I discovered your infamy, and let myself be poisoned, and threw the doctors off the scent? Do you really hope that I did this to prepare a scene of heartrending farewells, and to give you my benediction at the end? Ah, know me better!"

Bertha was sobbing; she tried to take her husband's hand, but he rudely repulsed her.

"Enough of these falsehoods," said he. "Enough of these perfidies. I hate you! You don't seem to perceive that hate is all that is still living in me."

Sauvresy's expression was at this moment ferocious.

"It is almost two months since I learned the truth; it broke me up, soul and body. Ah, it cost me a good deal to keep quiet—it almost killed me. But one thought sustained me; I longed to avenge myself. My mind was always bent on that; I searched for a punishment as great as this crime; I found none, could find none. Then you resolved to poison me. Mark this—

that the very day when I guessed about the poison I had a thrill of joy, for I had discovered my vengeance! "

.A constantly increasing terror possessed Bertha, and now stupefied her, as well as Trémorel.

" Why do you wish for my death? To be free and marry each other? Very well; I wish that also. The Count de Trémorel will be Madame Sauvresy's second husband."

" Never! " cried Bertha. " No, never! "

" Never! " echoed Hector.

" It shall be so, nevertheless, because I wish it. Oh, my precautions have been well taken, and you can't escape me. Now hear me. When I became certain that I was being poisoned, I began to write a minute history of all three of us; I did more—I have kept a journal day by day and hour by hour, narrating all the particulars of my illness ; then I kept some of the poison which you gave me——"

Bertha made a gesture of denial. Sauvresy proceeded:

" Certainly, I kept it, and I will tell you how. Every time that Bertha gave me a suspicious potion, I kept a portion of it in my mouth, and carefully ejected it into a bottle which I kept hid under the bolster. Ah, you ask how I could have done all this without your suspecting it, or without being seen by any of the servants. Know that hate is stronger than love, be sure that I have left nothing to chance, nor have I forgotten anything."

Hector and Bertha looked at Sauvresy with a dull, fixed gaze. They forced themselves to understand him, but could scarcely do so.

" Let's finish," resumed the dying man, " my strength is waning. This very morning, the bottle containing the poison I have preserved, our biographies, and the narrative of my poisoning, have been put in the hands of a trustworthy and devoted person, whom, even if you knew him, you could not corrupt. He does not know the contents of what has been confided to him. The day that you get married this friend will give them all up to you. If, however, you are not married in a year from to-day, he has instructions to put these papers and this bottle into the hands of the officers of the law."

A double cry of horror and anguish told Sauvresy that he had well chosen his vengeance.

"And reflect," added he, "that this package once delivered up to justice, means the galleys, if not the scaffold for both of you."

Sauvresy had overtasked his strength. He fell panting upon the bed, his mouth open, his eyes filmy, and his features so distorted that he seemed to be on the point of death. But neither Bertha nor Trémorel thought of trying to relieve him. They remained opposite each other with dilated eyes, stupefied, as if their thoughts were bent upon the torments of that future which the implacable vengeance of the man whom they had outraged imposed upon them. They were indissolubly united, confounded in a common destiny; nothing could separate them but death. A chain stronger and harder than that of the galley-slave bound them together; a chain of infamies and crimes, of which the first link was a kiss, and the last a murder by poison. Now Sauvresy might die; his vengeance was on their heads, casting a cloud upon their sun. Free in appearance, they would go through life crushed by the burden of the past, more slaves than the blacks in the American rice-fields. Separated by mutual hate and contempt, they saw themselves riveted together by the common terror of punishment, condemned to an eternal embrace.

Bertha at this moment admired her husband. Now that he was so feeble that he breathed as painfully as an infant, she looked upon him as something superhuman. She had had no idea of such constancy and courage allied with so much dissimulation and genius. How cunningly he had found them out! How well he had known how to avenge himself! To be the master, he had only to will it. In a certain way she rejoiced in the strange atrocity of this scene; she felt something like a bitter pride in being one of the actors in it. At the same time she was transported with rage and sorrow in thinking that she had had this man in her power, that he had been at her feet. She almost loved him. Of all men, it was he whom she would have chosen were she mistress of her destinies; and he was going to escape her.

Trémorel, while these strange ideas crowded upon Bertha's mind, began to come to himself. The certainty that Laurence was now forever lost for him occurred to him, and his despair was without bounds. The silence continued a full quarter of an hour. Sauvresy at last subdued the spasm which had exhausted him, and spoke.

"I have not said all yet," he commenced.

His voice was as feeble as a murmur, and yet it seemed terrible to his hearers.

"You shall see whether I have reckoned and foreseen well. Perhaps, when I was dead, the idea of flying and going abroad would strike you. I shall not permit that. You must stay at Orcival—at Valfeuillu. A friend—not he with the package—is charged, without knowing the reason for it, with the task of watching you. Mark well what I say—if either of you should disappear for eight days, on the ninth, the man who has the package would receive a letter which would cause him to resort at once to the police."

Yes, he had foreseen all, and Trémorel, who had already thought of flight, was overwhelmed.

" I have so arranged, besides, that the idea of flight shall not tempt you too much. It is true I have left all my fortune to Bertha, but I only give her the use of it; the property itself will not be hers until the day after your marriage."

Bertha made a gesture of repugnance which her husband misinterpreted.

" You are thinking of the copy of my will which is in your possession. It is a useless one, and I only added to it some valueless words because I wanted to put your suspicions to sleep. My true will is in the notary's hands, and bears a date two days later. I can read you the rough draft of it."

He took a sheet of paper from a portfolio which was concealed, like the revolver, under the bolster, and read :

" Being stricken with a fatal malady, I here set down freely, and in the fulness of my faculties, my last wishes :

" My dearest wish is that my well-beloved widow, Bertha, should espouse, as soon as the delay enjoined by law has expired, my dear friend, the Count Hector de Trémorel. Having appreciated the grandeur of soul and nobleness of sentiment which belong to my wife and friend, I know that they are worthy of each other, and that each will be happy in the other. I die the more peacefully, as I leave my Bertha to a protector whose——"

It was impossible for Bertha to hear more.

" For pity's sake," cried she, " enough."

" Enough ? Well, let it be so," responded Sauvresy.
" I have read this paper to you to show you that while
I have arranged everything to insure the execution of
my will; I have also done all that can preserve to you
the world's respect. Yes, I wish that you should be
esteemed and honored, for it is you alone upon whom I
rely for my vengeance. I have knit around you a net-
work which you can never burst asunder. You
triumph; my tombstone shall be, as you hoped, the
altar of your nuptials, or else—the galleys."

Trémorel's pride at last revolted against so many
humiliations, so many whip-strokes lashing his face.

" You have only forgotten one thing, Sauvresy; that
a man can die."

" Pardon me," replied the sick man, coldly. " I have
foreseen that also, and was just going to tell you so.
Should one of you die suddenly before the marriage,
the police will be called in."

" You misunderstood me; I meant that a man can
kill himself."

" You kill yourself? Humph! Jenny, who disdains
you almost as much as I do, has told me about your
threats to kill yourself. You! See here; here is my
revolver; shoot yourself, and I will forgive my wife ! "

Hector made a gesture of anger, but did not take the
pistol.

" You see," said Sauvresy, " I knew it well. You are
afraid." Turning to Bertha, he added, " This is your
lover."

Extraordinary situations like this are so unwonted
and strange that the actors in them almost always remain composed and natural, as if stupefied. Bertha,

Hector, and Sauvresy accepted, without taking note of it, the strange position in which they found themselves; and they talked naturally, as if of matters of every-day life, and not of terrible events. But the hours flew, and Sauvresy perceived his life to be ebbing from him.

"There only remains one more act to play," said he. "Hector, go and call the servants, have those who have gone to bed aroused, I want to see them before dying."

Trémorel hesitated.

"Come, go along; or shall I ring, or fire a pistol to bring them here?"

Hector went out; Bertha remained alone with her husband—alone! She had a hope that perhaps she might succeed in making him change his purpose, and that she might obtain his forgiveness. She knelt beside the bed. Never had she been so beautiful, so seductive, so irresistible. The keen emotions of the evening had brought her whole soul into her face, and her lovely eyes supplicated, her breast heaved, her mouth was held out as if for a kiss, and her new-born passion for Sauvresy burst out into delirium.

"Clement," she stammered, in a voice full of tenderness, "my husband, Clement!"

He directed toward her a glance of hatred.

"What do you wish?"

She did not know how to begin—she hesitated, trembled and sobbed.

"Hector would not kill himself," said she, "but I——"

"Well, what do you wish to say? Speak!"

"It was I, a wretch, who have killed you. I will not survive you."

An inexpressible anguish distorted Sauvresy's features. She kill herself! If so, his vengeance was vain;

his own death would then appear only ridiculous and absurd. And he knew that Bertha would not be wanting in courage at the critical moment.

She waited, while he reflected.

" You are free," said he, at last, " this would merely be a sacrifice to Hector. If you died, he would marry Laurence Courtois, and in a year would forget even our name."

Bertha sprang to her feet; she pictured Hector to herself married and happy. A triumphant smile, like a sun's ray, brightened Sauvresy's pale face. He had touched the right chord. He might sleep in peace as to his vengeance. Bertha would live. He knew how hateful to each other were these enemies whom he left linked together.

The servants came in one by one; nearly all of them had been long in Sauvresy's service, and they loved him as a good master. They wept and groaned to see him lying there so pale and haggard, with the stamp of death already on his forehead. Sauvresy spoke to them in a feeble voice, which was occasionally interrupted by distressing hiccoughs. He thanked them, he said, for their attachment and fidelity, and wished to apprise them that he had left each of them a goodly sum in his will. Then turning to Bertha and Hector, he resumed:

" You have witnessed, my people, the care and solicitude with which my bedside has been surrounded by this incomparable friend and my adored Bertha. You have seen their devotion. Alas, I know how keen their sorrow will be! But if they wish to soothe my last moments and give me a happy death, they will assent to the prayer which I earnestly make to them, and will swear to espouse each other after I am gone. Oh, my beloved friends, this seems cruel to you now; but you know not how all human pain is dulled in me. You are young, life has yet much happiness in store for you. I conjure you yield to a dying man's entreaties!"

They approached the bed, and Sauvresy put Bertha's hand into Hector's.

"Do you swear to obey me?" asked he.

They shuddered to hold each other's hands, and seemed near fainting; but they answered, and were heard to murmur:

"We swear it."

The servants retired, grieved at this distressing scene, and Bertha muttered:

"Oh, 'tis infamous, 'tis horrible!"

"Infamous—yes," returned Sauvresy, "but not more so than your caresses, Bertha, or than your hand-pressures, Hector; not more horrible than your plans, than your hopes——"

His voice sank into a rattle. Soon the agony commenced. Horrible convulsions distorted his limbs; twice or thrice he cried out:

"I am cold; I am cold!"

His body was indeed stiff, and nothing could warm it.

Despair filled the house, for a death so sudden was not looked for. The domestics came and went, whispering to each other, "He is going, poor monsieur; poor madame!"

Soon the convulsions ceased. He lay extended on his back, breathing so feebly that twice they thought his breath had ceased forever. At last, a little before ten o'clock, his cheeks suddenly colored and he shuddered. He rose up in bed, his eye staring, his arm stretched out toward the window, and he cried:

"There—behind the curtain—I see them—I see them!"

A last convulsion stretched him again on his pillow. Clement Sauvresy was dead!

XXI

The old justice of the peace ceased reading his voluminous record. His hearers, the detective and the doctor remained silent under the influence of this distressing narrative. M. Plantat had read it impressively, throwing himself into the recital as if he had been personally an actor in the scenes described.

M. Lecoq was the first to recover himself.

"A strange man, Sauvresy," said he.

It was Sauvresy's extraordinary idea of vengeance which struck him in the story. He admired his " good playing " in a drama in which he knew he was going to yield up his life.

"I don't know many people," pursued the detective, " capable of so fearful a firmness. To let himself be poisoned so slowly and gently by his wife! Brrr! It makes a man shiver all over!"

"He knew how to avenge himself," muttered the doctor.

"Yes," answered M. Plantat, "yes, Doctor; he knew how to avenge himself, and more terribly than he supposed, or than you can imagine."

The detective rose from his seat. He had remained motionless, glued to his chair for more than three hours, and his legs were benumbed.

"For my part," said he, " I can very well conceive what an infernal existence the murderers began to suffer the day after their victim's death. You have depicted them, Monsieur Plantat, with the hand of a master. I know them as well after your description as if I had studied them face to face for ten years."

He spoke deliberately, and watched for the effect of what he said in M. Plantat's countenance.

"Where on earth did this old fellow get all these details?" he asked himself. "Did he write this narrative, and if not, who did? How was it, if he had all this information, that he has said nothing?"

M. Plantat appeared to be unconscious of the detective's searching look.

"I know that Sauvresy's body was not cold," said he, "before his murderers began to threaten each other with death."

"Unhappily for them," observed Dr. Gendron, "Sauvresy had foreseen the probability of his widow's using up the rest of the vial of poison."

"Ah, he was shrewd," said M. Lecoq, in a tone of conviction, "very shrewd."

"Bertha could not pardon Hector," continued M. Plantat, "for refusing to take the revolver and blow his brains out; Sauvresy, you see, had foreseen that. Bertha thought that if her lover were dead, her husband would have forgotten all; and it is impossible to tell whether she was mistaken or not."

"And nobody knew anything of this horrible struggle that was going on in the house?"

"No one ever suspected anything."

"It's marvellous!"

"Say, Monsieur Lecoq, that is scarcely credible. Never was dissimulation so crafty, and above all, so wonderfully sustained. If you should question the first person you met in Orcival, he would tell you, as our worthy Courtois this morning told Monsieur Domini, that the count and countess were a model pair and adored each other. Why I, who knew—or suspected, I should say—what had passed, was deceived myself."

Promptly as M. Plantat had corrected himself, his slip of the tongue did not escape M. Lecoq.

" Was it really a slip, or not? " he asked himself.

" These wretches have been terribly punished," pursued M. Plantat, " and it is impossible to pity them ; all would have gone rightly if Sauvresy, intoxicated by his hatred, had not committed a blunder which was almost a crime."

" A crime ! " exclaimed the doctor.

M. Lecoq smiled and muttered in a low tone :

" Laurence."

But low as he had spoken, M. Plantat heard him.

" Yes, Monsieur Lecoq," said he severely.   " Yes, Laurence. Sauvresy did a detestable thing when he thought of making this poor girl the accomplice, or I should say, the instrument of his wrath.   He piteously threw her between these two wretches, without asking himself whether she would be broken.   It was by using Laurence's name that he persuaded Bertha not to kill herself.   Yet he knew of Trémorel's passion for her, he knew her love for him, and he knew that his friend was capable of anything.   He, who had so well foreseen all that could serve his vengeance, did not deign to foresee that Laurence might be dishonored ; and yet he left her disarmed before this most cowardly and infamous of men ! "

The detective reflected.

" There is one thing," said he, " that I can't explain. Why was it that these two, who execrated each other, and whom the implacable will of their victim chained together despite themselves, did not separate of one

accord the day after their marriage, when they had fulfilled the condition which had established their crime?"

The old justice of the peace shook his head.

"I see," he answered, "that I have not yet made you
understand Bertha's resolute character. Hector would
have been delighted with a separation; his wife could
not consent to it. Ah, Sauvresy knew her well! She
saw her life ruined, a horrible remorse lacerated her;
she must have a victim upon whom to expiate her
errors and crimes; this victim was Hector. Ravenous
for her prey, she would not let him go for anything in
the world."

"I' faith," observed Dr. Gendron, "your Trémorel
was a chicken-hearted wretch. What had he to fear
when Sauvresy's manuscript was once destroyed?"

"Who told you it had been destroyed?" interrupted
M. Plantat.

M. Lecoq at this stopped promenading up and down
the room, and sat down opposite M. Plantat.

"The whole case lies there," said he, "whether these
proofs have or have not been destroyed."

M. Plantat did not choose to answer directly.

"Do you know," asked he, "to whom Sauvresy confided them for keeping?"

"Ah," cried the detective, as if a sudden idea had en-
lightened him, "it was you."

He added to himself, "Now, my good man, I begin
to see where all your information comes from."

"Yes, it was I," resumed M. Plantat. "On the day
of the marriage of Madame Sauvresy and Count Hector, in conformity with the last wishes of my dying
friend, I went to Valfeuillu and asked to see Monsieur
and Madame de Trémorel. Although they were full of
company, they received me at once in the little room

on the ground-floor where Sauvresy was murdered. They were both very pale and terribly troubled. They evidently guessed the purpose of my visit, for they lost no time in admitting me to an interview. After saluting them I addressed myself to Bertha, being enjoined to do so by the written instructions I had received; this was another instance of Sauvresy's foresight. 'Madame,' said I, 'I was charged by your late husband to hand to you, on the day of your second marriage, this package, which he confided to my care.' She took the package, in which the bottle and the manuscript were enclosed, with a smiling, even joyous air, thanked me warmly, and went out. The count's expression instantly changed; he appeared very restless and agitated; he seemed to be on coals. I saw well enough that he burned to rush after his wife, but dared not. I was going to retire; but he stopped me. 'Pardon me,' said he, abruptly, 'you will permit me, will you not? I will return immediately,' with which he ran out. When I saw him and his wife a few minutes afterward, they were both very red; their eyes had a strange expression and their voices trembled, as they accompanied me to the door. They had certainly been having a violent altercation."

"The rest may be conjectured," interrupted M. Lecoq. "She had gone to secrete the manuscript in some safe place; and when her new husband asked her to give it up to him, she replied, 'Look for it.'"

"Sauvresy had enjoined on me to give it only into her hands."

"Oh, he knew how to work his revenge. He had it given to his wife so that she might hold a terrible arm against Trémorel, all ready to crush him. If he revolted, she always had this instrument of torture at

18

hand. Ah, the man was a miserable wretch, and she must have made him suffer terribly."

"Yes," said Dr. Gendron, "up to the very day he killed her."

The detective had resumed his promenade up and down the library.

"The question as to the poison," said he, "remains. It is a simple one to resolve, because we've got the man who sold it to her in that closet."

"Besides," returned the doctor, "I can tell something about the poison. This rascal of a Robelot stole it from my laboratory, and I know only too well what it is, even if the symptoms, so well described by our friend Plantat, had not indicated its name to me. I was at work upon aconite when Sauvresy died; and he was poisoned with aconitine."

"Ah, with aconitine," said M. Lecoq, surprised. "It's the first time that I ever met with that poison. Is it a new thing?"

"Not exactly. Medea is said to have extracted her deadliest poisons from aconite, and it was employed in Rome and Greece in criminal executions."

"And I did not know of it! But I have very little time to study. Besides, this poison of Medea's was perhaps lost, as was that of the Borgias; so many of these things are!"

"No, it was not lost, be assured. But we only know of it nowadays by Mathiole's experiments on felons sentenced to death, in the sixteenth century; by Hers, who isolated the active principle, the alkaloid, in 1833, and lastly by certain experiments made by Bouchardat, who pretends——"

Unfortunately, when Dr. Gendron was set agoing on poisons, it was difficult to stop him; but M. Lecoq, on the other hand, never lost sight of the end he had in view.

"Pardon me for interrupting you, Doctor," said he. "But would traces of aconitine be found in a body which had been two years buried? For Monsieur Domini is going to order the exhumation of Sauvresy."

"The tests of aconitine are not sufficiently well known to permit of the isolation of it in a body. Bouchardat tried ioduret of potassium, but his experiment was not successful."

"The deuce!" said M. Lecoq. "That's annoying."

The doctor smiled benignly.

"Reassure yourself," said he. "No such process was in existence—so I invented one."

"Ah," cried Plantat. "Your sensitive paper!"

"Precisely."

"And could you find aconitine in Sauvresy's body?"

"Undoubtedly."

M. Lecoq was radiant, as if he were now certain of fulfilling what had seemed to him a very difficult task.

"Very well," said he. "Our inquest seems to be complete. The history of the victims imparted to us by Monsieur Plantat gives us the key to all the events which have followed the unhappy Sauvresy's death. Thus, the hatred of this pair, who were in appearance so united, is explained; and it is also clear why Hector has ruined a charming young girl with a splendid dowry, instead of making her his wife. There is nothing surprising in Trémorel's casting aside his name and personality to reappear under another guise; he killed his wife because he was constrained to do so by the logic of events. He could not fly while she was alive, and yet he could not continue to live at Valfeuillu. And above all, the paper for which he searched with such desperation, when every moment was an affair of life and death to him, was none other than Sauvresy's manuscript, his condemnation and the proof of his first crime."

M. Lecoq talked eagerly, as if he had a personal animosity against the Count de Trémorel; such was his nature; and he always avowed laughingly that he could not help having a grudge against the criminals whom he pursued. There was an account to settle between him and them; hence the ardor of his pursuit. Perhaps it was a simple matter of instinct with him, like that which impels the hunting hound on the track of his game.

"It is clear enough now," he went on, "that it was Mademoiselle Courtois who put an end to his hesitation and eternal delay. His passion for her, irritated by obstacles, goaded him to delirium. On learning her condition, he lost his head and forgot all prudence and reason. He was wearied, too, of a punishment which began anew each morning; he saw himself lost, and his wife sacrificing herself for the malignant pleasure of sacrificing him. Terrified, he took the resolution to commit this murder."

Many of the circumstances which had established M. Lecoq's conviction had escaped Dr. Gendron.

"What!" cried he, stupefied. "Do you believe in Mademoiselle Laurence's complicity?"

The detective earnestly protested by a gesture.

"No, Doctor, certainly not; heaven forbid that I should have such an idea. Mademoiselle Courtois was and is still ignorant of this crime. But she knew that Trémorel would abandon his wife for her. This flight had been discussed, planned, and agreed upon between them ; they made an appointment to meet at a certain place, on a certain day."

" But this letter," said the doctor.

M. Plantat could scarcely conceal his emotion when Laurence was being talked about.

" This letter," cried he, " which has plunged her family into the deepest grief, and which will perhaps kill poor Courtois, is only one more scene of the infamous drama which the count has planned."

" Oh," said the doctor, " is it possible ? "

" I am firmly of Monsieur Plantat's opinion," said the detective. " Last evening we had the same suspicion at the same moment at the mayor's. I read and re-read her letter, and could have sworn that it did not emanate from herself. The count gave her a rough draft from which she copied it. We mustn't deceive ourselves ; this letter was meditated, pondered on, and composed at leisure. Those were not the expressions of an unhappy young girl of twenty who was going to kill herself to escape dishonor."

" Perhaps you are right," remarked the doctor visibly moved. " But how can you imagine that Trémorel succeeded in persuading her to do this wretched act ? "

" How ? See here, Doctor, I am not much experienced in such things, having seldom had occasion to study the characters of well-brought-up young girls ; yet it seems to me very simple. Mademoiselle Courtois saw the time coming when her disgrace would be public, and so prepared for it, and was even ready to die if necessary."

M. Plantat shuddered ; a conversation which he had had with Laurence occurred to him. She had asked him, he remembered, about certain poisonous plants which he was cultivating, and had been anxious to know how the poisonous juices could be extracted from them.

"Yes," said he, " she has thought of dying."

"Well," resumed the detective, "the count took her in one of the moods when these sad thoughts haunted the poor girl, and was easily able to complete his work of ruin. She undoubtedly told him that she preferred death to shame, and he proved to her that, being in the condition in which she was, she had no right to kill herself. He said that he was very unhappy; and that not being free, he could not repair his fault; but he offered to sacrifice his life for her. What should she do to save both of them? Abandon her parents, make them believe that she had committed suicide, while he, on his side, would desert his house and his wife. Doubtless she resisted for awhile; but she finally consented to everything; she fled, and copied and posted the infamous letter dictated by her lover."

The doctor was convinced.

"Yes," he muttered, " those are doubtless the means he employed."

"But what an idiot he was," resumed M. Lecoq, " not to perceive that the strange coincidence between his disappearance and Laurence's suicide would be remarked! He said to himself, ' Probably people will think that I, as well as my wife, have been murdered; and the law, having its victim in Guespin, will not look for any other.' "

M. Plantat made a gesture of impotent rage.

"Ah," cried he, " and we know not where the wretch has hid himself and Laurence."

The detective took him by the arm and pressed it.

"Reassure yourself," said he, coolly. " We'll find

him, or my name's not Lecoq ; and to be honest, I must say that our task does not seem to me a difficult one."

Several timid knocks at the door interrupted the speaker. It was late, and the household was already awake and about. Mme. Petit in her anxiety and curiosity had put her ear to the key-hole at least ten times, but in vain.

"What can they be' up to in there?" said she to Louis. "Here they've been shut up these twelve hours without eating or drinking. At all events I'll get breakfast."

It was not Mme. Petit, however, who dared to knock on the door, but Louis, the gardener, who came to tell his master of the ravages which had been made in his flower-pots and shrubs. At the same time he brought in certain singular articles which he had picked up on the sward, and which M. Lecoq recognized at once.

"Heavens!" cried he, "I forgot myself. Here I go on quietly talking with my face exposed, as if it was not broad daylight ; and people might come in at any moment!" And turning to Louis, who was very much surprised to see this dark young man whom he had certainly not admitted the night before, he added:

"Give me those little toilet articles, my good fellow ; they belong to me."

Then, by a turn of his hand, he readjusted his physiognomy of last night, while the master of the house went out to give some orders, which M. Lecoq did so deftly, that when M. Plantat returned, he could scarcely believe his eyes.

They sat down to breakfast and ate their meal as silently as they had done the dinner of the evening before, losing no time about it. They appreciated the value of the passing moments ; M. Domini was waiting for them at Corbeil, and was doubtless getting impatient at their delay.

Louis had just placed a sumptuous dish of fruit upon the table, when it occurred to M. Lecoq that Robelot was still shut up in the closet.

" Probably the rascal needs something," said he.

M. Plantat wished to send his servant to him ; but M. Lecoq objected.

" He's a dangerous rogue," said he. " I'll go myself."

He went out, but almost instantly his voice was heard :

" Messieurs ! Messieurs, see here ! "

The doctor and M. Plantat hastened into the library.

Across the threshold of the closet was stretched the body of the bone-setter. He had killed himself.

XXII

Robelot must have had rare presence of mind and courage to kill himself in that obscure closet, without making enough noise to arouse the attention of those in the library. He had wound a string tightly around his neck, and had used a piece of pencil as a twister, and so had strangled himself. He did not, however, betray the hideous look which the popular belief attributes to those who have died by strangulation. His face was pale, his eyes and mouth half open, and he had the appearance of one who has gradually and without much pain lost his consciousness by congestion of the brain.

" Perhaps he is not quite dead yet," said the doctor.

He quickly pulled out his case of instruments and knelt beside the motionless body.

This incident seemed to annoy M. Lecoq very much; just as everything was, as he said, " running on wheels," his principal witness, whom he had caught at the peril of his life, had escaped him. M. Plantat, on the contrary, seemed tolerably well satisfied, as if the death of Robelot furthered projects which he was secretly nourishing, and fulfilled his secret hopes. Besides, it little mattered if the object was to oppose M. Domini's theories and induce him to change his opinion. This corpse had more eloquence in it than the most explicit of confessions.

The doctor, seeing the uselessness of his pains, got up.

" It's all over," said he. " The asphyxia was accomplished in a very few moments."

The bone-setter's body was carefully laid on the floor in the library.

" There is nothing more to be done," said M. Plantat, " but to carry him home; we will follow on so as to seal up his effects, which perhaps contain important papers. Run to the mairie," he added, turning to his servant, " and get a litter and two stout men."

Dr. Gendron's presence being no longer necessary, he promised M. Plantat to rejoin him at Robelot's, and started off to inquire after M. Courtois's condition.

Louis lost no time, and soon reappeared followed not by two, but ten men. The body was placed on a litter and carried away. Robelot occupied a little house of three rooms, where he lived by himself; one of the rooms served as a shop, and was full of plants, dried herbs, grain, and other articles appertaining to his vocation as an herbist. He slept in the back room, which was better furnished than most country rooms. His body was placed upon the bed. Among the men who had brought it was the " drummer of the town," who was at the same time the grave-digger. This man, expert in everything pertaining to funerals, gave all the necessary instructions on the present occasion, himself taking part in the lugubrious task.

Meanwhile M. Plantat examined the furniture, the keys of which had been taken from the deceased's pocket. The value of the property found in the possession of this man, who had, two years before, lived from day to day on what he could pick up, were an overwhelming proof against him in addition to the others already discovered. But M. Plantat looked in vain for any new indications of which he was ignorant. He found deeds of the Morin property and of the Frapesle and Peyron lands ; there were also two bonds, for one hundred and fifty and eight hundred and twenty francs, signed by two Orcival citizens in Robelot's favor. M. Plantat could scarcely conceal his disappointment.

" Nothing of importance," whispered he in M. Lecoq's ear. " How do you explain that ? "

" Perfectly," responded the detective. " He was a sly rogue, this Robelot, and he was cunning enough to conceal his sudden fortune and patient enough to appear to be years accumulating it. You only find in his secretary effects which he thought he could avow without danger. How much is there in all ? "

Plantat rapidly added up the different sums, and said :

" About fourteen thousand five hundred francs."

" Madame Sauvresy gave him more than that," said the detective, positively. " If he had no more than this, he would not have been such a fool as to put it all into land. He must have a hoard of money concealed somewhere."

" Of course he must. But where ? "

" Ah, let me look."

He began to rummage about, peering into every-thing in the room, moving the furniture, sounding the floor with his heels, and rapping on the wall here and there. Finally he came to the fireplace, before which he stopped.

" This is July," said he. " And yet there are cinders here in the fireplace."

" People sometimes neglect to clean them out in the spring."

" True ; but are not these very clean and distinct ? I don't find any of the light dust and soot on them which ought to be there after they have lain several months."

He went into the second room whither he had sent the men after they had completed their task, and said :

" I wish one of you would get me a pickaxe."

All the men rushed out ; M. Lecoq returned to his companion.

" Surely," muttered he, as if apart, " these cinders have been disturbed recently, and if they have been——"

He knelt down, and pushing the cinders away, laid bare the stones of the fireplace. Then taking a thin piece of wood, he easily inserted it into the cracks be-tween the stones.

" See here, Monsieur Plantat," said he. " There is no cement between these stones, and they are movable ; the treasure must be here."

When the pickaxe was brought, he gave a single blow with it ; the stones gaped apart, and betrayed a wide and deep hole between them.

" Ah," cried he, with a triumphant air, " I knew it well enough."

The hole was full of rouleaux of twenty-franc pieces ;

on counting them, M. Lecoq found that there were nineteen thousand five hundred francs.

The old justice's face betrayed an expression of profound grief.

" That," thought he, " is the price of my poor Sauvresy's life."

M. Lecoq found a small piece of paper, covered with figures, deposited with the gold; it seemed to be Robelot's accounts. He had put on the left hand the sum of forty thousand francs; on the right hand, various sums were inscribed, the total of which was twenty-one thousand five hundred francs. It was only too clear; Mme. Sauvresy had paid Robelot forty thousand francs for the bottle of poison. There was nothing more to learn at his house. They locked the money up in the secretary, and affixed seals everywhere, leaving two men on guard.

But M. Lecoq was not quite satisfied yet. What was the manuscript which Plantat had read? At first he had thought that it was simply a copy of the papers confided to him by Sauvresy; but it could not be that; Sauvresy couldn't have thus described the last agonizing scenes of his life. This mystery mightily worried the detective and dampened the joy he felt at having solved the crime at Valfeuillu. He made one more attempt to surprise Plantat into satisfying his curiosity. Taking him by the coat-lapel, he drew him into the embrasure of a window, and with his most innocent air, said:

" I beg your pardon, are we going back to your house ? "

" Why should we ? You know the doctor is going to meet us here."

"I think we may need the papers you read to us, to convince Monsieur Domini."

M. Plantat smiled sadly, and looking steadily at him, replied:

"You are very sly, Monsieur Lecoq; but I too am sly enough to keep the last key of the mystery of which you hold all the others."

"Believe me—" stammered M. Lecoq.

"I believe," interrupted his companion, "that you would like very well to know the source of my information. Your memory is too good for you to forget that when I began last evening I told you that this narrative was for your ear alone, and that I had only one object in disclosing it—to aid our search. Why should you wish the judge of instruction to see these notes, which are purely personal, and have no legal or authentic character?"

He reflected a few moments, and added:

"I have too much confidence in you, Monsieur Lecoq, and esteem you too much, not to have every trust that you will not divulge these strict confidences. What you will say will be of as much weight as anything I might divulge—especially now that you have Robelot's body to back your assertions, as well as the money found in his possession. If Monsieur Domini still hesitates to believe you, you know that the doctor promises to find the poison which killed Sauvresy——"

M. Plantat stopped and hesitated.

"In short," he resumed, "I think you will be able to keep silence as to what you have heard from me."

M. Lecoq took him by the hand, and pressing it significantly, said:

"Count on me, Monsieur."

At this moment Dr. Gendron appeared at the door.

"Courtois is better," said he. "He weeps like a child; but he will come out of it."

"Heaven be praised!" cried the old justice of the peace. "Now, since you've come, let us hurry off to Corbeil; Monsieur Domini, who is waiting for us this morning, must be mad with impatience."

XXIII

M. Plantat, in speaking of M. Domini's impatience, did not exaggerate the truth. That personage was furious; he could not comprehend the reason of the prolonged absence of his three fellow-workers of the previous evening. He had installed himself early in the morning in his cabinet, at the court-house, enveloped in his judicial robe; and he counted the minutes as they passed. His reflections during the night, far from shaking, had only confirmed his opinion. As he receded from the period of the crime, he found it very simple and natural—indeed, the easiest thing in the world to account for. He was annoyed that the rest did not share his convictions, and he awaited their report in a state of irritation which his clerk only too well perceived. He had eaten his breakfast in his cabinet, so as to be sure and be beforehand with M. Lecoq. It was a usless precaution; for the hours passed on and no one arrived.

To kill time, he sent for Guespin and Bertaud and questioned them anew, but learned nothing more than he had extracted from them the night before. One of the prisoners swore by all things sacred that he knew nothing except what he had already told; the other preserved an obstinate and ferocious silence, confining himself to the remark: "I know that I am lost; do with me what you please."

M. Domini was just going to send a mounted gendarme to Orcival to find out the cause of the delay, when those whom he awaited were announced. He quickly gave the order to admit them, and so keen was his curiosity, despite what he called his dignity, that he got up and went forward to meet them.

"How late you are!" said he.

"And yet we haven't lost a minute," replied M. Plantat. "We haven't even been in bed."

"There is news, then? Has the count's body been found?"

"There is much news, Monsieur," said M. Lecoq. "But the count's body has not been found, and I dare even say that it will not be found—for the very simple fact that he has not been killed. The reason is that he was not one of the victims, as at first supposed, but the assassin."

At this distinct declaration on M. Lecoq's part, the judge started in his seat.

"Why, this is folly!" cried he.

M. Lecoq never smiled in a magistrate's presence.

"I do not think so," said he, coolly. "I am persuaded that if Monsieur Domini will grant me his attention for half an hour I will have the honor of persuading him to share my opinion."

M. Domini's slight shrug of the shoulders did not escape the detective, but he calmly continued:

"More; I am sure that Monsieur Domini will not permit me to leave his cabinet without a warrant to arrest Count Hector de Trémorel, whom at present he thinks to be dead."

"Possibly," said M. Domini. "Proceed."

M. Lecoq then rapidly detailed the facts gathered by himself and M. Plantat from the beginning of the inquest. He narrated them not as if he had guessed or been told of them, but in their order of time and in such a manner that each new incident which he mentioned followed naturally from the preceding one. He had completely resumed his character of a retired haberdasher, with a little piping voice, and such obsequious expressions as, " I have the honor," and " If Monsieur the Judge will deign to permit me ; " he resorted to the candy-box with the portrait, and, as the night before at Valfeuillu, chewed a lozenge when he came to the more striking points. M. Domini's surprise increased every minute as he proceeded ; while at times, exclamations of astonishment passed his lips: " Is it possible? " " That is hard to believe ! "

M. Lecoq finished his recital ; he tranquilly munched a lozenge, and added :

" What does Monsieur the Judge of Instruction think now ? "

M. Domini was fain to confess that he was almost satisfied. A man, however, never permits an opinion deliberately and carefully formed to be refuted by one whom he looks on as an inferior, without a secret chagrin. But in this case the evidence was too abundant, and too positive to be resisted.

" I am convinced," said he, " that a crime was committed on Monsieur Sauvresy with the dearly paid assistance of this Robelot. To-morrow I shall give instructions to Doctor Gendron to proceed at once to an exhumation and autopsy of the late master of Valfeuillu."

" And you may be sure that I shall find the poison," chimed in the doctor.

"Very well," resumed M. Domini. "But does it necessarily follow that because Monsieur Trémorel poisoned his friend to marry his widow, he yesterday killed his wife and then fled? I don't think so."

"Pardon me," objected Lecoq, gently. "It seems to me that Mademoiselle Courtois's supposed suicide proves at least something."

"That needs clearing up. This coincidence can only be a matter of pure chance."

"But I am sure that Monsieur Trémorel shaved himself—of that we have proof; then, we did not find the boots which, according to the valet, he put on the morning of the murder."

"Softly, softly," interrupted the judge. "I don't pretend that you are absolutely wrong; it must be as you say; only I give you my objections. Let us admit that Trémorel killed his wife, that he fled and is alive. Does that clear Guespin, and show that he took no part in the murder?"

This was evidently the flaw in Lecoq's case; but being convinced of Hector's guilt, he had given little heed to the poor gardener, thinking that his innocence would appear of itself when the real criminal was arrested. He was about to reply, when footsteps and voices were heard in the corridor.

"Stop," said M. Domini. "Doubtless we shall now hear something important about Guespin."

"Are you expecting some new witness?" asked M. Plantat.

"No; I expect one of the Corbeil police to whom I have given an important mission."

"Regarding Guespin?"

"Yes. Very early this morning a young working-woman of the town, whom Guespin has been courting,

19

brought me an excellent photograph of him. I gave this portrait to the agent with instructions to go to the Vulcan's Forges and ascertain if Guespin had been seen there, and whether he bought anything there night before last."

M. Lecoq was inclined to be jealous; the judge's proceeding ruffled him, and he could not conceal an expressive grimace.

" I am truly grieved," said he, dryly, " that Monsieur the Judge has so little confidence in me that he thinks it necessary to give me assistance."

This sensitiveness aroused M. Domini, who replied:

" Eh! my dear man, you can't be everywhere at once. I think you very shrewd, but you were not here, and I was in a hurry."

" A false step is often irreparable."

" Make yourself easy; I've sent an intelligent man."

At this moment the door opened, and the policeman referred to by the judge appeared on the threshold. He was a muscular man about forty years old, with a military pose, a heavy mustache, and thick brows, meeting over the nose. He had a sly rather than a shrewd expression, so that his appearance alone seemed to awake all sorts of suspicions and put one instinctively on his guard.

" Good news!" said he in a big voice. " I didn't make the journey to Paris for the King of Prussia; we are right on the track of this rogue of a Guespin."

M. Domini encouraged him with an approving gesture.

" See here, Goulard," said he, " let us go on in order if we can. You went then, according to my instructions, to the Vulcan's Forges?"

" At once, Monsieur."

" Precisely. Had they seen the prisoner there ? "

" Yes ; on the evening of Wednesday, July 8th."

" At what hour ? "

" About ten o'clock, a few minutes before they shut up ; so that he was remarked, and the more distinctly observed."

The judge moved his lips as if to make an objection, but was stopped by a gesture from M. Lecoq.

" And who recognized the photograph ? "

" Three of the clerks. Guespin's manner first attracted their attention. It was strange, so they said, and they thought he was drunk, or at least tipsy. Then their recollection was fixed by his talking very fast, saying that he was going to patronize them a great deal, and that if they would make a reduction in their prices he would procure for them the custom of an establishment whose confidence he possessed, the Gentil Jardinier, which bought a great many gardening tools."

M. Domini interrupted the examination to consult some papers which lay before him on his desk. It was, he found, the Gentil Jardinier which had procured Guespin his place in Trémorel's household. The judge remarked this aloud, and added :

" The question of identity seems to be settled. Guespin was undoubtedly at the Vulcan's Forges on Wednesday night."

" So much the better for him," M. Lecoq could not help muttering.

The judge heard him, but though the remark seemed singular to him he did not notice it, and went on questioning the agent.

" Well, did they tell you what Guespin went there to obtain ? "

" The clerks recollected it perfectly. He first bought a hammer, a cold chisel, and a file."

" I knew it," exclaimed the judge. " And then? "

" Then——"

Here the man, ambitious to make a sensation among his hearers, rolled his eyes tragically, and in a dramatic tone, added:

" Then he bought a dirk knife! "

The judge felt that he was triumphing over M. Lecoq.

" Well," said he to the detective in his most ironical tone, " what do you think of your friend now? What do you say to this honest and worthy young man, who, on the very night of the crime, leaves a wedding where he would have had a good time, to go and buy a hammer, a chisel, and a dirk—everything, in short, used in the murder and the mutilation of the body? "

Dr. Gendron seemed a little disconcerted at this, but a sly smile overspread M. Plantat's face. As for M. Lecoq, he had the air of one who is shocked by objections which he knows he ought to annihilate by a word, and yet who is fain to be resigned to waste time in useless talk, which he might put to great profit.

" I think, Monsieur," said he, very humbly, " that the murderers at Valfeuillu did not use either a hammer or a chisel, or a file, and that they brought no instrument at all from outside—since they used a hammer."

" And didn't they have a dirk besides? " asked the judge in a bantering tone, confident that he was on the right path.

" That is another question, I confess; but it is a difficult one to answer."

He began to lose patience. He turned toward the Corbeil policeman, and abruptly asked him:

" Is this all you know? "

The big man with the thick eyebrows superciliously eyed this little Parisian who dared to question him thus. He hesitated so long that M. Lecoq, more rudely than before, repeated his question.

" Yes, that's all," said Goulard at last, " and I think it's sufficient; the judge thinks so too; and he is the only person who gives me orders, and whose approbation I wish for."

M. Lecoq shrugged his shoulders, and proceeded:

" Let's see; did you ask what was the shape of the dirk bought by Guespin? Was it long or short, wide or narrow? "

" Faith, no. What was the use? "

" Simply, my brave fellow, to compare this weapon with the victim's wounds, and to see whether its handle corresponds to that which left a distinct and visible imprint between the victim's shoulders."

" I forgot it; but it is easily remedied."

" An oversight may, of course, be pardoned; but you can at least tell us in what sort of money Guespin paid for his purchases? "

The poor man seemed so embarrassed, humiliated, and vexed, that the judge hastened to his assistance.

" The money is of little consequence, it seems to me," said he.

" I beg you to excuse me if I don't agree with you," returned M. Lecoq. " This matter may be a very grave one. What is the most serious evidence against Guespin? The money found in his pocket. Let us suppose for a moment that night before last, at ten o'clock, he changed a one-thousand-franc note in Paris. Could the obtaining of that note have been the motive of the crime at Valfeuillu? No, for up to that hour the crime had not been committed. Where could it have come from? That is no concern of mine, at present. But if my theory is correct, justice will be forced to agree that the several hundred francs found in Guespin's possession can and must be the change for the note."

"That is only a theory," urged M. Domini in an irritated tone.

"That is true; but one which may turn out a certainty. It remains for me to ask this man how Guespin carried away the articles which he bought? Did he simply slip them into his pocket, or did he have them done up in a bundle, and if so, how?"

The detective spoke in a sharp, hard, freezing tone, with a bitter raillery in it, frightening his Corbeil colleague out of his assurance.

"I don't know," stammered the latter. "They didn't tell me—I thought——"

M. Lecoq raised his hands as if to call the heavens to witness: in his heart, he was charmed with this fine occasion to revenge himself for M. Domini's disdain. He could not, dared not say anything to the judge; but he had the right to banter the agent and visit his wrath upon him.

"Ah so, my lad," said he, "what did you go to Paris for? To show Guespin's picture and detail the crime to the people at Vulcan's Forges? They ought to be very grateful to you; but Madame Petit, Monsieur Plantat's housekeeper, would have done as much."

At this stroke the man began to get angry; he frowned, and in his bluffest tone, began:

"Look here now, you——"

"Ta, ta, ta," interrupted M. Lecoq. "Let me alone, and know who is talking to you. I am Monsieur Lecoq."

The effect of the famous detective's name on his antagonist was magical. He naturally laid down his arms and surrendered, straightway becoming respectful and obsequious. It almost flattered him to be roughly handled by such a celebrity. He muttered, in an abashed and admiring tone:

"What, is it possible? You, Monsieur Lecoq!"

"Yes, it is I, young man; but console yourself; I bear no grudge against you. You don't know your trade, but you have done me a service and you have brought us a convincing proof of Guespin's innocence."

M. Domini looked on at this scene with secret chagrin. His recruit went over to the enemy, yielding without a struggle to a confessed superiority. M. Lecoq's presumption, in speaking of a prisoner's innocence whose guilt seemed to the judge indisputable, exasperated him.

"And what is this tremendous proof, if you please?" asked he.

"It is simple and striking," answered M. Lecoq, putting on his most frivolous air as his conclusions narrowed the field of probabilities.

"You doubtless recollect that when we were at Valfeuillu we found the hands of the clock in the bedroom stopped at twenty minutes past three. Distrusting foul play, I put the striking apparatus in motion—do you recall it? What happened? The clock struck eleven. That convinced us that the crime was committed before that hour. But don't you see that if Guespin was at the Vulcan's Forges at ten he could not have got back to Valfeuillu before midnight? Therefore it was not he who did the deed."

The detective, as he came to this conclusion, pulled out the inevitable box and helped himself to a lozenge, at the same time bestowing upon the judge a smile which said :

" Get out of that, if you can."

The judge's whole theory tumbled to pieces if M. Lecoq's deductions were right ; but he could not admit that he had been so much deceived ; he could not renounce an opinion formed by deliberate reflection.

" I don't pretend that Guespin is the only criminal," said he. " He could only have been an accomplice ; and that he was."

" An accomplice ? No, Judge, he was a victim. Ah, Trémorel is a great rascal ! Don't you see now why he put forward the hands ? At first I didn't perceive the object of advancing the time five hours ; now it is clear. In order to implicate Guespin the crime must appear to have been committed after midnight, and——"

He suddenly checked himself and stopped with open mouth and fixed eyes as a new idea crossed his mind. The judge, who was bending over his papers trying to find something to sustain his position, did not perceive this.

" But then," said the latter, " how do you explain Guespin's refusal to speak and to give an account of where he spent the night ? "

M. Lecoq had now recovered from his emotion, and Dr. Gendron and M. Plantat, who were watching him with the deepest attention, saw a triumphant light in his eyes. Doubtless he had just found a solution of the problem which had been put to him.

" I understand," replied he, " and can explain Guespin's obstinate silence. I should be perfectly amazed if he decided to speak just now."

M. Domini misconstrued the meaning of this ; he thought he saw in it a covert intention to banter him.

" He has had a night to reflect upon it," he answered.
" Is not twelve hours enough to mature a system of
defence ? "

The detective shook his head doubtfully.

" It is certain that he does not need it," said he.
" Our prisoner doesn't trouble himself about a system
of defence, that I'll swear to."

" He keeps quiet, because he hasn't been able to get
up a plausible story."

" No, no ; believe me, he isn't trying to get up one.
In my opinion, Guespin is a victim; that is, I suspect
Trémorel of having set an infamous trap for him, into
which he has fallen, and in which he sees himself so
completely caught that he thinks it useless to struggle.
The poor wretch is convinced that the more he resists
the more surely he will tighten the web that is woven
around him."

" I think so, too," said M. Plantat.

" The true criminal, Count Hector," resumed the
detective, " lost his presence of mind at the last moment, and thus lost all the advantages which his previous caution had gained. Don't let us forget that he
is an able man, perfidious enough to mature the most
infamous stratagems, and unscrupulous enough to execute them. He knows that justice must have its victims, one for every crime ; he does not forget that the
police, as long as it has not the criminal, is always on
the search with eye and ear open ; and he has thrown us
Guespin as a huntsman, closely pressed, throws his
glove to the bear that is close upon him. Perhaps he
thought that the innocent man would not be in danger
of his life ; at all events he hoped to gain time by this
ruse ; while the bear is smelling and turning over the
glove, the huntsman gains ground, escapes and reaches

his place of refuge ; that was what Trémorel proposed to do."

The Corbeil policeman was now undoubtedly Lecoq's most enthusiastic listener. Goulard literally drank in his chief's words. He had never heard any of his colleagues express themselves with such fervor and authority ; he had had no idea of such eloquence, and he stood erect, as if some of the admiration which he saw in all the faces were reflected back on him. He grew in his own esteem as he thought that he was a soldier in an army commanded by such generals. He had no longer any opinion excepting that of his superior. It was not so easy to persuade, subjugate, and convince the judge.

" But," objected the latter, " you saw Guespin's countenance ? "

" Ah, what matters the countenance—what does that prove? Don't we know if you and I were arrested to-morrow on a terrible charge, what our bearing would be ? "

M. Domini gave a significant start ; this hypothesis scarcely pleased him.

" And yet you and I are familiar with the machinery of justice. When I arrested Lanscot, the poor servant in the Rue Marignan, his first words were : ' Come on, my account is good.' The morning that Papa Tabaret and I took the Viscount de Commarin as he was getting out of bed, on the accusation of having murdered the widow Lerouge, he cried : ' I am lost.' Yet neither of them were guilty ; but both of them, the viscount and the valet, equal before the terror of a possible mistake of justice, and running over in their thoughts the charges which would be brought against them, had a moment of overwhelming discouragement."

" But such discouragement does not last two days,"
said M. Domini.

M. Lecoq did not answer this; he went on, growing
more animated as he proceeded.

" You and I have seen enough prisoners to know
how deceitful appearances are, and how little they are to
be trusted. It would be foolish to base a theory upon
a prisoner's bearing. He who talked about ' the cry
of innocence ' was an idiot, just as the man was who
prated about the ' pale stupor ' of guilt. Neither crime
nor virtue have, unhappily, any especial countenance.
The Simon girl, who was accused of having killed her
father, absolutely refused to answer any questions for
twenty-two days; on the twenty-third, the murderer
was caught. As to the Sylvain affair——"

M. Domini rapped lightly on his desk to check the
detective. As a man, the judge held too obstinately
to his opinions; as a magistrate he was equally obstinate, but was at the same time ready to make any
sacrifice of his self-esteem if the voice of duty prompted
it. M. Lecoq's arguments had not shaken his convictions, but they imposed on him the duty of informing
himself at once, and to either conquer the detective or
avow himself conquered.

" You seem to be pleading," said he to M. Lecoq.
" There is no need of that here. We are not counsel
and judge; the same honorable intentions animate us
both. Each, in his sphere, is searching after the truth.
You think you see it shining where I only discern
clouds; and you may be mistaken as well as I."

Then by an act of heroism, he condescended to add:
" What do you think I ought to do? "

The judge was at least rewarded for the effort he
made by approving glances from M. Plantat and the

doctor. But M. Lecoq did not hasten to respond; he had many weighty reasons to advance; that, he saw, was not what was necessary. He ought to present the facts, there and at once, and produce one of those proofs which can be touched with the finger. How should he do it? His active mind searched eagerly for such a proof.

"Well?" insisted M. Domini.

"Ah," cried the detective. "Why can't I ask Guespin two or three questions?"

The judge frowned; the suggestion seemed to him rather presumptuous. It is formally laid down that the questioning of the accused should be done in secret, and by the judge alone, aided by his clerk. On the other hand it is decided, that after he has once been interrogated he may be confronted with witnesses. There are, besides, exceptions in favor of the members of the police force. M. Domini reflected whether there were any precedents to apply to the case.

"I don't know," he answered at last, "to what point the law permits me to consent to what you ask. However, as I am convinced the interests of truth outweigh all rules, I shall take it on myself to let you question Guespin."

He rang; a bailiff appeared.

"Has Guespin been carried back to prison?"

"Not yet, Monsieur."

"So much the better; have him brought in here."

M. Lecoq was beside himself with joy; he had not hoped to achieve such a victory over one so determined as M. Domini.

"He will speak now," said he, so full of confidence that his eyes shone, and he forgot the portrait of the dear defunct, "for I have three means of unloosening his tongue, one of which is sure to succeed. But before he comes I should like to know one thing. Do you know whether Trémorel saw Jenny after Sauvresy's death?"

"Jenny?" asked M. Plantat, a little surprised.

"Yes."

"Certainly he did."

"Several times?"

"Pretty often. After the scene at the Belle Image the poor girl plunged into terrible dissipation. Whether she was smitten with remorse, or understood that it was her conduct which had killed Sauvresy, or suspected the crime, I don't know. She began, however, to drink furiously, falling lower and lower every week——"

"And the count really consented to see her again?"

"He was forced to do so; she tormented him, and he was afraid of her. When she had spent all her money she sent to him for more, and he gave it. Once he refused; and that very evening she went to him the worse for wine, and he had the greatest difficulty in the world to send her away again. In short, she knew what his relations with Madame Sauvresy had been, and she threatened him; it was a regular black-mailing operation. He told me all about the trouble she gave him, and added that he would not be able to get rid of her without shutting her up, which he could not bring himself to do."

"How long ago was their last interview?"

"Why," answered the doctor, "not three weeks ago, when I had a consultation at Melun, I saw the count and this demoiselle at a hotel window; when he saw me he suddenly drew back."

"Then," said the detective, "there is no longer any doubt——"

He stopped. Guespin came in between two gendarmes.

The unhappy gardener had aged twenty years in twenty-four hours. His eyes were haggard, his dry lips were bordered with foam.

"Let us see," said the judge. "Have you changed your mind about speaking?"

The prisoner did not answer.

"Have you decided to tell us about yourself?"

Guespin's rage made him tremble from head to foot, and his eyes became fiery.

"Speak!" said he hoarsely. "Why should I?"

He added with the gesture of a desperate man who abandons himself, renounces all struggling and all hope:

"What have I done to you, my God, that you torture me this way? What do you want me to say? That I did this crime—is that what you want? Well, then—yes—it was I. Now you are satisfied. Now cut my head off, and do it quick—for I don't want to suffer any longer."

A mournful silence welcomed Guespin's declaration. What, he confessed it!

M. Domini had at least the good taste not to exult; he kept still, and yet this avowal surprised him beyond all expression.

M. Lecoq alone, although surprised, was not absolutely put out of countenance. He approached Guespin and tapping him on the shoulder, said in a paternal tone:

"Come, comrade, what you are telling us is absurd. Do you think the judge has any secret grudge against you? No, eh? Do you suppose I am interested to have you guillotined? Not at all. A crime has been committed, and we are trying to find the assassin. If you are innocent, help us to find the man who isn't. What were you doing from Wednesday evening till Thursday morning?"

But Guespin persisted in his ferocious and stupid obstinacy.

"I've said what I have to say," said he.

M. Lecoq changed his tone to one of severity, stepping back to watch the effect he was about to produce upon Guespin.

"You haven't any right to hold your tongue. And even if you do, you fool, the police know everything. Your master sent you on an errand, didn't he, on Wednesday night; what did he give you? A one-thousand-franc note?"

The prisoner looked at M. Lecoq in speechless amazement.

"No," he stammered. "It was a five-hundred-franc note."

The detective, like all great artists in a critical scene, was really moved. His surprising genius for investigation had just inspired him with a bold stroke, which, if it succeeded, would assure him the victory.

"Now," said he, "tell me the woman's name."

"I don't know."

"You are only a fool then. She is short, isn't she, quite pretty, brown and pale, with very large eyes?"

"You know her, then?" said Guespin, in a voice trembling with emotion.

"Yes, comrade, and if you want to know her name, to put in your prayers, she is called—Jenny."

Men who are really able in some specialty, whatever

it may be, never uselessly abuse their superiority; their satisfaction at seeing it recognized is sufficient reward. M. Lecoq softly enjoyed his triumph, while his hearers wondered at his perspicacity. A rapid chain of reasoning had shown him not only Trémorel's thoughts, but also the means he had employed to accomplish his purpose.

Guespin's astonishment soon changed to anger. He asked himself how this man could have been informed of things which he had every reason to believe were secret. Lecoq continued:

" Since I have told you the woman's name, tell me now, how and why the count gave you a five-hundred-franc note."

" It was just as I was going out. The count had no change, and did not want to send me to Orcival for it. I was to bring back the rest."

" And why didn't you rejoin your companions at the wedding in the Batignolles? "

No answer.

" What was the errand which you were to do for the count? "

Guespin hesitated. His eyes wandered from one to another of those present, and he seemed to discover an ironical expression on all the faces. It occurred to him that they were making sport of him, and had set a snare into which he had fallen. A great despair took possession of him.

" Ah," cried he, addressing M. Lecoq, " you have deceived me. You have been lying so as to find out the truth. I have been such a fool as to answer you, and you are going to turn it all against me."

" What? Are you going to talk nonsense again? "

" No, but I see just how it is, and you won't catch me again ! Now I'd rather die than say a word."

The detective tried to reassure him ; but he added :

" Besides, I'm as sly as you ; I've told you nothing but lies."

This sudden whim surprised no one. Some prisoners intrench themselves behind a system of defence, and nothing can divert them from it ; others vary with each new question, denying what they have just affirmed, and constantly inventing some new absurdity which anon they reject again. M. Lecoq tried in vain to draw Guespin from his silence ; M. Domini made the same attempt, and also failed ; to all questions he only answered, " I don't know."

At last the detective waxed impatient.

" See here," said he to Guespin, " I took you for a young man of sense, and you are only an ass. Do you imagine that we don't know anything? Listen : On the night of Madame Denis's wedding, you were getting ready to go off with your comrades, and had just borrowed twenty francs from the valet, when the count called you. He made you promise absolute secrecy (a promise which to do you justice, you kept) ; he told you to leave the other servants at the station and go to Vulcan's Forges, where you were to buy for him a hammer, a file, a chisel, and a dirk ; these you were to carry to a certain woman. Then he gave you this famous five-hundred-franc note, telling you to bring him back the change when you returned next day. Isn't that so ? "

An affirmative response glistened in the prisoner's eyes ; still, he answered, " I don't recollect it."

" Now," pursued M. Lecoq, " I'm going to tell you what happened afterwards. You drank something and

20

got tipsy, and in short spent a part of the change of the
note. That explains your fright when you were seized
yesterday morning, before anybody said a word to
you. You thought you were being arrested for spending that money. Then, when you learned that the count
had been murdered during the night, recollecting that
on the evening before you had bought all kinds of instruments of theft and murder, and that you didn't
know either the address or the name of the woman to
whom you gave up the package, convinced that if you
explained the source of the money found in your
pocket, you would not be believed—then, instead of
thinking of the means to prove your innocence, you became afraid, and thought you would save yourself by
holding your tongue."

The prisoner's countenance visibly changed; his
nerves relaxed; his tight lips fell apart; his mind
opened itself to hope. But he still resisted.

" Do with me as you like," said he.

" Eh ! What should we do with such a fool as you ? "
cried M. Lecoq angrily. " I begin to think you are a
rascal too. A decent fellow would see that we wanted
to get him out of a scrape, and he'd tell us the truth.
You are prolonging your imprisonment by your own
will. You'd better learn that the greatest shrewdness
consists in telling the truth. A last time, will you
answer ? "

Guespin shook his head; no.

" Go back to prison, then, since it pleases you," concluded the detective. He looked at the judge for his
approval, and added:

" Gendarmes, remove the prisoner."

The judge's last doubt was dissipated like the mist
before the sun. He was, to tell the truth, a little un-

easy at having treated the detective so rudely; and he tried to repair it as much as he could.

"You are an able man, Monsieur Lecoq," said he. "Without speaking of your clearsightedness, which is so prompt as to seem almost like second sight, your examination just now was a master-piece of its kind. Receive my congratulations, to say nothing of the reward which I propose to recommend in your favor to your chiefs."

The detective at these compliments cast down his eyes with the abashed air of a virgin. He looked tenderly at the dear defunct's portrait, and doubtless said to it:

"At last, darling, we have defeated him—this austere judge who so heartily detests the force of which we are the brightest ornament, makes his apologies; he recognizes and applauds our services."

He answered aloud:

"I can only accept half of your eulogies, Monsieur; permit me to offer the other half to my friend Monsieur Plantat."

M. Plantat tried to protest.

"Oh," said he, "only for some bits of information! You would have ferreted out the truth without me all the same."

The judge arose and graciously, but not without effort, extended his hand to M. Lecoq, who respectfully pressed it.

"You have spared me," said the judge, "a great remorse. Guespin's innocence would surely sooner or later have been recognized; but the idea of having imprisoned an innocent man and harassed him with my interrogatories, would have disturbed my sleep and tormented my conscience for a long time."

"God knows this poor Guespin is not an interesting youth," returned the detective. "I should be disposed to press him hard were I not certain that he's half a fool."

M. Domini gave a start.

"I shall discharge him this very day," said he, "this very hour."

"It will be an act of charity," said M. Lecoq; "but confound his obstinacy; it was so easy for him to simplify my task. I might be able, by the aid of chance, to collect the principal facts—the errand, and a woman being mixed up in the affair; but as I'm no magician, I couldn't guess all the details. How is Jenny mixed up in this affair? Is she an accomplice, or has she only been made to play an ignorant part in it? Where did she meet Guespin and whither did she lead him? It is clear that she made the poor fellow tipsy so as to prevent his going to the Batignolles. Trémorel must have told her some false story—but what?"

"I don't think Trémorel troubled his head about so small a matter," said M. Plantat. "He gave Guespin and Jenny some task, without explaining it at all."

M. Lecoq reflected a moment.

"Perhaps you are right. But Jenny must have had special orders to prevent Guespin from putting in an alibi."

"But," said M. Domini, "Jenny will explain it all to us."

"That is what I rely on; and I hope that within forty-eight hours I shall have found her and brought her safely to Corbeil."

He rose at these words, took his cane and hat, and turning to the judge, said:

"Before retiring——"

"Yes, I know," interrupted M. Domini, "you want a warrant to arrest Hector de Trémorel."

"I do, as you are now of my opinion that he is still alive."

"I am sure of it."

M. Domini opened his portfolio and wrote off a warrant as follows:

"By the law:

"We, judge of instruction of the first tribunal, etc., considering articles 91 and 94 of the code of criminal instruction, command and ordain to all the agents of the police to arrest, in conformity with the law, one Hector de Trémorel, etc."

When he had finished, he said:

"Here it is, and may you succeed in speedily finding this great criminal."

"Oh, *he'll* find him," cried the Corbeil policeman.

"I hope so, at least. As to how I shall go to work, I don't know yet. I will arrange my plan of battle tonight."

The detective then took leave of M. Domini and retired, followed by M. Plantat. The doctor remained with the judge to make arrangements for Sauvresy's exhumation.

M. Lecoq was just leaving the court-house when he felt himself pulled by the arm. He turned and found that it was Goulard who came to beg his favor and to ask him to take him along, persuaded that after having served under so great a captain he must inevitably become a famous man himself. M. Lecoq had some difficulty in getting rid of him; but he at length found himself alone in the street with the old justice of the peace.

"It is late," said the latter. "Would it be agreeable

to you to partake of another modest dinner with me, and accept my cordial hospitality? "

" I am chagrined to be obliged to refuse you," replied M. Lecoq. " But I ought to be in Paris this evening."

" But I—in fact, I—was very anxious to talk to you —about——"

" About Mademoiselle Laurence? "

" Yes ; I have a plan, and if you would help me——"

M. Lecoq affectionately pressed his friend's hand.

" I have only known you a few hours," said he, " and yet I am as devoted to you as I would be to an old friend. All that is humanly possible for me to do to serve you, I shall certainly do."

" But where shall I see you? They expect me to-day at Orcival."

" Very well ; to-morrow morning at nine, at my rooms, No — Rue Montmartre."

" A thousand thanks ; I shall be there."

When they had reached the Belle Image they separated.

XXIV

Nine o'clock had just struck in the belfry of the church of St. Eustache, when M. Plantat reached Rue Montmartre, and entered the house bearing the number which M. Lecoq had given him.

" Monsieur Lecoq? " said he to an old woman who was engaged in getting breakfast for three large cats which were mewing around her. The woman scanned him with a surprised and suspicious air. M. Plantat, when he was dressed up, had much more the appearance of a fine old gentleman than of a country attorney ; and though the detective received many visits from all

Nine o'clock had just struck in the belfry of the church of St.
Eustache when M. Plantat reached the Rue Montmartre.

sorts of people, it was rarely that the denizens of the
Faubourg Saint Germaine rung his bell.

"Monsieur Lecoq's apartments," answered the old
woman, "are on the third story, the door facing the
stairs."

The justice of the peace slowly ascended the narrow,
ill-lighted staircase, which in its dark corners was almost dangerous. He was thinking of the strange step
he was about to take. An idea had occurred to him,
but he did not know whether it were practicable, and
at all events he needed the aid and advice of the detective. He was forced to disclose his most secret
thoughts, as it were, to confess himself; and his heart
beat fast. The door opposite the staircase on the third
story was not like other doors; it was of plain oak,
thick, without mouldings, and fastened with iron bars.
It would have looked like a prison door had not its
sombreness been lightened by a heavily colored en-
graving of a cock crowing, with the legend "Always
Vigilant." Had the detective put his coat of arms up
there? Was it not more likely that one of his men had
done it? After examining the door more than a minute, and hesitating like a youth before his beloved's
gate, he rang the bell. A creaking of locks responded,
and through the narrow bars of the peephole he saw
the hairy face of an old crone.

"What do you want?" said the woman, in a deep,
bass voice.

"Monsieur Lecoq."

"What do you want of him?"

"He made an appointment with me for this morning."

"Your name and business?"

"Monsieur Plantat, justice of the peace at Orcival."

" All right. Wait."

The peephole was closed and the old man waited.

" Peste! " growled he. " Everybody can't get in
here, it seems." Hardly had this reflection passed
through his mind when the door opened with a noise as
of chains and locks. He entered, and the old crone,
after leading him through a dining-room whose sole
furniture was a table and six chairs, introduced him
to a large room, half toilet-room and half working-
room, lighted by two windows looking on the court,
and guarded by strong, close bars.

" If you will take the trouble to sit," said the servant, " Monsieur Lecoq will soon be here ; he is giving
orders to one of his men."

But M. Plantat did not take a seat ; he preferred to
examine the curious apartment in which he found himself. The whole of one side of the wall was taken up
with a long rack, where hung the strangest and most in-
congruous suits of clothes. There were costumes belonging to all grades of society ; and on some wooden
pegs above, wigs of all colors were hanging ; while
boots and shoes of various styles were ranged on the
floor. A toilet-table, covered with powders, essences,
and paints, stood between the fireplace and the window.
On the other side of the room was a bookcase full of
scientific works, especially of physic and chemistry.
The most singular piece of furniture in the apartment,
however, was a large ball, shaped like a lozenge, in
black velvet, suspended beside the looking-glass. A
quantity of pins were stuck in this ball, so as to form
the letters composing these two names: HECTOR—
JENNY.

These names glittering on the black background attracted the old man's attention at once. This must

have been M. Lecoq's reminder. The ball was meant
to recall to him perpetually the people of whom he was
in pursuit. Many names, doubtless, had in turn glittered on that velvet, for it was much frayed and perfor-
ated. An unfinished letter lay open upon the bureau;
M. Plantat leaned over to read it; but he took his
trouble for nothing, for it was written in cipher.

He had no sooner finished his inspection of the room
than the noise of a door opening made him turn round.
He saw before him a man of his own age, of respectable
mien, and polite manners, a little bald, with gold spectacles and a light-colored flannel dressing-gown.

M. Plantat bowed, saying:

" I am waiting here for Monsieur Lecoq——"

The man in gold spectacles burst out laughing, and
clapped his hands with glee.

"What, dear sir," said he, "don't you know me?
Look at me well—it is I—Monsieur Lecoq!" And to
convince him, he took off his spectacles. Those might,
indeed, be Lecoq's eyes, and that his voice; M. Plantat
was confounded.

" I never should have recognized you," said he.

" It's true, I have changed a little—but what would
you have? It's my trade."

And pushing a chair toward his visitor, he pursued:

" I have to beg a thousand pardons for the formali-
ties you've had to endure to get in here; it's a dire
necessity, but one I can't help. I have told you of the
dangers to which I am exposed; they pursue me to my
very door. Why, last week a railway porter brought a
package here addressed to me. Janouille—that's my
old woman—suspected nothing, though she has a sharp
nose, and told him to come in. He held out the package, I went up to take it, when pif! paf! off went two

pistol-shots. The package was a revolver wrapped up in oilcloth, and the porter was a convict escaped from Cayenne, caught by me last year. Ah, I put him through for this though!"

He told this adventure carelessly, as if it were the most natural thing in the world.

" But let's not starve ourselves to death," he continued, ringing the bell. The old hag appeared, and he ordered her to bring on breakfast forthwith, and above all, some good wine.

" You are observing my Janouille," remarked he, seeing that M. Plantat looked curiously at the servant. " She's a pearl, my dear friend, who watches over me as if I were her child, and would go through the fire for me. I had a good deal of trouble the other day to prevent her strangling the false railway porter. I picked her out of three or four thousand convicts. She had been convicted of infanticide and arson. I would bet a hundred to one that, during the three years that she has been in my service, she has not even thought of robbing me of so much as a centime."

But M. Plantat only listened to him with one ear; he was trying to find an excuse for cutting Janouille's story short, and to lead the conversation to the events of the day before.

" I have, perhaps, incommoded you a little this morning, Monsieur Lecoq?"

" Me? then you did not see my motto—'always vigilant?' Why, I've been out ten times this morning, besides marking out work for three of my men. Ah, we have little time to ourselves, I can tell you. I went to the Vulcan's Forges to see what news I could get of that poor devil of a Guespin."

" And what did you hear?"

"That I had guessed right. He changed a five-hundred-franc note there last Wednesday evening at a quarter before ten."

"That is to say, he is saved?"

"Well, you may say so. He will be, as soon as we have found Miss Jenny."

The old justice of the peace could not avoid showing his uneasiness.

"That will, perhaps, be long and difficult?"

"Bast! Why so? She is on my black ball there—we shall have her, accidents excepted, before night."

"You really think so?"

"I should say I was sure, to anybody but you. Reflect that this girl has been connected with the Count de Trémorel, a man of the world, a prince of the mode. When a girl falls to the gutter, after having, as they say, dazzled all Paris for six months with her luxury, she does not disappear entirely, like a stone in the mud. When she has lost all her friends there are still her creditors, who follow and watch her, awaiting the day when fortune will smile on her once more. She doesn't trouble herself about them, she thinks they've forgotten her; a mistake! I know a milliner whose head is a perfect dictionary of the fashionable world; she has often done me a good turn. We will go and see her if you say so, after breakfast, and in two hours she will give us Jenny's address. Ah, if I were only as sure of pinching Trémorel!"

M. Plantat gave a sigh of relief. The conversation at last took the turn he wished.

"You are thinking of him, then?" asked he.

"Am I?" shouted M. Lecoq, who started from his seat at the question. "Now just look at my black ball there. I haven't thought of anybody else, mark you, since yesterday; I haven't had a wink of sleep all night for thinking of him. I must have him, and I will!"

" I don't doubt it; but when?"

" Ah, there it is! Perhaps to-morrow, perhaps in a month; it depends on the correctness of my calculations and the exactness of my plan."

" What, is your plan made?"

" And decided on."

M. Plantat became attention itself.

" I start from the principle that it is impossible for a man, accompanied by a woman, to hide from the police. In this case, the woman is young, pretty, and in a noticeable condition; three impossibilities more. Admit this, and we'll study Hector's character. He isn't a man of superior shrewdness, for we have found out all his dodges. He isn't a fool, because his dodges deceived people who are by no means fools. He is then a medium sort of a man, and his education, reading, relations, and daily conversation have procured him a number of acquaintances whom he will try to use. Now for his mind. We know the weakness of his char- acter; soft, feeble, vacillating, only acting in the last ex- tremity. We have seen him shrinking from decisive steps, trying always to delay matters. He is given to being deceived by illusions, and to taking his desires for accomplished events. In short, he is a coward. And what is his situation? He has killed his wife, he hopes he has created a belief in his own death, he has eloped with a young girl, and he has got nearly or quite a mill- ion of francs in his pocket. Now, this position admit- ted, as well as the man's character and mind, can we by an effort of thought, reasoning from his known actions, discover what he has done in such and such a case? I think so, and I hope I shall prove it to you."

M. Lecoq rose and promenaded, as his habit was, up and down the room. " Now let's see," he continued, " how I ought to proceed in order to discover the probable conduct of a man whose antecedents, traits, and mind are known to me. To begin with, I throw off my own ·individuality and try to assume his. I substitute his will for my own. I cease to be a detective and become this man, whatever he is. In this case, for instance, I know very well what I should do if I were Trémorel. I should take such measures as would throw all the detectives in the universe off the scent. But I must forget Monsieur Lecoq in order to become Hector de Trémorel. How would a man reason who was base enough to rob his friend of his wife, and then see her poison her husband before his very eyes? We already know that Trémorel hesitated a good while before deciding to commit this crime. The logic of events, which fools call fatality, urged him on. It is certain that he looked upon the murder in every point of view, studied its results, and tried to find means to escape from justice. All his acts were determined on long beforehand, and neither immediate necessity nor unforeseen circumstances disturbed his mind. The moment he had decided on the crime, he said to himself : ' Grant that Bertha has been murdered ; thanks to my precautions, they think that I have been killed too ; Laurence, with whom I elope, writes a letter in which she announces her suicide ; I have money, what must I do? ' The problem, it seems to me, is fairly put in this way."

" Perfectly so," approved M. Plantat.

" Naturally, Trémorel would choose from among all the methods of flight of which he had ever heard, or which he could imagine, that which seemed to him the surest and most prompt. Did he meditate leaving the country? That is more than probable. Only, as he was not quite out of his senses, he saw that it was most difficult, in a foreign country, to put justice off the track. If a man flies from France to escape punishment, he acts absurdly. Fancy a man and woman wandering about a country of whose language they are ignorant; they attract attention at once, are observed, talked about, followed. They do not make a purchase which is not remarked; they cannot make any movement without exciting curiosity. The further they go the greater their danger. If they choose to cross the ocean and go to free America, they must go aboard a vessel; and the moment they do that they may be considered as good as lost. You might bet twenty to one they would find, on landing on the other side, a detective on the pier armed with a warrant to arrest them. I would engage to find a Frenchman in eight days, even in London, unless he spoke pure enough English to pass for a citizen of the United Kingdom. Such were Trémorel's reflections. He recollected a thousand futile attempts, a hundred surprising adventures, narrated by the papers; and it is certain that he gave up the idea of going abroad."

"It's clear," cried M. Plantat, " perfectly plain and precise. We must look for the fugitives in France."

"Yes," replied M. Lecoq. "Now let's find out where and how people can hide themselves in France. Would it be in the provinces? Evidently not. In Bordeaux, one of our largest cities, people stare at a man who is not a Bordelais. The shopkeepers on the quays say to their neighbors: 'Eh! do you know that man?' There are two cities, however, where a man may pass unnoticed—Marseilles and Lyons; but both of these are distant, and to reach them a long journey must be risked—and nothing is so dangerous as the railway since the telegraph was established.   One can fly quickly, it's true; but on entering a railway carriage a man shuts himself in, and until he gets out of it he remains under the thumb of the police.   Trémorel knows all this as well as we do.   We will put all the large towns, including Lyons and Marseilles, out of the question."

"In short, it's impossible to hide in the provinces."

"Excuse me—there is one means; that is, simply to buy a modest little place at a distance from towns and railways, and to go and reside on it under a false name. But this excellent project is quite above Trémorel's capacity, and requires preparatory steps which he could not risk, watched as he was by his wife.   The field of investigation is thus much narrowed.   Putting aside foreign parts, the provinces, the cities, the country, Paris remains.   It is in Paris that we must look for Trémorel."

M. Lecoq spoke with the certainty and positiveness of a mathematical professor; the old justice of the peace listened, as do the professor's scholars.   But he was already accustomed to the detective's surprising clearness, and was no longer astonished.   During the four-and-twenty hours that he had been witnessing M. Lecoq's calculations and gropings, he had seized the process and almost appropriated it to himself.   He found this method of reasoning very simple, and could now explain to himself certain exploits of the police which had hitherto seemed to him miraculous.   But M. Lecoq's " narrow field " of observation appeared still immense.

"Paris is a large place," observed the old justice.

M. Lecoq smiled loftily.

" Perhaps so; but it is mine. All Paris is under the eye of the police, just as an ant is under that of the naturalist with his microscope. How is it, you may ask, that Paris still holds so many professional rogues? Ah, that is because we are hampered by legal forms. The law compels us to use only polite weapons against those to whom all weapons are serviceable. The courts tie our hands. The rogues are clever, but be sure that our cleverness is much greater than theirs."

" But," interrupted M. Plantat, " Trémorel is now outside the law; we have the warrant."

" What matters it? Does the warrant give me the right to search any house in which I may have reason to suppose he is hiding himself? No. If I should go to the house of one of Hector's old friends he would kick me out of doors. You must know that in France the police have to contend not only with the rogues, but also with the honest people."

M. Lecoq always waxed warm on this subject; he felt a strong resentment against the injustice prac-tised on his profession. Fortunately, at the moment when he was most excited, the black ball suddenly caught his eye.

" The devil! " exclaimed he, " I was forgetting Hec-tor."

M. Plantat, though listening patiently to his com-panion's indignant utterances, could not help thinking of the murderer.

" You said that we must look for Trémorel in Paris," he remarked.

" And I said truly," responded M. Lecoq in a calmer tone. " I have come to the conclusion that here, per-haps within two streets of us, perhaps in the next house, the fugitives are hid. But let's go on with our calculation of probabilities. Hector knows Paris too well to hope to conceal himself even for a week in a hotel or lodging-house; he knows these are too sharply watched by the police. He had plenty of time before him, and so arranged to hire apartments in some convenient house."

"He came to Paris three or four times some weeks ago."

"Then there's no longer any doubt about it. He hired some apartments under a false name, paid in advance, and to-day he is comfortably ensconced in his new residence."

M. Plantat seemed to feel extremely distressed at this.

"I know it only too well, Monsieur Lecoq," said he, sadly. "You must be right. But is not the wretch thus securely hidden from us? Must we wait till some accident reveals him to us? Can you search one by one all the houses in Paris?"

The detective's nose wriggled under his gold spectacles, and the justice of the peace, who observed it, and took it for a good sign, felt all his hopes reviving in him.

"I've cudgelled my brain in vain—" he began.

"Pardon me," interrupted M. Lecoq. "Having hired apartments, Trémorel naturally set about furnishing them."

"Evidently."

"Of course he would furnish them sumptuously, both because he is fond of luxury and has plenty of money, and because he couldn't carry a young girl from a luxurious home to a garret. I'd wager that they have as fine a drawing-room as that at Valfeuillu."

21

" Alas ! How can that help us ? "

" Peste ! It helps us much, my dear friend, as you shall see. Hector, as he wished for a good deal of expensive furniture, did not have recourse to a broker; nor had he time to go to the Faubourg St. Antoine. Therefore, he simply went to an upholsterer."

" Some fashionable upholsterer——"

" No, he would have risked being recognized. It is clear that he assumed a false name, the same in which he had hired his rooms. He chose some shrewd and humble upholsterer, ordered his goods, made sure that they would be delivered on a certain day, and paid for them."

M. Plantat could not repress a joyful exclamation; he began to see M. Lecoq's drift.

" This merchant," pursued the latter, " must have retained his rich customer in his memory, this customer who did not beat him down, and paid cash. If he saw him again, he would recognize him."

" What an idea ! " cried M. Plantat, delighted. " Let's get photographs and portraits of Trémorel as quick as we can—let's send a man to Orcival for them."

M. Lecoq smiled shrewdly and proceeded:

" Keep yourself easy; I have done what was necessary. I slipped three of the count's cartes-de-visite in my pocket yesterday during the inquest. This morning I took down, out of the directory, the names of all the upholsterers in Paris, and made three lists of them. At this moment three of my men, each with a list and a photograph, are going from upholsterer to upholsterer showing them the picture and asking them if they recognize it as the portrait of one of their customers. If one of them answers ' yes,' we've got our man."

"And we will get him!" cried the old man, pale with emotion.

"Not yet; don't shout victory too soon. It is possible that Hector was prudent enough not to go to the upholsterer's himself. In this case we are beaten in that direction. But no, he was not so sly as that——"

M. Lecoq checked himself. Janouille, for the third time, opened the door, and said, in a deep bass voice:

"Breakfast is ready."

Janouille was a remarkable cook; M. Plantat had ample experience of the fact when he began upon her dishes. But he was not hungry, and could not force himself to eat; he could not think of anything but a plan which he had to propose to his host, and he had that oppressive feeling which is experienced when one is about to do something which has been decided on with hesitation and regret. The detective, who, like all men of great activity, was a great eater, vainly essayed to entertain his guest, and filled his glass with the choicest Château Margaux; the old man sat silent and sad, and only responded by monosyllables. He tried to speak out and to struggle against the hesitation he felt. He did not think, when he came, that he should have this reluctance; he had said to himself that he would go in and explain himself. Did he fear to be ridiculed? No. His passion was above the fear of sarcasm or irony. And what did he risk? Nothing. Had not M. Lecoq already divined the secret thoughts he dared not impart to him, and read his heart from the first? He was reflecting thus when the door-bell rang. Janouille went to the door, and speedily returned with the announcement that Goulard begged to speak with M. Lecoq, and asked if she should admit him.

" Certainly."

The chains clanked and the locks scraped, and presently Goulard made his appearance. He had donned his
best clothes, with spotless linen, and a very high collar. He was respectful, and stood as stiffly as a well-
drilled grenadier before his sergeant.

" What the deuce brought you here? " said M.
Lecoq, sternly. " And who dared to give you my address? "

" Monsieur," said Goulard, visibly intimidated by
his reception, " please excuse me; I was sent by Doctor
Gendron with this letter for Monsieur Plantat."

" Oh," cried M. Plantat, " I asked the doctor, last
evening, to let me know the result of the autopsy, and
not knowing where I should put up, took the liberty of
giving your address."

M. Lecoq took the letter and handed it to his guest.

" Read it, read it," said the latter. " There is nothing in it to conceal."

" All right; but come into the other room. Janouille,
give this man some breakfast. Make yourself at home,
Goulard, and empty a bottle to my health."

When the door of the other room was closed, M.
Lecoq broke the seal of the letter, and read:

" MY DEAR PLANTAT:

" You asked me for a word, so I scratch off a line or
two which I shall send to our sorcerer's——"

" Oh, ho," cried M. Lecoq. " Monsieur Gendron is
too good, too flattering, really! "

No matter, the compliment touched his heart. He
resumed the letter:

" At three this morning we exhumed poor Sauvresy's body. I certainly deplore the frightful circum-

stances of this worthy man's death as much as anyone; but on the other hand, I cannot help rejoicing at this excellent opportunity to test the efficacy of my sensitive paper——"

"Confound these men of science," cried the indignant Plantat. "They are all alike!"

"Why so? I can very well comprehend the doctor's involuntary sensations. Am I not ravished when I encounter a fine crime?"

And without waiting for his guest's reply, he continued reading the letter:

"The experiments promised to be all the more conclusive as aconitine is one of those drugs which conceal themselves most obstinately from analysis. I proceed thus: After heating the suspected substances in twice their weight of alcohol, I drop the liquid gently into a vase with edges a little elevated, at the bottom of which is a piece of paper on which I have placed my tests. If my paper retains its color, there is no poison; if it changes, the poison is there. In this case my paper was of a light yellow color, and if we were not mistaken, it ought either to become covered with brown spots, or completely brown. I explained this experiment beforehand to the judge of instruction and the experts who were assisting me. Ah, my friend, what a success I had! When the first drops of alcohol fell, the paper at once became a dark brown; your suspicions are thus proved to be quite correct. The substances which I submitted to the test were liberally saturated with aconitine. I never obtained more decisive results in my laboratory. I expect that my conclusions will be disputed in court; but I have means of verifying them, so that I shall surely confound all the chemists who oppose me. I think, my dear friend, that you will not be indifferent to the satisfaction I feel——"

M. Plantat lost patience.

"This is unheard-of!" cried he. "Incredible! Would you say, now, that this poison which he found in Sauvresy's body was stolen from his own laboratory? Why, that body is nothing more to him than 'suspected matter!' And he already imagines himself discussing the merits of his sensitive paper in court!"

"He has reason to look for antagonists in court."

"And meanwhile he makes his experiments, and analyzes with the coolest blood in the world; he continues his abominable cooking, boiling and filtering, and preparing his arguments——!"

M. Lecoq did not share in his friend's indignation; he was not sorry at the prospect of a bitter struggle in court, and he imagined a great scientific duel, like that between Orfila and Raspail, the provincial and Parisian chemists.

"If Trémorel has the face to deny his part in Sauvresy's murder," said he, "we shall have a superb trial of it."

This word "trial" put an end to M. Plantat's long hesitation.

"We mustn't have any trial," cried he.

The old man's violence, from one who was usually so calm and self-possessed, seemed to amaze M. Lecoq.

"Ah ha," thought he, "I'm going to know all." He added aloud:

"What, no trial?"

M. Plantat had turned whiter than a sheet; he was trembling, and his voice was hoarse, as if broken by sobs.

"I would give my fortune," resumed he, "to avoid

a trial—every centime of it, though it doesn't amount
to much. But how can we secure this wretch Trémorel
from a conviction? What subterfuge shall we invent?
You alone, my friend, can advise me in the frightful
extremity to which you see me reduced, and aid me to
accomplish what I wish. If there is any way in the
world, you will find it and save me——"

"But, my——"

"Pardon—hear me, and you will comprehend me.
I am going to be frank with you, as I would be with
myself; and you will see the reason of my hesitation,
my silence, in short, of all my conduct since the discovery of the crime."

"I am listening."

"It's a sad history, Lecoq. I had reached an age at
which a man's career is, as they say, finished, when I
suddenly lost my wife and my two sons, my whole joy,
my whole hope in this world. I found myself alone in
life, more lost than the shipwrecked man in the midst
of the sea, without a plank to sustain me. I was a soul-
less body, when chance brought me to settle down at
Orcival. There I saw Laurence; she was just fifteen,
and never lived there a creature who united in herself
so much intelligence, grace, innocence, and beauty.
Courtois became my friend, and soon Laurence was
like a daughter to me. I doubtless loved her then, but
I did not confess it to myself, for I did not read my
heart clearly. She was so young, and I had gray hairs!
I persuaded myself that my love for her was like that
of a father, and it was as a father that she cherished
me. Ah, I passed many a delicious hour listening to
her gentle prattle and her innocent confidences; I was
happy when I saw her skipping about in my garden,
picking the roses I had reared for her, and laying waste

my parterres; and I said to myself that existence is a precious gift from God. My dream then was to follow her through life. I fancied her wedded to some good man who made her happy, while I remained the friend of the wife, after having been the confidant of the maiden. I took good care of my fortune, which is considerable, because I thought of her children, and wished to hoard up treasures for them. Poor, poor Laurence!"

M. Lecoq fidgeted in his chair, rubbed his face with his handkerchief, and seemed ill at ease. He was really much more touched than he wished to appear.

"One day," pursued the old man, "my friend Courtois spoke to me of her marriage with Trémorel; then I measured the depth of my love. I felt terrible agonies which it is impossible to describe; it was like a long-smothered fire which suddenly breaks forth and devours everything. To be old, and to love a child! I thought I was going crazy; I tried to reason, to upbraid myself, but it was of no avail. What can reason or irony do against passion? I kept silent and suffered. To crown all, Laurence selected me as her confidant—what torture! She came to me to talk of Hector; she admired in him all that seemed to her superior to other men, so that none could be compared with him. She was enchanted with his bold horseback riding, and thought everything he said sublime."

"Did you know what a wretch Trémorel was?"

"Alas, I did not yet know it. What was this man who lived at Valfeuillu to me? But from the day that I learned that he was going to deprive me of my most precious treasure, I began to study him. I should have been somewhat consoled if I had found him worthy of her; so I dogged him, as you, Monsieur Lecoq, cling to

the criminal whom you are pursuing. I went often to
Paris to learn what I could of his past life; I became
a detective, and went about questioning everybody who
had known him, and the more I heard of him the more
I despised him. It was thus that I found out his in-
terviews with Jenny and his relations with Bertha."

"Why didn't you divulge them?"

"Honor commanded silence. Had I a right to dishonor my friend and ruin his happiness and life, because of this ridiculous, hopeless love? I kept my own
counsel after speaking to Courtois about Jenny, at
which he only laughed. When I hinted something
against Hector to Laurence, she almost ceased coming
to see me."

"Ah! I shouldn't have had either your patience or
your generosity."

"Because you are not as old as I, Monsieur Lecoq.
Oh, I cruelly hated this Trémorel! I said to myself,
when I saw three women of such different characters
smitten with him, 'what is there in him to be so
loved?'"

"Yes," answered M. Lecoq, responding to a secret
thought, "women often err; they don't judge men as
we do."

"Many a time," resumed the justice of the peace,
"I thought of provoking him to fight with me, that I
might kill him; but then Laurence would not have
looked at me any more. However, I should perhaps
have spoken at last, had not Sauvresy fallen ill and
died. I knew that he had made his wife and Trémorel
swear to marry each other; I knew that a terrible reason forced them to keep their oath; and I thought Laurence saved. Alas, on the contrary she was lost! One
evening, as I was passing the mayor's house, I saw a

man getting over the wall into the garden ; it was Trémorel. I recognized him perfectly. I was beside myself with rage, and swore that I would wait and murder him. I did wait, but he did not come out that
night."

M. Plantat hid his face in his hands ; his heart bled
at the recollection of that night of anguish, the whole
of which he had passed in waiting for a man in order
to kill him. M. Lecoq trembled with indignation.

" This Trémorel," cried he, " is the most abominable
of scoundrels. There is no excuse for his infamies and
crimes. And yet you want to save him from trial, the
galleys, the scaffold which await him."

The old man paused a moment before replying. Of
the thoughts which now crowded tumultuously in his
mind, he did not know which to utter first. Words
seemed powerless to betray his sensations ; he wanted
to express all that he felt in a single sentence.

" What matters Trémorel to me ? " said he at last.
" Do you think I care about him ? I don't care whether
he lives or dies, whether he succeeds in flying or ends
his life some morning in the Place Roquette."

" Then why have you such a horror of a trial ? "

" Because——"

" Are you a friend to his family, and anxious to preserve the great name which he has covered with mud
and devoted to infamy ? "

" No, but I am anxious for Laurence, my friend ; the
thought of *her* never leaves me."

" But she is not his accomplice ; she is totally ignorant—there's no doubt of it—that he has killed his
wife."

" Yes," resumed .M. Plantat, " Laurence is innocent ; she is only the victim of an odious villain. It is

none the less true, though, that she would be more cruelly punished than he. If Trémorel is brought before the court, she will have to appear too, as a witness, if not as a prisoner. And who knows that her truth will not be suspected? She will be asked whether she really had no knowledge of the project to murder Bertha, and whether she did not encourage it. Bertha was her rival; it were natural to suppose that she hated her. If I were the judge I should not hesitate to include Laurence in the indictment."

"With our aid she will prove victoriously that she was ignorant of all, and has been outrageously deceived."

"May be; but will she be any the less dishonored and forever lost? Must she not, in that case, appear in public, answer the judge's questions, and narrate the story of her shame and misfortunes? Must not she say where, when, and how she fell, and repeat the villain's words to her? Can you imagine that of her own free will she compelled herself to announce her suicide at the risk of killing her parents with grief? No. Then she must explain what menaces forced her to do this, which surely was not her own idea. And worse than all, she will be compelled to confess her love for Trémorel."

"No," answered the detective. "Let us not exaggerate anything. You know as well as I do that justice is most considerate with the innocent victims of affairs of this sort."

"Consideration? Eh! Could justice protect her, even if it would, from the publicity in which trials are conducted? You might touch the magistrates' hearts; but there are fifty journalists who, since this crime, have been cutting their pens and getting their paper ready. Do you think that, to please us, they would suppress the scandalous proceedings which I am anxious to avoid, and which the noble name of the murderer would make a great sensation? Does not this case unite every feature which gives success to judicial dramas? Oh, there's nothing wanting, neither unworthy passion, nor poison, nor vengeance, nor murder. Laurence represents in it the romantic and sentimental element; she—my darling girl—will become a heroine of the assizes; it is she who will attract the readers of the *Police Gazette;* the reporters will tell when she blushes and when she weeps; they will rival each other in describing her toilet and bearing. Then there will be the photographers besieging her, and if she refuses to sit, portraits of some hussy of the street will be sold as hers. She will yearn to hide herself—but where? Can a few locks and bars shelter her from eager curiosity? She will become famous. What shame and misery! If she is to be saved, Monsieur Lecoq, her name must not be spoken. I ask of you, is it possible? Answer me."

The old man was very violent, yet his speech was simple, devoid of the pompous phrases of passion. Anger lit up his eyes with a strange fire; he seemed young again—he loved, and defended his beloved.

M. Lecoq was silent; his companion insisted.

" Answer me."

" Who knows? "

" Why seek to mislead me? Haven't I as well as you had experience in these things? If Trémorel is brought to trial, all is over with Laurence. And I love her! Yes, I dare to confess it to you, and let you see the depth of my grief, I love her now as I have never loved her. She is dishonored, an object of contempt,

perhaps still adores this wretch—what matters it? I
love her a thousand times more than before her fall, for
then I loved her without hope, while now——"

He stopped, shocked at what he was going to say.
His eyes fell before M. Lecoq's steady gaze, and he
blushed for this shameful yet human hope that he had
betrayed.

" You know all, now," resumed he, in a calmer tone;
" consent to aid me, won't you? Ah, if you only would,
I should not think I had repaid you were I to give you
half my fortune—and I am rich——"

M. Lecoq stopped him with a haughty gesture.

" Enough, Monsieur Plantat," said he, in a bitter
tone, " I can do a service to a person whom I esteem,
love and pity with all my soul; but I cannot *sell* such
a service."

" Believe that I did not wish——"

" Yes, yes, you wished to pay me. Oh, don't excuse
yourself, don't deny it. There are professions, I know,
in which manhood and integrity seem to count for
nothing. Why offer me money? What reason have
you for judging me so mean as to sell my favors? You
are like the rest, who can't fancy what a man in my
position is. If I wanted to be rich—richer than you—
I could be so in a fortnight. Don't you see that I hold
in my hands the honor and lives of fifty people? Do
you think I tell all I know? I have here," added he,
tapping his forehead, " twenty secrets that I could sell
to-morrow, if I would, for a plump hundred thousand
apiece."

He was indignant, but beneath his anger a certain
sad resignation might be perceived. He had often to
reject such offers.

" If you go and resist this prejudice established for

ages, and say that a detective is honest and cannot be otherwise, that he is tenfold more honest than any merchant or notary, because he has tenfold the temptations, without the benefits of his honesty; if you say this, they'll laugh in your face. I could get together to-morrow, with impunity, without any risk, at least a million. Who would mistrust it? I have a conscience, it's true; but a little consideration for these things would not be unpleasant. When it would be so easy for me to divulge what I know of those who have been obliged to trust me, or things which I have surprised, there is perhaps a merit in holding my tongue. And still, the first man who should come along to-morrow—a defaulting banker, a ruined merchant, a notary who has gambled on 'change—would feel himself compromised by walking up the boulevard with me! A policeman—fie! But old Tabaret used to say to me, that the contempt of such people was only one form of fear."

M. Plantat was dismayed. How could he, a man of delicacy, prudence and finesse, have committed such an awkward mistake? He had just cruelly wounded this man, who was so well disposed toward him, and he had everything to fear from his resentment.

"Far be it from me, dear friend," he commenced, "to intend the offence you imagine. You have misunderstood an insignificant phrase, which I let escape carelessly, and had no meaning at all."

M. Lecoq grew calmer.

"Perhaps so. You will forgive my being so susceptible, as I am more exposed to insults than most people. Let's leave the subject, which is a painful one, and return to Trémorel."

M. Plantat was just thinking whether he should dare to broach his projects again, and he was singularly

touched by M. Lecoq's delicately resuming the subject
of them.

"I have only to await your decision," said the justice of the peace.

"I will not conceal from you," resumed M. Lecoq,
"that you are asking a very difficult thing, and one
which is contrary to my duty, which commands me to
search for Trémorel, to arrest him, and deliver him up
to justice. You ask me to protect him from the
law——"

"In the name of an innocent creature whom you will
thereby save."

"Once in my life I sacrificed my duty. I could not
resist the tears of a poor old mother, who clung to my
knees and implored pardon for her son. To-day I am
going to exceed my right, and to risk an attempt for
which my conscience will perhaps reproach me. I
yield to your entreaty."

"Oh, my dear Lecoq, how grateful I am!" cried M.
Plantat, transported with joy.

But the detective remained grave, almost sad, and
reflected.

"Don't let us encourage a hope which may be dis-
appointed," he resumed. "I have but one means of
keeping a criminal like Trémorel out of the courts; will
it succeed?"

"Yes, yes. If you wish it, it will!"

M. Lecoq could not help smiling at the old man's
faith.

"I am certainly a clever detective," said he. "But I
am only a man after all, and I can't answer for the
actions of another man. All depends upon Hector. If
it were another criminal, I should say I was sure. I am
doubtful about him, I frankly confess. We ought,

above all, to count upon the firmness of Mademoiselle
Courtois; can we, think you?"

" She is firmness itself."

" Then there's hope. But can we really suppress this
affair? What will happen when Sauvresy's narrative
is found? It must be concealed somewhere in Valfeuillu, and Trémorel, at least, did not find it."

" It will not be found," said M. Plantat, quickly.

" You think so?"

" I am sure of it."

M. Lecoq gazed intently at his companion, and simply said:

" Ah!"

But this is what he thought: " At last I am going to
find out where the manuscript which we heard read the
other night, and which is in two handwritings, came
from."

After a moment's hesitation, M. Plantat went on:

" I have put my life in your hands, Monsieur Lecoq;
I can, of course, confide my honor to you. I know you.
I know that, happen what may——"

" I shall keep my mouth shut, on my honor."

" Very well. The day that I caught Trémorel at the
mayor's, I wished to verify the suspicions I had, and
so I broke the seal of Sauvresy's package of papers."

" And you did not use them?"

" I was dismayed at my abuse of confidence. Besides, had I the right to deprive poor Sauvresy, who
was dying in order to avenge himself, of his vengeance?"

" But you gave the papers to Madame de Trémorel?"

" True; but Bertha had a vague presentiment of the
fate that was in store for her. About a fortnight before

her death she came and confided to me her husband's manuscript, which she had taken care to complete. I broke the seals and read it, to see if he had died a violent death."

"Why, then, didn't you tell me? Why did you let me hunt, hesitate, grope about——"

"I love Laurence, Monsieur Lecoq, and to deliver up Trémorel was to open an abyss between her and me."

The detective bowed. "The deuce," thought he, "the old justice is shrewd—as shrewd as I am. Well, I like him, and I'm going to give him a surprise."

M. Plantat yearned to question his host and to know what the sole means of which he spoke were, which might be successful in preventing a trial and saving Laurence, but he did not dare to do so.

The detective bent over his desk lost in thought. He held a pencil in his hand and mechanically drew fantastic figures on a large sheet of white paper which lay before him. He suddenly came out of his revery. He had just solved a last difficulty; his plan was now entire and complete. He glanced at the clock.

"Two o'clock," cried he, "and I have an appointment between three and four with Madame Charman about Jenny."

"I am at your disposal," returned his guest.

"All right. When Jenny is disposed of we must look after Trémorel; so let's take our measures to finish it up to-day."

"What! do you hope to do everything to-day——"

"Certainly. Rapidity is above all necessary in our profession. It often takes a month to regain an hour lost. We've a chance now of catching Hector by surprise; to-morrow it will be too late. Either we shall have him within four-and-twenty hours or we must change our batteries. Each of my three men has a carriage and a good horse; they may be able to finish with the upholsterers within an hour from now. If I calculate aright, we shall have the address in an hour, or at most in two hours, and then we will act."

Lecoq, as he spoke, took a sheet of paper surmounted by his arms out of his portfolio, and rapidly wrote several lines.

" See here," said he, " what I've written to one of my lieutenants."

" MONSIEUR JOB—
" Get together six or eight of our men at once and take them to the wine merchant's at the corner of the Rue des Martyrs and the Rue Lamartine; await my orders there."

" Why there and not here? "

" Because we must avoid needless excursions. At the place I have designated we are only two steps from Madame Charman's and near Trémorel's retreat; for the wretch has hired his rooms in the quarter of Notre Dame de Lorette."

M. Plantat gave an exclamation of surprise.

" What makes you think that? "

The detective smiled, as if the question seemed foolish to him.

" Don't you recollect that the envelope of the letter addressed by Mademoiselle Courtois to her family to announce her suicide bore the Paris postmark, and that of the branch office of Rue St. Lazare? Now listen to this: On leaving her aunt's house, Laurence must have gone directly to Trémorel's apartments, the address of

which he had given her, and where he had promised
to meet her on Thursday morning. She wrote the letter, then, in his apartments. Can we admit that she had
the presence of mind to post the letter in another quarter than that in which she was? It is at least probable
that she was ignorant of the terrible reasons which Trémorel had to fear a search and pursuit. Had Hector
foresight enough to suggest this trick to her? No,
for if he wasn't a fool he would have told her to post the
letter somewhere outside of Paris.   It is therefore
scarcely possible that it was posted anywhere else than
at the nearest branch office."

These suppositions were so simple that M. Plantat
wondered he had not thought of them before. But men
do not see clearly in affairs in which they are deeply interested; passion dims the eyes, as heat in a room dims
a pair of spectacles. He had lost, with his coolness, a
part of his clearsightedness.   His anxiety was very
great; for he thought M. Lecoq had a singular mode of
keeping his promise.

" It seems to me," he could not help remarking, " that
if you wish to keep Hector from trial, the men you
have summoned together will be more embarrassing
than useful."

M. Lecoq thought that his guest's tone and look betrayed a certain doubt, and was irritated by it.

" Do you distrust me, Monsieur Plantat? "

The old man tried to protest.

" Believe me——"

" You have my word," resumed M. Lecoq, " and if
you knew me better you would know that I always keep
it when I have given it. I have told you that I would do
my best to save Mademoiselle Laurence; but remember
that I have promised you my assistance, not absolute

success. Let me, then, take such measures as I think best."

So saying, he rang for Janouille.

" Here's a letter," said he when she appeared, " which must be sent to Job at once."

" I will carry it."

" By no means. You will be pleased to remain here and wait for the men that I sent out this morning. As they come in, send them to the wine merchant's at the corner of the Rue des Martyrs; you know it—opposite the church. They'll find a numerous company there."

As he gave his orders, he took off his gown, assumed a long black coat, and carefully adjusted his wig.

" Will Monsieur be back this evening?" asked Janouille.

" I don't know."

" And if anybody comes from over yonder?"

" Over yonder " with a detective, always means " the house "—otherwise the prefecture of police.

" Say that I am out on the Corbeil affair."

M. Lecoq was soon ready. He had the air, physiognomy, and manners of a highly respectable chief clerk of fifty. Gold spectacles, an umbrella, everything about him exhaled an odor of the ledger.

" Now," said he to M. Plantat. " Let's hurry away."

Goulard, who had made a hearty breakfast, was waiting for his hero in the dining-room.

" Ah ha, old fellow," said M. Lecoq. " So you've had a few words with my wine. How do you find it?"

" Delicious, my chief; perfect—that is to say, a true nectar."

" It's cheered you up, I hope."

" Oh, yes, my chief."

" Then you may follow us a few steps and mount

guard at the door of the house where you see us go in. I shall probably have to confide a pretty little girl to your care whom you will carry to Monsieur Domini. And open your eyes; for she's a sly creature, and very apt to inveigle you on the way and slip through your fingers."

They went out, and Janouille stoutly barricaded herself behind them.

XXV

Whosoever needs a loan of money, or a complete suit of clothes in the top of the fashion, a pair of ladies' boots, or an Indian cashmere, a porcelain table service or a good picture; whosoever desires diamonds, curtains, laces, a house in the country, or a provision of wood for winter fires—may procure all these, and many other things besides, at Mme. Charman's.

Mme. Charman lives at 136, Rue Notre Dame de Lorette, on the first story above the ground-floor. Her customers must give madame some guarantee of their credit; a woman, if she be young and pretty, may be accommodated at madame's at the reasonable rate of two hundred per cent. interest. Madame has, at these rates, considerable custom, and yet has not made a large fortune. She must necessarily risk a great deal, and bears heavy losses as well as receives large profits. Then she is, as she is pleased to say, too honest; and true enough, she is honest—she would rather sell her dress off her back than let her signature go to protest.

Madame is a blonde, slight, gentle, and not wanting in a certain distinction of manner; she invariably wears, whether it be summer or winter, a black silk dress. They say she has a husband, but no one has ever seen him, which does not prevent his reputation for good conduct from being above suspicion. However, honorable as may be Mme. Charman's profession, she has more than once had business with M. Lecoq; she has need of him, and fears him as she does fire. She, therefore, welcomed the detective and his companion—whom she took for one of his colleagues—somewhat as the supernumerary of a theatre would greet his manager if the latter chanced to pay him a visit in his humble lodgings.

She was expecting them. When they rang, she advanced to meet them in the ante-chamber, and greeted M. Lecoq graciously and smilingly. She conducted them into her drawing-room, invited them to sit in her best arm-chairs, and pressed some refreshments upon them.

"I see, dear Madame," began M. Lecoq, "that you have received my little note."

"Yes, Monsieur Lecoq, early this morning; I was not up."

"Very good. And have you been so kind as to do the service I asked?"

"How can you ask me, when you know that I would go through the fire for you? I set about it at once, getting up expressly for the purpose."

"Then you've got the address of Pélagie Taponnet, called Jenny?"

"Yes, I have," returned Mme. Charman, with an obsequious bow. "If I were the kind of woman to magnify my services, I would tell you what trouble it cost me to find this address, and how I ran all over Paris and spent ten francs in cab hire."

"Well, let's come to the point."

" The truth is, I had the pleasure of seeing Miss Jenny day before yesterday."

" You are joking ! "

" Not the least in the world. And let me tell you that she is a very courageous and honest girl."

" Really ! "

" She is, indeed. Why, she has owed me four hundred and eighty francs for two years. I hardly thought the debt worth much, as you may imagine. But Jenny came to me day before yesterday all out of breath and told me that she had inherited some money, and had brought me what she owed me. And she was not joking, either ; for her purse was full of bank notes, and she paid me the whole of my bill. She's a good girl ! " added Mme. Charman, as if profoundly convinced of the truth of her encomium.

M. Lecoq exchanged a significant glance with the old justice ; the same idea struck them both at the same moment. These bank-notes could only be the payment for some important service rendered by Jenny to Trémorel. M. Lecoq, however, wished for more precise information.

" What was Jenny's condition before this windfall ? " asked he.

" Ah, Monsieur Lecoq, she was in a dreadful condition. Since the count deserted her she has been constantly falling lower and lower. She sold all she had piece by piece. At last, she mixed with the worst kind of people, drank absinthe, they say, and had nothing to put to her back. When she got any money she spent it on a parcel of hussies instead of buying clothes."

" And where is she living ? "

" Right by, in a house in the Rue Vintimille."

"If that is so," replied M. Lecoq, severely, "I am astonished that she is not here."

"It's not my fault, dear Monsieur Lecoq; I know where the nest is, but not where the bird is. She was away this morning when I sent for her."

"The deuce! But then—it's very annoying; I must hunt her up at once."

"You needn't disturb yourself. Jenny ought to return before four o'clock, and one of my girls is waiting for her with orders to bring her here as soon as she comes in, without even letting her go up to her room."

"We'll wait for her then."

M. Lecoq and his friend waited about a quarter of an hour, when Mme. Charman suddenly got up.

"I hear my girl's step on the stairs," said she.

"Listen to me," answered M. Lecoq, "if it is she, manage to make Jenny think that it was you who sent for her; we will seem to have come in by the merest chance."

Mme. Charman responded by a gesture of assent. She was going towards the door when the detective detained her by the arm.

"One word more. When you see me fairly engaged in conversation with her, please be so good as to go and overlook your work-people in the shops. What I have to say will not interest you in the least."

"I understand."

"But no trickery, you know. I know where the closet of your bedroom is, well enough to be sure that everything that is said here may be overheard in it."

Mme. Charman's emissary opened the door; there was a loud rustling of silks along the corridor; and Jenny appeared in all her glory. She was no longer the fresh and pretty minx whom Hector had known—

the provoking large-eyed Parisian demoiselle, with
haughty head and petulant grace. A single year had
withered her, as a too hot summer does the roses, and
had destroyed her fragile beauty beyond recall. She
was not twenty, and still it was hard to discern that she
had been charming, and was yet young. For she had
grown old like vice; her worn features and hollow
cheeks betrayed the dissipations of her life; her eyes
had lost their long, languishing lids; her mouth had a
pitiful expression of stupefaction; and absinthe had
broken the clear tone of her voice. She was richly
dressed in a new robe, with a great deal of lace and a
jaunty hat; yet she had a wretched expression; she was
all besmeared with rouge and paint.

When she came in she seemed very angry.

"What an idea!" she cried, without taking the
trouble to bow to anyone; "what sense is there in
sending for me to come here in this way, almost by
force, and by a very impudent young woman?"

Mme. Charman hastened to meet her old customer,
embraced her in spite of herself, and pressed her to
her heart.

"Why, don't be so angry, dear—I thought you
would be delighted and overwhelm me with thanks."

"I? What for?"

"Because, my dear girl, I had a surprise in store for
you. Ah, I'm not ungrateful; you came here yesterday
and settled your account with me, and to-day I mean
to reward you for it. Come, cheer up; you're going to
have a splendid chance, because just at this moment I
happen to have a piece of exquisite velvet——"

"A pretty thing to bring me here for!"

"All silk, my dear, at thirty francs the yard. Ha,
'tis wonderfully cheap, the best——"

"Eh! What care I for your 'chance?' Velvet in July—are you making fun of me?"

"Let me show it to you, now."

"Never! I am expected to dinner at Asniéres, and so——"

She was about to go away despite Mme. Charman's attempts to detain her, when M. Lecoq thought it was time to interfere.

"Why, am I mistaken?" cried he, as if amazed; "is it really Miss Jenny whom I have the honor of seeing?"

She scanned him with a half-angry, half-surprised air, and said:

"Yes, it's I; what of it?"

"What! Are you so forgetful? Don't you recognize me?"

"No, not at all."

"Yet I was one of your admirers once, my dear, and used to breakfast with you when you lived near the Madeleine; in the count's time, you know."

He took off his spectacles as if to wipe them, but really to launch a furious look at Mme. Charman, who, not daring to resist, beat a hasty retreat.

"I knew Trémorel well in other days," resumed the detective. "And—by the bye, have you heard any news of him lately?"

"I saw him about a week ago."

"Stop, though—haven't you heard of that horrible affair?"

"No. What was it?"

"Really, now, haven't you heard? Don't you read the papers? It was a dreadful thing, and has been the talk of all Paris for the past forty-eight hours."

"Tell me about it, quick!"

"You know that he married the widow of one of his

friends. He was thought to be very happy at home;
not at all; he has murdered his wife with a knife."

Jenny grew pale under her paint.

" Is it possible? " stammered she. She seemed much
affected, but not very greatly surprised, which M.
Lecoq did not fail to remark.

" It is so possible," he resumed, " that he is at this
moment in prison, will soon be tried, and without a
doubt will be convicted."

M. Plantat narrowly observed Jenny; he looked for
an explosion of despair, screams, tears, at least a light
nervous attack; he was mistaken.

Jenny now detested Trémorel. Sometimes she felt
the weight of her degradation, and she accused Hector
of her present ignominy. She heartily hated him,
though she smiled when she saw him, got as much
money out of him as she could, and cursed him behind
his back. Instead of bursting into tears, she therefore
laughed aloud.

" Well done for Trémorel," said she. " Why did he
leave me? Good for her too."

" Why so? "

" What did she deceive her husband for? It was
she who took Hector from me—she, a rich, married
woman! But I've always said Hector was a poor
wretch."

" Frankly, that's my notion too. When a man acts
as Trémorel has toward you, he's a villain."

" It's so, isn't it? "

" Parbleu! But I'm not surprised at his conduct.
For his wife's murder is the least of his crimes; why,
he tried to put it off upon somebody else! "

" That doesn't surprise me."

" He accused a poor devil as innocent as you or I,

who might have been condemned to death if he hadn't been able to tell where he was on Wednesday night."

M. Lecoq said this lightly, with intended deliberation, so as to watch the impression he produced on Jenny.

" Do you know who the man was? " asked she in a tremulous voice.

" The papers said it was a poor lad who was his gardener."

" A little man, wasn't he, thin, very dark, with black hair? "

" Just so."

" And whose name was—wait now—was—Guespin."

" Ah ha, you know him then? "

Jenny hesitated. She was trembling very much, and evidently regretted that she had gone so far.

" Bah! " said she at last. " I don't see why I shouldn't tell what I know. I'm an honest girl, if Trémorel is a rogue; and I don't want them to condemn a poor wretch who is innocent."

" You know something about it, then? "

" Well, I know nearly all about it—that's honest, ain't it? About a week ago Hector wrote to me to meet him at Melun; I went, found him, and we breakfasted together. Then he told me that he was very much annoyed about his cook's marriage; for one of his servants was deeply in love with her, and might go and raise a rumpus at the wedding."

" Ah, he spoke to you about the wedding, then? "

" Wait a minute. Hector seemed very much embarrassed, not knowing how to avoid the disturbance he feared. Then I advised him to send the servant off out of the way on the wedding-day. He thought a moment, and said that my advice was good. He added that he had found a means of doing this; on the evening of the marriage he would send the man on an errand for me, telling him that the affair was to be concealed from the countess. I was to dress up as a chambermaid, and wait for the man at the café in the Place du Chatelet, between half-past nine and ten that evening; I was to sit at the table nearest the entrance on the right, with a bouquet in my hand, so that he should recognize me. He would come in and give me a package; then I was to ask him to take something, and so get him tipsy if possible, and then walk about Paris with him till morning."

Jenny expressed herself with difficulty, hesitating, choosing her words, and trying to remember exactly what Trémorel said.

" And you," interrupted M. Lecoq, " did you believe all this story about a jealous servant? "

" Not quite; but I fancied that he had some intrigue on foot, and I wasn't sorry to help him deceive a woman whom I detested, and who had wronged me."

" So you did as he told you? "

" Exactly, from beginning to end; everything happened just as Hector had foreseen. The man came along at just ten o'clock, took me for a maid, and gave me the package. I naturally offered him a glass of beer; he took it and proposed another, which I also accepted. He is a very nice fellow, this gardener, and I passed a very pleasant evening with him. He knew lots of queer things, and——"

" Never mind that. What did you do then? "

" After the beer we had some wine, then some beer again, then some punch, then some more wine—the gardener had his pockets full of money. He was very tipsy by eleven and invited me to go and have a dance with him at the Batignolles. I refused, and asked him to escort me back to my mistress at the upper end of the Champs Elysées. We went out of the café and walked up the Rue de Rivoli, stopping every now and then for more wine and beer. By two o'clock the fellow was so far gone that he fell like a lump on a bench near the Arc de Triomphe, where he went to sleep; and there I left him."

" Well, where did you go?"

" Home."

" What has become of the package?"

" Oh, I intended to throw it into the Seine, as Hector wished, but I forgot it; you see, I had drunk almost as much as the gardener—so I carried it back home with me, and it is in my room now."

" Have you opened it?"

" Well—what do you think?"

" What did it contain?"

" A hammer, two other tools and a large knife."

Guespin's innocence was now evident, and the detective's foresight was realized.

" Guespin's all right," said M. Plantat. " But we must know——"

M. Lecoq interrupted him; he knew now all he wished. Jenny could tell him nothing more, so he suddenly changed his tone from a wheedling one to abrupt severity.

" My fine young woman," said he, " you have saved an innocent man, but you must repeat what you have just said to the judge of instruction at Corbeil. And as you might lose yourself on the way, I'll give you a guide."

He went to the window and opened it; perceiving Goulard on the sidewalk, he cried out to him:

"Goulard, come up here."

He turned to the astonished Jenny, who was so frightened that she dared not either question him or get angry, and said:

"Tell me how much Trémorel paid you for the service you rendered him."

"Ten thousand francs; but it is my due, I swear to you; for he promised it to me long ago, and owed it to me."

"Very good; it can't be taken away from you." He added, pointing out Goulard who entered just then: "Go with this man to your room, take the package which Guespin brought you, and set out at once for Corbeil. Above all, no tricks, Miss—or beware of me!"

Mme. Charman came in just in time to see Jenny leave the room with Goulard.

"Lord, what's the matter?" she asked M. Lecoq.

"Nothing, my dear Madame, nothing that concerns you in the least. And so, thank you and good-evening; we are in a great hurry."

XXVI

When M. Lecoq was in a hurry he walked fast. He almost ran down the Rue Notre Dame de Lorette, so that Plantat had great difficulty in keeping up with him; and as he went along he pursued his train of reflection, half aloud, so that his companion caught here and there a snatch of it.

"All goes well," he muttered, "and we shall succeed. It's seldom that a campaign which commences

so well ends badly. If Job is at the wine merchant's,
and if one of my men has succeeded in his search, the
crime of Valfeuillu is solved, and in a week people will
have forgotten it."

He stopped short on reaching the foot of the street
opposite the church.

" I must ask you to pardon me," said he to the old
justice, " for hurrying you on so and making you one
of my trade; but your assistance might have been very
useful at Madame Charman's, and will be indispensable
when we get fairly on Trémorel's track."

They went across the square and into the wine shop
at the corner of the Rue des Martyrs. Its keeper was
standing behind his counter turning wine out of a large
jug into some litres, and did not seem much astonished
at seeing his new visitors. M. Lecoq was quite at home
(as he was everywhere), and spoke to the man with an
air of easy familiarity.

" Aren't there six or eight men waiting for somebody here? " he asked.

" Yes, they came about an hour ago."

" Are they in the big back room? "

" Just so, Monsieur," responded the wine merchant,
obsequiously.

He didn't exactly know who was talking to him, but
he suspected him to be some superior officer from the
prefecture; and he was not surprised to see that this
distinguished personage knew the ins and outs of his
house. He opened the door of the room referred to
without hesitation. Ten men in various guises were
drinking there and playing cards. On M. Lecoq's entrance with M. Plantat, they respectfully got up and
took off their hats.

" Good for you, Job," said M. Lecoq to him who

seemed to be their chief, "you are prompt, and it pleases me. Your ten men will be quite enough, for I shall have the three besides whom I sent out this morning."

M. Job bowed, happy at having pleased a master who was not very prodigal in his praises.

"I want you to wait here a while longer," resumed M. Lecoq, "for my orders will depend on a report which I am expecting." He turned to the men whom he had sent out among the upholsterers:

"Which of you was successful?"

"I, Monsieur," replied a big white-faced fellow, with insignificant mustaches.

"What, you again, Palot? really, my lad, you are lucky. Step into this side room—first, though, order a bottle of wine, and ask the proprietor to see to it that we are not disturbed."

These orders were soon executed, and M. Plantat being duly ensconced with them in the little room, the detective turned the key.

"Speak up now," said he to Palot, "and be brief."

"I showed the photograph to at least a dozen upholsterers without any result; but at last a merchant in the Faubourg St. Germain, named Rech, recognized it."

"Tell me just what he said, if you can."

"He told me that it was the portrait of one of his customers. A month ago this customer came to him to buy a complete set of furniture—drawing-room, dining-room, bed-room, and the rest—for a little house which he had just rented. He did not beat him down at all, and only made one condition to the purchase, and that was, that everything should be ready and in place,

23

and the curtains and carpets put in, within three weeks from that time; that is a week ago last Monday."

" And what was the sum-total of the purchase?"

" Eighteen thousand francs, half paid down in advance, and half on the day of delivery."

" And who carried the last half of the money to the upholsterer?"

" A servant."

" What name did this customer give?"

" He called himself Monsieur James Wilson; but Monsieur Rech said he did not seem like an Englishman."

" Where does he live?"

" The furniture was carried to a small house, No. 34 Rue St. Lazare, near the Havre station."

M. Lecoq's face, which had up to that moment worn an anxious expression, beamed with joy. He felt the natural pride of a captain who has succeeded in his plans for the enemy's destruction. He tapped the old justice of the peace familiarly on the shoulder, and pronounced a single word:

" Nipped!"

Palot shook his head.

" It isn't certain," said he.

" Why?"

" You may imagine, Monsieur Lecoq, that when I got the address, having some time on my hands, I went to reconnoitre the house."

" Well?"

" The tenant's name is really Wilson, but it's not the man of the photograph, I'm certain."

M. Plantat gave a groan of disappointment, but M. Lecoq was not so easily discouraged.

" How did you find out?"

"I pumped one of the servants."

"Confound you!" cried M. Plantat. "Perhaps you roused suspicions."

"Oh, no," answered M. Lecoq. "I'll answer for him. Palot is a pupil of mine. Explain yourself, Palot."

"Recognizing the house—an elegant affair it is, too—I said to myself: 'I' faith, here's the cage; let's see if the bird is in it.' I luckily happened to have a napoleon in my pocket; and I slipped it without hesitation into the drain which led from the house to the street-gutter."

"Then you rang?"

"Exactly. The porter—there is a porter—opened the door, and with my most vexed air I told him how, in pulling out my handkerchief, I had dropped a twenty-franc piece in the drain, and begged him to lend me something to try to get it out. He lent me a poker and took another himself, and we got the money out with no difficulty; I began to jump about as if I were delighted, and begged him to let me treat him to a glass of wine."

"Not bad."

"Oh, Monsieur Lecoq, it is one of your tricks, you know. My porter accepted my invitation, and we soon got to be the best friends in the world over some wine in a shop just across the street from the house. We were having a jolly talk together when, all of a sudden, I leaned over as if I had just espied something on the floor, and picked up—the photograph, which I had dropped and soiled a little with my foot. 'What,' cried I, 'a portrait?'. My new friend took it, looked at it, and didn't seem to recognize it. Then, to be certain, I said, 'He's a very good-looking fellow, ain't he now?

Your master must be some such a man.' But he said no, that the photograph was of a man who was bearded, while his master was as clean-faced as an abbé. ' Besides,' he added, ' my master is an American; he gives us our orders in French, but Madame and he always talk English together.' "

M. Lecoq's eye glistened as Palot proceeded.

" Trémorel speaks English, doesn't he ? " asked he *of* M. Plantat.

" Quite well; and Laurence too."

" If that is so, we are on the right track, for we know that Trémorel shaved his beard off on the night of the murder. We can go on———"

Palot meanwhile seemed a little uneasy at not receiving the praise he expected.

" My lad," said M. Lecoq, turning to him, " I think you have done admirably, and a good reward shall prove it to you. Being ignorant of what we know, your conclusions were perfectly right. But let's go to the house at once; have you got a plan of the ground-floor ? "

" Yes, and also of the first floor above. The porter was not dumb, and so he gave me a good deal of information about his master and mistress, though he has only been there two days. The lady is dreadfully melancholy, and cries all the time."

" We know it; the plan———"

" Below, there is a large and high paved arch for the carriages to pass through ; on the other side is a good-sized courtyard, at the end of which are the stable and carriage-house. The porter's lodge is on the left of the arch ; on the right a glass door opens on a staircase with six steps, which conducts to a vestibule into which the drawing-room, dining-room, and two other little rooms open.   The chambers are on the first floor, a study, a——"

"Enough," M. Lecoq said, "my plan is made."

And rising abruptly, he opened the door, and followed by M. Plantat and Palot, went into the large room.   All the men rose at his approach as before.

"Monsieur Job," said the detective, "listen attentively to what I have to say.   As soon as I am gone, pay up what you owe here, and then, as I must have you all within reach, go and install yourselves in the first wine-shop on the right as you go up the Rue d'Amsterdam.   Take your dinner there, for you will have time —but soberly, you understand."

He took two napoleons out of his pocket and placed them on the table, adding:

"That's for the dinner."

M. Lecoq and the old justice went into the street, followed closely by Palot.   The detective was anxious above all to see for himself the house inhabited by Trémorel.   He saw at a glance that the interior must be as Palot had described.

"That's it, undoubtedly," said he to M. Plantat; "we've got the game in our hands.   Our chances at this moment are ninety to ten."

"What are you going to do?" asked the justice, whose emotion increased as the decisive moment approached.

"Nothing, just yet.   I must wait for night before I act.   As it is two hours yet before dark, let's imitate my men; I know a restaurant just by here where you can dine capitally; we'll patronize it."

And without awaiting a reply, he led M. Plantat to a restaurant in the Passage du Havre.   But at the moment he was about to open the door, he stopped and made a signal. Palot immediately appeared.

"I give you two hours to get yourself up so that the porter won't recognize you, and to have some dinner. You are an upholsterer's apprentice. Now clear out; I shall wait for you here."

M. Lecoq was right when he said that a capital dinner was to be had in the Passage du Havre; unfortunately M. Plantat was not in a state to appreciate it. As in the morning, he found it difficult to swallow anything, he was so anxious and depressed. He longed to know the detective's plans; but M. Lecoq remained impenetrable, answering all inquiries with:

"Let me act, and trust me."

M. Plantat's confidence was indeed very great; but the more he reflected, the more perilous and difficult seemed the attempt to save Trémorel from a trial. The most poignant doubts troubled and tortured his mind. His own life was at stake; for he had sworn to himself that he would not survive the ruin of Laurence in being forced to confess in full court her dishonor and her love for Hector.

M. Lecoq tried hard to make his companion eat something, to take at least some soup and a glass of old Bordeaux; but he soon saw the uselessness of his efforts and went on with his dinner as if he were alone. He was very thoughtful, but any uncertainty of the result of his plans never entered his head. He drank much and often, and soon emptied his bottle of Léoville. Night having now come on, the waiters began to light the chandeliers, and the two friends found themselves almost alone.

"Isn't it time to begin?" asked the old justice, timidly.

"We have still nearly an hour," replied M. Lecoq, consulting his watch; "but I shall make my preparations now."

He called a waiter, and ordered a cup of coffee and writing materials.

"You see," said he, while they were waiting to be served, "we must try to get at Laurence without Trémorel's knowing it. We must have a ten minutes' talk with her alone, and in the house. That is a condition absolutely necessary to our success."

M. Plantat had evidently been expecting some immediate and decisive action, for M. Lecoq's remark filled him with alarm.

"If that's so," said he mournfully, "it's all over with our project."

"How so?"

"Because Trémorel will not leave Laurence by herself for a moment."

"Then I'll try to entice him out."

"And you, you who are usually so clear-sighted, really think that he will let himself be taken in by a trick! You don't consider his situation at this moment. He must be a prey to boundless terrors. We know that Sauvresy's declaration will not be found, but he does not; he thinks that perhaps it has been found, that suspicions have been aroused, and that he is already being searched for and pursued by the police."

"I've considered all that," responded M. Lecoq with a triumphant smile, "and many other things besides. Well, it isn't easy to decoy Trémorel out of the house. I've been cudgelling my brain about it a good deal, and have found a way at last. The idea occurred to me just as we were coming in here. The Count de Trémorel, in an hour from now, will be in the Faubourg St. Germain. It's true it will cost me a forgery, but you will forgive me under the circumstances. Besides, he who seeks the end must use the means."

He took up a pen, and as he smoked his cigar, rapidly wrote the following:

" MONSIEUR WILSON:

" Four of the thousand-franc notes which you paid me are counterfeits; I have just found it out by sending them to my banker's. If you are not here to explain the matter before ten o'clock, I shall be obliged to put in a complaint this evening before the procureur.

" RECH."

" Now," said M. Lecoq, passing the letter to his companion. " Do you comprehend?"

The old justice read it at a glance and could not repress a joyful exclamation, which caused the waiters to turn around and stare at him.

" Yes," said he, " this letter will catch him; it'll frighten him out of all his other terrors. He will say to himself that he might have slipped some counterfeit notes among those paid to the upholsterer, that a complaint against him will provoke an inquiry, and that he will have to prove that he is really Monsieur Wilson or he is lost."

" So you think he'll come out?"

" I'm sure of it, unless he has become a fool."

" I tell you we shall succeed then, for this is the only serious obstacle——"

He suddenly interrupted himself. The restaurant door opened ajar, and a man passed his head in and withdrew it immediately.

" That's my man," said M. Lecoq, calling the waiter

to pay for the dinner, " he is waiting for us in the passage ; let us go."

A young man dressed like a journeyman upholsterer was standing in the passage looking in at the shop-windows. He had long brown locks, and his mustache and eyebrows were coal-black. M. Plantat certainly did not recognize him as Palot, but M. Lecoq did, and even seemed dissatisfied with his get-up.

" Bad," growled he, " pitiable. Do you think it is enough, in order to disguise yourself, to change the color of your beard? Look in that glass, and tell me if the expression of your face is not just what it was before? Aren't your eye and smile the same? Then your cap is too much on one side, it is not natural ; and your hand is put in your pocket awkwardly."

" I'll try to do better another time, Monsieur Lecoq," Palot modestly replied.

" I hope so ; but I guess your porter won't recognize you to-night, and that is all we want."

" And now what must I do? "

" I'll give you your orders ; and be very careful not to blunder. First, hire a carriage, with a good horse ; then go to the wine-shop for one of our men, who will accompany you to Monsieur Wilson's house. When you get there ring, enter alone and give the porter this letter, saying that it is of the utmost importance. This done, put yourself with your companion in ambuscade before the house. If Monsieur Wilson goes out—and he will go out or I am not Lecoq—send your comrade to me at once. As for you, you will follow Monsieur Wilson and not lose sight of him. He will take a carriage, and you will follow him with yours, getting up on the hackman's seat and keeping a lookout from there. Have your eyes open, for he is a rascal who may feel inclined to jump out of his cab and leave you in pursuit of an empty vehicle."

" Yes, and the moment I am informed——"

"' Silence, please, when I am speaking. He will probably go to the upholsterer's in the Rue des Saints-Pères, but I may be mistaken. He may order himself to be carried to one of the railway stations, and may take the first train which leaves. In this case, you must get into the same railway carriage that he does, and follow him everywhere he goes ; and be sure and send me a despatch as soon as you can."

" Very well, Monsieur Lecoq ;. only if I have to take a train——"

" What, haven't you any money ? "

" Well—no, my chief."

" Then take this five-hundred-franc note ; that's more than is necessary to make the tour of the world. Do you comprehend everything ? "

" I beg your pardon—what shall I do if Monsieur Wilson simply returns to his house ? "

" In that case I will finish with him. If he returns, you will come back with him, and the moment his cab stops before the house give two loud whistles, you know. Then wait for me in the street, taking care to retain your cab, which you will lend to Monsieur Plantat if he needs it."

" All right," said Palot, who hastened off without more ado.

M. Plantat and the detective, left alone, began to walk up and down the gallery ; both were grave and silent, as men are at a decisive moment ; there is no chatting about a gaming-table. M. Lecoq suddenly started ; he had just seen his agent at the end of the gallery.   His impatience was so great that he ran toward him, saying:

" Well? "

" Monsieur, the game has flown, and Palot after him! ".

" On foot or in a cab? "

" In a cab."

" Enough. Return to your comrades, and tell them to hold themselves ready."

Everything was going as Lecoq wished, and he grasped the old justice's hand, when he was struck by the alteration in his features.

" What, are you ill? " asked he, anxiously.

" No, but I am fifty-five years old, Monsieur Lecoq, and at that age there are emotions which kill one. Look, I am trembling at the moment when I see my wishes being realized, and I feel as if a disappointment would be the death of me. I'm afraid, yes, I'm afraid. Ah, why can't I dispense with following you? "

" But your presence is indispensable; without your help I can do nothing."

" What could I do? "

" Save Laurence, Monsieur Plantat."

This name restored a part of his courage.

" If that is so—" said he. He began to walk firmly toward the street, but M. Lecoq stopped him.

" Not yet," said the detective, " not yet; the battle now depends on the precision of our movements.   A single fault miserably upsets all my combinations, and then I shall be forced to arrest and deliver up the criminal.   We must have a ten minutes' interview with Mademoiselle Laurence, but not much more, and it is absolutely necessary that this interview should be suddenly interrupted by Trémorel's return. Let's make

our calculations. It will take the rascal half an hour
to go to the Rue des Saints-Pères, where he will find
nobody; as long to get back; let us throw in fifteen
minutes as a margin; in all, an hour and a quarter.
There are forty minutes left us."

M. Plantat did not reply, but his companion said that
he could not stay so long on his feet after the fatigues
of the day, agitated as he was, and having eaten nothing since the evening before. He led him into a neighboring café, and forced him to eat a biscuit and drink a
glass of wine. Then seeing that conversation would be
annoying to the unhappy old man, he took up an evening paper and soon seemed to be absorbed in the latest
news from Germany. The old justice, his head leaning
on the back of his chair and his eyes wandering over
the ceiling, passed in mental review the events of the
past four years. It seemed to him but yesterday that
Laurence, still a child, ran up his garden-path and
picked his roses and honeysuckles. How pretty she
was, and how divine were her great eyes! Then, as it
seemed, between dusk and dawn, as a rose blooms on
a June night, the pretty child had become a sweet and
radiant young girl. She was timid and reserved with
all but him—was he not her old friend, the confidant of
all her little griefs and her innocent hopes? How
frank and pure she was then; what a heavenly ignorance of evil!

Nine o'clock struck; M. Lecoq laid down his paper.
"Let us go," said he.

M. Plantat followed him with a firmer step, and they
soon reached M. Wilson's house, accompanied by Job
and his men.

"You men," said M. Lecoq, "wait till I call before
you go in; I will leave the door ajar."

He rang; the door swung open; and M. Plantat and the detective went in under the arch.   The porter was on the threshold of his lodge.

" Monsieur Wilson? " asked M. Lecoq.

" He is out."

" I will speak to Madame, then."

" She is also out."

" Very well.   Only, as I must positively speak with Madame Wilson, I'm going upstairs."

The porter seemed about to resist him by force; but, as Lecoq now called in his men, he thought better of it and kept quiet.

M. Lecoq posted six of his men in the court, in such a position that they could be easily seen from the windows on the first floor, and instructed the others to place themselves on the opposite sidewalk, telling them to look ostentatiously at the house.   These measures taken, he returned to the porter.

" Attend to me, my man.   When your master, who has gone out, comes in again, beware that you don't tell him that we are upstairs; a single word would get you into terribly hot water——"

" I am blind," he answered, " and deaf."

" How many servants are there in the house? "

" Three; but they have all gone out."

The detective then took M. Plantat by the arm, and holding him firmly:

" You see, my dear friend;" said he, " the game is ours.   Come along—and in Laurence's name, have courage ! "

XXVII

All M. Lecoq's anticipations were realized. Laurence was not dead, and her letter to her parents was an odious trick. It was really she who lived in the house as Mme. Wilson. How had the lovely young girl, so much beloved by the old justice, come to such a dreadful extremity? The logic of life, alas, fatally enchains all our determinations to each other. Often an indifferent action, little wrongful in itself, is the beginning of an atrocious crime. Each of our new resolutions depends upon those which have preceded it, and is their logical sequence just as the sum-total is the product of the added figures. Woe to him who, being seized with a dizziness at the brink of the abyss, does not fly as fast as possible, without turning his head; for soon, yielding to an irresistible attraction, he approaches, braves the danger, slips, and is lost. Whatever thereafter he does or attempts he will roll down the faster, until he reaches the very bottom of the gulf.

Trémorel had by no means the implacable character of an assassin; he was only feeble and cowardly; yet he had committed abominable crimes. All his guilt came from the first feeling of envy with which he regarded Sauvresy, and which he had not taken the pains to subdue. Laurence, when, on the day that she became enamoured of Trémorel, she permitted him to press her hand, and kept it from her mother, was lost. The hand-pressure led to the pretence of suicide in order to fly with her lover. It might also lead to infanticide.

Poor Laurence, when she was left alone by Hector's departure to the Faubourg St. Germain, on receiving M.

Lecoq's letter, began to reflect upon the events of the past year.   How unlooked-for and rapidly succeeding they had been!   It seemed to her that she had been whirled along in a tempest, without a second to think or act freely.   She asked herself if she were not a prey to some hideous nightmare, and if she should not presently awake in her pretty maidenly chamber at Orcival. Was it really she who was there in a strange house, dead to everyone, leaving behind a withered memory, reduced to live under a false name, without family or friends henceforth, or anyone in the world to help her feebleness, at the mercy of a fugitive like herself, who was free to break to-morrow the bonds of caprice which to-day bound him to her?   Was it she, too, who was about to become a mother, and found herself suffering from the excessive misery of blushing for that maternity which is the pride of pure young wives?   A thousand memories of her past life flocked through her brain and cruelly revived her despair.   Her heart sank as she thought of her old friendships, of her mother, her sister, the pride of her innocence, and the pure joys of the home fireside.

As she half reclined on a divan in Hector's library, she wept freely.   She bewailed her life, broken at twenty, her lost youth, her vanished, once radiant hopes, the world's esteem, and her own self-respect, which she should never recover.

Of a sudden the door was abruptly opened.

Laurence thought it was Hector returned, and she hastily rose, passing her handkerchief across her face to try to conceal her tears.

A man whom she did not know stood upon the threshold, respectfully bowing.   She was afraid, for Trémorel had said to her many times within the past

two days, "We are pursued; let us hide well;" and
though it seemed to her that she had nothing to fear,
she trembled without knowing why.

"Who are you?" she asked, haughtily, "and who
has admitted you here? What do you want?"

M. Lecoq left nothing to chance or inspiration; he
foresaw everything, and regulated affairs in real life as
he would the scenes in a theatre. He expected this very
natural indignation and these questions, and was prepared for them. The only reply he made was to step
one side, thus revealing M. Plantat behind him.

Laurence was so much overcome on recognizing her
old friend, that, in spite of her resolution, she came near
falling.

"You!" she stammered; "you!"

The old justice was, if possible, more agitated than
Laurence. Was that really his Laurence there before
him? Grief had done its work so well that she seemed
old.

"Why did you seek for me?" she resumed. "Why
add another grief to my life? Ah, I told Hector that
the letter he dictated to me would not be believed.
There are misfortunes for which death is the only refuge."

M. Plantat was about to reply, but Lecoq was determined to take the lead in the interview.

"It is not you, Madame, that we seek," said he, "but
Monsieur de Trémorel."

"Hector! And why, if you please? Is he not
free?"

M. Lecoq hesitated before shocking the poor girl,
who had been but too credulous in trusting to a scoun-
drel's oaths of fidelity. But he thought that the cruel
truth is less harrowing than the suspense of intimations.

"Monsieur de Trémorel," he answered, "has committed a great crime."

"He! You lie, sir."

The detective sorrowfully shook his head.

"Unhappily I have told you the truth. Monsieur de Trémorel murdered his wife on Wednesday night. I am a detective and I have a warrant to arrest him."

He thought this terrible charge would overwhelm Laurence; he was mistaken. She was thunderstruck, but she stood firm. The crime horrified her, but it did not seem to her entirely improbable, knowing as she did the hatred with which Hector was inspired by Bertha.

"Well, perhaps he did," cried she, sublime in her energy and despair; "I am his accomplice, then—arrest me."

This cry, which seemed to proceed from the most senseless passion, amazed the old justice, but did not surprise M. Lecoq.

"No, Madame," he resumed, "you are not this man's accomplice. Besides, the murder of his wife is the least of his crimes. Do you know why he did not marry you? Because in concert with Bertha, he poisoned Monsieur Sauvresy, who saved his life and was his best friend. We have the proof of it."

This was more than poor Laurence could bear; she staggered and fell upon a sofa. But she did not doubt the truth of what M. Lecoq said. This terrible revelation tore away the veil which, till then, had hidden the past from her. The poisoning of Sauvresy explained all Hector's conduct, his position, his fears, his promises, his lies, his hate, his recklessness, his marriage, his flight. Still she tried not to defend him, but to share the odium of his crimes.

24

"I knew it," she stammered, in a voice broken by sobs, "I knew it all."

The old justice was in despair.

"How you love him, poor child!" murmured he.

This mournful exclamation restored to Laurence all her energy; she made an effort and rose, her eyes glittering with indignation:

"I love him!" cried she. "I! Ah, I can explain my conduct to you, my old friend, for you are worthy of hearing it. Yes, I *did* love him, it is true—loved him to the forgetfulness of duty, to self-abandonment. But one day he showed himself to me as he was; I judged him, and my love did not survive my contempt. I was ignorant of Sauvresy's horrible death. Hector confessed to me that his life and honor were in Bertha's hands—and that she loved him. I left him free to abandon me, to marry, thus sacrificing more than my life to what I thought was his happiness; yet I was not deceived. When I fled with him I once more sacrificed myself, when I saw that it was impossible to conceal my shame. I wanted to die. I lived, and wrote an infamous letter to my mother, and yielded to Hector's prayers, because he pleaded with me in the name of my—of our child!"

M. Lecoq, impatient at the loss of time, tried to say something; but Laurence would not listen to him.

"But what matter?" she continued. "I loved him, followed him, and am his. Constancy at all hazards is the only excuse for a fault like mine. I will do my duty. I cannot be innocent when Hector has committed a crime; I desire to suffer half the punishment."

She spoke with such remarkable animation that the detective despaired of calming her, when two whistles in the street struck his ear. Trémorel was returning and there was not a moment to be lost. He suddenly seized Laurence by the arm.

"You will tell all this to the judges, Madame," said he, sternly. "My orders are only for M. de Trémorel. Here is the warrant to arrest him."

He took out the warrant and laid it upon the table. Laurence, by the force of her will, had become almost calm.

"You will let me speak five minutes with the Count de Trémorel, will you not?" she asked.

M. Lecoq was delighted; he had looked for this request, and expected it.

"Five minutes? Yes," he replied. "But abandon all hope, Madame, of saving the prisoner; the house is watched; if you look in the court and in the street you will see my men in ambuscade. Besides, I am going to stay here in the next room."

The count was heard ascending the stairs.

"There's Hector!" cried Laurence, "quick, quick! conceal yourselves!"

She added, as they were retiring, in a low tone, but not so low as to prevent the detective from hearing her:

"Be sure, we will not try to escape."

She let the door-curtain drop; it was time. Hector entered. He was paler than death, and his eyes had a fearful, wandering expression.

"We are lost!" said he, "they are pursuing us. See, this letter which I received just now is not from the man whose signature it professes to bear; he told me so himself. Come, let us go, let us leave this house——"

Laurence overwhelmed him with a look full of hate and contempt, and said:

"It is too late."

Her countenance and voice were so strange that
Trémorel, despite his distress, was struck by it, and
asked:

"What is the matter?"

"Everything is known; it is known that you killed
your wife."

"It's false!"

She shrugged her shoulders.

"Well, then, it is true," he added, "for I loved you
so——"

"Really! And it was for love of me that you poisoned Sauvresy?"

He saw that he was discovered, that he had been
caught in a trap, that they had come, in his absence, and
told Laurence all. He did not attempt to deny anything.

"What shall I do?" cried he, "what shall I do?"

Laurence drew him to her, and muttered in a shuddering voice:

"Save the name of Trémorel; there are pistols
here."

He recoiled, as if he had seen death itself.

"No," said he. "I can yet fly and conceal myself;
I will go alone, and you can rejoin me afterward."

"I have already told you that it is too late. The police have surrounded the house. And—you know—it
is the galleys, or—the scaffold!"

"I can get away by the courtyard."

"It is guarded; look."

He ran to the window, saw M. Lecoq's men, and returned half mad and hideous with terror.

"I can at least try," said he, "by disguising myself——"

" Fool! A detective is in there, and it was he who left that warrant to arrest you on the table."

He saw that he was lost beyond hope.

" Must I die, then? " he muttered.

" Yes, you must; but before you die write a confession of your crimes, for the innocent may be suspected——"

He sat down mechanically, took the pen which Laurence held out to him, and wrote:

" Being about to appear before God, I declare that I alone, and without accomplices, poisoned Sauvresy and murdered the Countess de Trémorel, my wife."

When he had signed and dated this, Laurence opened a bureau drawer; Hector seized one of the brace of pistols which were lying in it, and she took the other. But Trémorel, as before at the hotel, and then in the dying Sauvresy's chamber, felt his heart fail him as he placed the pistol against his forehead. He was livid, his teeth chattered, and he trembled so violently that he let the pistol drop.

" Laurence, my love," he stammered, " what will—become of you? "

" Me! I have sworn that I will follow you always and everywhere. Do you understand? "

" Ah, 'tis horrible! " said he. " It was not I who poisoned Sauvresy—it was she—there are proofs of it; perhaps, with a good advocate——"

M. Lecoq did not lose a word or a gesture of this tragical scene. Either purposely or by accident, he pushed the door-curtain, which made a slight noise.

Laurence thought the door was being opened, that the detective was returning, and that Hector would fall alive into their hands.

"Miserable coward!" she cried, pointing her pistol at him, "shoot, or else——"

He hesitated; there was another rustle at the door; she fired.

Trémorel fell dead.

Laurence, with a rapid movement, took up the other pistol, and was turning it against herself, when M. Lecoq sprung upon her and tore the weapon from her grasp.

"Unhappy girl!" cried he, "what would you do?"

"Die. Can I live now?"

"Yes, you can live," responded M. Lecoq. "And more, you ought to live."

"I am a lost woman——"

"No, you are a poor child lured away by a wretch. You say you are very guilty; perhaps so; live to repent of it. Great sorrows like yours have their missions in this world, one of devotion and charity. Live, and the good you do will attach you once more to life. You have yielded to the deceitful promises of a villain; remember, when you are rich, that there are poor innocent girls forced to lead a life of miserable shame for a morsel of bread. Go to these unhappy creatures, rescue them from debauchery, and their honor will be yours."

M. Lecoq narrowly watched Laurence as he spoke, and perceived that he had touched her. Still, her eyes were dry, and were lit up with a strange light.

"Besides, your life is not your own—you know."

"Ah," she returned, "I must die now, even for my child, if I would not die of shame when he asks for his father——"

"You will reply, Madame, by showing him an honest man and an old friend, who is ready to give him his name—Monsieur Plantat."

The old justice was broken with grief; yet he had the strength to say:

"Laurence, my beloved child, I beg you accept me——"

These simple words, pronounced with infinite gentleness and sweetness, at last melted the unhappy young girl, and determined her.   She burst into tears.

She was saved.

M. Lecoq hastened to throw a shawl which he saw on a chair about her shoulders, and passed her arm through M. Plantat's, saying to the latter:

"Go, lead her away; my men have orders to let you pass, and Palot will lend you his carriage."

"But where shall we go?"

"To Orcival; Monsieur Courtois has been informed by a letter from me that his daughter is living, and he is expecting her.   Come, lose no time."

M. Lecoq, when he was left alone, listened to the departure of the carriage which took M. Plantat and Laurence away; then he returned to Trémorel's body.

"There," said he to himself, "lies a wretch whom I have killed instead of arresting and delivering him up to justice.   Have I done my duty?   No; but my conscience will not reproach me, because I have acted rightly."

And running to the staircase, he called his men.

XXVIII

The day after Trémorel's death, old Bertaud and Guespin were set at liberty, and received, the former four thousand francs to buy a boat and new tackle, and the latter ten thousand francs, with a promise of a like sum at the end of the year, if he would go and live in his own province.   Fifteen days later, to the great surprise of the Orcival gossips, who had never learned the details of these events, M. Plantat wedded Mlle. Laurence Courtois; and the groom and bride departed that very evening for Italy, where it was announced they would linger at least a year.

As for Papa Courtois, he has offered his beautiful domain at Orcival for sale; he proposes to settle in the middle of France, and is on the lookout for a commune in need of a good mayor.

M. Lecoq, like everybody else, would, doubtless, have forgotten the Valfeuillu affair, had it not been that a notary called on him personally the other morning with a very gracious letter from Laurence, and an enormous sheet of stamped paper.   This was no other than a title deed to M. Plantat's pretty estate at Orcival, " with furniture, stable, carriage-house, garden, and other dependencies and appurtenances thereunto belonging," and some neighboring acres of pleasant fields.

" Prodigious!" cried M. Lecoq.   " I didn't help ingrates, after all!   I *am* willing to become a landed proprietor, just for the rarity of the thing."